THE GOOD OLD HOCKEY GAME

B.E. Russell

For more information, or to book an event, contact:
press@blairedwardrussell.com
www.BlairEdwardRussell.com

ISBN - Paperback 978-1-966245-17-9

First Paperback Edition: Februrary 5, 2018

CONTENTS

1

ON THE POND

Eleven year-old Doug Mansfield pressed his nose to the frosted window, his warm breath making small circles of condensation on the glass. Outside, a fresh blanket of snow gleamed under the late afternoon sun. The sky was that particular shade of winter blue, where the sunlight took on a faint golden glow. In the backyard, a narrow path his father had shoveled zigzagged to the wooden gate. Beyond the gate, a small, tree-lined field stretched out toward a local pond that had frozen over during a cold snap. Doug felt a mixture of excitement and unease swirling in his stomach. He had never really skated before—not outside of a few wobbly attempts at the local indoor rink. Today, he would lace up real hockey skates on the pond for the first time.

His older brother, Mike, who had turned fourteen at the start of winter, rummaged through their cramped hallway closet in search of some gear. Mike was lean, a couple of inches taller, and far more confident. Where Doug was shy and reserved, Mike seemed to carry himself with an easy self-assurance, at least when it came to hockey. The older boy's passion for the sport was evident in the way he spoke about it, the posters of Maple Leafs players that covered his bedroom walls, and the battered hockey stick he took everywhere like a treasured appendage.

"Here," Mike said, pulling out a pair of skates that had definitely seen better days. They were black with white cowlings, a brand Doug didn't recognize, and a few dings and scuff marks showed the mileage. They were also slightly bigger than Doug's shoe size, but might just fit with a couple pairs of wool socks. Mike tossed the skates near Doug's feet and grabbed his own, newer ones. "These will work," he added, arching an eyebrow. "You sure you wanna try this, Dougie?"

Doug gave a small nod, swallowing hard. "I—I'm sure," he said, trying to steady the quiver in his voice. A little pang of embarrassment settled in his chest. He didn't want to look foolish in front of Mike or, potentially, the other neighborhood kids who might be out on the pond. But something in him craved this. Hockey, in a vague and thrilling sense, called to him—especially after nights spent watching the Leafs on TV with his dad. He could still feel the vibration of the cheering crowds as though it had traveled through the television screen and lodged in his soul. But being on the ice, actually experiencing the game in some tangible way, was entirely different.

Mike tugged a black knitted cap over his short brown hair and motioned for Doug to follow him through the back door. The chill hit them instantly. Doug pulled his red parka tighter around his skinny frame and tucked his hands into thick, homemade mittens. His mother watched from the kitchen window, smiling in that knowing, maternal way that signaled both pride and a hint of concern. She tapped the glass, waved at them, and turned back to her dinner preparations.

The backyard gate squeaked as Mike nudged it open with a quick push. Doug could see puffs of white breath escaping his brother's mouth. The path leading to the pond looked well-trodden—likely from older kids who had already been skating. In the crisp, biting air, Doug's cheeks began to tingle. The snow crunching beneath his boots sounded like muffled styrofoam. The sun was low, resting just above the treetops, painting the world in a gentle winter glow.

"I heard Tommy and a couple of the guys might be here today," Mike said casually. "Probably practicing for that peewee tournament in February."

Doug said nothing but felt a slight knot of nerves. Tommy was Mike's friend, a sturdy fourteen-year-old who already had a reputation for being a decent hockey player—and a big talker about his achievements. If Tommy and his friends were there, Doug feared he would only embarrass himself. But Mike cast him a reassuring glance. "Don't worry," he said. "It's all in fun. No one's gonna judge you for being new."

Doug tried to believe it. They trudged along until the pond came into full view. He inhaled sharply. The surface looked like a wide, gleaming mirror, a pure expanse of ice catching the final rays of sunlight. At the far end of the pond, a handful of tall evergreen trees stood guard, their branches weighed down by clumps of snow. A couple of kids, too distant to identify, zipped around the center, leaving faint white lines where their blades carved the ice. Their distant laughter and the echoing scrape of skates carried on the breeze.

"It's so...open," Doug murmured. He'd been to the indoor rink countless times as a spectator, but that space was confined—boards, plexiglass, a scoreboard, the usual hum of fluorescent lights. The pond felt infinite.

"Grab a spot, let's lace up," Mike instructed, dropping a worn backpack onto a small patch of cleared snow near the edge. Doug knelt down, removing his boots gingerly. The cold seeped into his knees, but he didn't mind. Pulling the skates on, he found them a bit loose. He reached for the laces and tried to tie them as tightly as possible, wriggling his toes through two layers of socks. Mike finished tying his own laces in record time, a skill he'd perfected over years of playing.

When Doug finally stood, his ankles wobbled uncertainly. The ice at the edge was bumpy, marked by footprints and chipped spots. Mike braced Doug's arm. "Take a step or two. See how it feels."

Doug attempted a tentative half-step, his skate sliding on a patch of ice that wasn't as smooth as he'd expected. He nearly toppled forward, but Mike steadied him. Heat flared in Doug's cheeks, though Mike didn't laugh or tease him—he just nodded, as if to say *everyone has to start somewhere.* The two slowly shuffled away from the bank, careful of the rough edges until they reached the smoother center.

"Okay," Mike said with an encouraging smile, "just push off with one foot and glide with the other. Remember, keep your knees bent a bit. Don't lock 'em."

Doug took a breath, forced himself to relax, and did as instructed. He pushed off with his right foot, letting the left glide forward. A breeze rustled the winter air, stinging his face in the best possible way. The next push felt more confident, and within a few moments, Doug found a subtle rhythm: right push, left glide, right push, left glide. The pond's frozen surface wasn't perfect—there were tiny cracks and rough patches—but it was more forgiving than he'd expected.

Mike circled around him, skates moving in long, lazy arcs. "Nice, Dougie, nice," he called. "Try to pick up a bit of speed, if you can." With that, Mike demonstrated a few powerful strides, accelerating seamlessly.

Feeling the bite of the cold air on his cheeks, Doug tried to mimic his brother's form. He pressed his edges a bit harder into the ice, pushing off with more vigor. His heart hammered, not just with fear of falling but with a sudden exhilaration he'd never quite felt before. This was more than just moving from point A to point B—there was a sense of freedom, almost like flying, but with his skates grounded in the ice.

Within minutes, that earlier trepidation gave way to an astounding sense of comfort. He wasn't a natural at many things—always overshadowed by Mike's achievements in sports and academics—but on the ice, he felt an innate understanding. He felt each muscle in his legs responding, each push building momentum. A small grin tugged at the corners of his mouth. He was doing it. He was really skating.

As he gained confidence, Doug glanced around. A few older kids were at the far side of the pond, where they'd set up a makeshift goal using two branches as posts. They batted a puck around, chanting hockey jargon, lost in their own little game. He recognized a boy named Eric from down the street, sporting a Toronto Maple Leafs jersey over his winter coat. Another, somewhat shorter boy was wearing a Montreal Canadiens knit cap. They were so consumed by their own scrimmage that they hadn't even noticed Doug yet.

Mike came to a stop with a flourish of ice shavings near Doug. "Ready for a bit more challenge?" he asked. Doug's grin widened, and he nodded. Mike reached into the backpack they'd brought and pulled out two hockey sticks—one was Mike's usual, fairly well-worn with black tape, and the other a smaller wooden stick, probably a leftover from a few seasons ago.

Doug accepted the smaller stick. It was a bit dinged-up, but he cradled it with reverence. Holding a hockey stick on a frozen pond made him feel like he was stepping into a new world. Mike fetched a battered puck from the bag, dropped it onto the ice, and gave it a light tap toward Doug. He stiffened with nerves, but managed to stop the puck by placing his stick in front of it.

"Give it a push, see if you can skate and handle it at the same time," Mike suggested. Then he backed away a few feet.

Doug gingerly nudged the puck forward with the blade of his stick. It wobbled on the uneven surface, and he skated forward, leaning in. His eyes flicked from the puck to the ice in front of him to ensure he didn't slip on a rough patch. His knees shook slightly, but he was determined. He pushed the puck ahead, then pulled it back, trying to maintain some semblance of control.

Little by little, his movements gained stability. Doug found that the instincts guiding his feet also began to help with his stickhandling. Sure, the puck bounced unpredictably at times, but he was able to correct course, tapping it side to side. He glanced up, seeing Mike's approving nod, and felt a swell of pride. The skate blades made a pleasant scraping sound, like a whispered promise that something incredible was starting to blossom.

Mike joined in, sending the puck back and forth between them. At first, Doug found passing while skating to be tricky—he often lost his balance or overshot the puck—but after a half-dozen tries, he managed a decent pass right to Mike's tape. Mike caught it neatly and grinned. "Awesome, Dougie!" he shouted. "You pick this up fast!"

A surge of warmth ignited in Doug's chest. He might've blushed under his cap. It was rare to hear such open praise from his brother. He felt that if he could stay in this moment forever, he would—just a boy discovering the thrill of the sport under the open sky, the winter wind nipping at his nose.

Soon, their informal practice drew the attention of the other kids on the pond. The small group from across the ice skated over, curiosity evident in their faces. Eric, wearing the Leafs jersey, gave a friendly nod. "Mike! Didn't know you were coming out today." He eyed Doug and added, "Who's this? Your cousin or something?"

"My little brother, Doug," Mike replied, hooking a thumb in Doug's direction. "He's giving pond hockey a try."

"Nice," Eric said with a slight grin, and a couple of the others nodded politely. Doug caught Tommy's eye—a tall kid with a noticeable swagger. Tommy had been playing with Mike in a local league, so Doug recognized him from a distance. They'd rarely spoken, but Tommy gave him a quick once-over and shrugged, as if assessing whether Doug was worth a second glance. Doug suddenly felt small, his new burst of confidence threatening to deflate.

Eric pointed to the makeshift net they'd set up. "We were just messing around. Why don't you guys join in? Five or six of us can do three-on-three. We'll keep it casual."

Doug's stomach lurched. A game? Already? He'd only just started skating. The idea of being thrown into a scrimmage with kids who had years of experience was daunting. But before he could protest, Mike answered for both of them. "Sure, sounds good," Mike said. "Doug's new, though, so take it easy on him, all right?"

"Course," Eric said, though there was a mischievous gleam in his eye. He spun around and glided back toward the far end, letting the others know it was time to pick teams.

Doug quietly followed Mike, pressing his lips together in apprehension. "I—I'm not sure I'm ready for a game," he whispered.

"You'll do fine," Mike assured him. "We'll keep it friendly. Just stay near me, and keep your eyes on the puck. Biggest thing is to have fun. We're not playing for the Cup."

Doug tried to laugh, but it came out more like a strangled cough. Still, there was a spark of excitement in him. Only a half-hour ago, he'd never skated on a pond before, and now he was about to play his first ever pick-up game of hockey. Maybe this was how big dreams started—with a single, nervous step out of one's comfort zone.

They divided into teams. Mike, Doug, and a boy named Scott ended up on one side. Tommy, Eric, and the younger boy in the Canadiens cap took the opposing side. Scott, a burly kid of about thirteen, grinned at Doug. "You any good?" he asked good-naturedly, not out of judgment but out of curiosity.

Doug managed a half smile. "Not really," he admitted. "Just started skating today."

"Hey, no biggie," Scott replied. "We'll pass you the puck. Just do your best."

They agreed that the first team to five goals would win, a simple enough structure for a friendly game. Eric dropped the puck at center ice and tapped it with his stick. Then, with a quick countdown—"Three... two... one..."—the game was on. Eric and Mike vied for possession, their sticks clacking against each other as the puck skittered around. Doug hovered nearby, uncertain of how best to help. Out of the corner of his eye, he could see Tommy leaning forward intently, waiting to break away.

Mike finally freed the puck from Eric's stick, but nearly lost his footing on a rough patch. Tommy snatched the puck and took off, his strides confident and strong. Doug tried to skate after him, but felt like he was moving in slow motion compared to Tommy. Within seconds, Tommy had slipped around an imaginary defense and snapped a shot toward the branches serving as the net. The puck slapped the ice and slid in between the crude posts. One-nothing, the other side.

Scott exhaled, pumping his arms in a half-laugh. "Dang, that was fast. Let's get it back." He took the puck from Tommy, who tossed it over with a cocky grin.

Doug's heart hammered. He reminded himself that this was all in good fun. The scoreboard didn't matter. Still, a little part of him wanted to prove something—to show that he wasn't just the new kid with shaky ankles. He hovered near the center, scanning for an opening while Mike passed the puck to Scott. Scott made a beeline toward Eric, who lunged in for a steal. At the last moment, Scott flicked the puck sideways, and it skidded right toward Doug's skates.

Doug fumbled. His eyes widened, and he jabbed his stick forward, barely managing to trap the puck. In that moment, he felt every nerve in his body go on high alert. Keep it moving, keep it moving. He turned on his skates and awkwardly propelled himself forward. Miraculously, he made it past Tommy, who had been momentarily distracted by Mike's movement on the other side. The puck bounced on a crack, but Doug recovered, giving it a gentle push ahead.

His body felt unbelievably alive—legs pumping, lungs inhaling the frigid air, heart pounding. He was skating faster than he ever had before, chasing that black puck. The wind whipped at his cheeks and ears, but he barely noticed. He could sense the presence of the others behind him. Time seemed to slow down as he neared the makeshift net. In that instant, he heard Mike's voice: "Shoot it, Dougie!"

His eyes flicked to the net. The branches were only a few strides away. The puck wobbled in front of him. In a surge of newfound determination, he lifted his stick and took a shot, more of a forward shove than a real slapshot. The puck slid swiftly across the ice, heading directly between the improvised posts. It banged lightly against the broken branch on the other side.

Goal.

Doug's breath caught. He stopped in his tracks—well, more like stumbled to a halt—and just stared at the puck. For a second, he wondered if this was all in his imagination. But the others confirmed it with cheers and exclamations. Mike raised his arms. "Holy smokes, Dougie!" he shouted. "Nice shot!"

Eric skated over, a playful smirk on his face. "Beginner's luck," he teased lightly, but there was an undeniable trace of respect in his voice.

Doug broke into a grin, cheeks burning with a mix of cold air and excitement. A wave of warmth—pride, maybe—flooded him. He'd actually scored a goal in a game with older kids. Sure, it was just a casual pick-up game on a frozen pond, but the moment felt monumental. He wondered if this was the same thrill that real players felt when they scored in front of thousands of fans—something about the puck hitting its target, the crisp air, and the camaraderie among players. It felt magical.

The game pressed on, filled with lighthearted jabs and dramatic attempts at breakaways. Doug found himself improving bit by bit with every shift, getting used to skating while handling the puck, adjusting to the natural lumps in the ice. Whenever he stumbled, he scrambled right back to his feet, fueled by excitement rather than fear. Mike would shout small pieces of advice—"Keep your stick on the ice, Dougie!" or "Look where you're passing!"—and each tip clicked into place.

By the time the sun dipped lower, painting the horizon with a wash of pink and orange, the teams were tied at four goals apiece. Doug had managed two goals for his side, one more than he ever would have dared to imagine. Now, the next goal would decide the winner. Tommy, who was fiercely competitive, wiped sweat from his brow, even though the temperature was well below freezing. "Next goal wins," he declared, his breath coming out in clouds.

They faced off at center ice, the tension suddenly tangible, even though it was a simple, friendly scrimmage. Mike tapped Doug's stick. "Let's do this," he said quietly, a grin lighting his face. "You've already impressed everyone. Let's finish strong."

The puck dropped. Mike and Eric battled for control, their sticks whacking against the ice and each other. Eric got the better position and flung the puck toward the Canadiens-capped boy, who flew down the ice with surprising speed. Scott rushed to intercept, but the kid flicked a clever pass behind him. Tommy took over, weaving skillfully. Doug raced to keep up, sweat trickling under his cap despite the cold.

Tommy was dangerously close to the net now. Mike lunged, hooking the puck off Tommy's stick. It shot out to the side, bouncing awkwardly. Doug, heart pounding, spotted it first. He veered around, positioning himself between the puck and a swiftly approaching Eric. With shaky confidence, Doug corralled the puck. Then he pushed forward, crossing the center line, feeling adrenaline surge in his veins. Through the corner of his eye, he saw Mike calling for a pass, but a small voice in Doug's head whispered, *You can do this.*

He aimed for an opening between Eric and Tommy, crossing to the right. Tommy lunged, but Doug sidestepped and kept going. His legs burned with the strain of skating fast, but he pressed on. The net loomed. He pulled back for a shot, praying it wouldn't fly off to the side. Then something unexpected happened—Eric caught up with him and managed to get his stick under Doug's blade. The puck slid away, and Doug lost his balance. He toppled onto the ice, landing on his side. Pain jolted through his hip and elbow.

For a moment, Doug just lay there, gasping, feeling the ice's chill seep into his bones. He thought he'd blown it. But then, he heard Mike's voice. "I got it!" Mike snatched the loose puck, dodged a flailing Tommy, and hammered a shot. Time seemed to slow as the puck soared across the ice, sliding cleanly between the two branches. The sound of it striking the far edge of the stick serving as a makeshift crossbar reverberated like a bell.

Goal. Their team had won.

Mike let out a whoop and skated over to Doug, offering him a hand. "We did it!" he laughed breathlessly. Doug allowed himself to be pulled up, wincing a bit at the ache in his side. But even that dull throb was drowned out by the surge of excitement in his chest.

Scott skated over and gave Mike a congratulatory bump before ruffling Doug's cap. "Not bad, rook," he said with a grin.

The opposing team shook their heads, panting with exertion. Tommy shrugged good-naturedly, though he clearly disliked losing. "All right, all right," he said. "Nice job, guys." He turned to Doug, giving him a short nod of acknowledgment. Doug felt a flash of surprise—he'd half expected a snide remark. Instead, he sensed respect in Tommy's gesture.

In the fading light, the group of boys decided it was time to wrap up. As they drifted back to the pond's edge to retrieve their boots, Doug felt a twinge of disappointment that the game was over. He still wanted to do more laps, to test how far he could push himself, maybe perfect that shot. But all good things come to an end, he told himself. Tomorrow was another day.

They sat in a rough circle on the edge, huddled close to each other, untying skates and slipping numb toes into warm boots. The chatter was energetic, with everyone dissecting the best plays of their impromptu match. Doug's attention drifted to the setting sun. The last stretch of golden light reflected off the ice, a faint shimmer that made the entire pond look like a precious jewel. The place felt magical, as though it existed in a separate pocket of the world where time and worry were suspended. He could've easily spent an entire day right there on the ice.

"You're a natural," Mike said quietly, so only Doug could hear. He bumped Doug's shoulder. "You really are."

Doug blinked. The compliment sent a wave of warmth through him. He never thought of himself as 'a natural' at anything, let alone something as challenging as hockey. But the strange sense of rightness he'd felt while skating—like his body finally discovered its true rhythm—told him Mike might be right.

"Thanks," Doug murmured, a half-smile on his chapped lips. He didn't know how else to respond, but he hoped his gratitude showed in his eyes.

They parted ways with the other kids, each trudging along a separate snow-packed path toward home. Mike and Doug walked side by side, breath still coming in little clouds. The sky had deepened into a purplish twilight. Their boots sank into the crunchy snow. A comforting hush fell over the neighborhood—windows glowed softly, smoke curled from chimneys, and the scent of wood-burning stoves lingered in the air.

Mike cleared his throat. "We should do this again tomorrow. Or whenever we can. Right, Dougie?"

Doug nodded enthusiastically, feeling a fresh jolt of anticipation. "Yeah," he replied, his voice cracking slightly. "I—I'd like that."

When they finally reached the backyard gate, the porch light cast a warm cone of illumination on the snow. Doug's body ached pleasantly, but his spirits soared higher than he could remember. That sense of calm and satisfaction coursed through him, tinted with an eager excitement for what might come next. He understood now, on a visceral level, why people loved this sport so deeply. It was more than just a game of skill; it was an experience, a community, a dance with the elements themselves. The scrape of blade on ice, the sting of cold air on flushed cheeks, the wild excitement of chasing a puck across a vast frozen surface—he felt it all, and it resonated within him like a chord struck on a perfectly tuned guitar.

Inside the house, their mother met them with steaming mugs of hot chocolate. She gave Doug's elbow a concerned glance when she saw he was favoring it slightly. "Are you hurt?" she asked, touching the spot gently.

"It's just a bruise," Doug said, offering a small grin. "I fell a couple times, but I'm okay."

She nodded and smiled back, tousling his hair. "Well, that's part of learning, I suppose. You boys hungry? Dinner's almost ready."

Mike peeled off his coat, letting out a huge sigh. "Starving," he declared, then turned to Doug. "First goal, Dougie. That's something you won't forget."

Doug's mother looked at him, eyes sparkling. "Your first goal? Really? That's wonderful, honey."

Doug felt a spark of pride. "Yeah," he managed, still feeling a bit shy about the attention. "It was just a little game on the pond, but... I scored."

She beamed, patting him on the back. "Well, you can tell us all about it over dinner."

Doug slipped out of his snow pants and coat, relishing the warm air on his chilly skin. As he trudged upstairs to his room to drop off the borrowed skates, he noticed how every muscle in his legs felt used. Standing in his small bedroom, with posters of cartoons still on the walls and a mess of books on the floor, he found himself replaying the afternoon in his mind— the sensation of gliding effortlessly, the puck sliding on ice, the success of that goal. A thrill spread through him, making him feel oddly invincible, even if just for a moment.

He stared down at the battered skates. They weren't fancy, and they belonged to Mike once upon a time, but they felt like a treasure—like they possessed some enchantment that allowed him to do something he never thought possible. Suddenly, the idea of playing hockey—really playing it—didn't seem so far-fetched. For the first time, he let himself imagine stepping onto the ice in a real rink, wearing a uniform, hearing the roar of fans. The spark of the dream took hold.

That night, Doug's dreams were filled with visions of gliding on endless ice fields. He dreamt of swirling snow and bright stadium lights, of scoring a winning goal in an arena bursting with cheers. And somewhere in that dream, he heard a soft whisper that sounded like a promise: *You belong here.*

—

The next morning, the entire world seemed dusted with a fresh coat of snow, and the temperature had dropped another few degrees. Doug woke early, itching to revisit the pond. It took considerable patience to make it through breakfast, chores, and the other small tasks his mother laid out for him. Once he and Mike were finally free, they dashed to the backyard gate like giddy conspirators. The second day on the pond—how would it feel? Would that same magic still be there?

But when they arrived, they found the pond empty. The cold snap must have deterred most of the other kids. A biting wind whipped across the ice, carrying tiny crystals of snow that stung the face. Doug glanced at Mike, uncertain if they'd brave the elements on their own. Mike's answer was a grin as he pulled on his skates. That was all the encouragement Doug needed.

There, under a pale winter sun, they took turns passing the puck and doing little one-on-one drills. Doug discovered he could turn sharper, stop quicker, and even maneuver around Mike—at least sometimes. They had the entire pond to themselves. The wind howled, but the sense of joy in Doug's heart kept him warm. Every once in a while, a gust would blow so hard they had to pause, but the moment it eased, they returned to practice.

They stayed until their fingers numbed inside their gloves and their cheeks burned red from the cold. By the time they tramped home, they were half-frozen but elated. Doug felt that a whole new chapter of his life had begun, the day he first stepped onto that frozen pond. The house was the same, the world outside looked the same, but he felt different—like he had tapped into a piece of himself that he never knew existed.

That night, after dinner, Doug found himself poring over old hockey magazines that Mike kept stuffed in his room. Though the pages were creased and dog-eared, the images leapt out at him: high-stakes games, triumphant goals, the Maple Leafs battling bitter rivals. He read about techniques like the slapshot, the wrist shot, the butterfly save for goalies—names for moves he didn't fully understand but was eager to learn. Mike dropped by, noticing Doug's fascination, and the two spent an hour discussing what a real hockey league might look like for Doug in the future. Could he make a house league team? Would he need better equipment? Doug's eyes glowed with excitement at every question.

As the days turned into weeks, the pond became Doug's sanctuary. Almost every free moment after school, he'd rush home, finish homework at breakneck speed, and beg Mike to head out with him. Sometimes their father came along, watching from a distance. At times, other neighborhood kids joined in, and soon the pick-up games became regular events. Doug's skill improved rapidly—he learned to shoot with more accuracy, to pass swiftly, to skate with confidence. Each small victory—like mastering a crossover step or cleanly catching a pass on his blade—fueled his desire for more.

Yet, it wasn't all effortless progress. He fell plenty of times, winding up with bruises on his knees and elbows. There were moments when older kids would steal the puck effortlessly, or he'd miss a wide-open shot. But none of those stumbles could extinguish the spark he felt. Every misstep was just motivation to try again, to push harder.

Even the coldest winter nights couldn't keep him away. On weekends, if the pond wasn't already crowded with families and local teens, Doug would stand out there in the twilight, letting the near-silence of a snowy evening wrap around him. The frozen surface lit faintly by porch lights or the moon, the hiss of skates cutting across the ice—it had become his personal haven. Each time he stepped onto the pond, that old mixture of nervousness and excitement faded, replaced by a growing sense of belonging.

Before long, word spread that Doug—young, quiet, reserved Doug—actually had a knack for hockey. One neighbor who regularly played on the pond jokingly called him "the secret sniper" after a game where Doug scored a handful of goals. Another teased that Doug should be careful or scouts would show up at the Mansfield backyard any day now. It was all in jest, of course, but it made Doug's heart soar. It was the first time he'd felt recognized for a talent. No longer just "Mike's little brother," he was slowly building a reputation of his own.

The highlight of any pond session was still playing alongside Mike. Something about having an older brother who believed in him was more empowering than Doug ever expected. Mike wasn't perfect—he teased Doug about his height, about how awkward he could be in social settings—but on the ice, the teasing vanished. They were co-conspirators, creating plays, feeding each other passes, celebrating each other's goals with unbridled joy. The moments they shared skating under a broad winter sky became etched into Doug's mind as some of the best he'd ever known.

And so, the season carried on—Doug forging an unbreakable bond with the game. Each day, as he raced to the pond, he would recall that first magical afternoon, the quickening of his pulse, the awe he felt gliding over the untouched surface. He replayed that initial taste of success—scoring a goal in his first game—and how it seemed to ignite an insatiable hunger for more. Hockey, he realized, was unlike anything else he'd experienced: it demanded strength, but also finesse; it required speed, but also self-control. It allowed him to be part of a team, yet express himself in a way that felt deeply personal.

Perhaps what he loved most was the raw, unfiltered joy of it. No tests to ace, no teachers to please, no crowds of strangers to impress. Just him, Mike, and a few friends, slicing across the ice in a swirl of winter air. His breath puffing in front of him, his lungs burning from the cold, and that puck—always that little black disk—rolling ahead, daring him to keep chasing.

It was on this frozen pond that Doug's dream quietly unfurled, a seed taking root in the depths of his heart. He wouldn't be able to name it precisely yet—to say, *I want to play at the highest level someday*—but a faint whisper of that ambition had begun. Each time he felt the blade of his skate grip the ice, each time the puck found the back of the net, he sensed a possibility ripening. It was the beginning of a long, winding journey that neither he nor anyone else could fully comprehend yet. But it had started, right there on that frozen pond.

He didn't know it at the time, but one day he would look back on this very chapter of his life with absolute clarity. He'd recall the row of stately evergreens bordering the pond, the crisp winter air that stung his cheeks, the sound of skates carving fresh tracks, the swirl of snow kicked up by sharp turns, and the rush of accomplishing something he never dreamed possible. He'd remember the exact moment when, as a shy eleven-year-old, he discovered the spark of a lifelong passion—and in that memory, he'd smile at how it all began so simply, so purely, on a patch of ice just beyond his own backyard gate.

2

THE OBSESSION BEGINS

Doug's alarm rang well before dawn, echoing through his small bedroom like a clarion call. He slapped at the clock, silencing the tinny bells. The frosty chill of his room hit him the moment he kicked off the covers. Wiping the sleep from his eyes, he felt something stir deep in his chest—an eagerness, electric and fresh. It had been building for weeks now, steadily consuming his thoughts ever since that day on the pond. He couldn't ignore it: he wanted more hockey.

He dressed quickly in a thermal shirt, heavy sweatshirt, and well-worn jeans. Downstairs, the house was quiet except for the soft hum of the furnace. His mother hadn't started breakfast yet, and his father was still asleep, so Doug tiptoed through the hall, trying not to let the floorboards creak under his weight. Pulling on a pair of thick socks, he stuffed his feet into boots. He pushed open the back door carefully, letting in a gust of icy air that stung his cheeks and made his eyes water.

Outside, the sky was a deep navy-blue fading to gray, with the faintest hint of light on the horizon. The temperature must have dipped well below freezing overnight, creating a silver crust on the snow. Doug inhaled deeply, the cold almost painful, but it awakened something in him—a sense of purpose that had started to define his every waking moment. Hockey. He needed to get the yard's small makeshift rink ready. Mike and Doug had spent part of the previous week tampering with a patch of flat ground behind their house, using plywood boards and a plastic liner to create a modest backyard rink. It wasn't perfect—there were lumps and the occasional bubble—but it was theirs.

Doug reached for the shovel resting against the side of the garage. The metal handle was cold to the touch, so he gripped it with gloved hands. He trudged to the rink's edge, finding a thin dusting of snow covering the ice. The wind had blown some small drifts into the corners. He started scraping, clearing a path from one end of the boards to the other. In the predawn stillness, the rhythmic scrape-scrape of the shovel against ice was oddly soothing.

All around him, the world was still. Clouds of vapor hovered with each breath he exhaled. He remembered how, just a few weeks earlier, the idea of waking up this early—especially in the winter—would have been unthinkable. But that was before hockey had taken root in his mind. Now, the desire to see a smooth sheet of ice waiting for him each day eclipsed the comfort of his warm bed.

When he finished shoveling, he set the shovel aside and surveyed his work. The rink was far from pristine; lumps of snow clung to spots he hadn't thoroughly cleared. Doug frowned, grabbed a broom, and started sweeping to smooth it further. In those moments, lost in the mechanical act of clearing and prepping the ice, he barely noticed time passing. His hands grew numb, but he pressed on.

Eventually, the sun peeked over the horizon, bathing the backyard in a soft, golden glow. He heard the back door open and glanced over to see Mike stepping outside, arms wrapped around his torso to keep warm. Doug flashed a grin.

"Morning," he called, leaning on the broom.

Mike hopped off the small step, eyebrows raised. "Didn't expect you to be up this early," he said, though his smirk suggested otherwise. "Couldn't sleep?"

Doug shrugged. "I wanted to fix up the rink. Figured we could skate before school if you're up for it."

Mike laughed, a white puff of vapor trailing from his lips. "You're obsessed, you know that?" But there was affection in his voice, not disapproval. He clapped a hand on Doug's shoulder, then glanced at the rink. "Looks good. Let's see how it feels."

They each went back inside for a moment to grab their skates. Their mother, awake by now, eyed them in the kitchen as they tugged on laces and rummaged through the pantry for cereal bars. "Boys, you're not seriously skating at this hour, are you?" She gave a mild sigh, half amused, half exasperated.

Mike grinned at her over his shoulder. "Just for a bit, Mom. Promise we'll be ready for school on time."

Doug's mother shook her head, but an indulgent smile flickered across her face. She was used to Mike's passion for hockey; now, she had to accept Doug's new dedication as well. "Don't freeze out there," she said, turning back to the stove to start breakfast.

Once suited up, Doug and Mike stepped onto the backyard rink. The wood boards barely came up to their knees, but it gave just enough of a boundary to keep pucks from sliding too far away. Doug tested the surface with a few careful strides. The ice was rough in spots, and his skates scraped a bit. Still, it was playable. A sense of triumph blossomed in his chest; he'd helped make this. And now he could practice whenever he wanted—no need to wait for the pond to freeze perfectly or other kids to show up.

Mike took a gentle pass from Doug and stickhandled, weaving from one end of the small rink to the other. Doug watched how Mike shifted his weight, how he angled his blade to keep the puck close. Doug tried to mimic those moves, though there wasn't much room to pick up speed in such a cramped space. Still, it was better than sitting around inside, waiting for the next time they could go to the pond or an indoor public skate.

They only stayed out for fifteen minutes—just enough to work up a slight sweat under their layers—but it felt glorious. Doug left the ice with his cheeks tingling, mind buzzing with excitement. Every day, he told himself, he was going to get a little better.

Later that evening, after school, Doug found himself gravitating toward the living room TV. It was Wednesday, which meant the local sports network would rerun highlights from past Maple Leafs games. Doug dropped his backpack by the couch and flicked on the television. The footage was old— he recognized some of the players from the 1970s and 80s, men with bushy mustaches and simpler equipment. But he watched hungrily, absorbing details about positioning, passing, and even the fights. His mother's footsteps resonated in the hallway behind him.

"Doug, don't you have homework?" she asked, her tone wary.

"I'll do it in a bit," Doug mumbled, barely taking his eyes off the screen. "Just need to watch this one segment."

When the highlight reel ended, it cut to a panel of commentators discussing power-play strategies. Doug inched closer, turning up the volume. Words like "forecheck," "zone entry," and "neutral zone trap" floated through the air. He only half-understood them, but he was determined to learn. Something about the technical side of hockey—the intricacies that made the difference between a dominating team and a struggling one—captivated him. It wasn't just about skating fast and shooting hard; it was about systems, creativity, timing, synergy. Doug wanted to know it all.

A few minutes later, he sensed someone behind him again. Glancing back, he saw his father standing there, arms crossed. "Getting pretty serious about this, huh?" he asked. There was no accusation in his voice, just an observation.

Doug felt a mild surge of defensiveness; was he spending too much time on this? He swallowed and nodded. "I—I guess so. I really like it, Dad."

His father's expression softened, and he walked around to sit next to Doug. On the screen, an old clip showed a highlight of the Maple Leafs playing against the Montreal Canadiens at the old Forum. The footage was grainy, the scoreboard flickering in and out. "I remember watching these games when I was about your age," his father reminisced. "We didn't have fancy replays, though. Just had to catch what we could on the live broadcast."

The two fell silent, watching as a Leafs winger scored a top-shelf goal. Doug felt a flutter of excitement, wondering if he could ever pull off a shot like that. Finally, his father cleared his throat. "Listen," he began cautiously, "I'm glad you've found something you love. Just don't lose sight of everything else, okay? School, family, keeping some balance..."

Doug managed a sheepish nod, feeling a pang of guilt. "I will," he promised. He meant it, though a small voice in the back of his mind insisted that hockey was more important than anything else. His father seemed to accept the answer, ruffling Doug's hair before he rose to check on dinner.

As weeks turned into a month, Doug's obsession only deepened. Every spare moment was spent reading about hockey, watching hockey, or actually playing hockey. When he wasn't on the backyard rink or the pond, he was in his room, scanning old magazines for tips on skating drills and shot techniques. Mike had quite a collection of books and magazines piled on his bookshelf—some about famous players, others filled with advanced strategies. Doug devoured them all.

One early morning, Doug was halfway through clearing fresh snow off the backyard rink when his mother's voice drifted from the back step. "You'll be late for the bus, honey."

Breathless, Doug paused. His heart pounded, not just from the shoveling but from the frustration of leaving the rink unfinished. "Can I stay just a bit longer?" he called back, batting a chunk of snow away.

"You've got five minutes, Doug. Then get inside. I won't write you a note if you miss the bus."

With a sigh, he realized he had no choice. He took the final few swipes with the shovel, then propped it against the boards. Glancing back over his shoulder at the rink, he felt that now-familiar pull: a wish that he could skip school and skate all day. He pictured himself like the pros on TV—gliding smoothly, deking around defenders, unleashing a perfect wrist shot. That fantasy lit up his thoughts as he trudged inside to gulp down breakfast and catch the bus, daydreaming about the next time he'd be able to lace up.

It wasn't just his parents who noticed the change. At school, Doug found himself zoning out during classes, doodling little sketches of hockey sticks and Maple Leaf crests in the margins of his notebook. A friend, Jordan, poked him in the ribs during math class one day. "You okay, man? You've been spacey."

Doug offered a shrug and a faint grin. "Just thinking about hockey."

Jordan smirked. "Again? Dude, you gotta teach me sometime. Maybe we can play street hockey after school?"

Doug nodded politely, though his mind was too fixated on real ice to muster enthusiasm for street hockey. By lunchtime, he was leafing through a sports magazine he'd borrowed from Mike. Inside was a breakdown of Wayne Gretzky's passing strategies—though the article was old, having been published when Gretzky was still with the Edmonton Oilers. Doug read each paragraph twice, absorbing every detail, every hint of genius behind "The Great One's" approach.

Meanwhile, Mike watched his younger brother with a mix of pride and concern. He had always been the hockey-obsessed one in the house, but now Doug had doubled, maybe tripled, that intensity. He admired Doug's drive and recognized a budding talent that might carry him to real opportunities. On the other hand, he worried about Doug's all-or-nothing focus. Mike, after all, had learned the hard way that there were times to skate, times to study, and times to just be a normal kid.

One Saturday afternoon, when the two of them were returning from a particularly long session on the pond, Mike pulled Doug aside. "So, I was thinking," he began, voice cautious. "You know how you've been improving? Scoring all those goals against us older guys?"

Doug blushed, feeling a surge of pride. "Yeah?"

Mike nodded. "I was talking to Coach Loring—my old peewee coach—yesterday. He's still around, running the local peewee team. They could use a solid forward, especially one with potential. I mentioned your name." Mike paused, trying to gauge Doug's reaction. "He said you could come to a practice session, just to see if it's something you'd want to do."

Doug's face lit up, though immediately, nerves fluttered in his stomach. "Practice with a real team?" he asked, voice edged with both eagerness and apprehension.

"Yeah, real team," Mike confirmed, grinning. "You're good enough for it. Probably better than I was at your age, to be honest."

Doug let that sink in, trying to picture himself on a proper team with jerseys, coaches, organized games. The thought thrilled him and terrified him in equal measure. He swallowed. "Mom and Dad... do they know?"

Mike shrugged. "Not yet. But I'm sure they'd be okay with it. Dad always says he wants us to do whatever we love, and Mom... well, she'll worry, but she usually comes around."

Doug nodded, already feeling the exhilaration of possibility. Yet a shadow of uncertainty loomed. What if he wasn't good enough in a structured environment? Pick-up games on the pond were one thing—no pressure, no real consequences. A real team meant competition, tryouts, coaches who expected results. And it might demand more time, more focus. Could he handle that while still managing school and everything else?

But the doubt melted under the heat of excitement. He thought of the rush of scoring, of the feeling he got gliding down the ice, faking out a defender, unleashing a perfectly aimed shot. That feeling was worth the risk. "I'll do it," he told Mike. "I really want to."

Mike's grin broadened. "Awesome. Let's talk to them together."

That evening, over a dinner of roast chicken and potatoes, Mike raised the topic. He explained that Doug had been invited to a peewee practice. Their father looked at Doug with raised eyebrows. "You're serious about this?" he asked. "It's a big commitment."

Doug took a breath, fighting the anxiety that churned in his stomach. "I—I am. I mean, I think about hockey all day, every day. I want to see if I can make a team."

His mother pursed her lips. "Doug, we've barely been able to get you away from the backyard rink or the pond as it is," she said, her gaze flicking to his father. "If he joins an organized team, that means even more time. Practices, traveling to games, tournaments... Are you sure you can handle your schoolwork with all this?"

Doug nodded, perhaps more emphatically than he intended. "I promise I'll keep my grades up. I'll do my homework as soon as I get home. Just... please, let me try."

His father exhaled, exchanging a glance with his mother. "You know, we've always tried to support you and Mike in whatever you wanted to do. Hockey's not cheap, though—equipment, fees, all that."

"We can get used gear," Doug hurried to say. "I don't need new stuff. I just want to play."

A tense moment passed, but Mike chimed in, "I can help him, Dad. We can figure it out together." He shot Doug a reassuring smile.

Finally, their mother let out a small sigh. "Well, if you're both willing to share the responsibility... and if your father is okay with it... I suppose I can't say no."

Doug's heart soared, a pulse of relief. His father nodded. "All right, we'll give it a shot. But if your grades slip, or if this becomes too overwhelming, we're going to have a serious talk, understood?"

"Yes!" Doug said, perhaps too eagerly. "Thank you. I promise—I won't let you down."

The days leading up to the first practice felt agonizingly slow. Doug's mind was so fixated on hockey that he found himself counting hours until he could be on the ice again. School became a blur, his classmates and teachers background noise. Each night, after finishing his homework at lightning speed, he'd pore over YouTube clips on Mike's old laptop, studying tutorials on stickhandling drills, shooting form, and skating technique. He practiced these moves in the backyard rink whenever possible, even if it meant staying outside until his toes went numb.

His parents grew more concerned with each passing day, though they tried not to dampen Doug's enthusiasm. He heard the hush of their murmured conversations—worries that he was "too consumed," that he might "burn out." But Doug felt unstoppable, like a rocket already launched. He kept repeating to himself that if he could just impress the coach, everything would fall into place.

The evening of the practice arrived with a gust of biting wind rattling the windows. Doug paced the living room floor, newly purchased secondhand hockey bag at his feet. His father had driven him to a local sports consignment shop a few days earlier. They'd painstakingly picked out each piece of equipment: shoulder pads with slightly torn stitching, elbow pads missing a strap, gloves with some worn-down palms, and a helmet with a scuffed cage. None of it matched, but Doug didn't care—this gear was his. He'd never owned a full set of hockey equipment in his life. Now, every bump and scratch on the gear felt like a story waiting to happen.

Mike was in the kitchen, double-checking the directions to the rink, while Doug's mother fiddled with the zipper on his hockey bag. "Got everything? Skates, pads, helmet?" she asked in a brisk tone that thinly veiled her nervousness.

Doug nodded so many times his neck hurt. "Yes, everything."

"Stick?" she pressed.

Doug blinked, then smacked his forehead. "It's in my room!" He ran upstairs, heart pounding. *Imagine if I forgot my stick on my first real practice!* That would be humiliating beyond measure. He snatched the stick from the corner of his room and hurried back down, nearly tripping on the last step. Mike greeted him with a wry grin.

"Good thing Mom asked," Mike teased, pushing open the door. "We can't have a hockey star without a stick."

The mention of "hockey star" made Doug's stomach churn with a mix of excitement and dread. He couldn't think of himself as a star yet, but he loved the idea that maybe, just maybe, he was on the path to becoming something more than just a backyard rink kid.

They piled into the family's old sedan, father at the wheel, mother up front, and Mike in the back with Doug. The air smelled like cold leather from the seats. During the short drive, no one spoke much. The only sounds were the hum of the heater and the faint radio playing. Doug's father finally broke the silence as they turned onto the main road toward the community arena.

"This place used to be my stomping grounds," he said quietly. "When I was your age, I took figure skating lessons here—your grandfather insisted I learn how to skate properly before I picked up a hockey stick."

Doug peeked over the seat, surprised. "Figure skating? Really?"

His father chuckled. "Yeah, but I didn't stick with it for long. Once I tried hockey, that was it. The rest was just for show."

Doug smiled, imagining his father doing spins and jumps, then realized he shouldn't be too critical—after all, figure skating taught footwork and balance. Maybe that's why his dad always looked so smooth skating on the pond.

They arrived at the arena, a single-story building of weathered brick and a corrugated metal roof. A tall sign by the entrance read *Northside Community Rink.* The parking lot was dotted with cars despite the lateness of the hour. Doug recognized some from the neighborhood—fellow kids or families who had year-round memberships. The overhead lights in the lot cast circles of pale yellow on the asphalt, and Doug's breath misted in front of his face as he stepped outside.

Inside, warm air tinged with the smell of rubber mats and old popcorn enveloped them. A faint roar from another rink— there were two in the facility—echoed down the hall, along with the sound of whistles and the scratch of skates. Doug followed Mike, lugging his hockey bag, helmet, and stick. His father and mother trailed them, scanning the corridors lined with trophy cases and bulletin boards.

They found the correct dressing room labeled with a piece of paper: *Peewee Practice – Coach Loring.* Doug hesitated at the threshold, heart racing. Mike patted him on the back.

"You'll be fine," he whispered. "Go on in, I'll be nearby if you need me."

Trying to project confidence he didn't quite feel, Doug swallowed hard and nudged the door open. The room was a swirl of activity—kids around his age wrestling with hockey gear, a few parents lacing skates, the smell of sweat and wet equipment thick in the air. Doug spotted Coach Loring immediately. He recognized him from old photos Mike had, and from around town: a tall, broad-shouldered man with salt-and-pepper hair, wearing a windbreaker with the local team's logo. The coach caught Doug's eye and offered a grin.

"You must be Doug," he said, loud enough to be heard over the chatter. "Mike's brother, right?"

Doug nodded, his voice sticking in his throat for a moment. "Yes, sir. Thanks for letting me...um, come out."

Coach Loring waved off the formality. "Happy to have you. Let's get you suited up. Practice starts in ten." He pointed to an empty spot on the wooden bench.

Doug set his bag down, took a deep breath, and started pulling on his equipment. Overhearing the chatter of other boys—some discussing a big game they had last weekend, others comparing new sticks—Doug felt a pang of self-consciousness. He was an unknown here, a guest. Would they resent him if he showed up and played well? Or laugh at him if he wasn't good enough?

He forced those worries aside, focusing on the methodical process of gearing up: shin pads first, then socks, pants, shoulder pads, elbow pads, jersey, and finally his skates. Adjusting the laces as tight as he could, he tried to recall everything Mike had told him about comfort versus circulation. Once he strapped on his helmet, Doug felt enclosed in a world of muffled sounds and narrow vision. But somehow, that also helped; it blocked out the noise and reminded him he was here for one reason: hockey.

Coach Loring tapped a whistle against his palm. "All right, everyone, let's go!" he barked. The kids, about a dozen in total, rose from the benches in a swirl of plastic and fiberglass. Doug shouldered his stick, following them out to the rink.

A wave of cold air and bright fluorescent lighting greeted him. The ice gleamed under overhead lights, ringed by boards plastered with local business advertisements. A scoreboard hung on one end, though it was off for practice. Doug's heart thudded as he stepped onto the ice, feeling that familiar rush. He took a few cautious strides—more out of nerves than needing to test his footing. But the same excitement that had seized him on the pond quickly returned, surging through his veins.

Coach Loring led them in a warm-up skate. The group formed a line, striding in unison around the perimeter, building speed with each lap. Doug noticed a few kids accelerate ahead, weaving in and out like they owned the place. Others hung back, chatting. He tried to find a middle ground, not wanting to draw attention but also not wanting to lag behind.

After warm-ups, the coach introduced a series of drills. They started with basic puck-handling—skate in a zig-zag from the blue line to the end boards, controlling the puck through cones. Doug took his turn, determined to show he belonged. His nerves jittered, but the moment the puck touched his stick, muscle memory kicked in. He focused on small, quick taps, guiding the puck around each cone. His turns were tighter than some of the other kids', his posture lower, his eyes on the puck but also darting forward to plan his path. By the time he finished, he was breathing heavily but felt a bloom of pride. That had gone okay.

Next, they practiced shooting on a goalie, who looked not much taller than Doug but was bulked up by thick pads and a bright red mask. The goalie smacked his glove against his thigh, beckoning shooters to bring it on. Standing at the top of the circle, Doug hesitated. This was different from a casual pond setup. There were lines on the ice, a real net, a real goalie. He could feel eyes on him—Coach Loring, teammates, maybe even Mike watching from the benches.

He swung the puck out in front of him, took a breath, and snapped a quick wrist shot aimed for the lower stick side. The goalie reacted fast, dropping to the butterfly, and the puck clanged off a pad. The ricochet slid away. Doug's heart dropped—he'd missed. It wasn't a total whiff, but still a missed shot.

"Not bad," Coach Loring said, leaning on his stick. "Pick your spot earlier, and really commit to it."

Doug nodded, retrieving the puck. Another skater was up next. He watched, analyzing the boy's stance and shot, trying to glean pointers for his next attempt. As the practice went on, Doug loosened up. He scored a couple of times, found a decent rhythm in passing drills, and even connected on a neat give-and-go with one of the returning players, who gave him a nod of appreciation. By the time Coach Loring blew the final whistle for a cooldown, Doug's jersey was soaked with sweat and his lungs burned, but he felt euphoric.

Coach Loring gathered them at center ice. "All right, that's good for tonight," he announced. "Couple things before we go: We have a scrimmage on Saturday morning. If you're on this roster, be here by eight. If you're new—" he looked at Doug, "—and you want to come, you're welcome to watch or even suit up if you can finalize your paperwork. Up to you."

Doug met the coach's gaze and managed a small, determined smile. "I'd like to play, sir."

"Great," the coach said, giving a curt nod. "See you then."

Afterward, in the hallway by the locker rooms, Doug found Mike waiting near a trophy case. Mike's face lit up when he saw Doug approach, gear clutched in both arms. "So?" Mike asked eagerly. "How'd it go?"

Doug exhaled, pulling off his helmet. A swirl of steam rose from his hair. "Good," he said, his voice trembling with adrenaline. "Really good. Coach wants me to come back Saturday."

Mike's grin broadened. "I knew it. You were keeping up out there, Dougie—I saw you weave through those cones. Some of those guys couldn't control the puck half as well." He clapped Doug on the shoulder.

Their parents emerged from the stands, braving the frigid arena air to meet them. Doug's father still wore that cautious expression, as though he was proud but measuring how far this might go. Doug's mother gave him a tight smile, looking relieved that he was in one piece. "Peewee practice seems serious," she commented softly. "But you handled yourself well out there."

Doug swallowed, searching her face for approval. "Thanks, Mom."

As they walked out to the car, each breath Doug took seemed more exhilarating than the last. The exhaustion in his muscles was overshadowed by a deep sense of accomplishment. Hockey wasn't just a pastime—it was becoming an inseparable part of him. Despite his father's and mother's reservations, he knew they were seeing him in a new light: not just a daydreaming kid, but a kid with purpose. With a goal.

In the days leading to Saturday, Doug ramped up his routine. He woke earlier and stayed out on the backyard rink longer. He practiced shooting against a plywood board he'd set up in the driveway, aiming for chalk-drawn targets that represented the goalie's weak spots: top shelf, between the pads, blocker side. Each shot repeated a hundred times, each attempt an incremental step toward the control he craved. He studied advanced stickhandling moves online—like toe drags and backhand dekes—and tried to replicate them on the ice, often losing the puck or stumbling, but getting a bit better each time.

His parents watched from the kitchen window. Doug often caught a glimpse of their faces—his father's neutral, analyzing expression; his mother's concerned but slightly curious gaze. Occasionally, one would come out to remind him about chores or homework, but otherwise, they let him be. Mike joined him whenever he could, giving pointers or just playing mini one-on-one games. They'd rattle the boards with mock hits, all the while grinning so hard their cheeks ached.

Yet at school, Doug's teachers began commenting on his daydreaming. His math teacher, Mr. Gilbert, asked him to stay after class one afternoon. "Doug, you seem... elsewhere," Mr. Gilbert said gently, tapping a pencil on his grade book. "Your test scores are still okay, but they've slipped a bit from earlier in the year. Everything all right?"

Doug squirmed. He hadn't realized his grades were slipping, though he supposed it made sense. Night after night, his mind was on hockey; homework had become more of an afterthought. He mumbled something about having a lot going on, to which Mr. Gilbert offered a sympathetic nod. "Just keep on top of it, all right? You're a bright kid. Don't let your focus drift too far."

Doug walked away feeling a small pang of guilt. For a moment, he worried about the vow he'd made to his parents—that he'd balance hockey and school. *I'll try harder,* he promised himself. But as soon as the final bell rang that day, his thoughts drifted immediately to the backyard rink.

Saturday came at last, bright and early. Doug could hardly contain himself. The scrimmage was scheduled for eight in the morning, which meant leaving the house by seven to get dressed, warm up, and do any last-minute instructions. He barely slept, jolting awake before his alarm. By six-thirty, he was dressed in warm sweats, jacket, and a Maple Leafs beanie, standing by the front door with his hockey bag, practically bouncing on the balls of his feet.

His father and mother exchanged bleary-eyed glances over coffee mugs. Mike, who'd volunteered to come along for moral support, stifled a yawn as he pulled on his sneakers. The drive to the rink felt interminable. Doug's father navigated the empty streets, the sky still streaked with pale pinks from the rising sun. In the back seat, Doug stared out the window, tapping his foot incessantly.

"Relax," Mike said, leaning over. "It's just a scrimmage. You've played pickup games that were probably more intense."

Doug knew Mike was trying to help, but his stomach churned. *This is different,* he wanted to say. *This is organized. This is my chance to prove I belong.* But he didn't voice it; he just forced a nod and tried not to imagine all the ways he could mess up.

They arrived at the rink, where a handful of parents and kids were already unloading gear. Doug said a quick goodbye to his parents and headed straight for the dressing room. Some of the same boys from practice were there, including the friendly goalie, who gave Doug a nod. A taller kid Doug hadn't met was regaling everyone with a story about a recent hockey tournament in a neighboring town. Doug quietly found a spot to change, meticulously putting on each piece of equipment like armor.

Coach Loring popped in, clipboard in hand. "Glad you're back, Doug," he said with a firm pat on Doug's shoulder pad. "You'll skate on the second line with Alex and Trevor." He pointed to two boys lacing their skates a few seats away. "Don't worry, you'll do fine."

Doug managed a shaky smile. The second line. That meant he'd get a decent amount of ice time, not just scraps. He glanced at Alex and Trevor—two boys who looked about his age, maybe a year older. Both had the casual confidence of kids who'd been playing for years. Alex offered a quick nod, while Trevor mumbled a greeting. Doug wondered if they resented having to line up with the new kid, but neither seemed bothered. If anything, they looked curious.

When everyone was dressed, the team trooped out to the ice. The stands were mostly empty, save for a handful of parents scattered around. Doug spotted his father, mother, and Mike settling in the top row. His parents waved awkwardly; Mike gave a thumbs-up. Doug fought the urge to wave back, feeling self-conscious. Instead, he skated a few laps around the rink, exhaling nervously into the frosty air.

The scrimmage was against another local peewee group, also around a dozen kids. Coach Loring explained that they'd play three short periods, each around ten minutes of running clock, with the scoreboard actually turned on. Doug felt his heart hammer the moment the clock lit up: *10:00* in bright red digits.

The first line started, and Doug's line stood at the bench, waiting. He leaned against the boards, trying to calm his breathing, while Alex and Trevor chatted about their favorite NHL players. Two minutes in, Coach hollered, "Second line—go!"

Doug hopped the boards carefully, stick in hand. The shift began. The other team had the puck, their forward skating swiftly into Doug's zone. Doug positioned himself near the point, remembering the diagrams he'd studied in magazines: cover your man, keep an eye on the puck carrier, watch for passes. The defenseman took a shot from the blue line; Doug automatically stuck out his stick, deflecting the puck away from the net. He felt a surge of pride—he'd done the right thing.

Trevor picked up the loose puck, firing a quick pass to Alex, who started up the ice. Doug sprinted to join the rush, knees pumping, adrenaline flaring through every muscle. Alex, seeing a defender approach, slid the puck to Doug. It bobbled momentarily, but Doug recovered it with a deft flick of his wrist. The path to the net wasn't clear—two defenders converged on him. In a flash of instinct, Doug feigned a shot, then pulled the puck back, slipping it to Trevor on his left. Trevor's eyes widened in surprise but he took it in stride, unleashing a shot that soared over the goalie's pad and into the net.

Goal. Only a minute into their first shift, and they'd scored. Doug felt a powerful rush of elation. He pumped his fist quietly, not wanting to over-celebrate, but Trevor turned to him with a wide grin, tapping gloves. "Nice pass, man!"

Alex joined them, ruffling Doug's helmet. "Great play. Keep it up."

They skated back to the bench, adrenaline surging. Coach Loring gave them each a nod, grinning around his whistle. "Textbook," he said simply. Doug caught Mike's eye in the stands, and Mike gave a vigorous thumbs-up. Doug's chest felt light, almost buoyant. This was exactly where he wanted to be.

As the scrimmage went on, Doug's nerves faded. He wasn't perfect—he missed some passes, lost a faceoff or two—but his line created more chances than they allowed. By the end of the second period, they were leading 3–1. Doug even rang a shot off the crossbar that left him reeling with excitement (and a bit of disappointment).

Coach Loring called them over during a short break. "You see how each of you has a role out there?" he said, pointing at Alex, Trevor, then Doug. "Alex's speed is key. Trevor's got a quick release on his shot. Doug, you're reading the play well, anticipating. Use that. Keep focusing on moving your feet and making those crisp passes. Good things happen when you hustle."

Doug nodded, soaking in every word. He felt a fierce joy in the coach's praise—recognition that he wasn't just tagging along, but contributing in a real way. It was the validation he'd been craving without even fully knowing it.

When the final buzzer sounded, the scoreboard read 4–2. Their team had won. The kids glided around, tapping gloves, exchanging cheers. Doug's face hurt from grinning. He made eye contact with Trevor, who winked playfully. "We gotta keep you around," Trevor said. "That pass was sweet."

Alex patted Doug's back. "You ever play in a league before?"

Doug shook his head. "No, just... pond hockey and backyard stuff."

Alex's eyebrows rose. "Seriously? Dude, that's wild. Keep it up."

Feeling a bit shy under the praise, Doug ducked his head. But inside, his heart hammered with pride. Maybe he truly belonged here.

After changing out of his gear and packing up, Doug stepped into the hallway to find his parents and Mike waiting. His father wore a rare, open smile. "You looked good out there," he said in an uncharacteristically enthusiastic tone. "That pass was impressive."

His mother chimed in, eyes bright. "You seemed so... comfortable, Doug. Like you've been doing this for years."

Doug shrugged, trying to hide how thrilled he was. "Thanks, guys. I still have a lot to learn."

Mike slung an arm around his shoulders. "You did great, Dougie. I'm telling you, you're a natural."

Coach Loring appeared from the locker room behind them, nodding a greeting to Doug's father and mother. "He's got a good feel for the game," he told them. "If Doug wants to join the team for the rest of the season, we'd be happy to have him. I'll get you the paperwork and schedule." He looked at Doug. "We've got practice Mondays and Wednesdays, and games most Saturdays. Think you can handle it?"

Doug felt a burst of excitement. *I have to handle it,* he thought, bobbing his head. "Yes, Coach. Absolutely."

Coach Loring smiled, handing a small folder of forms to Doug's father. "Welcome aboard. We'll see you Monday, Doug."

That night, Doug could hardly concentrate on anything else. He sat at his desk, attempting to do his math homework, but his mind replayed each moment from the scrimmage—the slick pass to Trevor, the crossbar shot that almost went in, the swirl of voices on the bench, the quick instructions from the coach. He felt more alive on the ice than he ever had anywhere else. Was this what it meant to truly love a sport?

He heard a light knock on his bedroom door. "Yeah?" Doug called, snapping out of his reverie.

Mike stuck his head in. "Just wanted to check on you, see if you're still riding that high from the game." He entered and leaned against the edge of Doug's desk. "You know, you can rest a little, right?"

Doug laughed softly, closing his math book. "I know, I know. I just keep thinking about how to get better. I want to work on my shot accuracy, my speed, everything."

Mike studied him a moment. "I get it. Trust me, I do. Hockey's amazing, but... remember to pace yourself. Don't lose sight of other stuff, all right? I'm saying this because I've been there."

Doug nodded, but a flicker of stubbornness sparked within him. "Sure, but I can balance it. I won't slack on school."

Mike shrugged in a good-natured way, pushing off the desk. "All right, hotshot. Just remember if you ever feel overwhelmed, you've got me, you've got Mom and Dad. You're not alone in this."

"Thanks, Mike," Doug said quietly. He meant it. Having Mike's support made him feel safer, like he wasn't just charging blindly into a new world.

When Mike left, Doug sighed and reopened his math book. He forced himself to concentrate, but every few minutes, his mind drifted to hockey. In the margins of his notebook, he doodled a tiny jersey with a scribbled leaf logo and the number 9—his favorite number for reasons he could barely articulate, aside from hearing legends like Gordie Howe wore it. Doug wondered if, someday, he might wear that number in a bigger game, in front of an even bigger crowd.

By the time Doug finally crawled into bed, exhaustion crept into his limbs. But rather than feeling drained, he felt a sense of fulfillment. The memory of that morning's scrimmage had rooted itself into his mind. He stared at the dark ceiling, listening to the faint sounds of his family moving around the house. *This is just the beginning,* he told himself. *I've got a long way to go.*

Outside, the wind whistled through the trees. Maybe snow would fall overnight, dusting the backyard rink. If it did, Doug knew he'd be out there at first light, shovel in hand. The cold morning air beckoned him. The ice called to him.

And as sleep slowly claimed him, images of the puck dancing on his stick, the glow of arena lights, and the echoing cheers of a crowd filled his dreams. The obsession had begun, and Doug embraced it wholeheartedly, convinced that on the ice—whether it was a humble backyard rink, the local pond, or a sparkling arena—he was finally where he belonged.

3

MAPLES LEAFS VS. THE MONTREAL CANADIENS

The cold winter sun crept through the slats of Doug's bedroom blinds on a Saturday morning that promised both excitement and biting chill. He blinked awake, momentarily disoriented, then remembered what night it was—*Hockey Night in Canada*, featuring none other than the Toronto Maple Leafs versus the Montreal Canadiens. A jolt of energy shot through him, banishing any lingering sleepiness.

He had grown up hearing about this rivalry—a storied clash that cut deep into the history of Canadian hockey. He'd read about it in dog-eared magazines and old newspaper clippings, listened to Mike recount legendary games from the past, and even overheard heated bar debates among adults about which team boasted the more illustrious heritage. Now, after weeks of immersing himself in all things hockey, Doug felt newly attuned to the drama that was about to unfold on the TV screen that night.

But morning came first, and with it the routines Doug had forced himself to adopt: finishing chores, juggling homework, and maybe squeezing in some time on the backyard rink. He trudged downstairs, the smell of oatmeal and bacon greeting him. His mother stood at the stove, flipping bacon strips. She flashed him a smile. "Morning, hockey fanatic," she teased gently, aware of how glued Doug had been to every piece of hockey news since he'd joined the peewee team.

"Morning, Mom," Doug mumbled, still shaking off the last remnants of sleep. He slid onto a kitchen chair and reached for the juice pitcher. "Is Dad still asleep?"

"He's up," she replied, nodding toward the living room. "He's reading the paper, I think."

Doug polished off a glass of orange juice and made his way around the corner. Sure enough, his father was in the worn recliner, flipping through the local sports section. He looked up as Doug entered. "Excited for tonight?" his dad asked, a small grin tugging at his lips.

Doug nodded, feeling a spark leap inside him. "Definitely. Leafs vs. Habs. I can't wait."

His father closed the paper, folding it neatly. "I was your age the first time I really appreciated that rivalry. It's in our blood, son. My father used to say it went back to the very beginnings of the NHL—Toronto and Montreal, always at each other's throats." He paused, a nostalgic gleam in his eye. "I'm glad you'll be watching with me tonight."

Doug settled onto the couch. "Me too," he said quietly, imagining how, in just a few hours, they'd both be huddled in front of the TV, dissecting every faceoff, every hit, every scoring chance. The day yawned ahead, but Doug wished he could fast-forward straight to puck drop.

After breakfast, Doug dutifully tackled his chores. He helped shovel the driveway, where the overnight wind had blown a fine layer of snow into swirling drifts. With each thrust of the shovel, his breath puffed out in cloudy bursts, his legs still a bit stiff from the previous day's peewee practice. Yet the memory of that practice fueled him with excitement: he'd made a nice cross-ice pass that had led to a scrimmage goal, earning a pat on the back from Coach Loring. Every moment on the ice reminded him that he was inching closer to understanding the complexities of the game he loved.

As soon as he finished his outdoor duties, he hustled inside and raced upstairs to chip away at some homework. Though he was anxious to do something hockey-related, he also remembered his father's warning about keeping his grades up. So he cracked open his math textbook, scanning the problems for that evening's assignment. But in the quiet of his room, it wasn't equations that filled his head—it was the upcoming Leafs vs. Habs matchup. He thought of top lines, special teams, star players, and the swirl of the crowd roaring at the Scotiabank Arena (or the Bell Centre, depending on who had home ice). In his imagination, the scene was vivid: the organ music, the flash of cameras, and the anxious hush before a big faceoff.

He forced himself to focus, scribbling out solutions until he reached the final problem. Over an hour had passed, and though he couldn't fully recall how he'd arrived at each answer, he had at least completed the worksheet. Satisfied, Doug sprang to his feet and checked the clock: still hours to go until the game. Maybe he could get in some practice outside.

Huddled in his coat and gloves, Doug trudged to the backyard rink. The sun was brighter now, though still stingy with its warmth. Thin streams of vapor rose from the ice's surface where morning dew had frozen. He skated in lazy circles for a while, warming up. Then he set up a small patch of plywood along one side—the "goal." He used a rubber ball instead of a puck, figuring it would handle the bumps on the makeshift rink better.

He practiced his shooting, aiming for marked spots with chalk: top-left corner, top-right, low five-hole, and so on. Each time, he visualized an NHL goalie at the other end, imagining the roar of the crowd if he scored. The yard was silent, but in Doug's mind, thousands of voices rose and fell with each shot. He pictured the Maple Leafs crest on his chest, the feel of crisp air in a packed arena, the rival Canadiens glaring from across the faceoff circle. The daydreams ignited a warmth in his chest that transcended the cold.

After half an hour, his arms ached from repetitive shots. He paused, bent over to catch his breath, and realized he was dripping with sweat beneath his jacket. That was enough for now—he needed to save energy for the emotional marathon of watching the big game that night. As he unlaced his skates, he felt a twinge of embarrassment at how seriously he was taking all this. It was just a game on TV. But for him, it represented so much more: tradition, aspiration, and the flickering dream of one day stepping onto that ice himself.

Mid-afternoon brought a subtle change to the house's atmosphere. Doug's father disappeared briefly to run errands, promising he'd be back well before puck drop. His mother tackled some laundry, and Mike was out with friends, likely playing street hockey or browsing the local sports shop for new sticks. Doug found himself pacing through the living room, flipping channels aimlessly, until he paused on a pre-game special analyzing the Leafs-Habs rivalry. Archive footage filled the screen: black-and-white clips of bygone eras, then the color-saturated 70s, 80s, 90s, all the way to modern day. Fierce hits, improbable comebacks, legendary goaltenders. Doug felt goosebumps prickle along his arms. *This is what it's all about,* he thought.

The commentator's voice droned on about how these two teams had faced each other numerous times in the playoffs, how their fanbases were among the most passionate in the league. Words like "historic," "fierce," and "unrivaled" kept popping up. Doug devoured each anecdote, each highlight, storing them away like precious keepsakes. So many stars had worn the Maple Leaf on their chests, fighting for pride and the chance to upstage the Canadiens. One day, maybe he could be among them. One day.

Darkness fell early, as it often did in winter. Doug's father returned with groceries, a special treat of potato chips, soda, and wings for the game. He placed them on the counter with a wink at Doug. "Figure we can make a night of it," he said. "It's tradition, after all." Doug beamed, the scent of freshly bought barbecue wings already filling the kitchen.

Mike appeared around dinnertime, shrugging off his coat in the hall. "Did I miss anything?" he asked, arching an eyebrow at Doug's father.

"Not yet," came the reply. "Puck drops at seven. Better eat fast—then we'll settle in."

Normally, dinner was a leisurely affair in the Mansfield house, but tonight, there was a shared urgency. They all sensed it was a big night—Doug's first time truly *invested* in the Leafs-Habs rivalry as more than just a casual observer. Even though the rest of the family had different levels of interest, Doug's excitement was contagious. Mother teased Doug about having the channels memorized, while Mike joked that if Doug got any more hyped, he might start painting his face blue and white. Their father just smiled through it all, offering recollections of the last Leafs-Habs game he'd watched in full.

Finally, dinner ended, dishes were stacked in the sink, and they migrated to the living room. Doug's father turned the TV on, flipping to the classic opening montage of *Hockey Night in Canada*. The iconic theme played, and Doug felt a pleasant buzz run through him, as though this was a ritual connecting him to millions of other Canadian fans, all huddled in living rooms, bars, or community centers. This was more than a sport—it was a unifying thread, weaving together strangers and families alike.

The pre-game show began with the usual commentary: experts dissecting each lineup, analyzing injury reports, and assessing which team had the advantage that night. Doug settled into the sofa, leaning forward, eyes glued to the screen. His father occupied the recliner as always, while Mike and his mother hovered between the living room and kitchen. The wings and chips were on the coffee table, tempting to anyone who walked by.

They showed the players during warm-ups, each Leafs skater cruising around in the classic blue-and-white sweaters, the Maple Leaf crest bold on their chests. Doug's heart thumped faster when the camera panned over the visiting Montreal Canadiens, decked out in red, white, and blue. The legendary "CH" on their jerseys seemed to vibrate with the same storied energy as Toronto's crest. Doug's father offered some background. "See that guy, their captain? One of the top goal-scorers in the league. Our defense needs to keep him in check tonight."

Doug nodded, soaking it in. Meanwhile, his own eyes flicked over the Leafs bench. He was particularly enthralled with the star forward—a flashy player known for highlight-reel goals. "He's unstoppable when he's on his game," Doug mused, half to himself. "But the Habs have a good goalie. It'll be tough." He loved that he could talk about it like he was part of the conversation. The nuances made sense now, thanks to his deep-dive into strategies, practice drills, and experiences with his peewee team.

Soon, the broadcast cut to the national anthem. The camera panned over the stands—thousands of fans packed into every seat. Some wore blue and white jerseys, others red and white. Many held signs, waved flags, or sported face paint. Doug's father turned up the volume, and a hush fell over the living room as the singer's voice soared through the arena. Doug felt chills. He could almost smell the popcorn and spilled beer, feel the rumble of collective voices singing in unison. It reminded him of why this rivalry was so special—two powerhouse fanbases, two proud franchises, all standing to honor the sport and the country, even if only for a minute.

When the puck finally dropped, Doug could barely sit still. The Leafs won the opening faceoff, the center cleanly drawing it back to the defense. A roar erupted from the crowd, though it was hard to tell from the broadcast if it was cheers or boos. Doug loved that chaotic swirl of noise, the living heartbeat of an NHL game. The defenseman reversed the puck behind the net, avoiding the forecheck from Montreal's speedy winger.

His father leaned forward, pointing at the screen. "Look at that gap control. He's not letting the Habs forward close in too fast."

Doug nodded, now able to grasp these subtleties. A couple of months ago, it might have just looked like random skating and chasing. Now, he understood that the Leafs were setting up a breakout play, the defenseman looking for a lane to pass. Sure enough, the puck zipped across to the right winger, who accelerated through the neutral zone.

Doug's mother, perched on the edge of the sofa, chuckled at Doug's intensity. "He's like a coach in miniature," she joked. Mike smirked, tossing a chip into his mouth.

"I'm learning," Doug said with a grin, not taking his eyes off the screen.

The first shift ended quietly, but soon enough, the tone set in. Montreal hammered the Leafs with physical play, landing big hits in open ice. One jarring collision rattled the boards, causing the Leafs forward to lose the puck. Doug winced at the impact, but also felt a strange excitement—it was part of the game's raw allure.

Within the first five minutes, Doug's father pointed at the scoreboard. "Shots are 4–1 in favor of Montreal. We need to get some pucks on net." He sounded like a second commentator, and Doug hung on every word. Indeed, Toronto looked a step behind, as if they were feeling out the game while Montreal pressed hard.

Then, in a sudden swing of momentum, the Leafs' second line managed a zone entry. Crisp passing along the boards, a drop pass to the trailing defenseman, a quick wrister from the blue line—deflected in front. The Montreal goalie scrambled, but the puck found its way under his pad. *Gooooal.* A storm of noise on TV: the home fans leaping out of their seats, horns blaring, the commentators' voices drowning in the commotion.

Doug let out a whoop, pounding his fist into a couch cushion. His father clapped excitedly, while Mike jumped up, arms raised. Even their mother smiled, caught in the contagious joy of seeing the Leafs score first against their longtime rival. Doug imagined for a split second being that player who found the puck in the slot, burying it behind the goalie, hearing the crowd erupt.

As the period wore on, the game stayed tight. The Habs responded with pressure, unleashing a flurry of shots on the Leafs netminder. Some rang off the posts, others required jaw-dropping saves. Doug marveled at the athleticism, noticing how the goalie tracked the puck so smoothly from left to right. The speed of an NHL game struck him in ways it never had before—bodies flying, passes zipping across the ice, the forecheck snapping at every opportunity.

"This is unreal," Doug muttered, more to himself than anyone else. "They move so fast."

His father nodded in agreement. "NHL hockey is something else. It's one thing to play peewee or watch highlights, but seeing these men up close—well, on TV but in real time—makes you realize the skill level."

Doug felt an odd mix of inspiration and intimidation. Could he ever hope to reach that stratosphere of speed and skill? Part of him dreamed about it so intensely that it felt like a physical ache—he wanted that more than anything. Another part reminded him just how far away it was. He was an 11-year-old in battered secondhand gear. But the dream wouldn't be quelled. Especially not on a night like this.

At the end of the first period, the score remained 1–0 Leafs. During the intermission, the broadcast crew dissected the period, praising Toronto's opportunistic play and Montreal's aggressive forecheck. Doug devoured their every word, noticing how the experts pointed out small defensive errors, complimented certain wingers for their "hustle," and predicted adjustments for the second period. The entire breakdown provided a mini coaching clinic, feeding Doug's growing strategic mind.

Early in the second period, Montreal came out hungry, dominating puck possession. Their top center managed to slip behind the Leafs' defense and blistered a shot toward the top corner. The Toronto goalie just barely got a piece of it, sending the puck fluttering wide. Doug exhaled, heart pounding. "That was close."

"Too close," his father agreed. "We can't give them that space."

Moments later, a Montreal forward delivered a crushing hit to the Leafs' defenseman along the boards. The defenseman sprawled onto the ice, and a pushing match ensued. Gloves flew, and the camera zoomed in on a swirl of fists and jerseys. A hush fell over the living room, except for Mike's exclamation—"Whoa!"—followed by some typical big-brother excitement. Doug stared, half in awe, half in discomfort. He knew fights were part of the game, but witnessing an all-out brawl was different.

"This rivalry brings out the passion," his father said, though he sounded less than thrilled with the violence. "But yeah, these teams have a lot of bad blood. Always have."

The referees intervened, handing out penalties, and the broadcast replayed the hit from different angles. Doug found himself strangely riveted—*that's* how far players would go to defend each other, to send a message. Peewee hockey was physical, but nowhere near that level. It struck Doug that if he truly aimed for the NHL, he'd have to face this intensity someday.

Once the dust settled, the Leafs found themselves on a power play. Doug's eyes lit up as their special teams unit took the ice. He watched how the defenseman quarterbacked from the blue line, how the forwards positioned themselves for deflections, one-timers, or rebounds. The synergy was beautiful, a well-oiled machine. For nearly two minutes, the Leafs swarmed the Canadiens' zone, peppering the goalie with shots—one clanged off the post, another was gobbled up in the goalie's glove, and a third skidded through the crease without finding a stick.

No goal, but the crowd roared its approval of the effort. Doug found himself bouncing on the couch cushion, fists clenched. This was as exciting as anything he'd ever seen.

Halfway through the second, Montreal broke loose on a 2-on-1. The Leafs defenseman sprawled to block the pass, but the puck slipped past him. The Montreal forward rifled a shot into the top corner, tying the game 1–1. The deafening hush from the home crowd was palpable—even through the TV broadcast. The Canadiens players swarmed each other, celebrating with a flurry of hugs and glove taps.

Doug sighed, sinking back into the couch. He felt the sting of disappointment as though he were on the Leafs' bench. Mike let out a low whistle, while Doug's father shook his head. "We got caught pinching. That's what can happen against a team with speed."

But if Doug had learned anything from playing hockey, it was that there was always another shift, another faceoff, another chance. And sure enough, the Leafs responded with a wave of offensive energy, culminating in a scramble around Montreal's net. Bodies piled in the crease, the goalie flailing. The puck squirted out to a Leafs winger at the side of the net. With a quick flick, he buried it.

"YEAH!" Doug leaped up, nearly spilling the bowl of chips. His father pumped a fist, and even Doug's mother cheered, caught in the moment. The scoreboard now read 2–1, in favor of Toronto. The tension was thick, and there was still half a game to go.

During the second intermission, Doug's mother gently reminded him he had a bedtime, to which he pleaded, "Just one night, please let me stay up to watch the whole thing. It's the Habs and the Leafs." She relented—partly because it was Saturday, and partly because she could see how much it mattered to him.

"I remember how Grandpa used to let me stay up for the third period if it was a big game," Doug's father said with a nostalgic smile. "A tradition worth keeping alive."

The third period opened with an explosion of energy. Montreal seemed determined to even things up, firing shots from all angles. Doug's father sighed every time the Leafs defense iced the puck, buying themselves a moment of respite. *They look tired,* Doug thought, noticing how the Leafs were content to dump it out and make quick changes.

Mike, who'd returned from a brief phone call with a friend, plopped down on the couch. "We can't sit back. If we let the Habs run the show, they'll tie it up in no time."

Sure enough, with about ten minutes remaining, Montreal pinned the Leafs in their own zone. A cycling play behind the net led to a quick wraparound attempt. The Leafs' goalie sprawled, but the puck squirted through his pads and trickled in. A collective groan rose from the home crowd, matched by a stunned silence in the Mansfield living room.

"2–2," Doug said softly, biting his lip. His father shook his head, but offered a pragmatic viewpoint: "Still time left. We just need to push."

The tension mounted with every shift. The hits got heavier, the forechecking more relentless. Doug felt his pulse in his ears, as if he were on the bench waiting for the coach to tap his shoulder. He imagined the pressure these NHL players must be facing—the hope of an entire city, the weight of a century-old rivalry. It was exhilarating, and it also underscored how mighty a dream it was to play at that level. But if anything, it fueled him further.

With under five minutes to go, Toronto's first line roared up the ice. The center shielded the puck along the boards, slipped a pass to the high slot. A defenseman crept in from the blue line, unleashed a slapper that soared through traffic. Doug leaned forward, heart in his throat. The puck found its way past the goalie, rattling the back of the net. A ferocious cheer erupted from the stands.

Doug and Mike jumped up, nearly colliding in midair. Their father let out a triumphant laugh. Even Doug's mother, usually more reserved, clapped and whooped. The scoreboard lit up: 3–2 Leafs. Four minutes left.

But the game wasn't done yet. Montreal, desperate to tie, pulled their goalie in the final minute. Six attackers swarmed Toronto's end, hurling shots. Doug sat on the edge of the couch, hardly breathing. The Leafs defenders blocked two attempts, the goalie smothered another. The final seconds ticked away. A last-second shot whistled wide. The horn sounded. Leafs win. 3–2.

The Mansfield household erupted in celebration. Doug flung his arms in the air, a grin splitting his face. The TV screen showed the Leafs players pouring off the bench, congratulating the goalie, while the Canadiens skated off, heads low. The cameras panned to the disappointed Habs fans in the crowd, then to the jubilant Leafs faithful. Doug's father clapped him on the shoulder. "That, my boy, is a classic rivalry game. Hard-fought, tight score. You don't get better hockey than that."

Doug nodded in exhilaration, but inside he felt something more profound: *This is what I want.* He craved the roar of that arena, the pulse-pounding final minutes, the swirl of adrenaline. He wanted to be one of those players slamming fists on the goalie's pads, celebrating a gritty victory.

When the post-game show wrapped up, the clock read nearly 10:00 PM—late for Doug, but he could hardly feel tired. He helped clean up the living room, gathering empty plates and cups. Mike gave him a playful nudge. "You look like you just won the Cup, Dougie."

Doug laughed. "I feel like it, almost."

Their mother collected the last few dishes. "All right, guys, wrap it up. Doug, you've earned your late night, but tomorrow is Sunday, so we'll let you sleep in a bit. Don't think you'll get out of chores, though," she teased.

Doug's father lingered by the TV, flipping channels briefly. "Nothing else on that can top a Leafs-Habs thriller," he said, turning it off. "I'm heading to bed. Night, everyone."

"Night, Dad." Doug made his way to his room, adrenaline still coursing through his veins. He flicked on the light, scanning the walls. Though his bedroom décor was still a mix of random posters and kid-friendly images, he'd started taping up pictures of hockey players. He had a photo of that Maple Leafs star forward, the one who'd made a crucial pass tonight.

He also had a Maple Leaf logo he'd drawn by hand, pinned near his desk.

Slumping onto the bed, he replayed the game in his mind. The defensive plays, the hits, the breathtaking saves, the triumphant goal with minutes left to play. The rivalry's intensity echoed in his thoughts. What must it feel like to stand on that ice, hearing the crowd erupt around you? The possibility felt both thrilling and impossible—like a distant star in the night sky, shimmering in unattainable grandeur. But as he gazed at his taped-up pictures, he allowed himself to dream. *One day,* he repeated to himself. *One day I could pull on that Leafs sweater, step onto the ice against the Canadiens, and live this rivalry firsthand.*

Just imagining it made his pulse quicken. He closed his eyes, letting the scenes swirl in his mind. The Habs' red sweaters across the faceoff circle, the Maple Leaf crest on his own chest, the whistle shrieking for the opening draw, the roar of thousands. He pictured his father in the stands, wearing a Toronto jersey, maybe holding a sign. The entire city of Toronto behind him, rooting for him to beat their oldest rival. He thought about the scuffles, the big hits, the critical goals. It was terrifying, yet he'd never felt a desire so strong.

He must have dozed off at some point, because the next thing Doug knew, it was morning and a soft gray light filtered through the blinds. He rubbed his eyes, feeling a pleasant warmth of memory: the Leafs had won. He hopped out of bed, body still buzzing with that post-game glow, and rummaged for some clothes. It was Sunday, which usually meant a slower pace in the Mansfield household—late breakfast, perhaps a trip to the grocery store, some time to relax or watch a midday broadcast of highlights.

When Doug walked into the kitchen, he found his father at the table with a steaming mug of coffee, reading an online recap of last night's game on his tablet. "Morning, champ," his father greeted, eyes crinkling. "Sleep well?"

Doug nodded, sliding into a chair across from him. "Yeah, had a pretty epic dream about playing in that game." He felt a slight flush creep up his neck. Admitting such a big aspiration felt vulnerable, but also strangely liberating.

His father set the tablet aside. "Tell me about it."

Doug shrugged, toying with a napkin. "I was on the Leafs, obviously. We were playing Montreal, just like last night. Except I was the one who scored the go-ahead goal late in the game. I remember the crowd was so loud it felt like the ice was shaking." He smiled sheepishly. "Then I woke up."

His father's expression softened with fondness. "That's a wonderful dream, Doug. And you know, it's not impossible. Long road, but you've got the passion. And that's where it all starts."

Doug studied his father's face, searching for any hint of dismissiveness. Instead, he found sincere encouragement. Maybe it was crazy to think an 11-year-old from a small Ontario town could make it big in the NHL, but his father's belief buoyed him. "Thanks, Dad."

They chatted a bit about the finer points of the game—how Toronto's penalty kill had stifled Montreal's power play, the questionable hooking call in the second period, the star forward's near-miss on a breakaway. Doug marveled at how these were the same tactics and strategies he was learning at the peewee level, just magnified a hundred times. If he kept studying, practicing, pushing himself...who knew?

Later that morning, Mike joined them, yawning dramatically. The conversation naturally circled back to the Leafs win. Doug's mother, wiping down the kitchen counters, rolled her eyes with mock exasperation at how everything in the house seemed to revolve around hockey now. But Doug noticed she wore a tiny smile. Despite her concerns about his obsession, she sensed how much joy it brought him.

Doug brought up a topic that had been simmering in his mind. "Dad, do you think we could go see a Leafs game in person someday? At Scotiabank Arena?"

A flicker of hesitation crossed his father's face. "I'd like that, Doug, but tickets can get pricey. Especially for a Montreal matchup."

"Oh," Doug said, crestfallen. Of course it would be expensive—everyone wanted seats when Toronto played Montreal.

Mike piped up. "We could always aim for a less flashy matchup. Maybe the next time a different team comes to town, the ticket prices might be cheaper."

Doug nodded. Even to watch a Leafs game against a non-rival would be incredible. The idea of stepping into that arena, hearing the national anthem echo through the rafters, and seeing his heroes up close thrilled him. "Yeah, that'd be amazing. I'm down for any game."

His father grinned, leaning back. "Then we'll see what we can do. No promises, but let's keep an eye out."

It wasn't the guarantee Doug craved, but it was enough for now. The mere possibility of seeing an NHL game live was exhilarating, and it deepened his resolve. One day, he wanted to be the one on the ice, not just the kid in the stands. *For now, though, I'll be grateful to watch from anywhere I can.*

By midday, the house had mostly returned to its quiet weekend rhythms. Doug worked on a school project in the living room, but the TV hummed softly in the background, replaying last night's highlights: *Leafs best Canadiens, 3–2, in a Saturday night thriller.* The montage showed the key goals, the big hits, the ecstatic celebrations. Doug paused his schoolwork to watch it again, even though he'd already witnessed it live. Each replay reignited that spark of ambition.

He thought of the difference between dreaming of an NHL future and *actively* pursuing it. So far, he had poured countless hours into practice, watching games, and learning strategies. But was that enough? He recalled the skill, speed, and grit he had seen on display. Perhaps he'd need to do more—work harder, train systematically, not just skate around for fun. The thought made him both excited and anxious.

While he mulled this over, Mike entered the room carrying two hockey sticks. "The backyard rink's still decent," he said. "Wanna go run a few drills? I've got some ideas from last night's game. We could replicate that pass up the boards to a quick shot scenario."

Doug's face lit up. "Yeah, absolutely." He abandoned his school project without a second thought, grabbing his coat and following Mike outside.

In the backyard, the two brothers worked through a series of improvised drills. They mimicked the breakout they'd seen on TV, passing the puck along the boards, circling behind the net. Of course, their rink was tiny compared to an NHL standard, but they adapted. Mike demonstrated how a forward should time his movement if the defenseman was pinching. Doug tried to apply the concept, though the space constraints were challenging. Even so, each successful pass, each effective shot made him feel a step closer to the dream.

Between drills, Mike teased Doug. "You were about to lose it last night during the final minute, weren't you?"

Doug laughed, breath steaming in the cold air. "I thought my heart would explode. I can't imagine how the players handle that pressure."

Mike shrugged, leaning on his stick. "They train for years. They live for those moments. You're on your way, Dougie. Keep working at it, and who knows?"

Doug inhaled, letting that confidence wash over him. The backyard rink might be rough and cramped, but in his mind, it expanded into an NHL arena. He could practically see fans in the stands, cheering his name. The vision fueled him with each stride.

By mid-afternoon, the sky began to cloud over, threatening more snow. Doug and Mike retreated inside, stamping off their boots and discarding gloves stiff with cold. Their father eyed them over the edge of the newspaper. "You two look frozen. Hot chocolate?"

"Sounds great," Doug said, cheeks numb.

While the hot chocolate warmed on the stove, Doug settled at the kitchen table, flipping through an old hockey magazine that listed the all-time greatest Leafs-Habs games. He pointed out a 1979 playoff match that ended in overtime, a 1967 Stanley Cup Final showdown, and various other epic clashes. His father joined him, occasionally reminiscing about the eras when players wore minimal gear and crazy facial hair.

"Back then, the rivalry was everything," his father said, stirring cocoa powder into mugs. "Half the country seemed split between Toronto and Montreal. Sure, there are other

Canadian teams now, but Leafs-Habs—there's nothing like it. Last night's game was just another chapter in a long story."

Doug's mother bustled by, reminding them not to let the hot chocolate boil over. She wore a gentle smile as she listened to them delve into old stats and stories. Although she didn't share the same fervor for the rivalry, she recognized its significance for the Mansfield men—and now, especially, for Doug.

Once the mugs were ready, the three—Doug, Mike, and their father—lingered in the kitchen, sipping the sweet, velvety cocoa. Outside the window, flakes of snow began drifting lazily. Doug gazed at them, feeling an almost overwhelming rush of gratitude. *I love this game,* he thought, *and I love these moments, too.* He pictured nights down the road, maybe even years away, when he'd still be talking about last night's tilt with Montreal, or a game from 2025 or 2030, if he was lucky enough to be playing in it.

Evening came on quietly, with no further games scheduled that the family was interested in watching. Mike and their mother took over the living room TV to watch a movie, while Doug's father migrated to the den to catch a western film. Doug decided to retreat to his room, where he clicked on his small desk lamp. There, he began rearranging the pictures on his wall. He placed the Maple Leafs crest front and center, pinned at eye level. Surrounding it, he tacked on smaller images: famous Leafs players, some celebrating goals, some posing for official headshots.

In a corner, he put a few photos of Montreal greats. Not because he was a Habs fan—far from it—but because he respected the rivalry. It felt right to acknowledge the other side of the coin, to remind himself of the level of competition he'd be facing if he truly pursued an NHL path. Once finished, he stepped back, surveying his new "Wall of Inspiration." The Maple Leaf in the middle, the Canadiens in the corner, and scattered around them, the essence of a dream that had sprouted in his heart like a seedling seeking the sun.

He pulled out his phone—a small, hand-me-down model—and snapped a picture of the arrangement, just for himself. Maybe in a few years, he'd look back on this moment. *I was that kid with big dreams,* he'd say. And with luck, he'd see how far he'd come.

Doug turned off the lamp and let his gaze settle on the silhouettes of the pictures in the darkness. His mind replayed the game's final moments one more time: The crisp pass to the defenseman, the winding slapshot that found twine, the crowd's thunderous outburst. In that single second, the Leafs overcame their arch-rivals. Doug closed his eyes, letting the echoes of that triumph fill him.

He remembered his father's words: *It's not impossible. You have the passion.* Passion—he felt it in every fiber of his being. Tomorrow, Monday, he'd have to get up early for school, pay attention in classes, and maybe do some chores afterward. But soon enough, there'd be more hockey practice, more nights watching the NHL, more steps on that path. *One day,* he promised himself again, *I'm going to skate onto that ice, wearing the Maple Leafs sweater, facing the Canadiens. And I'm going to make everyone proud—Dad, Mike, Mom... and myself.*

It was a wild, ambitious thought, but no less powerful for being so. With the hush of winter pressing close against the house and the memory of that thrilling 3–2 victory still pulsing in his veins, Doug drifted to sleep, lost in a tapestry of cheering crowds, shining ice, and the timeless magic of the Leafs versus the Habs.

4

THE HOCKEY CARD EXPO

Doug woke up on an overcast Saturday morning with a flutter of excitement in his belly. He had been anticipating this day all week, ever since Mike mentioned the upcoming hockey card expo at a nearby convention hall. At first, Doug wasn't entirely sure what a "card expo" entailed—he'd collected a few hockey cards here and there, mostly random packs from the local convenience store, but he'd never delved into the world of trading, vintage finds, and high-stakes collectibles. As the days rolled by, however, he couldn't help feeding on Mike's enthusiasm. Mike had told tales of rare rookie cards from legendary players selling for hundreds, sometimes thousands of dollars. Doug's father, too, had chimed in, reminiscing about the hockey cards he traded as a kid, flipping them in schoolyards or securing them with elastic bands that inevitably left marks on those now-priceless cardboard treasures.

That morning, Doug was the first to bound down the stairs and into the kitchen. His mother was leaning over a grocery list, pen in hand, ready to tackle her weekend errands. She arched an eyebrow when she saw Doug's wide grin and restless stance. "You're certainly up early," she teased. "You don't usually move this quickly unless it involves a hockey stick."

Doug grinned, grabbing a glass of orange juice from the fridge. "Or hockey cards," he quipped, voice tinged with excitement. "Dad said we'd leave by nine. I just can't wait."

His mother smiled knowingly. "I'm happy to see you spending time with your dad and Mike. Just don't come home with an entire trunk full of cards, all right? We have to save some money for groceries."

"Oh, I'm not planning anything big," Doug said, trying to sound casual, though in his mind, he was already picturing a table laden with Maple Leafs memorabilia, old pictures, and rare card sets. "I just want to look around. Maybe I'll find something special."

At eight-thirty, Doug and Mike were both sitting on the living room couch, tapping their feet impatiently. Their father appeared from the hallway, pulling on his jacket. "All set," he announced, jingling the car keys. "Ready to see some hockey history?"

The drive to the expo took about thirty minutes, winding through busy weekend traffic and then onto a smaller route that led to the local convention center on the outskirts of town. During the ride, Mike animatedly discussed the most valuable cards in circulation. He rattled off the names of legends: Gordie Howe, Maurice Richard, Bobby Orr, Wayne Gretzky. Doug listened intently, feeling a jolt of recognition whenever the conversation turned to Maple Leafs greats. Even though he was still relatively new to collecting, he was hungry to learn more.

Finally, they pulled into a parking lot filled with cars, many of them adorned with hockey-themed bumper stickers or flags. Doug noticed a father and son stepping out of the vehicle next to them, each wearing a Maple Leafs jersey. A group of teenagers in Montreal Canadiens hats hurried toward the entrance, comparing their latest trades in animated tones. Doug exchanged an excited glance with Mike as they followed the small throng of hockey fans into the building.

The moment Doug stepped inside, he was hit by the smell of popcorn, hot dogs, and a faint whiff of cardboard—a mix of concessions and the countless card boxes spread across rows of tables. The expo occupied a large, open space, partitioned into aisles that were jam-packed with vendors, collectors, and curious fans. Folding tables displayed glass cases with shimmering protective sleeves, each containing pristine, mint-condition cards. Others had towering stacks of lesser-known or more common cards, sold cheaply to those eager just to get their hands on anything hockey-related.

Doug felt his pulse quicken as he scanned the kaleidoscope of team colors. Everywhere he looked, there were jerseys—Leafs, Canadiens, Bruins, Red Wings, even some less-common Western Conference teams. There were vendors offering pucks, signed sticks, old hockey magazines, and even vintage gear like goalie masks from the 1970s. Voices melded into a hum of transactions and excited chatter, punctuated by calls like, "I've got a 1983 Gretzky here!" or "Any interest in a complete set of '92 O-Pee-Chee?"

"This is incredible," Doug whispered, sidling up next to Mike. Their father hovered behind, taking in the scene with an amused smile. "I never knew hockey cards could be so... big."

Mike nodded, face alight. "We should start at one end and work our way through," he suggested. "We don't want to miss anything. And you never know which table might have a hidden treasure."

Doug's father agreed, so the three of them meandered down the first aisle. Doug paused at nearly every table, drawn to the glint of plastic sleeves and top loaders, or the bright colors of team logos. One vendor proudly showcased an entire binder filled with Maple Leafs legends, each card carefully placed in a protective sheet. Doug flipped through it, marveling at the neat progression of years, from black-and-white sets of the early NHL days to vibrant modern cards featuring glossy action shots.

He was amazed by the prices, too—some cards were just a few dollars, while others, marked "RARE" or "ROOKIE," could be hundreds or even more. Doug felt a pang of longing when he saw a 1960s Maple Leafs card in near-mint condition, sporting the face of a player whose jersey number the team eventually retired. It was far beyond his budget, but just seeing it up close sent a thrill through him.

"Check this out," Mike said at one point, motioning Doug over to a stall showcasing limited-edition autograph inserts. The vendor, a friendly older gentleman, explained how players sometimes signed short-print cards, turning them into coveted collectibles. He pointed to a newly signed Maple Leafs forward's card, the signature scrawled in silver ink across the bottom. Doug let out a low whistle. He imagined how incredible it would be to one day sign his own cards. That notion flared a spark of excitement: maybe, just maybe, if he worked hard enough, he'd see his own face on a card at an expo like this.

After roaming the aisles for close to an hour, the three of them took a break near a small concession stand set up in one corner. Doug's father bought hot dogs and sodas, and they found a few rickety chairs to rest on. Doug's feet ached a bit, but his mind was far too keyed-up to relax. He couldn't stop replaying everything he'd seen: the array of cards, the enthusiastic collectors negotiating trades or deals, the historical glimpses into hockey's past.

"This is something else," Doug's father remarked, biting into his hot dog. "Back in my day, we traded cards in the schoolyard. No plastic cases, no grading systems. Just pocketed them and hoped they didn't get too beat up." He chuckled ruefully. "If only I'd known how valuable some would become. I probably ruined a fortune by flipping them against concrete walls."

Mike snorted. "Yeah, you and every other kid back then. You couldn't have known. Anyway, it's a good lesson: handle these cards with care."

Doug sipped his soda thoughtfully. "Dad, did you used to collect Maple Leafs cards? You know, from the big players?"

His father's expression softened. "Sure, I had a few. Nothing major. But I remember having a favorite Leafs center's rookie card back in the '70s. I used to keep it in a little tin box. Who knows what happened to it."

Doug thought about that as they finished up their snacks. The day felt ripe with possibility. Maybe he'd find something truly special—a card he could treasure in the way his father once had. The idea of forging a deeper connection to the Maple Leafs' storied history tugged at his heart.

They resumed their journey, weaving through tables they'd missed on the far side of the expo hall. The crowds seemed to thicken as midday approached, and vendors were in full swing. Doug lingered at one table displaying nothing but vintage O-Pee-Chee sets from the 1960s through the 1980s. The vendor, a man with a neat mustache and a Maple Leafs ball cap, noticed Doug's fascination and beckoned him closer.

"You a Leafs fan?" the man asked cheerfully.

Doug nodded. "Huge fan," he said, scanning the neatly arranged rows of cards in plastic sleeves. Each was labeled with year, set, and price. "I just started playing hockey a few months ago, and I'm learning all about the team's history."

"That's great," the vendor said. "The Leafs have such a legacy. My dad took me to Maple Leaf Gardens when I was a kid, back in the days of... well, let's just say the stands were different." He laughed. "I've got a few nice Leafs pieces here. Anything catch your eye?"

Doug carefully looked over the displayed cards. He paused on a slightly worn rookie card featuring a Maple Leafs forward he recognized from highlight reels—one of the fan-favorite players from the early 1990s who eventually became a star. The vendor followed Doug's gaze and fished the card out for a closer look.

"Ah, that one's not in perfect shape," the vendor admitted, pointing to the soft corners and a faint crease. "But it's an authentic rookie card from his first year. Considering the condition, I can let it go for a pretty reasonable price. Maybe twenty bucks."

Doug's heart fluttered. Twenty dollars. That was a decent sum, but not astronomical. He reached for his wallet, recalling the modest amount of money he'd saved from chores, plus a bit extra his father had given him for the expo. He had enough to cover it.

As Doug turned the card over in his hands, fascinated by the stats on the back, he heard someone behind him say, "That's a solid find, kid." He glanced up and saw a tall, stocky man with a bit of gray in his hair, wearing a jacket embroidered with a minor-league team logo Doug vaguely recognized. The man smiled kindly. "I remember that player's rookie season. He was a real spark plug on the ice—never gave up on a shift."

Doug blinked, not entirely sure who he was speaking with, but politely answered, "Yeah, he was one of the reasons I started following the Leafs more. I've seen old clips of him scoring some amazing goals."

The man nodded. "I played a few minor-league games in the same system. He was an inspiration to a lot of us who never made it big. Always worked his tail off, no matter the situation."

Doug's eyes widened. "You were a player?"

"Retired," the man clarified with a small chuckle. "Just a few years in the minors, nothing fancy. I got to skate in training camp with the big club once or twice, but I never cracked the NHL lineup. Too much competition, not enough luck, I guess." He shrugged, then extended his hand. "Name's Vince."

Doug shook Vince's hand, noticing his firm grip. Mike and Doug's father approached, intrigued by the conversation. Vince gave them a polite nod. "Seems your boy's got a good eye for Leafs history," Vince told Doug's father.

Doug's father smiled. "He's fallen head over heels for the sport—and for the Leafs."

Vince took a moment to examine Doug. "So you're playing hockey yourself?"

Doug nodded shyly. "Yeah, I'm on a peewee team this year. It's my first time playing competitively."

"Good for you." Vince's tone was warm but laced with a touch of seriousness. "Let me guess: You're hoping to make it to the NHL one day?"

Doug hesitated, feeling a little embarrassed to admit such a lofty dream to a total stranger. But something about Vince's demeanor encouraged honesty. "It's what I dream about," he said softly, glancing at Mike and his dad for reassurance.

Vince nodded as though he'd heard this aspiration a hundred times. "Happens to the best of us, that dream. Some see it through. Most don't. But even if you don't make it to the show, there's a lot of fulfillment in chasing it with all you've got."

Doug's father stepped in. "Any advice for him?"

Vince smiled thoughtfully. "Well, there's a ton of cliches I could offer—practice hard, never give up, all that. But the reality is that hockey's a game of seizing opportunities. In my career, I had a shot at making it to the NHL for a handful of games, but I got injured right before camp. Never fully recovered my form. That window of opportunity closed for me." He shrugged. "So if I'd give one piece of advice, it's this: you never know when your chance will come. Be ready for it— physically and mentally—and don't be afraid when it arrives."

Doug felt those words sink in, stirring something within him. He thought of the times he'd daydreamed about stepping onto the ice in a Maple Leafs uniform. Could he muster the courage and readiness if such a moment ever came? "Thank you," Doug said quietly. "I really appreciate that."

Vince nodded and glanced back at the well-worn rookie card in Doug's hands. "That card's a great reminder. That guy fought tooth and nail to earn his spot. People said he was too small, too injury-prone, but he refused to quit."

Doug looked at the creased card again, seeing it in a new light. It wasn't just an image of a player—it was a story of perseverance. He felt a swell of determination well up in his chest. *I need this card,* he thought. *It's like a symbol of what I'm working toward.*

Mike and their father hovered, eyeing the transaction. Doug turned to the vendor and asked softly, "Could I buy this one?"

The vendor smiled. "Sure thing, kid. That'll be twenty, but I'll include a protective sleeve."

Doug counted out the bills carefully from his wallet, his heart pounding. It felt monumental, like he was investing in more than just a collectible. After handing the money over, the vendor slid the card into a sturdy plastic holder. Doug gazed at his new treasure, the corners soft from time, the color a bit faded, yet brimming with meaning.

The conversation continued for another few minutes. Vince shared a couple of minor-league anecdotes—long bus rides, playing in half-empty arenas, forging lifelong friendships with teammates who shared the same dream. The stories gave Doug a glimpse into the gritty side of pursuing professional hockey. It wasn't all bright lights and roars of the crowd. It was also sweat, heartbreak, and dogged resilience.

"You keep that heart of yours strong," Vince told Doug before parting ways. "Don't get discouraged by setbacks or doubts. If you love this game, let that love push you forward."

Doug nodded, repeating the words in his head like a mantra. A swirl of gratitude and determination mingled, making him feel older somehow, as if the weight of this new advice was forging a more focused path. He watched Vince disappear into the crowd, thinking that one day he might pass the same wisdom to a younger player if he were lucky enough to have his own career in the sport.

Mike and Doug's father led him on through the expo, but Doug found it hard to concentrate on the rest of the tables. He was still reeling from meeting a retired player who shared real, tangible insights into the life Doug dreamed of living. For the next hour or so, they ambled among more stalls, occasionally pausing if something caught their eye—like a striking vintage poster of the Leafs from the 1950s or a partial set of 1980s O-Pee-Chee that Mike considered buying. But none of it felt quite as important to Doug as that single rookie card he now carried, gently tucked into his jacket pocket.

Eventually, lunchtime rolled around, and the trio decided to leave the expo for the day. They'd seen almost everything on offer, and though each of them could have lingered longer, the press of the crowd and the temptation to spend more money encouraged them to call it a day. Outside, the crisp air hit them, and Doug's father gave an exaggerated sigh of relief. "I could barely hear myself think in there," he joked, rubbing his ears.

Mike stretched his arms overhead. "That was awesome, though. I might come back next year with a bit more cash. Some of those sets were calling my name."

Doug trailed slightly behind, one hand carefully pressing the card through the fabric of his jacket, feeling the slight rectangular outline. He had already resolved that this card would go somewhere special—perhaps in a small frame on his desk, or maybe in a binder he'd start just for Maple Leafs memorabilia. But beyond mere placement, Doug wanted to remember the feeling he had as he bought it—the rush of possibility, the sensation that he was connecting with the sport's legacy at a deeper level.

The car ride back was filled with conversation about their various discoveries. Mike recounted how he'd almost snagged a rare Montreal Canadiens card for a friend of his, but the price was just too high. Doug's father found it hilarious that the expo was practically a microcosm of Canada itself: Leafs fans and Habs fans mingling, comparing notes, trading cards but still talking trash about each other's teams in good fun.

Doug mostly listened, gazing out the window at the gray sky. His mind flitted from the venders' displays to Vince's words. He pictured the retired minor-leaguer's earnest expression as he urged Doug never to take his opportunities for granted. That advice melded with Doug's own expanding view of hockey. Before, it had been pure excitement: the joy of skating, the dream of wearing a Maple Leafs sweater. Now, it also felt like a responsibility—to work hard, to be ready if a door ever opened.

He closed his eyes for a moment, imagining stepping onto an NHL ice surface while thousands of fans erupted in cheers. The Maple Leaf crest bright under the lights, the adrenaline pumping so hard he could scarcely breathe. But now he also pictured the behind-the-scenes: the early-morning practices, the bus rides, the bruises, the rejections. The image was both thrilling and daunting.

When they got home, his mother greeted them at the door. "Buy anything interesting?" she asked, smiling at the large bag of smaller items Mike carried—a few common sets, some protective sleeves, and a poster. Doug carefully pulled out his new card from his jacket, brandishing it with gentle pride.

His mother examined the protective sleeve. "It's a little worn," she commented, noticing the card's creases and softened edges.

Doug grinned. "That's part of what I love about it," he said. "It has a story."

His mother smiled at his enthusiasm, then handed them each a mug of hot chocolate she'd prepared. "I figured you could use something warm after a day of excitement."

They gathered around the kitchen table, sipping cocoa, rehashing expo highlights. Mike rattled off the most outrageous prices he'd seen for certain cards, while Doug's father asked Doug about meeting Vince. "He told me to never waste an opportunity," Doug explained, voice steady. "And to be ready, because you never know when your chance might come."

His father nodded, patting Doug's shoulder. "Sounds like sage advice. And you've got plenty of time to build your skills. But it's good to keep that mindset."

Doug mulled over those words as he brought the hot chocolate to his lips. He thought about his next peewee practice, how each drill, each shift, could be a chance to push himself. Sure, he was just a kid, far removed from the high-stakes world of professional hockey. But as Vince had said, if he truly loved the game, he should embrace every moment that propelled him forward.

Later that evening, after dinner and homework, Doug retreated to his room. He sat at his desk, switching on a small lamp that cast a warm glow over the scattered papers, notebooks, and a few hockey magazines. Carefully, he removed the rookie card from his pocket and studied it in the mellow light. The player's determined expression still jumped out from behind the protective sleeve, the Maple Leafs logo proudly displayed on his chest. The corners were bent, and a hairline crease ran across one edge, but Doug found that it only enhanced its charm.

He recalled the highlight reels he'd watched of that very player weaving through defenses, digging pucks out of corners, and firing quick shots under the goalie's glove. In one vintage video, the announcer's voice boomed: "He never quits on a play!" The same spirit Doug admired for his own game. *If only I could be that relentless*, he mused.

He opened a drawer in his desk, rummaging through pencils and a few stray items until he found a small plastic stand—something Mike had given him long ago for displaying a single card or photo. He placed the stand at the rear of his desk, propped the card upright, and sat back to admire it. It wasn't flashy or valuable in a monetary sense; yet to Doug, it felt priceless.

A soft knock sounded at his door. "Come in," Doug called.

Mike stepped inside, hands in his jean pockets. "Just wanted to see how you're settling in with your new prize," he said, eyes drifting to the desk where the card stood. "Looks good there."

Doug nodded. "I'm glad I didn't buy some super-expensive card. This one has character."

Mike leaned against the doorframe, a grin tugging at his mouth. "That's the best kind of collectible—the one that means something personal to you. So... how you feeling after meeting that retired guy, Vince?"

Doug's gaze flicked to the card, then back to Mike. "It made me realize... it's going to be hard. To make it, I mean. I've always known it's tough, but hearing him say how he missed his chance because of an injury reminded me that luck plays a role, too."

Mike nodded, expression thoughtful. "Yeah, sports can be cruel. But you're young, Dougie. Don't let that scare you. If anything, let it drive you to make the most of every practice, every game, every workout. Control what you can control."

Doug grinned. "I will. I promise."

Mike patted the doorframe. "All right, little bro, I'll let you get some rest. We've got a family day tomorrow, but we can hit the backyard rink on Monday if you're up for it."

As Mike disappeared into the hallway, Doug returned his gaze to the card. He felt a surge of motivation course through him, as if that bent piece of cardboard was whispering a challenge: *You want to be on a card someday? Show the world you deserve it.*

The next morning, Doug woke earlier than usual. Even though it was supposed to be a family day—visiting grandparents in town—he couldn't resist spending a few minutes alone with a stick in the backyard. He bundled up in a coat, gloves, and boots, stepping onto the frozen patch he and Mike had turned into a makeshift rink. It was too small to do any serious drills, but just feeling the scrape of ice underfoot reminded him of Vince's advice.

He dribbled a puck back and forth, imagining a defender in front of him. In his mind's eye, he was wearing a Maple Leafs jersey, with a roaring crowd cheering him on. He pictured the frenzy of an NHL game, the tension in the final moments. He practiced a quick spin move, losing his balance slightly on the uneven surface, stumbling but not falling. *Stay ready,* he told himself. *Opportunities come when you least expect them.*

After five minutes, his hands were numb, and he realized he risked running late for their family outing. Gritting his teeth against the cold, he stashed the puck and stick, then hurried back inside. Yet even as he warmed his hands under running water, that sense of purpose stayed with him. The battered rookie card on his desk wasn't just a souvenir—it was a symbol of perseverance.

Throughout the day, as he visited grandparents and made small talk over cups of tea, Doug kept thinking about hockey. He recalled how the famed player on that card had been considered undersized, had been traded, and then come back stronger. *Hard work, determination, a bit of luck.* That formula was repeating in Doug's head like a mantra.

That evening, back home again, he found time to catch the tail end of another NHL game on TV. Not the Leafs this time, but still a high-level match that showcased speed, precision, and the grit of professional hockey. Even watching teams he wasn't as passionate about stirred him. He studied the passing plays, the defensive zone coverage. A color commentator pointed out how the star winger never let up, constantly pressuring the opponent's breakout. Doug jotted a few notes in a small pad he'd started keeping for hockey insights, thinking he could try those tactics in his next practice or backyard rink session.

He couldn't wait to share some of these ideas with Coach Loring at their upcoming practice. He remembered Vince's words about being ready—this included mental readiness, too. For Doug, that meant soaking up every piece of knowledge he could.

As the week progressed, Doug's rookie card remained perched on the little stand, an ever-present reminder of what he was striving for. Sometimes, before going to bed, he'd pick it up, carefully removing it from its sleeve to examine the back. There, beneath the bold rookie stats, were basic facts about the player—his birthplace, his height and weight, some personal trivia. Doug would trace the crease with a fingertip, imagining the card's prior life: maybe it once belonged to another kid who carried it around, or a collector who finally decided to sell it. The idea that this card had a history comforted Doug. It reminded him that everyone, and everything, had a journey.

One afternoon, Mike poked his head into Doug's room. "Hey, I found something in my closet," he said, holding up a binder. "I used to keep my old hockey cards in here. Mostly random ones, but I think there's a page of Leafs players."

Doug accepted the binder, flipping through dusty plastic sheets. Most of the cards were from sets he didn't recognize, featuring lesser-known players or duplicates that Mike had cast aside. But sure enough, there was a single page dedicated to Maple Leafs. Doug recognized a couple of big names from the 2000s, but none matched the revered status of the star on Doug's new rookie card. Still, he was grateful for these little glimpses of Leafs history.

"Thanks, Mike. I'll keep them safe," Doug promised.

"All yours," Mike said with a smile. "I figure you're the bigger Leafs fan now."

Doug smirked. "No question."

By the time the weekend rolled around again, Doug felt a renewed sense of vigor. Peewee practice was on Saturday morning, and he was determined to bring the same intensity he'd been harboring all week. As he and Mike drove over with their father, Doug ran over in his mind all the small improvements he wanted to focus on: quicker feet, better puck protection along the boards, sharper passes.

During practice, Coach Loring ran them through a series of conditioning drills that left Doug gasping for air, but he pushed harder, remembering Vince's advice. When they split into lines for a scrimmage, Doug rushed onto the ice, heart pounding. He chased loose pucks with a tenacity that surprised even himself, dug them out from behind the net, and fed a crisp pass to a teammate who buried it. *Seize every chance,* he thought, feeling a wave of satisfaction as the puck hit twine.

After practice, as the kids peeled off their gear in the locker room, Doug's friend Trevor patted him on the back. "Man, you were flying out there," he said. "What's gotten into you?"

Doug just shrugged, grinning. "I've been learning from the best." He thought of Vince, of the newly acquired rookie card, and of the countless nights spent watching Leafs games. Perhaps "learning from the best" didn't only mean coaches or star athletes on TV—it also meant absorbing wisdom from anyone who'd walked the path before, be it a retired minor-leaguer or the intangible legacy embodied by an old piece of cardboard.

As he emerged from the locker room, helmet under his arm, Doug spotted his father waiting by the bench. "Ready, champ?" his father called, tossing Doug a water bottle.

Doug nodded, feeling pleasantly tired. "Ready."

As they walked to the car, Doug's father asked, "So, how do you feel about that expo card now? Still glad you bought it?"

"Definitely," Doug replied, a flash of a grin crossing his face. "It's more than just a card to me. It reminds me why I'm doing this."

His father nodded, unlocking the car. "That's good, Doug. Keep that drive alive. Never know where it might lead."

Doug slid into the backseat, setting his helmet on his lap. In his mind, he pictured the card resting on his desk at home, waiting for him like a quiet mentor, urging him forward. *One day,* he thought, *I'll have my own rookie card. And maybe some kid at an expo, years from now, will look at it with the same awe.*

The idea made him tingle with excitement. He buckled his seatbelt, feeling the pleasant ache of hard work in his legs. Each day, each practice, each fleeting conversation—it was all leading somewhere. And every time he looked at that well-worn card, he'd remember Vince's words about perseverance, about being ready, about loving the game so deeply that you never let a moment pass you by.

With his father starting the engine and Mike recounting a funny moment from practice, Doug smiled to himself. He might only be at the start of his journey, but he was building a foundation strong enough to hold all his aspirations. It began with the dream, and now it was fueled by a tangible reminder in the form of a creased rookie card—a symbol that even the underdog, the overlooked, and the under-sized could fight their way into greatness if they refused to let go. And Doug intended to hold on tight, every step of the way.

5

USED EQUIPMENT

Doug pressed the measuring tape against the inside of his forearm, squinting to read the tiny numbers. He tugged the tape a little, trying to smooth out the twists. His father, standing behind him, frowned slightly.

"It's definitely longer," Doug's dad said, stepping forward to hold the tape. "Your arms, your legs... no wonder your gear feels tight."

Doug's mother had noticed it first. Over the past month, she'd made casual remarks—"Your jeans look a bit short, Doug," or "You're outgrowing that shirt, aren't you?"—but Doug was so consumed by hockey that he barely registered the changes. Then, at a recent peewee practice, he'd tried to cinch his elbow pads only to discover he couldn't secure the Velcro. It was as if his arms had stretched overnight. His shin pads, too, felt snug, and his skates pinched at the toes. That night, after practice, he finally confessed to his parents that his equipment no longer fit.

Now, in the small upstairs hallway of their modest home, they did a quick measurement of Doug's arms and legs. His father made a note on a scrap piece of paper. "You've grown nearly an inch in about two months," he said, as though trying to confirm some kind of grand conspiracy.

Doug shifted uneasily. On one hand, the idea of growing was exhilarating—he wanted to be bigger, stronger, more physically capable on the ice. But with each half inch came the logistical problem of replacing gear. And hockey equipment, as Doug had learned, did not come cheap.

His mother poked her head out of Doug's bedroom. "Should we check your skates again?" she asked.

Doug nodded, trailing her into the room. The skates lay splayed on the floor, next to the closet where he stored his helmet, shoulder pads, gloves, and a battered old hockey bag. Doug reluctantly shoved his socked foot into the nearest skate, wincing at how his toes curled uncomfortably. "It's too small," he admitted. "I can feel it squishing my foot."

His mother sighed, sharing a look with Doug's father that spoke volumes about their finances. They both worked hard—his father as a mechanical technician, his mother as a part-time office clerk—but money was perpetually tight. Between household expenses, bills, and the general cost of raising two kids, the budget had little wiggle room for brand-new hockey gear.

"Okay," Doug's father said, trying to sound steady, "we can't put this off. If your gear is too small, you can't play safely. We'll figure something out."

Doug's mother forced a smile. "How about we check out that second-hand sports store? I've heard good things. Their prices should be more reasonable."

Doug felt a pang of mixed emotions: relief that they had a plan, and a prick of embarrassment. He knew some kids on his peewee team whose parents bought them top-of-the-line, brand-new equipment every season. Would showing up in used gear make him look like an amateur? He pushed the thought away—any gear was better than gear that didn't fit at all.

"Sounds good," Doug said, trying to sound cheerful.

The following Saturday, Doug, his father, and his mother piled into the car. Mike was off at a friend's house, so it was just the three of them. A late-winter wind rattled the bare trees lining their street, sending a few stray leaves tumbling across the pavement. Doug clutched his current skates in his lap, the ones that pinched his toes, as if to remind himself of why they were making this trek.

They drove to a part of town dotted with older storefronts—small businesses offering everything from dry cleaning to antique sales. Doug noticed a modest sign above one of the shops: **PLAY IT AGAIN SPORTS** in bright, if somewhat faded, letters. A sandwich board out front read: "Hockey Gear, Skis, Snowboards — Great Deals!"

"This is the place," Doug's father said, pulling into a cramped parking space. Doug's mother turned in her seat to smile reassuringly at Doug.

"It'll be fine," she said gently, as though sensing the swirl of emotions behind Doug's quiet demeanor.

Doug climbed out of the car, bracing himself against a cold gust of wind. A twinge of uncertainty pricked his stomach, but he forced a small smile. If there was decent gear here, he'd make it work. No sense worrying about what his teammates might think—he needed properly fitting equipment more than brand-new shine.

A bell tinkled as they pushed the glass door open. Inside, the shop smelled of rubber mats, metal racks, and a vague hint of sweat—likely clinging to the used sporting goods. Rows of hockey sticks lined one wall; next to them, wire bins overflowed with assorted elbow pads, shoulder pads, gloves, and helmets. Doug saw corners dedicated to other sports—

soccer cleats, baseball gloves, even golf clubs—but the hockey section dominated the middle of the store, a testament to Canadian priorities.

A woman in a black polo shirt greeted them. "Looking for anything in particular today?"

Doug's father stepped forward. "Yes, our son's had a growth spurt. We need new skates, probably new pads too. He's playing peewee hockey."

"Gotcha," the woman said with a nod. "We have a good selection of second-hand skates and protective gear. Let me show you."

Doug followed, marveling at the variety. Skates of all sizes perched on shelves, some looking nearly new, others with scuffed leather and chipped blade holders. Pads lay in bins, sorted roughly by size: small, medium, large. A few items had scribbled price tags that Doug found surprisingly low compared to the brand-new prices he'd seen at sporting goods superstores.

"Let's see," the shop employee said, pulling out a pair of skates from a shelf labeled 'Junior Sizes.' "These might be close to your size. Wanna try them on?"

Doug nodded, swallowing the wave of nerves that threatened to bubble up. He sank onto a metal bench in front of a small mirror, pulling off his sneaker, and pushed his foot into the second-hand skate. The interior felt a bit stiff, and there were minor nicks on the toe cap, but it was better than his old pair. His toe brushed the end, but not painfully so—just enough for a snug fit.

"They're a little tight," Doug admitted, lacing them experimentally. "Do you have something a half-size bigger?"

The employee rummaged through the shelves. Doug's mother and father hovered nearby, exchanging concerned glances as if to say, *We can't afford to be picky.* But the employee seemed unbothered, quickly locating another pair. This new pair, black with fading white stripes and some visible wear along the inside ankle, felt more comfortable. Doug tightened the laces, wiggling his toes. "This seems good," he said, relief slipping into his voice.

His father checked the price tag, raising his eyebrows at the sum—still a fraction of what new skates cost, but not trivial. Doug tried to ignore the tension in his father's posture. He reminded himself to be grateful that they could afford anything at all.

"Let's see pads next," Doug's father said, clearing his throat. "We'll compare our total after we gather everything."

They navigated to the bins of elbow and shin pads. Doug's mother pulled out a pair of shin pads, battered and sporting a few surface scratches. Doug slipped them on, relieved that they fit lengthwise but noticing they had one mismatched strap. "We can replace the strap easily," his mother said, voice brisk but encouraging.

Doug forced a smile. "I like them," he said, testing how they felt around his calves. The padding was a little worn but still cushioned. He couldn't help recalling how some of his peewee teammates bragged about newly released gear with advanced technology, designed for maximum protection and minimal weight. These, by contrast, looked like survivors of many seasons. But they'd protect his shins all the same.

They found elbow pads in a similar state—slightly worn fabric, a bit of fraying at the edges. One vendor sticker read, "$12.99 — Still Good!" in big letters. Doug tried them on and found that, while they weren't as sleek as newer models, they fit just right. *Good enough for me*, he thought, imagining how each scuff might tell a story from a past owner's hockey battles.

The helmet was next on the list. Doug had outgrown his old one—he'd noticed it compressing his temples in recent practices. As they sorted through the used helmets, his father frowned at a couple with visible cracks. The shop employee pointed them toward a newer batch. "We test these and ensure they're safe, but if there's any sign of structural damage, we can't sell them," she explained. "So this group is a little pricier, but still cheaper than buying new."

Doug tried on a black helmet with a steel cage, ignoring the scuff marks. The fit was snug, but not uncomfortable. "This one's good," he said quietly, flipping up the cage to test the hinges. *No squeaks, no cracks. Feels solid enough.* He could see the reflection of himself in a small mirror—he looked a bit ridiculous, wearing mismatched used gear, but he refused to let that dampen his resolve.

By the end of it, they had a pile: one pair of skates, shin pads, elbow pads, and a helmet. Doug still had a serviceable shoulder-pad set, and his gloves were only slightly snug—he could make do for now. They carried their haul to the front counter, where the cashier tallied everything.

"That'll be $75.50," she announced.

Doug heard his father exhale softly. That might not sound like a fortune to some, but for them, every penny counted. Doug's heart twisted in guilt, and a flicker of shame. *I shouldn't feel ashamed,* he told himself. *I need gear that fits.* He watched his father pull out his wallet, carefully counting the bills. Doug's mother stood beside him, offering a supportive pat on Doug's back. "We'll get you set, don't you worry," she whispered.

Doug mustered a thankful smile. "Thanks, Mom. Thanks, Dad."

They walked out of the store with a box and a large plastic bag of gear. As they headed to the car, Doug felt a swirl of gratitude—his parents were making sacrifices for his dream. But embarrassment lingered as well. He imagined how a few of the wealthier kids on his team might tease him if they noticed his obviously used gear. Then he remembered how Vince, the retired minor-leaguer he'd met at the card expo, spoke of seizing opportunities and working with what you have. Doug decided right there that he wouldn't let shame hold him back.

The next day, Doug hurried through his homework so he could test his second-hand equipment. He threw on a sweatshirt and sweatpants, then dragged his new acquisitions to the backyard rink. The temperature hovered around freezing, and a light dusting of snow sprinkled the boards Mike had helped set up that winter.

Doug strapped on the shin pads, noticing one strap hung a bit loose, but nothing some extra tape couldn't fix. He fit on the elbow pads, adjusting them until they covered the vulnerable spots just above his wrists. Finally, he slid the helmet over his head. The foam padding had a faint musty smell, but at least it wasn't pressing painfully against his temples. Good enough for now.

With the gear in place, he laced up the "new" skates. They'd definitely seen better days—scratches marred the black surfaces, and the steel blades were dull, probably needing a sharpening. But they felt better than the painfully small pair he'd outgrown. Doug stepped onto the ice, taking a few tentative strides.

At first, he wobbled, adjusting to the new fit. But within moments, the muscle memory kicked in. He glided across the backyard rink, feeling a distinct sense of relief that his toes weren't cramped. He tried a few quick turns, testing the edges. The dullness of the blades threw him off slightly; he resolved to ask his dad to get them sharpened soon. Still, he felt more mobile, less constrained.

Doug took out a hockey stick and began stickhandling a puck, weaving around small wooden cones he and Mike had set up. The elbow pads didn't hinder his arm movement, and the shin pads felt secure enough. With each shift of his weight, each pivot, Doug felt gratitude overshadowing any lingering embarrassment. This gear might not be flashy, but it let him do what he loved—play.

After about twenty minutes of hard skating and drills, Doug paused, breath puffing out in white clouds. He leaned on his stick, a small smile curling his lips. *I can make this work. I'm not going to let old gear hold me back.* He recalled how some of the best players in hockey history started with humble equipment. Skills and heart mattered more than brand-new padding.

That evening, Doug carried his gear back inside, carefully laying it out near a heating vent to dry. His mother noticed him rummaging through the boxes of old hockey tape, searching for extra strips to secure the loose strap on his shin pad. A worried expression crossed her face.

"Doug, are you okay with everything?" she asked, her tone gentle. "I know it might be tough seeing some of your teammates with fancy equipment."

Doug shrugged, focusing on wrapping tape around a frayed strap. "It's fine. The gear fits, that's what matters."

She gave a half-smile. "We'll see if we can save up for better stuff later on, but... you know how it is."

"I know," Doug said, glancing up to meet her eyes. "It's okay. Really." He paused, feeling a rush of earnestness. "Thank you for helping me. I know this isn't cheap."

His mother's eyes grew soft. "We just want you safe and happy, Dougie," she said, using the old nickname she rarely voiced now that he was older. "If you ever feel embarrassed—"

"I won't," Doug interrupted, forcing confidence. "Besides, if I work hard, it won't matter what brand of helmet I have."

She nodded, relief evident in the lines of her face. "That's the spirit. Now, let's call it a night—dinner's in ten."

As she walked away, Doug finished his taping, determined not to let thoughts of used gear overshadow the excitement of playing. *All that matters is how I perform on the ice,* he reminded himself.

A few days later, Doug had his first peewee game since acquiring his new (old) gear. He changed in the arena's cramped locker room, half-worried that his teammates would notice how beaten-up his equipment looked. But the reality of youth hockey was that everyone was busy focusing on their own routine—lacing skates, taping sticks, adjusting jerseys. A couple of kids chatted about new sticks they'd received for Christmas, but no one commented on Doug's gear.

As Doug finished suiting up, he saw Trevor, his friend and occasional line-mate, glance at Doug's elbow pads with a curious expression. Doug's gut tightened. *Here it comes,* he thought. But all Trevor did was grin.

"New gear?" Trevor asked, though the scuffs clearly told a different story.

Doug mustered a casual nod. "Yeah, I outgrew my old stuff. Picked this up used."

Trevor shrugged, finishing the tape on his stick. "Long as it protects you, right?"

Doug forced a breath of relief. "Exactly."

No one else seemed to care. Doug realized most of his teammates were too busy with their own concerns—skate tightness, laces snapping, last-minute advice from the coach. Doug took comfort in that. *They're not judging me. They just want to play.*

The game itself was intense—two well-matched peewee teams battling for position in the league standings. Doug's line took the ice early in the first period. He felt a renewed freedom in his movements, no longer cramped by undersized gear. Every stride felt more natural. He fought for pucks in the corner, using his elbows to shield the puck from opposing players. Although he absorbed a few hits, the pads held up fine, and he barely felt the stings.

Late in the second period, the puck squirted loose near the neutral zone. Doug seized the opportunity, bursting forward in a short-handed breakaway. He could hear the pounding of his heartbeat echoing in his helmet. The opposing goalie readied himself, but Doug was locked in—he pulled the puck to his backhand and slipped it five-hole. *Goal.*

He pumped his fist in celebration, gliding past the bench where his teammates cheered. It was a highlight moment, one he'd remember for a long time. As he skated back to center ice, he thought of his parents—working hard, sacrificing financially. He thought of Vince's words about never wasting an opportunity. *Used gear, new gear, it doesn't matter. I can do this.*

They ended up winning the game 3–1. In the locker room afterward, the mood was jubilant. Kids were high-fiving, the coach was praising their defensive play. Doug peeled off his helmet, sweat dripping down his face. Trevor gave him a congratulatory bump. "Nice breakaway," he said, beaming.

"Thanks." Doug returned the grin, feeling that surge of camaraderie.

As he unstrapped his elbow pads, Doug caught a glimpse of their frayed edges. In that moment, he felt only pride. These scuffs and worn edges were battle scars that represented the unstoppable drive inside him. *We're in this together, old gear,* he thought wryly. *And we're going to keep pushing forward.*

That evening, once Doug was home and showered, he found his parents in the living room. His father was tinkering with a small household project—a rickety shelf—while his mother jotted down expenses in a small ledger. Doug slipped onto the couch, hugging a cushion.

"We won," he announced quietly. "I scored, too."

His father looked up, smiling. "Hey, that's great!" He put down the screwdriver. "How'd the new gear feel?"

"Great," Doug said, truly meaning it. "Thanks again for getting it for me."

A hint of warmth lit his mother's gaze. "We're glad it worked out," she said. Then she glanced at the ledger, sighing. "Money's getting tight, but we'll manage. Your father and I will do what it takes to support you and Mike."

Doug's chest tightened. The reality of their finances weighed on him more than ever before. He wanted desperately to repay them somehow. "I... I'll work hard," Doug said, an unsteady thread of emotion in his voice. "I'll make sure it's worth it."

His father set aside the shelf and stood, walking over to put a hand on Doug's shoulder. "Son, we're proud of you whether you score a hundred goals or none. Hard work is all we ask. Passion, dedication... those are the real goals here."

Doug nodded, swallowing the lump in his throat. "I promise I'll keep pushing," he whispered.

Over the next few weeks, Doug's schedule felt packed—school, homework, peewee practices, occasional games. Despite the rush, he consistently found small slots of time to train in the backyard or watch NHL highlights. His used gear, once a source of mild embarrassment, became a badge of honor. He'd repair straps with tape, wipe the helmet down carefully after every game, and occasionally air out the pads in the garage to keep them from growing musty.

One afternoon, while Doug fiddled with the battered shin pads in the living room, Mike strolled in. "Hey, Dougie, got a second?"

Doug looked up. "What's up?"

Mike sat on the arm of the couch, crossing his arms. "I just want you to know— I think you're handling this gear thing really well. When I was your age, I might've whined a lot more if I had to wear used stuff."

Doug smirked. "It's not that bad. I'm just glad it fits."

Mike gave him a light punch on the shoulder. "Still, proud of you. A lot of kids care too much about brand names and having the latest gear. But you're focused on the game itself. That's what counts."

Doug felt a small swell of pride. Coming from Mike—who'd always been so put-together and confident—this meant a lot. "Thanks," he said quietly.

Late one evening, Doug sat at his desk, a single lamp illuminating the surface. Nearby, his prized rookie card of the Maple Leafs hero watched over him from its small stand. Doug had a notebook open, scribbling down small goals: "Improve snap shot," "Work on faster first stride," "Practice stickhandling in tight spaces." He'd gleaned these from online tutorials and from Coach Loring's recent tips.

He glanced at the old helmet perched on his desk, the cage slightly dented. A month ago, he would've worried it looked too shabby. Now, he saw only the lines of possibility it carried, the potential for better coverage, better sightlines. It was his, and it did the job.

His eyes flicked back to the rookie card. *Never waste an opportunity,* Vince had said. Doug thought of the night he'd walked away with that card, full of ambition. Now, armed with used gear and unwavering determination, he felt more ready than ever to chase his dream.

Someday, he might outgrow this equipment. He might move on to better pads, or brand-new skates, or maybe a new helmet if circumstances allowed. But for now, he was content with what he had—and he vowed to make every stride count.

Doug closed the notebook, yawned, and crawled into bed. Under the covers, he replayed the memory of that breakaway goal, hearing the echo of the cheering crowd. He pictured the Maple Leafs crest on his chest, not just as a daydream, but as a possibility he inched toward every time he stepped onto the ice, second-hand gear or not.

With a final deep breath, he let sleep claim him, carrying with it the promise of another day to hone his skills, to lean into the love of the game. Used equipment wouldn't stop him; nothing would, as long as he kept skating forward. And in the quiet darkness, he wore a small, certain smile—knowing that the path he was on, though challenging, was entirely his own to shape.

6

THE FIRST FIGHT

Doug leaned against the boards, his breath fogging the plexiglass as he watched his house-league teammates scramble in the neutral zone. He was halfway through his shift, legs burning from the furious pace of this late-season game. The league's end-of-year tournament was on the horizon, and every team wanted momentum heading in. Tonight's opponent—a scrappy, physical squad from a neighboring district—had come ready to set a tone. Doug could feel the tension the moment the puck dropped. Checks were harder, chirps on the ice more pointed. As a result, the game's temperature rose with each passing minute.

In the stands, a modest crowd hollered encouragement, a few parents banging thunder sticks as if this were the NHL playoffs. The boards rattled after nearly every collision. Doug's father was among the spectators, wearing a light jacket despite the ice-cold rink air, while Doug's mother held a thermos of hot chocolate in her lap. Mike was away at his own practice, meaning Doug had no older brother around to watch him tonight. Somehow that made Doug feel simultaneously more grown-up and more on edge, as if he needed to prove himself in a new way.

The scoreboard read 2–2, with about six minutes left in the second period. Doug's line, which included his friend Trevor on the left wing, stepped onto the ice for another shift. Coach

Wilkins had been rolling all lines to keep everyone fresh, but the game's physicality had left them all a bit bruised. Doug flexed his arms, feeling the pads that he'd recently bought second-hand—still holding up fine, though he worried about how well they'd absorb a truly massive hit.

He skated into position for the faceoff at center ice, bouncing on the balls of his skates to stay loose. His center, a stocky kid named Harrison, leaned over for the draw. Across the circle, the other team's center glared, and the referee dropped the puck. The black disk skittered across the ice, Harrison tying up the opposing center's stick just long enough for Doug to scoop the puck forward. He took a quick stride, sending the puck up to Trevor, who barrelled into the offensive zone. The opposing defensemen slid over, trying to box Trevor against the boards.

Doug followed the play, scanning for a pass or a rebound, adrenaline sizzling through his veins. Trevor cut inside, only to be muscled off the puck by a taller defenseman with a heavy shoulder check. Trevor spun off balance, stumbling but not falling. Doug recognized the number on that defenseman's jersey—Number 18. Even from earlier shifts, Doug had pegged him as a physically imposing, hotheaded player. Sure enough, as Trevor tried to corral the puck, Number 18 pinned him against the boards, giving an extra shove long after the puck slid away.

A spark of indignation flared inside Doug. Trevor was a friend—he wasn't the biggest kid on the ice, so he sometimes absorbed big hits. Usually, Trevor bounced right back. But this cross-check looked excessive. Doug changed direction, determined to help.

He reached the fray just as the puck squirted loose. Another teammate snagged it, but Doug saw that Trevor was still pressed awkwardly against the boards. Number 18 had an arm across Trevor's back, shoving. "Knock it off!" Doug blurted, jabbing his stick between them to separate the two.

Number 18 whipped around, eyes flashing with agitation. "Mind your business," he growled, giving Doug a small push with his free hand.

Doug felt a jolt as he staggered backward. For a brief moment, he hesitated. Fights happened in hockey, sure—but in the house-league setting, they were rare. Penalties for fighting were serious. The league strongly discouraged it, and Doug had never even considered himself a scrappy player. He was more about skill, passing, and the occasional well-timed check. But the raw aggression in Number 18's eyes ignited something inside Doug: anger, adrenaline, protectiveness.

Trevor finally slid away from the boards, looking rattled. Doug's immediate thought was to check if Trevor was okay, but before he could, Number 18 gave Trevor one more shove from behind, sending him sprawling to the ice. A roar rose from the stands—a mix of disapproval and alarm.

That was it. Instinct overrode caution. Doug dropped his stick and lunged, shoving Number 18 in the chest with both gloved hands. "Enough!" he barked. The bigger player skidded backward a foot, more from surprise than force. In the corners of his vision, Doug saw the linesman reacting, starting to move in.

But it was too late. Number 18 responded with a shove of his own, knocking Doug off balance. Doug's helmet rattled as he stumbled, knees flexing to keep upright. The ref's whistle shrilled, but in the heat of the moment, neither Doug nor

Number 18 heeded it. The big defenseman cocked a fist. Doug blinked—he had never been in a true fight before. A swirl of conflicting thoughts erupted: *Do I throw a punch? Do I just hold on?*

And then Number 18's glove connected with Doug's shoulder, hooking near the pad. Doug reacted by jabbing with his own gloved fist, trying to protect himself as much as he was retaliating. He felt the jolt of contact, though the padded glove softened the impact. A chorus of shouts echoed off the rink walls. Another punch flew from Number 18, grazing Doug's helmet cage. Doug, half in panic, half in fury, grabbed the front of the bigger player's jersey and swung again, this time connecting with the side of his helmet.

In seconds, the linesmen arrived, wedging themselves between the combatants. Doug's heart hammered. The tension in his arms was electric. Number 18 snarled, still trying to swing as the linesmen pinned his arms back. Doug breathed heavily, as if he'd run a full-ice sprint. A swirl of guilt and adrenaline brewed in his gut. *Did I really just do that?*

The ref skated over, arms outstretched, urging calm. "Hey, hey, that's enough!" he shouted, voice echoing. "Both of you, that's done. You're out of here!"

Doug realized, with sinking dread, that he was being ejected. House-league rules were strict about fighting. Even if you weren't the initial aggressor, dropping the gloves typically meant a game misconduct. Another linesman escorted Number 18 away, the big kid cursing under his breath. Meanwhile, Doug's teammates hovered, wide-eyed. Some looked impressed, others concerned.

Coach Wilkins wore a grim expression as he motioned Doug toward the penalty box. "We'll get this sorted," the coach said, his voice taut. "But you know the rules."

Trevor, still wincing, tried to skate close. "You okay, man?" he asked, voice laced with gratitude. Doug nodded, though his heart hammered so violently he thought it might burst. At that moment, the linesman coaxed him into the penalty box. Doug plopped down on the bench, unsteady and confused. The scoreboard's digital clock froze, presumably while the officials sorted out penalties. Doug gulped, taking in lungfuls of cold arena air that did little to calm the swirl of emotion.

He peered through the scratched plexiglass surrounding the box. Across the ice, Number 18 was being shepherded toward his own bench, no doubt receiving a similar lecture. Doug's gaze drifted up to where his father and mother sat. His mother looked stunned, one hand over her mouth, while his father's lips were pressed into a thin line. Doug felt a wave of guilt. *What must they be thinking?*

At the same time, an undercurrent of exhilaration buzzed through his veins. He'd never felt such a raw surge of adrenaline. For a split second—when he'd shoved Number 18— he'd realized how passionately he wanted to protect Trevor. Part of him, however small, felt an odd sense of pride: *I stood up for a teammate.*

The referee skated over to the penalty box, barking instructions to the timekeeper. "Fighting majors for both 15 in white and 18 in black—game misconducts. They're done for the night."

Doug sagged on the bench. So that was it. He was out, with a "fighting major" on his record. In house league. It was a serious infraction. By the time the linesman opened the penalty box door, Doug felt the weight of shame pressing down on him. The crowd watched as he stepped out, removing his gloves and carrying his stick, heading toward the exit. The scoreboard still read 2–2, but for Doug, the game was over.

He found his way into the narrow hallway behind the benches, heart in his throat. The old arena architecture made every sound echo: the scrape of skates, the clang of pucks hitting boards, muffled cheers from the stands. Doug hovered in front of the locker room, uncertain if he was allowed inside or if he should wait for the period to end. His father stepped through a side door, wearing a conflicted expression.

"Doug," he said quietly, glancing around to ensure no prying ears were nearby.

Doug's chest tightened. "Dad, I— I'm sorry," he blurted, voice trembling slightly. "He was going after Trevor. I didn't mean to make it a—"

His father held up a hand, halting Doug's words. "I know, son. I saw." He exhaled, shoulders tense. "This is complicated. Fighting in this league is a big no, you know that. But... I also saw how you were protecting your teammate. I'm not exactly proud of the fight, but I understand what happened."

Doug swallowed, relief and guilt tangling in his gut. "I didn't know what else to do. He kept shoving Trevor."

His father laid a hand on Doug's shoulder. "You need to go back to the locker room and wait. Coach will talk to you. Then we'll see if there's a suspension or something."

Doug nodded, throat tight. "Is Mom— I mean, how is she?"

His father's lips twitched in a pained grin. "A bit rattled. But she'll be all right." With that, he stepped aside to let Doug enter the locker room. "I'm heading back to watch the rest of the game. I'll come get you after. Hang in there."

"Thanks, Dad," Doug murmured, forcing a faint smile.

Once inside the locker room, the silence pressed on him like a weight. The overhead fluorescent lights buzzed softly. Doug slumped onto the bench along the wall, removing his helmet and gloves. His hands shook from adrenaline and leftover shock. Without the roar of the arena, the swirling emotions became more intense. *What have I done?* he thought. *Fighting... me?*

He had flashes of the scuffle: the bigger player, the anger in his own chest, the blur of fists. Doug had seen fights on TV, mostly in NHL games or highlight reels. Some fans cheered that sort of thing. But was that who he wanted to be? A tough guy dropping gloves in a low-level game? The question churned in his mind.

The game's next half hour felt like an eternity. Doug stayed glued to the bench in the locker room, occasionally pressing his ear to the door to catch the crowd's reaction. Once, he heard a roar—someone must have scored. But he had no idea which side.

Finally, the heavy door swung open, and Coach Wilkins entered, wearing a resigned expression. "Hey, Doug," he said, setting down a clipboard. "How're you holding up?"

Doug stood awkwardly. "I— I'm okay, Coach. Sorry, I—"

Coach Wilkins held up a hand. "Let me talk, all right?" He sat next to Doug, removing his baseball cap to run a hand through his thinning hair. "I spoke with the refs. You're looking at a one-game suspension at least, maybe two, because of the league's zero-tolerance policy for fighting. I can't say I disagree with them—house league or not, you threw punches."

Doug closed his eyes briefly, a pang stabbing his chest. "I understand," he whispered. "I didn't want it to escalate. I just saw him roughing up Trevor."

Coach Wilkins sighed. "I know. I get it. And the team appreciates that you stood up for Trevor. But as your coach, I have to remind you: fighting is not how you handle these things, especially in a league that's about sportsmanship first. The referees are there to call penalties for hits like that." He paused, brow furrowing. "You're a good kid, Doug. This is out of character."

Doug swallowed. "So... I'm out next game?"

"Most likely two," Coach Wilkins said. "The league's disciplinary committee will confirm, but that's my guess."

A flurry of disappointment and frustration welled in Doug's chest. He'd worked so hard all season—missing two games would hurt his development and his bond with the team. "Yes, sir," he said, voice subdued.

Coach Wilkins stood. "I need to address the team, but you head on home. We'll talk more soon. Keep your head up, all right?"

Doug nodded, though he felt anything but confident. As Coach left the locker room, Doug began removing his pads. He felt as if each strap symbolized a shred of his self-assurance, undone one by one. What would Mike say? *Well, you're tough now,* he might joke. But Doug didn't feel tough. He felt hollow.

When he finally emerged, his father and mother were waiting near the exit. His mother wrapped him in a brief hug. "You scared me," she said, her voice trembling. "I'm just glad no one was seriously hurt."

Doug leaned into her embrace, feeling a fresh pang of guilt. "Me too," he murmured. "I'm sorry, Mom."

She pulled back, brushing hair off his forehead. "We'll talk more at home," she said gently.

They trudged outside, the crisp night air hitting Doug's face like a slap of reality. Ice crystals clung to the edges of cars in the lot. Doug's father unlocked their sedan, and they all slid into the cold seats. No one spoke during the short drive home; the tension weighed too heavily.

Once inside the warmth of their living room, Doug realized how exhausted he was, physically and emotionally. He dropped his gear bag by the door with a soft thunk. His father set his keys on the kitchen counter, turning to face Doug. "You want to talk about it now or tomorrow?" he asked quietly.

Doug swallowed. "Now is fine," he said, wanting to get it over with.

They all moved to the living room couch. Doug's mother perched on an armchair, hands laced. His father took a seat on the sofa, gesturing for Doug to do the same. Doug sank down, heart thudding.

His father took a measured breath. "Doug, we saw you stand up for Trevor. We also saw you throw punches. Fighting is serious. Your league might suspend you. You know that."

Doug nodded, eyes downcast. "Coach said probably two games."

His mother made a soft sound, half dismay, half acceptance. "What matters now is how you move forward," she said. "We're not condoning fighting, but I know you felt you were defending your friend."

Doug looked up, tears pricking the corners of his eyes. "I didn't want to hurt anyone," he said. "But I was so angry. That guy... he was hurting Trevor."

His father cleared his throat, crossing his arms. "Hockey is physical, yes, but the rules exist to handle dirty hits. You have to let the refs handle it. If you go after the player yourself, you're the one who gets ejected, not him. Is that how you help your team?"

Doug shook his head, feeling those words sink in like stones. He realized the truth: by fighting, he might have left his team shorthanded, not to mention risking injury or a bigger meltdown. "I... I see your point," he mumbled.

His mother shifted in her seat. "It's okay to be passionate, Doug. But violence... it's never the real solution. Especially when you're just a kid learning the game."

Doug swallowed, voice trembling. "I get it." He paused, the memory of that surge of adrenaline still fresh. "But I also feel... I don't know... part of me feels like I had to stand up for him. I can't explain it."

His father's expression softened. "No one's saying you have to back down if you see an injustice. But in hockey, there's a difference between standing up for a teammate and dropping the gloves." He exhaled. "Tonight was a big lesson. It's how you handle it from here that matters."

A heavy silence followed. Finally, Doug's mother rose, placing a gentle hand on Doug's shoulder. "How about we get some rest, all right? We'll figure out the details of the suspension when Coach contacts us. In the meantime... let's just let this sink in."

Doug nodded wearily. He stood, letting his mother pull him into a quick hug. "I'm okay, Mom," he assured her, though his voice lacked conviction.

Doug retreated to his bedroom, flicking on the small lamp by his desk. The air felt stale, as if it, too, were holding its breath in judgement. He changed out of his sweat-dampened undershirt and into pajamas. Usually, he found solace in looking at his Maple Leafs rookie card, or flipping through hockey magazines, but tonight the idea of seeing images of the sport he loved only reminded him of the fight.

He threw himself onto his bed, exhaustion creeping through his limbs. The swirling cocktail of guilt, shame, and a vestige of adrenaline made it hard to relax. His phone buzzed—a message from Trevor.

TrevorTrevorTrevor. Hey man, thanks for having my back. Sorry it got crazy.

Doug typed back: *Yeah, sorry too. You okay?*

The response came quickly: *A bit sore, but good. Wish you hadn't gotten a penalty for me.*

Doug stared at the words. He realized, ironically, Trevor was probably carrying guilt of his own, feeling responsible that Doug was ejected. Another message popped up: *We'll talk tomorrow. Thanks again.*

Doug set the phone aside, thoughts churning. He was upset at himself, at the situation, but also a flicker of pride still lingered. He tried to remind himself that hockey was a contact sport, that fights occasionally happen, but a heavier truth overshadowed it: in house league, fights were not just frowned upon, they were actively punished. He might have cost his team a chance to place higher in the standings if his suspension overlapped crucial games.

Rolling onto his side, Doug flicked off the lamp. Darkness cloaked his room, broken only by a sliver of streetlight through the blinds. The fight replayed in his mind in slow motion: the hits, the yells, the moment he decided to swing. He recalled the numb shock as his glove made contact with the other player's helmet. That wasn't the kind of hockey Doug imagined when he daydreamed about playing for the Maple Leafs. That was ugly, clumsy, and fueled by rage.

He clenched his jaw. *I want to be better than that,* he told himself in the silence. *I want my skill to define me, not violence.*

Eventually, he drifted into a restless sleep, haunted by half-dreams of referees' whistles and scuffles in the corners.

The next morning, Doug awoke to the scent of toast and eggs drifting up the stairs. He trudged down, arms still sore from the previous night's tension. Entering the kitchen, he found his mother at the stove and his father reading the local newspaper at the table. She offered a small smile as Doug slipped into a chair.

"Morning," Doug mumbled, rubbing his eyes.

"Morning," his father replied, folding the newspaper. "I emailed Coach Wilkins. He said the league's disciplinary folks are meeting tomorrow."

Doug nodded, absently buttering a slice of toast. "Probably out two games," he said softly.

His mother turned off the stove, setting a plate of scrambled eggs in front of Doug. "We'll deal with it," she said. "And while you're off, you can still attend practices if Coach allows, keep your head in the game."

Doug forced a small nod. *That's something,* he thought.

They ate quietly, tension lacing the air. Doug's father occasionally asked questions about school, but Doug's answers were terse. The fight still occupied most of his thoughts—how it might damage his reputation, how Trevor and the team saw him now.

After breakfast, Doug slipped outside to the backyard, where the remnants of the homemade rink remained. Warmer days had left patches of slush on the ice. He stepped onto the boards carefully, wearing just boots and carrying a stick, nudging a puck back and forth. Skating wasn't really an option with the ice in that condition, but he needed some version of therapy—at least the motion of the stick soothed him.

He stared at the pockmarked ice, remembering how this very spot had ignited his passion, how he'd discovered his knack for skating. *What was I thinking last night?* He tapped the puck softly, the dull thunk echoing. A swirl of conflicting emotions came again: part regret, part a stubborn feeling that he'd done the right thing by defending Trevor.

Poking at a slushy patch with the blade of his stick, Doug exhaled a cloudy breath. *There has to be a balance,* he thought. *I can't let players get away with dirty hits, but I also can't turn into a brawler.*

Later that afternoon, Coach Wilkins called. Doug hurried to pick up the phone in the living room while his father hovered nearby.

"Hello?" Doug answered, voice tentative.

"Doug, it's Coach," came the measured voice on the other end. "Listen, I talked with the league official. They confirmed a two-game suspension. I'm sorry, but that's final."

Doug swallowed, nodding even though Coach couldn't see him. "I understand."

Coach sighed. "I want you at practices still—stay sharp, keep working. You can't sit on the bench during games, but I want you in the stands with the team to show support, okay?"

Doug's shoulders relaxed a bit. "Thanks for letting me still be part of it."

"We'll see you at practice on Tuesday. Hang in there, kid."

Click. The line went silent. Doug set the phone down. *Two games... I can handle that,* he thought, though disappointment still gnawed at him.

He relayed the news to his father, who patted him on the back. "At least you're not shut out entirely," he said. "Let's use the time to train, if you like."

Doug managed a faint smile. "That'd be good," he admitted.

Tuesday's practice arrived like a fresh start. Doug entered the locker room cautiously, half-expecting stares. But as he stepped in, the usual banter greeted him: guys complaining about homework, others bragging about a new curve on their sticks. Trevor waved him over, sporting a bruise on his forearm but otherwise looking fine.

"How you doing?" Trevor asked, eyes flicking to Doug's bag of gear.

Doug shrugged. "I'm all right. Suspended two games, though."

Trevor grimaced. "Man, sorry. That's rough. But thanks again for backing me up."

Doug mustered a tight grin. "Well, next time, I'll try to let the ref handle it." He felt a surge of conflicting pride and guilt swirl in his chest again. He clapped Trevor's shoulder, then found his usual spot on the bench to suit up.

Coach Wilkins gave Doug a nod as he strolled by, carrying a stack of cones for drills. "Glad you're here, Doug. Suit up—just remember, you won't be eligible for tomorrow's game."

"Yes, Coach," Doug replied.

They hit the ice, going through usual warm-ups: laps, stretching, then puck-handling drills. Doug poured his energy into each stride, each pivot. He wanted to reaffirm to everyone—and himself—that he was more than the kid who got into a fight. During a two-on-one drill, he skated fluidly, delivering crisp passes. That sense of calm control returned, overshadowing the tumult of the last few days. *This is what I love—the skill, the flow.*

A scrimmage followed, pitting half the team against the other. Doug's line flitted around, burying a few shots behind the goaltender. A defender bumped into Doug at one point, and Doug instinctively tensed, memories of the fight surging. But no fists flew, no anger sparked. Doug simply adjusted, kept skating. *See? It doesn't have to end in a brawl.*

After practice, the guys filed off the ice, breath steaming from under their cages. Doug headed to the locker room, removing his helmet to let the cold air hit his sweat-dampened hair. Trevor nudged him. "You looked good out there."

"Thanks," Doug said quietly. "I feel better, you know? Less messed up about the fight."

Trevor nodded, offering a small smile. "That's good, man. We need you."

Doug changed quickly, wanting to find Coach Wilkins to discuss any extra training he could do. But by the time he reached the hallway, Coach Wilkins was in conversation with one of the parents. Doug lingered near the vending machines, drumming his fingers on the metal side. He spotted Number 18 in his mind—a bigger, older memory that still felt fresh. *Why is the game so violent sometimes?* he asked himself. *Do I just accept that side of hockey or try to rise above it?*

Eventually, Coach Wilkins finished his conversation and turned to Doug. "What's up?" the coach asked, tucking a clipboard under his arm.

"Coach, I just wanted to see if there's anything extra I can work on. Since I'm out two games, I don't want to fall behind."

Coach Wilkins nodded thoughtfully. "Focus on skating drills, especially foot speed and agility. You're already good with puck-handling, but if you add more quickness, you'll be tough to stop. And, I'll be honest: it might help you avoid these big collisions that spark trouble."

Doug grimaced. "Yeah, I guess so."

The coach patted Doug on the shoulder. "Keep your nose clean. The best way to handle cheap shots is to outskate them, outscore them. Let the refs do their job."

Doug appreciated the coach's candor. "Thanks. I'll do that."

The next two games came and went without Doug on the bench. It felt surreal to sit in the stands, wearing street clothes while his teammates battled on the ice below. He cheered as loudly as any parent, biting his lip every time a big check rattled the boards. His team lost the first of those two games in a tight 1–0 affair, but they rebounded to win the second 4–2. Watching from the stands, Doug realized just how helpless it felt not to be able to do anything. *No matter how intense it gets, I'd rather be down there playing,* he thought.

On the final shift of the second game, a minor scuffle broke out behind the net—an opposing forward shoved one of Doug's defensemen after the whistle. Tensions flared, but his teammates mostly kept their cool, letting the referee handle it. *That could've been me two weeks ago,* Doug mused, heart pounding at the memory. Perhaps he was seeing the game in a new light. *Sometimes it's better to step back.*

When the buzzer sounded and his team sealed their 4–2 win, Doug hopped from his seat, cheering with the rest. He hurried downstairs to the locker room hallway to congratulate them. Trevor, removing a glove, clapped Doug's hand. "You're back next game, right?"

Doug nodded, grin stretching across his face. "Yeah. Can't wait."

Coach Wilkins gave a thumbs-up. "Nice to see you there cheering, Doug. We'll have you back on the ice next week."

Walking away with his father, who had attended both games by Doug's side in the stands, Doug felt an odd sense of closure forming around the fight incident. The suspension was over, he'd observed the game from a different perspective, and he realized that while physical play was a part of hockey, crossing the line into fights did more harm than good—especially at this level.

That night, Doug lay in bed, replaying the day's events. His return to the lineup was imminent, and he vowed to make the most of it. He could still be aggressive, still stand up for his teammates, but in a way that kept him in the game and out of the penalty box. *Hard checks, smart hockey, no fists.*

He thought of the conflicting rush of guilt and exhilaration from that fight. Part of him understood why fighting existed in the sport at higher levels—players policed each other, enforced respect. But in a youth league, it seemed out of place, overshadowing skill development and sportsmanship. *Maybe when I'm older, I'll understand it better,* Doug mused. *But for now, I'll focus on playing the right way.*

His phone buzzed again—another message from Trevor: *Congrats on finishing the suspension! We need you for the next game—big playoff push.*

Doug texted back: *Thanks. I'm ready to help us win.*

Then he set his phone aside, letting relief wash over him. He was still the same kid who loved hockey—the same dreamer who wanted to pull on a Maple Leafs sweater one day. The fight hadn't changed that. If anything, it forced him to confront a tougher reality: hockey could be violent, and how he responded to that violence was crucial. *I'll choose skill and heart, not fists,* he decided firmly.

In the coming days, Doug's renewed focus translated to extra time on the backyard rink—what remained of it as winter's end neared—and additional off-ice workouts. He practiced quick direction changes, mimicking the drills Coach had suggested. He honed his shot in the driveway, visualizing top-corner snipes. Each time he felt a surge of frustration or anger about the fight or anything else in life, he poured it into clean hockey moves.

His parents recognized the subtle shift, noticing how he channeled aggression into constructive training. Mike, whenever he saw Doug running sprints or practicing stickhandling in the basement, teased him: "No more fights, Rocky?" But he said it with a wink, letting Doug know he admired the dedication.

By the time Doug finally suited up for his first game post-suspension, nerves fluttered in his stomach. He entered the locker room, scanning the faces of his teammates. Harrison gave him a playful knock on the helmet. "Glad you're back, man," he said. "We need your speed out there."

Trevor, lacing up his skates, nodded in agreement. "Just don't go dropping the gloves on us," he joked, drawing light laughter.

Doug chuckled, cheeks flushing. "I'll keep it clean."

Coach Wilkins didn't give a grand speech about the suspension—he simply tapped Doug's shoulder as he passed, offering a reassuring nod. That gesture told Doug he'd been forgiven, and now it was time to just play hockey.

They took the ice for warm-ups, and Doug felt a surge of gratitude. *I'm here, not in the stands.* The arena lights glinted off the freshly resurfaced ice, the hum of fans settling into the bleachers. Doug eased into his laps, mindful of the tension in his shoulders. He told himself: *Channel your energy into the game. Show them what you can do.*

The opening faceoff saw the puck bounce deep into the opposing zone, and Doug immediately chased, weaving around a defenseman to force a turnover. The adrenaline that once drove him to throw punches now fueled a fierce forecheck. He forced the defenseman to cough up the puck, flicking it to Trevor, who rifled a quick shot on net. The goalie smothered it, stopping play. Doug and Trevor tapped gloves, grinning. That's how teamwork should look—aggressive but within the rules.

Midway through the first period, a tense moment arose. One of the opposing forwards delivered a borderline hit on Harrison along the boards. Doug tensed, heart pounding. He recognized the old anger creeping in—the desire to intervene. But this time, he checked himself. He glided toward the scene, ready to separate them if needed, but the refs promptly whistled the play dead, awarding a minor penalty to the aggressor. Doug hung back, letting the referees do their jobs. He and Harrison locked eyes briefly, and a silent understanding passed between them. *We'll stand up for each other by playing our game, not fighting.*

The power play that followed saw Doug's team cycle the puck brilliantly. Doug hovered near the right circle, awaiting a pass. When it came, he fired a low, hard shot that deflected off the goalie's pad, ricocheting out to Trevor, who buried the rebound. 1–0. The bench erupted, the crowd cheering. Doug felt a wave of joy. *This is the rush I want—the thrill of scoring, not punching.*

By the end of the night, they'd secured a 3–1 victory. Doug assisted on two of the three goals, playing some of his best hockey all season. As the final buzzer sounded, he skated to the handshake line with a weight lifted from his shoulders. No fights, no ejections—just skill, hustle, and sportsmanship.

As Doug and his teammates tapped gloves with the opposition, he briefly locked eyes with the kid who'd delivered that rough hit on Harrison. Rather than exchanging glares, they simply nodded. Doug realized that in youth hockey, hostility could flare quickly—but it could also dissolve just as fast. The game was done; time to move on.

Back in the locker room, the atmosphere was celebratory. Guys peeled off equipment with satisfied grins, some hooting about the upcoming tournament. Coach Wilkins clapped Doug on the back. "Excellent game. You used your energy in the right way."

Doug beamed. "Thanks, Coach."

Trevor sidled over. "You see? We need your passes more than your fists, man," he teased, although the warmth in his voice was sincere.

Doug laughed, shoulders finally relaxing. "Yeah, definitely." He sank onto the bench, sweat-soaked but relieved. *I can still play tough,* he told himself, *but tough doesn't have to mean fighting.*

In the days that followed, Doug reflected on that defining moment—the fight—and what it meant for his relationship with hockey. He understood now that while the sport was inherently physical, and standing up for teammates was part of the culture, there was a line he didn't want to cross again. If a time ever came in a higher-level game when fighting might be expected or tacitly allowed, he'd weigh his choices carefully.

For now, though, he was content to keep his gloves on, focusing on speed, skill, and teamwork. The memory of that brawl still stung, but it also served as a reminder of the power of adrenaline and the importance of self-control. He wasn't proud of throwing punches, but he also recognized the sincerity of his intention: to protect a friend. *I'll protect them in other ways now,* he resolved, *like out-hustling the opponent and playing the right way.*

His father later commended him for that bounce-back game, subtly acknowledging how proud he was that Doug had chosen discipline over aggression. His mother, relieved beyond words, no longer had to watch him get ejected or land in the penalty box for unsportsmanlike conduct. And Mike, for all his teasing, respected Doug's evolution. "You did what you felt you had to do," Mike said, "but now you see how better to handle it. That's what matters."

Most important, Doug's own conscience felt clearer. He could glance at the Maple Leafs poster on his wall and see the sport not through rose-colored glasses, but with an honest understanding: hockey was thrilling, fast, and occasionally rough. Yet it was also about skill and heart, about working together, about respect. If he someday made it to the bigger stages—junior hockey, maybe even the NHL—he hoped to carry that lesson with him.

And so, a single fight became a turning point in Doug's young hockey journey. Guilt and exhilaration had warred within him, forcing him to confront the sport's violent edge.

Emerging on the other side, he felt neither purely ashamed nor purely proud—rather, he felt more aware, more mature. He had glimpsed the heat of battle, and it had clarified his belief in the game's deeper essence: respect, camaraderie, and the pursuit of skillful play.

As he laced up for subsequent games, the memory of that tense scuffle never fully left him. But each time he stepped on the ice, he reminded himself what truly mattered: pushing his limits without losing sight of who he wanted to be. He'd hold that lesson close as he forged ahead—still a dreamer with visions of the Maple Leafs crest on his chest, still a kid navigating the complexities of a beloved sport, determined to find his own balance between grit and grace.

7

TRYOUTS

Doug exhaled slowly, leaning forward to tie his skates with methodical precision. He was seated on a worn wooden bench in the lobby of a large, modern hockey facility—a far cry from the quaint little arenas that housed his house-league games. Bright fluorescent lights hummed overhead, and the buzz of other aspiring players and their parents echoed in the cavernous space. This was it: tryouts for a competitive youth hockey team. The next step in Doug's budding career.

He'd only recently mustered the courage to sign up. The past year had been a roller coaster of new experiences: discovering his natural affinity for the game, playing on a house-league team, standing up for his friends—even getting into a scuffle. Yet, through all the ups and downs, Doug's love for the sport had only grown stronger. Now, stepping into a higher level, he was caught between a heady mix of excitement and nerve-wracking self-doubt.

He tightened the final lace on his left skate, then glanced up at his father, who stood nearby with crossed arms and an encouraging smile. "You've got this," his father said, his voice low but steady.

Doug forced a small grin. "Hope so."

Truth be told, he was anxious. For days, he'd been visualizing this moment—stepping onto the ice with more experienced players. His practices in house league had gone well enough, and he'd become a key player on his team. But that was house league. Now, he was leaping into a pool of players who'd possibly been training with private coaches, attending specialized camps, or skating since they could walk. *Don't psych yourself out,* he told himself. *Trust your skills.*

He stood, picking up his bag and stick. The sign taped to the rink door read: **"U14 Tryouts: Check In Here."** Younger kids were filing into an adjacent rink, older teens in another. Doug spotted a few players already in full gear, scuttling on rubber mats that led to the ice. A man with a clipboard—one of the assistant coaches, by the looks of it—handed each player a pinnie with a tryout number pinned to the front and back.

Doug approached, heart thumping. "Name?" the assistant coach asked.

"Doug Mansfield," Doug said, voice almost catching in his throat.

The coach ran a finger down a list. "Number 37," he said, ripping a pinnie off a rack. "Goalies in the locker room down the hall, skaters in the main locker room. Get dressed and be on the ice in ten minutes."

Doug took the pinnie—a plain white mesh vest with a black number 37 pinned at chest and spine. Nervous excitement churned in his stomach. *Number 37... that's me for the day.* He spotted his father out of the corner of his eye. "I'll wait out here," his father said gently, obviously reading Doug's jitters. "Go show them what you've got."

Doug nodded and headed to the locker room. There, he found a throng of players in various stages of dressing—some older-looking and tall, some about his size. The chatter was subdued, each kid clearly focused on the task ahead. Doug spotted a free spot on a bench, wedging himself and his gear into it.

He opened his hockey bag and carefully began to suit up: shin pads, socks, tape, pants, elbow pads, then pulling on the battered chest protector he still used from house league. It wasn't top-of-the-line, but it fit, and that was enough. He tried not to compare himself to the kids with brand-new gear. *It's about how you play, not how you look,* he reminded himself.

A hushed tension lay over the locker room. Everyone was here for the same reason: to impress the evaluators and earn a spot on the competitive team. Doug swallowed past the dryness in his throat. He remembered advice from his house-league coach: *Focus on your strengths. Skate hard, battle for the puck, don't try to be fancy if it's not your style.*

He secured the laces on his skates, slipping them into a short pre-game ritual of tapping each skate blade against the floor. Then he tugged his helmet on, snapped the chinstrap, and grabbed his stick. Following a stream of other players, Doug stepped out and made his way onto the ice.

The rink was immaculate, freshly resurfaced, with bright boards and glass panels polished to a near shine. Doug glided onto the ice, cutting a clean line with his blades. An immediate chill prickled his cheeks, the kind of bracing cold he loved. High above, a scoreboard glowed, though it was turned off for tryouts. A few parents dotted the bleachers, and behind the bench area stood several coaches and evaluators—clipboards in hand, eyes scanning each player intensely.

Doug's nerves flared as he joined a cluster of skaters at center ice. For a moment, they all looked at one another, sizing up the competition. Some kids offered subdued nods, others focused on adjusting their gloves or fiddling with their mouthguards. An older coach, wearing a jacket with the team's logo and a whistle around his neck, glided into the circle's center.

"All right, boys," the coach said, voice echoing in the stillness. "My name is Coach Hall. For the next two hours, we're going to see what you've got. We'll run drills, then scrimmage. Work hard, keep your heads up, show us your skills. Any questions?"

No one spoke. The tension was palpable. Doug's heart hammered in his chest.

"Good. Let's warm up."

He blew the whistle, and the group exploded into motion. Doug pushed off with purpose, reminding himself to skate with confidence. He found an open lane, pumping his legs, feeling that familiar rush of wind. They circled the rink, building speed with each lap. Doug forced himself to relax his shoulders, lengthen his stride, and concentrate on form.

Soon, Coach Hall directed them through standard drills—blue-line to red-line sprints, transitions, crossovers around cones. Doug struggled to keep pace in the first few sets, his stomach in knots. He felt stiff, mechanical. The players around him seemed so smooth, weaving through cones with effortless agility. Doug stumbled slightly during a transition from forward to backward skating, feeling frustration bloom in his chest. *Come on, Doug, settle down.*

A handful of evaluators stood along the boards, jotting notes on their clipboards. Doug glanced at one of them and felt a spike of anxiety. *Stop looking at them,* he told himself. *Focus on the ice.*

After the initial skating drills, the coaches introduced puck-handling work. Groups formed at the corners, weaving through cones that stretched across half the rink, aiming at small targets placed in the net. Doug's group included three bigger skaters, all of them older and apparently used to higher-level competition. They took their turns swiftly, each handling the puck with confidence. One kid fired a perfect top-corner shot that pinged off the crossbar and in.

Doug stepped up, the puck on his blade. He took a breath. The whistle sounded, and he darted forward. Cone one: a neat deke, the puck staying close to his blade. Cone two: a quick shift to backhand. Cone three: he misjudged the angle, clipping the cone's edge and nearly losing the puck. Doug's heart leapt into his throat. He recovered it before it slid too far but could practically feel the evaluators' eyes on him. Then, at the final cone, he rushed the pivot and stumbled, sending the puck just out of comfortable reach. His shot on net was off-balance, rolling weakly into the goalie's pads.

Disappointment surged through Doug. He heard faint murmurs in the stands—whether they were about him or not, it made his cheeks burn. The next kid raced up, pulling a fancy toe-drag move that wowed onlookers. Doug skated back in line, swallowing a bitter taste of self-doubt.

A wave of negativity whispered through his mind: *You're not good enough. These kids are older, faster, stronger.* But he shook his head, trying to cling to the knowledge that he belonged out here, that he'd earned a shot. *I can do better,* he insisted to himself.

Coach Hall and the assistants soon shifted the session to passing drills. Doug found some relief here—he'd always prided himself on crisp passes. They formed pairs, moving up the ice in sync, passing quickly back and forth. Doug was paired with a tall, lanky player named Xavier. Xavier had a wicked shot, but Doug noticed he sometimes struggled with puck control at top speed.

They set off together. Doug focused on each pass, aiming for the tape of Xavier's stick. The first three passes were spot-on, while Xavier's returns wobbled. Doug quickly corralled them, flicking each pass back smoothly. By the time they neared the blue line, they'd found a modest rhythm, culminating in a final pass that Doug caught fluidly and zipped back to Xavier for a shot on net. It was a small moment, but it buoyed Doug's confidence. *I can do this.*

They progressed to more complex drills—2-on-1s, 3-on-2s. Doug braced himself for the dreaded 1-on-1 battles where you had to defend or beat an opponent in open ice. He might not have the biggest frame, but he had determination. When Doug's turn came, facing a wiry defenseman, he remembered to keep his feet moving. With a burst of speed, he cut inside, faked left, and slipped around the defender. It was a fleeting victory, but a real one—Doug slid a quick wrist shot that slipped past the goalie's pad. A small flash of brilliance.

He heard a coach's voice: "Nice move, 37!" Doug's heartbeat soared. *They noticed me.* The sting of earlier mistakes dulled for a moment.

At last, Coach Hall blew his whistle and announced they'd split into two squads for a scrimmage. Doug was placed on a line with Xavier at center and a quick left-winger named Evan. Their job: to stand out in a structured 5-on-5 environment.

They lined up against a trio of physically imposing players, one of whom had that wicked top-corner shot Doug observed earlier. Doug's pulse thrummed as the puck dropped. Xavier lost the faceoff, and the other side barreled into the zone. Doug hustled to the boards to cut off the winger. He didn't flatten him—Doug wasn't a bruiser—but he kept his stick active, forcing a weak pass into neutral ice. Evan picked it off, quickly passing to Xavier, who turned up-ice with speed.

Doug sprinted forward, tapping his stick once to signal he was open. Xavier slid him a pass. The puck wobbled, but Doug corralled it and charged toward the net, adrenaline coursing through his veins. An opposing defender loomed, but Doug angled his body, shielded the puck, and managed to thread a short pass to Evan, who cranked a one-timer. The goalie made a flashy glove save, but Doug still felt exhilarated. It was a promising play.

As the scrimmage continued, Doug found that while these players were indeed bigger or more polished, he could keep up thanks to his hustle. Several times he raced in on the forecheck, causing turnovers. His passes were mostly tape-to-tape, fueling quick offensive bursts. And in one highlight moment, he managed to break up a cross-ice pass by dropping to his knees, intercepting the puck mid-lane. The assistant coaches clearly noticed—Doug caught them scribbling notes after that play.

But not all went smoothly. During one shift, Doug struggled to get the puck out of the zone, fumbling a clearing attempt that gave the opposing team a prime scoring chance. The goalie bailed Doug out with a glove save. Doug grimaced, feeling the sting of imperfection. *Can't make those mistakes in a tryout.*

Still, as the scrimmage wore on, Doug's heart pounded with a mixture of fatigue and excitement. *I'm proving I can belong,* he kept telling himself. *Don't stop now.*

By the time the final whistle blew, Doug's jersey was soaked, and his legs felt rubbery. He joined the other players in an informal line at center ice while Coach Hall skated out. The assistants gathered behind him, flipping through pages of notes.

"All right," Coach Hall announced, "nice work, everyone. We'll be finalizing cuts and rosters over the next couple of days. Keep an eye on your emails and phones." He paused, scanning the group. "We saw a lot of good things. Some of you are polished, some are raw with tons of potential. Either way, you should be proud you came out and gave it your all."

He dismissed them with a curt nod, blowing his whistle. Doug and the others peeled off toward the bench. A swirl of voices, shuffles, and a collective sense of relief filled the air—tryouts were exhausting, physically and mentally. Doug was about to head for the exit when he felt a firm hand on his shoulder pad. He turned to see Coach Hall.

"Number 37, right?" the coach said, pushing up the brim of his cap. "Doug Mansfield?"

Doug's stomach flipped. "Yes, sir."

The coach eyed him thoughtfully. "You had a shaky start out there—saw you lose the puck in the cone drill—but your effort was top-notch in the scrimmage. Good instincts, too. Keep working on your transitions. But overall, nice job."

Doug's chest flooded with warmth. "Thank you," he managed. "I'll do better next time."

Coach Hall nodded, a faint smile curving his lips. "We'll see how the roster shakes out." With that, he turned and skated away, leaving Doug frozen with a mix of relief and excitement. *He noticed me,* Doug thought, a grin tugging at his mouth. *He saw something, even if I wasn't perfect.*

Doug slogged back to the locker room, adrenaline wearing off. He removed his gear in a haze, replaying every moment of the tryout. Even the passing compliments were overshadowed by fear of potential cuts. Still, hearing the coach single him out in a positive way eased some of that anxiety.

The room buzzed with subdued chatter. Players compared notes about the scrimmage or their previous teams. Doug kept mostly quiet, stowing his equipment. Then, releasing a slow exhale, he grabbed his bag and headed to the lobby.

His father was there, leaning against a vending machine. He looked up with a question in his eyes. "How'd it go?"

Doug shrugged, but a slight smile cracked his features. "Okay, I think. I stumbled early, but the coach said I did well in the scrimmage."

His father's shoulders relaxed a fraction. "That's great. Let's get you home—get some rest."

They walked outside into the late-afternoon sun, which felt oddly warm after the rink's chill. Doug loaded his bag into the trunk, and they started the drive back. As they merged onto a main road, Doug's father glanced over. "No matter what happens, I'm proud of you for trying. Jumping into a more competitive league takes guts."

Doug nodded, the knot in his stomach beginning to unwind. "Thanks, Dad," he murmured. "I just hope it's enough."

At home, Doug's mother asked the same question: "How'd it go?" He repeated his answer, and she offered words of encouragement and a comforting hug. Mike, who was in the kitchen rummaging for a snack, raised an eyebrow.

"Competitive league, huh? Looks like you're moving up in the world," Mike teased with a grin. "Next step, the NHL draft?"

Doug rolled his eyes, but smiled all the same. "Sure, eventually. One step at a time, though."

He retreated to his room, letting the adrenaline crash morph into exhaustion. His muscles ached, and his mind was awash with images of cones, coaches, breakaways, and that fleeting moment of praise. He flopped onto his bed, staring at the poster of the Toronto Maple Leafs pinned above his desk. *I'm getting there,* he told himself. *One rung at a time.*

The next two days were agony. Doug went to school, but his mind kept drifting to the tryout. He checked his email constantly, waiting for the official communication from the club. Would it say, "Thank you, but we're unable to offer you a spot"? Or would it be the start of a new chapter in Doug's hockey journey? Every time he opened his phone, his stomach twisted with anticipation.

He also replayed any mistakes he could recall, gnawing on each misstep: the bungled puck at the cone drill, the fumbled clearing attempt. But then he reminded himself of the positives: the crisp passes, the intercepted cross-ice pass, that strong forecheck. *You did enough,* he whispered to his reflection in the bathroom mirror one morning. *You have to believe it.*

On the evening of the second day, Doug sat at the dinner table with his family. His mother had prepared a casserole; the rich aroma filled the house. But Doug barely tasted his food, jiggling his leg under the table. The phone sat in front of him, face-down, as if looking at it would conjure disappointment.

Finally, a ping. Doug's heart leapt into his throat. He snatched the phone, glancing at the screen: **New Email: Youth Hockey Club**. He stared at his parents, who both paused mid-bite. Mike, too, froze, wide-eyed.

"Well?" Doug's father said quietly.

Doug opened the email. His eyes skimmed the text, devouring the words. Then, a grin blossomed, bright as a new morning. "I made the first cut," he breathed. "They haven't finalized the entire roster, but they invited me back for a second round of tryouts."

A burst of joy rippled around the table. His mother let out a small cheer, setting her fork down. Mike gave Doug a playful punch on the shoulder. His father exhaled, relief crossing his face. "That's my boy," he said, voice thick with pride.

Doug read it again, slower: *'Doug Mansfield, #37, we'd like to invite you to the second phase of tryouts next week...'* He nearly vibrated with excitement. "Next week," he repeated. "I have another shot to secure a full roster spot."

His mother beamed. "We're so proud of you, Doug."

Doug's father nodded. "Absolutely. You put yourself out there, and it's paying off. Now, keep pushing."

Doug nodded vigorously. "I will," he said, feeling a wave of determination wash over him.

The days leading up to the second-round tryout were a blur of school, chores, and self-imposed extra training. Doug revisited the local outdoor rink near his neighborhood whenever it was free, working on his transitions and acceleration. He watched videos online of pro players executing tight turns, analyzing how they kept balance and speed. He even asked Mike to time him on sprints in the driveway, using cones to replicate the drill he'd struggled with.

"Quicker footwork," Mike advised at one point, hands in his hoodie pocket as Doug gasped for breath after a sprint. "The actual speed will come. Focus on your quick takeoff first."

Doug nodded, sweat beading on his forehead. He repeated each drill until his legs burned. Then he'd hobble inside, determined to do it all again the next day. His father watched this with a proud but concerned eye, cautioning Doug not to overdo it.

On the night before the second tryout, Doug could hardly sleep. He kept picturing the moment Coach Hall singled him out. *Sharp reflexes, good instincts,* he told himself. *Just show them more of that.*

Finally, the day arrived. Doug donned his gear in the same locker room as before, though the group was noticeably smaller this time—maybe half as many players had been invited back. An air of even greater intensity weighed on everyone, the stakes higher. One final audition for a precious spot on the competitive roster.

Coach Hall kept the structure similar: a brisk warm-up, advanced drills, then a scrimmage. Right from the warm-up laps, Doug felt a new sense of ease. Yes, the stakes were high, but he'd already proven he belonged in the second round. That knowledge helped calm his nerves. *Skate your game,* he reminded himself. *Just like last time, but smoother.*

He tackled the cone drills with laser focus. This time, he nailed the transitions without stumbling. While not the flashiest skater on the ice, he kept clean form, hitting the right angles. He even caught a glimpse of a coach making a small positive note on a clipboard.

In the puck-handling segment, Doug weaved confidently, placing each deke with purpose. When he shot at the end, he fired a low, hard wrister that rang off the post. He grimaced— so close—but the shot had power, accuracy just a hair off. *Better than a flubbed shot,* he consoled himself.

When the scrimmage started, Doug once again found himself on a line with Xavier and Evan. The chemistry from the last tryout seemed to remain, with each knowing the other's style a bit better now. Doug particularly focused on quick puck movement and supporting his linemates—he didn't want to hog the play, but he also wanted to demonstrate he could carry the puck with confidence.

Midway through the scrimmage, they forced a turnover in the neutral zone. Evan threaded a pass to Doug, who accelerated along the boards. One defender came at him fast. Doug feigned cutting inside, only to slip the puck between the defender's skates along the boards and dart around him on the outside—*a simple but effective move*, Doug thought. Catching up to the puck, he glanced toward the crease. Xavier was streaking in from the opposite side. Doug fired a cross-ice pass, tape to tape, and Xavier roofed the puck into the net.

The clang of the goal pipes was followed by a sharp cheer from a few onlookers. Doug's heart soared. *That's the kind of play that stands out,* he told himself. He exchanged glove taps with Xavier. For the next shifts, Doug rode that high, making sure not to get sloppy in defense.

When the final whistle ended the scrimmage, Doug's body hummed with equal parts fatigue and triumph. He'd made fewer mistakes this time, displayed solid passing and hustle, and even had a hand in a goal. *If that's not enough, I don't know what is.*

Coach Hall assembled the group. Once again, he offered minimal feedback, only promising they'd reach out within a few days with final decisions. Doug's heart thrummed, but he maintained a calm exterior. He'd done everything he could.

The next night found Doug at the dinner table again, phone beside him. This time, he was more at peace—he sensed he'd done well, and if the coaches decided otherwise, at least he had no regrets.

His father glanced at him. "Did they say exactly when they'd finalize the roster?"

Doug shook his head. "They said 'within a few days.'"

Just then, a new email notification lit up Doug's phone. He inhaled sharply, exchanging a look with his family. He tapped to open the message.

A rush of relief and excitement buzzed through him as he scanned the text: *"Congratulations, you have been selected for the U14 Competitive Roster..."* He nearly jumped from his seat.

"I got in!" he exclaimed, voice cracking. "I made the team!"

His mother let out a joyous laugh, hurrying around the table to hug him. His father gripped his shoulder, eyes gleaming with pride. Mike, who stood in the hallway, raised a triumphant fist. "There we go, Dougie! That's what I'm talking about!"

Doug's chest swelled. He read further details in the email: practice schedules, tournament plans, uniform fittings. All the responsibilities and commitments that came with being on a competitive team. Far from daunting him, it filled him with eager anticipation.

Later that night, Doug sat on his bed, phone in hand. He stared at the Maple Leafs poster pinned above his desk, reflecting on the journey so far: from shooting pucks on a frozen backyard rink, to house-league scraps, to the decision to try out for a higher-level team. *And now I'm in,* he told himself. *One step closer.*

He flicked through the email again, soaking in every detail. Then he pulled up a text message to Trevor, his friend and teammate from house league. Trevor had also been to various tryouts, though for a different organization. Doug typed: *Hey man, guess what—I made the U14 comp team! Let's train together soon.*

A minute later, Trevor's reply buzzed: *Congrats, dude! You earned it. Let's celebrate on the ice.*

Doug smiled to himself, setting the phone down. He thought of Coach Hall's final words at the rink: "Some of you are polished, some are raw with tons of potential." Doug considered himself among the raw, a work in progress. But he had shown flashes of brilliance—and that was enough to catch the eye of a coach looking for heart, hustle, and skill yet to be fully refined.

He turned off his lamp, darkness settling over the room. In the quiet, he felt the subtle ache in his muscles, the telltale sign of hours spent on the ice. *This is the life I want,* he reminded himself. *Hard practices, big games, the grind of competition—all of it.*

With a contented sigh, Doug closed his eyes. Tonight, he'd let himself savor the victory of making the team. Tomorrow, he'd wake up ready to tackle the next challenge: proving he belonged, day in and day out, on that competitive squad. Because in hockey—like in life—making the roster was only the beginning of the real work.

He drifted off to sleep with a smile, images of sharp cross-ice passes and breakaway rushes dancing in his dreams, confident that he was on the right path and determined to keep moving forward.

8

THE FIRST SEASON

Doug glanced up at the rink's large digital clock reading 5:59 a.m. The arena lights buzzed overhead, illuminating the freshly resurfaced ice. Even though he was half-asleep, clad in sweats and lugging his gear bag over one shoulder, a bolt of excitement shot through him. It was his first day of official practices for the competitive youth league team he'd fought so hard to join—and the new schedule was already making itself known.

He spotted two figures at the far side of the lobby, rummaging through a duffel bag of pucks: Coach Hall and one of the assistant coaches, Ms. Leclair. Doug's heart thumped at the sight of them. He still couldn't believe he'd made it onto this roster. *Now the real work begins,* he reminded himself, stepping onto the rubber mat that led toward the locker rooms.

Inside, half the team was already there, bleary-eyed from the early hour. Doug offered a tired grin in greeting, and a few kids he recognized from tryouts waved or nodded. Some rummaged for tape in the bottom of their bags, others sipped water or energy drinks. A heavy hush hung in the chilly air— nobody was quite awake enough for boisterous talk just yet, but there was a buzz of anticipation beneath the yawns.

Doug found an empty spot on the bench. He set his bag down, pulled off his hoodie, and began the methodical process of suiting up: shin pads, socks, hockey pants, then shoulder pads. Each piece of equipment felt more precious now that he was on a higher-level team. He remembered how close he'd come to doubting himself during tryouts. *No time for doubts now,* he told himself, carefully lacing his skates.

"Hey, man," came a voice from a few feet away. Doug looked up. It was Xavier, the tall, lanky center with whom he'd had some good chemistry during tryouts.

"Morning," Doug managed, stifling a yawn. "Ready for this?"

Xavier chuckled. "As ready as I can be before sunrise." He shoved a mouthguard case into his bag. "Coach Hall runs these early practices so we don't interfere with after-school stuff, but I swear it's brutal."

Doug nodded sympathetically. "Yeah, I get it."

In truth, Doug felt that same tension—knowing he'd have to juggle these early practices with school, homework, and possibly more. He thought about his father dropping him off in the dark, offering a sleepy yet encouraging good-luck wave before heading to his own job. The weight of this opportunity settled on Doug's shoulders in a tangible way. He was determined to prove it wasn't wasted.

Five minutes later, the entire team of about fifteen skaters and two goalies filed onto the ice. Coach Hall and Ms. Leclair called them into a half-circle at center ice, their breath creating tiny clouds in the cold air. Doug felt his muscles tighten in anticipation.

"Morning, everyone," Coach Hall said, voice echoing. "This is where we separate the good from the great. You all made this roster because we see potential, but now we need to push you further. We have a tough schedule and high expectations."

Ms. Leclair nodded in agreement. "We're focusing on conditioning, puck control, and discipline. We'll go hard from day one—if you can't keep up, we'll know."

No one spoke, but Doug could feel a current of determination run through the group. Everyone had made it this far; no one wanted to show weakness now.

They launched into skating drills that tested their endurance right out of the gate—lap after lap, forward, backward, crossovers, suicides. Doug's lungs burned, but he pushed through, leaning on the resolve he'd developed practicing on that backyard rink and in house league. Still, he quickly realized this was a different level of intensity. The coaches expected sharper turns, quicker transitions, and less recovery time between reps.

After the conditioning, they shifted to puck-handling sequences—zigzagging through cones, maneuvering in tight corners. Doug found a rhythm, grateful for the summer hours he'd spent practicing. Even so, his stick occasionally bobbled when he tried more advanced dekes at high speed. He noticed that Ms. Leclair jotted something on her clipboard each time he mishandled the puck. A spike of anxiety flared in his chest. *They're watching every detail,* he thought. *I can't slip up.*

The final portion of practice involved small-area scrimmages—3-on-3 battles in the corners, behind the net, and along the boards. Doug discovered quickly that the physicality was on another tier. Guys who had been relatively polite during tryouts were now leaning in with heavier checks, jostling for position, making sure no one got an easy shot. Doug caught an elbow in the ribs during one scrum, pain flaring momentarily. But instead of backing off, he dug in deeper, fighting for that puck with renewed tenacity. *If I'm going to belong here, I need to show I can handle the rough stuff,* he told himself, wincing as he pried the puck free and slipped it to Xavier.

By the time Coach Hall blew the final whistle, sweat drenched Doug's gear. He skated to the bench, muscles trembling with fatigue. As he bent over to catch his breath, he could sense that same weariness in his teammates. Yet in their eyes, he also saw the spark of camaraderie already taking root: they were in this together, hammered by the same punishing drills, united by the shared goal of excelling as a team.

"Good job, folks," Coach Hall said. "Shower, head to school, and we'll see you again tomorrow."

Doug peeled off his helmet. The thought of repeating this grueling routine before sunrise for weeks on end was daunting, but a flicker of pride ignited within him. *I survived Day One,* he thought, exhausted yet exhilarated. *I can survive the next.*

The season's first month flew by, peppered with more early-morning practices, weekend sessions, and occasional team meetings. Doug discovered an entirely new dimension of hockey life that extended beyond the ice—film sessions, strategy talks, nutritional advice. Coach Hall sometimes projected game footage on a wall at the rink, highlighting flaws in positioning or praising a well-executed breakout. Doug felt like he was stepping into a miniature version of professional hockey, and the immersion thrilled him.

He also started to forge relationships with his teammates. Most were from various corners of the region—some from city suburbs, others from small towns like Doug's. They ranged in personality: quiet types who rarely spoke unless it was about tactics, and outgoing jokesters who kept the locker room lively. Regardless of background, they bonded over bruised knees and sore shoulders, shared triumphs and mutual complaints about 5:30 a.m. alarms.

Xavier, the lanky center, became one of Doug's closest friends on the team. Despite having different personalities—Doug was more cautious, Xavier more laid-back—they connected over their love for puck movement and setting each other up for plays. There was also Jeremy, a short but extremely agile defenseman, whose chirpy humor kept everyone entertained, and Cameron, a stoic goalie who seldom said a word unless it was to critique his own performance.

Their first real off-ice bonding occurred one Saturday afternoon, after a brutal two-hour skate. Jeremy casually invited Doug and a few others to his house for an NHL video game tournament. They crowded around a TV in Jeremy's basement, hollering at pixelated players, munching on chips, and swapping stories about their earliest hockey memories. In that moment—surrounded by laughter, friendly taunts, and the occasional bag of frozen peas pressed against a bruised shoulder—Doug felt the true essence of a team forming. *We're more than just hockey players on the same roster; we're a family in the making.*

When the league's opening weekend finally arrived, Doug felt the familiar swirl of nervous excitement. Their first official game was at a sleek suburban arena against a formidable rival. Rumor had it this rival team boasted several returning players who had been together for years, forging chemistry that new squads like Doug's found daunting.

Doug remembered pulling on the crisp, newly issued jersey for the first time—blue and gold with a bold crest on the front, his number (37) stitched on the back. He smoothed the fabric, heart pounding. *I'm really part of this now,* he thought.

The game started at a frantic pace. Doug's line took the ice early, the puck zipping from stick to stick at speeds that felt faster than any house-league match he'd played. Within minutes, the opposing squad demonstrated their chemistry with a quick passing sequence that ended in a laser shot into the top corner, beating Cameron's glove. 1–0 against them.

Doug's spirits dipped, but a surge of determination shot through him. On his next shift, he pressured the opposing defenseman in their zone, forcing a turnover that Xavier scooped up. Xavier snapped a shot that clanged off the post, missing by a hair. *So close,* Doug thought.

Despite their efforts, the game spiraled into a lesson in synergy and experience. The opposing team's lines seemed to read each other's minds. Each time Doug's squad mustered an attack, they were countered by crisp, organized defense. By the final buzzer, the scoreboard showed a 4–1 loss.

Dejected, Doug filed off the ice with his teammates. Yet, in the locker room, Coach Hall delivered a calm talk: "They're a seasoned group. We're still gelling. Learn from this, because we'll see them again."

Doug sat, unfastening his helmet. His shoulders slumped in disappointment, but he also felt a strange sense of readiness to improve—like the loss was fueling a fire in his belly. *We'll be better next time.*

The next few games ran the gamut of emotions. In one matchup, they faced a younger, less-polished team, dominating with a 6–0 shutout that showcased their raw potential. Doug himself contributed two assists, threading passes through seams that left the opposing defense floundering. That victory felt sweet, especially after the stinging loss from the previous week.

However, the following game proved a heartbreaker—an overtime loss to a mid-level team they should have beaten. Doug's line poured on shots, but the opposing goalie stood on his head, making acrobatic saves. In OT, a miscommunication on defense led to a breakaway, sealing the defeat 3–2. Frustration brewed, and Doug witnessed the intensity of his teammates' disappointment. Xavier slammed his stick against the boards, Jeremy scowled in silence, and Cameron uncharacteristically muttered curses under his breath.

But with each setback, Coach Hall guided them back to the fundamental question: *What did we learn?* He dissected their defensive lapses, their neutral-zone turnovers, their inability to convert on power plays. He praised small positives—like Doug's continued hustle on the forecheck—and hammered home the idea that improvement was a marathon, not a sprint.

As weeks turned into a month, Doug began noticing incremental changes. Their breakouts became cleaner. They timed their zone entries better. Xavier developed a knack for winning key faceoffs, and Jeremy refined his poke-check timing. Their chemistry solidified, especially among the forward lines. Doug emerged as a reliable right-wing presence who could retrieve pucks from dirty areas and create scoring chances.

Beyond game days, the rigorous schedule tested everyone's dedication. In addition to the early practices, Coach Hall often scheduled evening video sessions or weekend "optional" skates that never truly felt optional if you wanted to keep up. Doug found himself juggling homework on bus rides to away games, studying vocab lists in the stands while waiting for his shift in warmups.

Fatigue became a constant companion. Doug woke some mornings with knots in his calves, bruises on his forearms, and a stiff back. On Monday nights, after a weekend doubleheader, all he wanted to do was collapse. His parents stepped in, reminding him to stay on top of rest, nutrition, and school responsibilities. "Don't burn out," his father warned gently. "It's okay to pace yourself."

Doug nodded whenever his parents expressed concern, but he also harbored a fierce drive to prove he could handle this schedule. *If I want to go even further—junior hockey, maybe pro—I have to endure these early challenges,* he told himself. The result was a mixture of constant exhaustion and relentless perseverance.

Yet, despite the aches, Doug felt more alive than ever. The team environment was infectious. Carpooling to distant arenas brought them closer together—laughing at each other's jokes, sharing headphones, mocking Jeremy's choice in music. Those bus rides echoed with the excited chatter of adolescent players forging deep bonds through a mutual dream.

As the regular season barreled forward, Doug's team found itself in the midst of intensifying rivalries. Their matches with the first team that had crushed them (the 4–1 fiasco) became must-watch affairs. In their second meeting, Doug's squad pulled off a thrilling 3–2 win. Doug notched a goal—a wrist shot that slipped just under the goalie's blocker—and joined in a massive celebration at center ice. He'd rarely felt such vindication. *We've come a long way.*

Another rivalry emerged against a chippy team known for borderline hits. One game, a particularly vicious elbow knocked Xavier out of the game early, leaving Doug's line scrambled. Anger simmered among Doug's teammates, but

Coach Hall insisted they channel that emotion into disciplined play. They ended up grinding out a 2–1 victory, leaving the other team fuming about penalties they'd racked up. In the handshake line, Doug sensed the tension in every stare, a silent vow that next time would be even tougher.

Through these battles, Doug discovered an intense camaraderie he hadn't experienced in house league. Teammates literally bled together after catching pucks in the face or body checks gone wrong. They hoisted each other up, fended off cheap shots, and celebrated even small successes— a key block, a well-timed backcheck, a go-ahead goal. It was hockey at a level of synergy and brotherhood that thrilled Doug to his core. *Every bruise has a story,* he thought, *and every story binds us closer.*

Inevitably, the season also dished out its share of slumps. Doug experienced a stretch where he couldn't buy a goal, no matter how many shots he took. Coach Hall tried mixing up lines, giving Doug different centermen to spark something new. The result only frustrated him more as he struggled to adjust to new linemates' styles.

One night, after a particularly poor showing, Doug found himself in the empty locker room long after everyone else had left. He stared at the dented floor, sweaty hair plastered to his forehead. A swirl of self-doubt nibbled at him: *Am I cut out for this?*

Then Xavier stuck his head back in. "Hey, Mansfield, you good?"

Doug sighed, forcing a small grin. "Yeah, just frustrated."

Xavier stepped inside, leaning on a metal locker. "Slumps happen. You'll snap out of it."

Doug shrugged. "I just feel like I'm letting everyone down."

Xavier gave him a gentle punch on the shoulder pad. "Man, you're one of the hardest workers on this team. We all see it. Don't let a couple games of bad luck eat you alive."

Those words gave Doug a jolt of comfort. He offered a faint grin. "Thanks," he whispered. "I appreciate it."

As the weeks progressed, the slump eventually lifted. In a pivotal game against a mid-tier rival, Doug found himself in a 2-on-1 break with Jeremy. With the defenseman sliding to block a pass, Doug faked a shot, then slid the puck across at the last second. Jeremy buried it top shelf. The bench erupted, and Doug felt the weight of the slump fall away. Coach Hall patted Doug's helmet afterward: "That's the killer instinct I knew you had."

By mid-season, Doug's resilience began to pay off in tangible results. He developed a reputation for tenacious puck retrieval in the corners—his house-league roots had taught him not to shy away from dirty work. His forechecking style disrupted opponents, causing turnovers and leading to prime scoring chances.

Coach Hall started leaning on Doug's line in key situations, especially when they needed a momentum shift. Doug's stats quietly blossomed: a steady stream of assists from his crisp passing, plus timely goals whenever he found open space or capitalized on rebounds. He wasn't the flashiest player, but his consistency stood out.

In the locker room, the older guys began to see Doug as more than just a newcomer. They recognized his commitment, the hours he put in, his willingness to absorb hits to make a play. Teammates started giving him small compliments or playful nicknames—like "Scrapper" when he emerged from a corner battle with the puck, or "Fisher" because he seemed to fish out loose pucks wherever they lurked.

During one memorable game, Doug netted his first multi-goal performance—a pair of well-placed shots that found twine. After the final horn, Cameron, the usually silent goalie, skated up and tapped Doug's pads. "That was huge," Cameron said simply, a rare grin crossing his face. Doug realized that recognition from this quiet netminder meant the world.

The season's home stretch delivered a roller coaster of results. A dramatic overtime win against the top-ranked team placed Doug's squad on everyone's radar. The local hockey forum buzzed about this new contender, praising the cohesive forecheck and the emergent star forward wearing #37, who never seemed to quit on a play. Doug's heart soared at such mentions—though he tried not to let it inflate his ego too much.

But just as they climbed the standings, a crushing setback loomed. In a game that could have cemented their playoff seeding, they collapsed against a lower-ranked team. Sloppy turnovers and defensive miscues led to an embarrassing 5–2 defeat. The locker room afterward felt like a funeral. Xavier kicked the wall in frustration, Jeremy shook his head in disbelief, and Doug slumped in front of his stall, replaying every blown pass in his mind.

Coach Hall addressed them sternly, but not unkindly: "We lost focus. We let ourselves get comfortable after a few big wins. This is the cost."

The hardest part was confronting the reality that they weren't invincible. The league was balanced, and any slip in intensity could cost them. Doug took it particularly hard, feeling the sting of letting the team down. But as usual, hockey offered no time for wallowing—there was always another game, another practice. And so, they picked themselves up, bound by the shared determination to bounce back.

By the final weeks of the regular season, Doug's consistent production and relentless style of play became impossible to ignore. He was no longer just the new kid adjusting to a competitive level—he was an integral part of the offense. The local sports blogger who covered youth hockey wrote a short piece calling Doug "one of the league's most promising two-way forwards," citing his ability to both create scoring chances and hustle back on defense.

His teammates noticed the shift, too. In a crucial rematch with that chippy team they'd beaten 2–1 earlier, Doug was tasked with shadowing the opponent's top scorer. Though smaller, Doug pestered him all night, intercepting passes, angling him off the puck, and chipping pucks off the boards to start rushes the other way. By the third period, the frustrated scorer took a careless penalty, giving Doug's squad a power play that sealed the game with a late goal.

Afterward, as they high-fived in the handshake line, that same top scorer gave Doug a curt nod, a sign of grudging respect. Doug, breathing heavily, realized he'd never felt more confident in his role.

In the locker room, Coach Hall singled Doug out in front of everyone: "Mansfield, that was a clinic in hustle. Well done." Applause rippled around the stall. Doug, cheeks red, felt immense pride. He realized how far he'd come since tryouts, when he was just hoping not to embarrass himself. Now, he was a pillar of the team.

In between intense games and punishing practices, Doug savored the off-ice moments that made the season special.

Team dinners at a local pizza joint after a big win, bus rides where they belted out off-key songs, impromptu pep talks from veterans who recognized Doug's potential.

He also realized how much he owed to his parents. They rearranged schedules to drive him to distant arenas, paid extra fees for tournaments, and made sure he kept his grades afloat. One night, as Doug iced his sore knee in the living room, his mother gently placed a blanket over him. "We're proud of you," she said quietly. "But remember to take care of yourself. You're more than just hockey."

Doug nodded, gratitude filling his chest. *I'll keep pushing—both for me and for them,* he thought.

And push he did. In the final stretch, the team secured a playoff berth. It felt surreal—Doug recalled daydreaming about moments like this back when he was playing on a backyard rink. Now he was part of a legitimate playoff-bound squad, wearing a jersey that signified more than just a team; it was a symbol of shared sacrifice and ambition.

As the regular season ended, Doug found himself reflecting on the months of brutal wake-up calls, battered knees, thrilling wins, and crushing losses. The practice schedule was unrelenting, the physical toll was high, and the emotional roller coaster never ceased. Yet, in the midst of it all, he had emerged as a standout forward, forging memories and friendships he knew would last.

Coach Hall called the team together after their final regular-season game, a tense 2–2 tie that ended in a shootout win. Standing in the locker room, the coach paced in front of them, expression unreadable. "You all have come a long way," he said finally, voice echoing in the hushed space. "You've formed something special—a brotherhood built on sweat, bruises, and belief in one another. Now we go into playoffs. Keep the intensity, keep the unity, and we'll see where it takes us."

Doug sat next to Xavier, who gave him a grin and offered a fist bump. Doug returned it, heart swelling with anticipation. *Playoffs,* he thought. *This is what we've worked for.*

Later, as he peeled off his damp gear, Doug recalled the sense of wonder he'd felt at his first house-league game, then that leap to a competitive tryout, and now this. He felt older, more grounded, and yet the same excitement still thrummed in his veins. He might not know exactly how far hockey would carry him, but he was certain that this season—his first season in a truly competitive league—had changed him forever.

He'd discovered a level of camaraderie that went beyond mere friendship: it was forged in the crucible of shared exhaustion, a desire to outwork opponents, and the unwavering trust that every guy wearing that jersey had each other's backs. Doug was proud to be a part of it, eager to see how the playoffs would unfold, and determined to keep proving his worth.

As the final echoes of skates and chatter faded in the locker room, Doug slung his gear bag over his shoulder. He stepped out into the corridor, where his father was waiting, a proud smile lighting his face. Doug reciprocated with a grin. Together, they headed into the cold night air, mind already turning to the next step in this journey. *I can't wait for the playoffs,* he thought, the flicker of ambition bright in his chest.

He might have started the season as just another rookie kid, but now he walked away as a recognized standout forward—one whose hustle, skill, and heart might just carry him and his team deeper into the path he'd always dreamed of treading. And, in the process, Doug realized he'd found something priceless: a sense of belonging and purpose that fueled him to lace up his skates again and again, no matter how early the morning call.

9

SCOUTS TAKE NOTICE

The chatter in the locker room was unusually hushed before the big game. Usually, Doug's competitive youth team thrived on a loose, bantering atmosphere before hitting the ice—but not tonight. Something electric hung in the air, stirring a mix of anxiety and excitement. Doug swore he could hear every tap of tape on shin guards, every nervous shuffle of skates on the worn rubber floor. It was the final game of the regular season, and although they'd already locked up a playoff berth, rumors buzzed that junior scouts had shown up in the stands to get a look at certain rising talents.

Doug tried to block out the swirling gossip as he pulled on his blue-and-gold jersey. The new crest, which had once felt stiff and foreign against his chest, now felt like a second skin. He'd grown so much this season—stronger, faster, more confident—and it showed in his stats. Already considered one of the top forwards on the team, he was a go-to player for vital shifts. But now, as he laced his skates, the knowledge that scouts were in the building tightened a knot in his stomach. *One game shouldn't define me,* he told himself, *but it might.*

His linemate, Xavier, sidled up next to him. "You hear that a couple OHL scouts are up there?" he asked under his breath, eyebrows raised.

Doug swallowed. "Yeah, I heard. Trying not to think about it."

Xavier nodded. "Me too. But, man... can you imagine if we really get noticed?" He exhaled slowly, attempting to keep his voice casual. "Like, the big leagues—maybe not the NHL, but the step before that. A major junior team. That's how you get on the radar."

Doug recognized the glimmer in Xavier's eye: ambition. He felt it, too, a quiet spark he'd harbored ever since he first realized he might be good enough to play at a higher level. But he'd also felt the weight of real-life concerns pressing on him— like money for equipment, travel, and the possibility of living away from home at a young age. Yet, hearing Xavier's excitement made Doug's heart race with the same "what-if" scenarios he'd entertained countless times. *What if this is the chance?*

He smoothed out a kink in his shin tape and forced a smile. "Let's focus on the game first," he said. "We've got a job to do out there."

Xavier grinned back, giving a short nod. "Yeah. Let's do it."

Their home arena was packed. Parents, friends, and local fans jammed into the modest bleachers. At the far top row, Doug recognized a few unfamiliar figures: men in coats with notepads, some wearing hats bearing the logos of junior hockey clubs. He tried not to stare. Instead, he picked out his father and mother among the crowd, seated midway up as usual. His father, arms folded, wore a proud but thoughtful expression; his mother clutched a thermos of coffee, half-smiling in that worried way she often did when something momentous loomed.

Just last night, Doug had overheard his parents discussing finances in hushed tones. He hadn't meant to eavesdrop—but the walls of their small house could only conceal so much. His father had mentioned rising costs: new skates, away-tournament fees, the possibility of further expenses if Doug moved up into a junior league. Doug had crept back to his room, heart heavy. *Am I imposing too much on them?* Yet his parents had always told him to chase his dream, to do what he loved—even if it meant sacrificing luxuries.

Now, stepping onto the ice for warm-ups, Doug felt torn. A swirl of excitement about the scouts. A pang of guilt at the weight it would add to his family's financial load. *Don't let it distract you,* he reminded himself. *Play your game.*

Warm-up laps began, each stride slicing across fresh ice. Doug inhaled the crisp arena air, focusing on the comforting rhythm of his skates. He fired a few shots at the goalie, feeling relief with each solid hit of puck on stick. *Yes, I'm ready,* he told himself. *I can do this.*

The scoreboard counted down the minutes to puck drop. A low hum of conversation spread across the stands. Rumors about scouts had circulated all week: the local sports blog had posted a piece hinting that a handful of players in the league—including Doug—were on the radar for OHL teams. Doug's phone had buzzed nonstop with messages from teammates, half-joking about an "NHL star in our midst," half-serious about the magnitude of such an opportunity.

But with that excitement came Doug's internal conflict. *What if a junior team does come calling?* He pictured himself in a new jersey, living in a billet house in some distant city, away from his parents and older brother, Mike. The idea thrilled and terrified him. And then there was the cost: bigger leagues often covered some expenses, but not all. He'd seen families go into debt traveling the junior circuit, hoping their kid might stand out. He wondered if that was fair to his family.

He glided around, faking a small deke around an imaginary defender. His mother's words from last night buzzed in his ear: *If it happens, we'll figure it out.* She'd said it softly, with love, but Doug knew how careful they had to be. He exhaled, pushing the thought away as best he could. For now, there was only this game, the final of the regular season. A chance to show—maybe for the first time—that he was genuinely ready for the next level.

The referee blew his whistle. The national anthem played, echoing in the anxious hush. Doug stood at the blue line with his teammates, heart pounding in his chest. As the anthem ended, the teams lined up for the faceoff. Doug's line would start tonight—a testament to how much trust Coach Hall had placed in him. Doug bent his knees, leaning in, scanning the opposing players. *Let's set the tone.*

The puck dropped, and the opposing center won the draw, sending the puck back to his defenseman. Doug and Xavier charged forward on the forecheck. Immediately, Doug felt the intensity: no one was holding back, not with scouts watching and playoff seeding implications on the line. The defenseman rifled an outlet pass, but Doug got a piece of it with his stick, forcing a loose puck in the neutral zone. He scrambled for possession, but the other team's winger swooped in and collected it, racing into Doug's zone.

That winger was talented—one of the top scorers in the league. Doug's defensemen quickly engaged, but the winger twisted free, snapping a shot that tested their goalie. A quick glove saved the day. The whistle blew, and Doug skated to the faceoff circle, adrenaline spiking. *They're not messing around.*

On the next shift, Doug found himself pinned against the boards in the offensive zone, battling for the puck with a tall, lanky defenseman. The physicality was relentless. Doug gritted his teeth, using the strength he'd gained all season to hold his ground. He managed to poke the puck loose, sending it to Xavier in the corner. No goal materialized, but it was a small win—a show of grit in front of watchful eyes.

Still, despite some decent pushes, the scoreboard remained 0–0. The tension ratcheted up. Doug's legs felt heavy, weighed down by the pressure. He tried to remind himself to breathe, to trust his instincts. Each time he caught sight of those mysterious figures in the top row—scouts scribbling or simply observing—his nerves jangled.

Late in the first period, Doug's line found itself hemmed into the defensive zone. Their opponents unleashed a flurry of shots. Doug scrambled to block a pass, but the puck deflected off his skate and soared right onto an opposing player's stick. *Danger.* A quick wrister sailed over their goalie's shoulder. 1–0.

Doug's heart sank as he glided back to the bench. He felt partly responsible. If he'd better controlled that puck, maybe they wouldn't be trailing. Coach Hall patted him on the back. "Shake it off, Mansfield. Be ready next shift."

But Doug couldn't entirely shake it off. As he took a seat, he spotted one of the scouts scribbling something. *Great— probably noting my turnover.* A sick feeling stirred in his gut. He cast a sidelong glance at the stands, locking eyes with his father for a moment. His father nodded, mouthing something like "It's okay," but Doug's face burned. *Dad's sacrificing so much for me—and I'm screwing up under the spotlight.*

The period ended with the score 1–0. Doug trudged to the locker room, plagued by self-doubt. If this was the performance he gave in front of scouts, how could he justify the financial strain it might cause his family? *If I can't handle the pressure at this level, how would I handle junior hockey?*

Inside the locker room, Coach Hall quickly addressed them: "We're only down by one. Don't overthink it. Keep playing our system. Forecheck harder. Doug, Xavier, you had a couple good looks—keep hustling." The coach's eyes flicked to Doug. "Don't let that bounce get in your head."

Doug nodded stiffly, sipping water to clear the dryness in his throat. He resolved to make the next period count. *One bounce doesn't define me.* Even so, the knot of worry refused to completely loosen.

Stepping onto the ice for the second period, Doug forced himself to breathe deeper, center his thoughts. He reminded himself of the work he'd put in over the season—the punishing practices, the hours spent refining his shot, the extra gym sessions to build strength. *That's who I am, not just some turnover.* He dropped into a crouch at the faceoff dot, mentally wiping the slate clean.

It helped. Early in the period, Doug's line executed a fluid breakout, with Jeremy (the chirpy defenseman) sending a perfect pass up the boards to Xavier. Doug bolted through center ice, pushing off with all the energy he could muster. Xavier saw him, flicking a lead pass that landed right on Doug's tape. Doug caught the puck in stride, crossing the blue line with pace. A defenseman converged, but Doug shifted the puck to his backhand, sliding around the opponent's hip. For a heartbeat, time seemed to slow. The goalie squared up, and Doug snapped a low wrister aiming five-hole.

Clank. The puck ricocheted off the goalie's pad, but the rebound skittered into the slot. Xavier, trailing the play, poked it home. *Goal!* A roar erupted from the stands. Doug pumped his fist, euphoria rushing through him. 1–1. The bench whooped, banging sticks on the boards. *Yes,* Doug thought, *this is how we do it.*

When he returned to the bench, Coach Hall nodded approvingly. "Nice drive, Mansfield." Another assistant coach gave him a tap on the shoulder. Doug risked a glance toward the stands, glimpsing the scouts again. One seemed to be exchanging words with another. Doug couldn't read their expressions, but the idea that they noticed him setting up the tying goal sent a thrill through his veins.

Their momentum swelled. The team poured on pressure, outshooting the opposition by a wide margin for the rest of the period. Doug's line nearly struck again on a power play, with Doug circling behind the net and sliding a pass across the crease that just barely missed Xavier's stick. Even so, the energy felt different—they were controlling the play, dictating pace.

As the period wound down, the scoreboard remained locked at 1–1. Doug returned to the locker room with a lighter step, a sense of possibility returning. Perhaps the scouts had seen enough good to forgive his earlier mistake. *But let's not settle,* he told himself. *We can close this out with a win.*

During the second intermission, Doug slipped out of the locker room to catch a breath in the hallway. He wasn't prepared for what he found: one of the scouts, a middle-aged man in a team jacket, talking quietly with Coach Hall near the vending machines. Doug froze, heart pounding. *They're talking about me, or about the team, or...*

Before Doug could turn away, Coach Hall spotted him and beckoned him over. The scout offered a friendly smile. "So this is Mansfield?" he asked, eyeing Doug's jersey.

Coach Hall nodded. "Yes. Doug, this is Mr. Latimer, a scout for the OHL's Western Wolves."

Doug's tongue felt stuck to the roof of his mouth. "Uh, hi," he managed, cheeks burning.

Mr. Latimer extended a hand. "I've watched you a bit this season. You've got a nice blend of speed and hockey sense. A few details to polish, of course, but you're definitely on our radar. Keep it up."

Doug shook the scout's hand, heart rattling. "Thank you," he said quietly, unsure what else to add. *On our radar.* The words spun in his head like a dream.

Coach Hall patted Doug on the shoulder. "Doug, we still have a period to play," he reminded, a small smile tugging at his lips. "Go finish strong. Mr. Latimer was just telling me they're going to keep an eye on a few players for next year's minor-junior draft."

Doug swallowed, nodding vigorously. "Yes, Coach." He forced a grin, adrenaline surging at the scout's presence. Then he excused himself, hurrying back to the locker room, mind buzzing like a hive. *He's seen me. He thinks I'm good enough. This is real.*

When the third period began, Doug felt both invigorated and jittery. He had to remind himself not to force plays just to impress the scout. *Play your game,* he told himself, *like you have all season.* Nonetheless, an undercurrent of excitement thrummed in his every stride.

The opposing team came out hungry, determined to regain the momentum they lost in the second. Their top line generated sustained pressure, peppering shot after shot on Doug's goalie. Doug's shift changed quickly into a defensive posture. Twice, he managed to break up passes, using his stick in passing lanes—small, vital plays that seldom show up on stat sheets but matter deeply to coaches and scouts.

Still, the scoreboard refused to budge. As the clock ticked under five minutes, the tension in the arena rose to a fever pitch. A draw in the final game might be anti-climactic, but for the scouts and for Doug's sense of accomplishment, a game-winner was right there for the taking.

Then, with 2:14 remaining, the coach double-shifted Doug's line. The game was still tied 1–1. If any line could tilt it, it was the combination of Doug, Xavier, and their left winger, Evan. They hopped over the boards with their usual synergy, determined to bury one.

Doug received a pass from Jeremy at center ice. He burst into the attacking zone, scanning for a lane. Evan cut to the net, drawing a defender with him. Xavier hovered in the high slot. Doug drew the second defender, faking a shot, then threaded a pass toward Xavier. The puck skittered off a defender's skate—*a near interception*—but landed softly on Xavier's stick.

Xavier hesitated for a split second, then snapped a quick release, aiming top shelf. The goalie, screened by Evan, didn't pick it up until it was too late. The lamp lit up. **Goal!** 2–1 with just over two minutes left.

The crowd erupted, and Doug's bench hollered, sticks clashing against the boards in celebration. Doug leaped into Xavier's arms, fueled by euphoria. *We did it!*

The final two minutes felt like an eternity. The opposing team pulled their goalie, swarming Doug's zone. Doug, nearly out of breath, took short shifts, giving everything in each shift. With three seconds left, their goalie gloved a last-gasp shot. The buzzer sounded—Doug's team had won 2–1.

The handshake line was a blur of sweaty, beaming faces. Doug tore off his helmet, hair matted with sweat. He could hardly process the swirling emotions—relief at the win, pride at having performed in front of the scouts, and a curious sense of foreboding about what it all meant for his future.

He skated to his teammates at center ice, raising his stick in salute to the cheering crowd. Xavier nearly tackled him in a congratulatory hug. "That pass, man! Clutch!" he shouted. Doug laughed, still reeling. The scoreboard above blinked final: 2–1. They'd ended the season on a high note.

Coach Hall called them to the locker room for a final address. Doug glanced up at the stands one last time, searching for the scouts. They were already gone, perhaps off to another arena or stepping outside to make phone calls. The fact that they'd left so quickly gave Doug a jolt of anxiety. *Did I do enough?*

He forced the thought aside as he trudged off the ice with the rest of the team. *I gave it everything tonight,* he told himself, *that's all I can do.*

Back in the locker room, the atmosphere was jubilant. Shouts, laughter, the metallic clang of sticks being placed in racks. Doug sank onto a bench, exhausted in the best way. Coach Hall stood in the middle, arms folded, waiting for the chaos to settle.

"Great finish to the regular season," he said. "A tough, grinding win. We overcame early adversity, we stuck to our game plan, and we earned it. I'm proud of every single one of you. Playoffs are next, but take a moment to enjoy tonight. You've shown the league—and some important eyes—what you're capable of."

He turned, pointing at Doug and Xavier. "Great job on that winning goal. Mansfield, you hustled back on defense like a pro, too. Keep it up."

Doug felt a flush of pride as teammates whooped. He exchanged wide-eyed looks with Xavier. They'd done something special tonight, validated by Coach Hall's praise.

As players eventually peeled off equipment, Doug lingered, lost in thought. The victory felt incredible, but the seeds planted by the scout's presence had grown into a swirl of questions: *Would he call? Would there be an invitation to try out for a junior team? Was Doug even ready for that step?*

Exiting the locker room, Doug found his parents waiting near the main doors. His father wore a wide grin. His mother's eyes shone with pride. She stepped forward to envelop Doug in a quick hug, ignoring the sweat soaking his undershirt.

"Well done, honey," she murmured, stepping back to examine him. "That was a great game."

His father nodded in agreement. "Heck of a pass on that winner."

Doug smiled, heart full. "Thanks. I'm so happy we pulled it off."

They began walking through the corridor, weaving around other families. "We noticed someone talking to Coach Hall earlier—looked like a scout," his father said carefully, watching Doug's reaction. "Any truth to that rumor?"

Doug exhaled. "Yeah. He's from the Western Wolves in the OHL. He said he's been watching me." A wave of giddiness washed over him just saying it aloud, tempered only by the memory of his parents' financial conversation.

His mother exchanged a glance with Doug's father, a complicated swirl of emotions in her eyes—pride, worry, love.

"That's incredible," she said softly. "But... how do you feel about it?"

Doug shrugged, trying to articulate the jumble in his mind. "I'm excited, of course, but also... it's a big step, if anything comes of it. It's time away from home, costs... I'm not sure if it's the right time. I don't want to burden you guys."

His father's expression softened. "We'll figure out finances together if that door opens," he said gently. "Don't let that be your main worry. You've worked too hard to throw away an opportunity because of money. We'll make it work, if it's the path you choose."

His mother nodded, adding, "We'll be cautious, but we'll support you, Doug."

A wave of relief flooded him, tears prickling the edges of his eyes. "Thanks," he whispered. "I just... it's everything I've dreamed of, but also a lot of pressure."

His father wrapped an arm around Doug's shoulders. "One step at a time, champ. Let's see what the next few weeks bring. For now, celebrate your season and get ready for playoffs. Scouts or no scouts, you're an amazing player. We're proud."

Doug leaned into his father's side, warmth blossoming in his chest. *They're with me,* he thought gratefully. He might not have all the answers yet, but at least he wouldn't have to face them alone.

At home that evening, Doug found it impossible to sleep. He tossed and turned, replaying the game's key moments, the scout's handshake, and the final words his parents had offered. Finally, he got up, tiptoed downstairs, and poured himself a glass of water. The house was still, the only sound the faint hum of the fridge.

He stared at the worn family photo on the living room shelf—his father and mother, smiling broadly at a much-younger Doug clutching a mini hockey stick. *They've always been in my corner,* he realized. He recalled how they'd scraped together funds for used equipment, how they'd driven him to away games in snowstorms, how they'd consoled him after tough losses and cheered the biggest wins.

The idea of leaving them to pursue hockey in a far-off city felt surreal. Yet, the chance to climb the ranks in junior hockey could be the best route to a pro career—and that was the dream, right? *Yes, it is,* Doug reminded himself. *But I must be sure I'm ready, and that it's truly what I want.*

He returned upstairs, mind still whirling with possibilities. His phone buzzed—a message from Xavier: *Still buzzing from that game. We going all the way in playoffs or what?*

Doug grinned, tapping back: *Absolutely. Let's keep the good vibes.* He hesitated, then added: *Heard anything else about scouts?*

A moment later, a response: *Not yet. But keep your phone on, man. This is just the beginning.*

Doug set down his phone, heart fluttering. *Just the beginning.* He breathed deeply, letting a mixture of excitement and resolve settle over him. *I'll handle the next step when it comes.*

The final game was done, the regular season wrapped, but Doug's journey was just entering its next phase. In the coming days, he'd juggle playoff preparation, end-of-season commitments, and the underlying hum of "what comes after." Scouts might call, or they might not. Junior teams might extend an invitation, or they might wait another year to see his development.

Still, that night, as Doug drifted off to sleep, he allowed himself a moment of quiet pride. He'd stepped onto the ice determined to show everyone—and himself—that he wasn't just a fluke of skill or hustle. He'd proven he could handle the spotlight, bounce back from mistakes, and be a game-changer in crucial moments. The final game had been a testament to his growth: from a shy house-league kid who once worried about fighting and finances, to a standout forward confident enough to attract serious attention.

And if or when that phone call or email came, offering him a chance at junior hockey, Doug knew he had his parents' cautious blessing to explore it. The uncertainty remained—about money, about leaving home, about the real demands of chasing a pro hockey dream—but for the first time, Doug felt genuinely ready to face that uncertainty. *I can do this,* he thought. *One shift, one stride, one game at a time. I'll keep pushing.*

As he finally closed his eyes, he pictured the next day's practice, the roaring crowds of a possible junior arena, maybe even the glint of NHL lights in some distant future. The road would be long and hard, no doubt. Yet, he embraced it with open arms. A small smile formed on his lips: *Let the scouts watch. I'm ready for them.*

10

JUNIOR TRYOUTS

Doug clenched his fists, trying to still the tremor in his hands. He was standing in the same cramped hallway that dozens of aspiring hockey players had paced in before him, all with sweaty palms and nerves dancing in their stomachs. But this wasn't the local youth circuit; he'd been invited to try out for both Junior 'A' and Major Junior 'A' OHL teams, and he could feel the difference in the air. Posters of legendary alumni hung on the walls, reminding Doug of the hallowed ground he was treading.

He swallowed. *This is it,* he told himself. *No more house-league or small-time. This is the real deal.*

It had all happened so fast. One moment he was finishing up a stellar season in a competitive youth league, and the next he was fielding calls from scouts who'd seen his hustle, his knack for winning puck battles, his timely goals in crucial games. Junior teams, always on the lookout for young talent, invited him to show his stuff at their upcoming camps. Doug's parents had worried about finances, about the pressure, about him leaving home—but they'd also recognized the door that was opening. They told him to go for it, to throw himself into these tryouts head-on, no matter how intimidating.

Now he was here, his gear bag weighing heavily on one shoulder as he waited to register. Down the hall, he could see other players—many older, taller, more physically imposing.

Some wore jackets emblazoned with logos from top-level minor or junior programs. One or two had their names on the back, obviously big deals from their hometowns. *They look huge,* Doug noted, feeling a twinge of doubt.

A tall team official holding a clipboard beckoned him forward. "Name?"

"Doug Mansfield," he said, his voice betraying just the smallest wobble.

The official checked the list, then handed Doug a practice jersey. It bore no name or sponsor, just a bold number—*81*—stitched on the back. Doug stared at it with reverence. He'd never worn a number that high in a tryout. *Welcome to the big leagues, I guess.*

"Locker room 3," the official said, pointing down a corridor. "You'll be on Group B for the first on-ice session. Good luck."

Doug thanked him and made his way through the labyrinth of hallways, eventually finding the door labeled **3**. He paused for a second, inhaling. *Remember what Coach Hall said: play your game, keep your feet moving, don't get intimidated.* Then he nudged the door open.

The locker room smelled of fresh tape, sharpened steel, and that underlying tang of ammonia from deep-cleaned floors. A handful of players were already inside, half-dressed, chatting in low tones. Some looked a year or two older than Doug—17 or 18—but others were even older. These were men, not boys, each with powerful legs and broad shoulders, the result of intense off-ice training.

Doug found an unoccupied bench and set his gear bag down. He introduced himself to the kid next to him, who seemed similarly wide-eyed. "Hey, I'm Doug," he offered.

"Luke," the kid replied, giving a tight smile. "From out west. You?"

"Small town, near here," Doug said, tugging out his skates. He paused, wondering if Luke had also played in a youth league or if he'd come from some AAA pipeline. The big question lodged in Doug's mind was whether either of them felt ready to compete with the bigger, stronger returning players who'd already made a name for themselves in Junior 'A' or Major Junior 'A' programs.

A coach stuck his head in, clipboard in hand. "We're on the ice in fifteen. Be sharp. You know what's at stake here."

The door slammed shut behind him. Doug heard one of the older players remark, "Yeah, no pressure," prompting a ripple of sarcastic laughter. But the tension remained.

Doug dressed quickly, forcing himself not to rush through each piece of equipment. He reminded himself how to calm the nerves: breathe deep, double-check laces, keep track of the little details. By the time he pulled on the practice jersey with #81 across the chest, he felt a jolt of adrenaline. *This jersey represents a real shot at junior hockey. Don't waste it.*

The first on-ice session was a whirlwind. Almost immediately, Doug felt the difference in level: the coaches ran complex, high-tempo drills that tested his skating, stickhandling, and split-second decision-making. These weren't the standard cone weaves and casual scrimmages he'd seen in local tryouts. Here, everything was about intensity and execution.

A beep sounded through the loudspeaker, and a coach's voice bellowed: "Go, go, GO!"

Doug joined a line of forwards at the blue line, waiting for his turn in a breakout drill. When the whistle blew, he sprinted into the neutral zone, receiving a pass from a defenseman while at top speed. The puck bobbled on his stick—it was slightly harder and faster than what he was used to. He fumbled for a second, then regained control. He looked up, scanning for an outlet or a lane to enter the offensive zone. Another defender rushed in, larger by a full head. Doug felt a surge of panic but cut sharply, slipping the puck between the defender's legs and darting around him.

A small spark of triumph ignited in Doug's chest. But as soon as he set his sights on the net, a second defender—a grizzled, returning junior player—slid over and checked him off the puck. Doug grunted, nearly losing his balance from the force. The puck trickled away, and the next drill rep began.

He skated back into line, chest heaving. *Man, they're fast—and strong.* He tried not to show the swirl of insecurity in his expression. *Shake it off. Keep going.*

As the session wore on, Doug got a feel for the pace. He managed a few good plays—some slick passes, a decent shot that smacked the goalie's pads. But he also felt the sting of failed breakouts, turnovers under pressure, and the sheer physicality whenever he ventured too close to the boards. Each time he was shoved or pinned, Doug reminded himself to stand his ground.

At the end of the hour, the coaches barked a final whistle. Everyone glided to the bench, panting. One of the assistant coaches clapped his hands. "All right, that's the first taste. Hit the locker room for a break. Next group is up, then we'll bring you out again."

Doug peeled off his helmet, sweat dripping from his hair. He could barely register how quickly that hour had passed. The trials of junior-level hockey had become glaringly real. Still, he couldn't deny the thrill. *I'm here,* he thought, *competing with guys who are bigger, older, more polished—and I'm holding my own.* It wasn't perfect, but it was a start.

Later in the day, as Doug waited for his second on-ice stint, he wandered the corridors. He spotted a group of media members—local reporters, a few hockey bloggers—chatting about who had impressed them. Words like "size," "presence," and "finishing touch" floated through the air. Doug overheard one voice mention a kid named Fraser who already had a 90 mph slapshot. Another praised a returning forward from the Junior 'A' club who led the league in points the previous season.

A small part of Doug bristled. He knew he wasn't going to command that kind of immediate hype, not with his average frame and fewer accolades. But that didn't mean he couldn't prove himself. *Let your play speak,* he reminded himself, ignoring a flicker of self-doubt that threatened to creep in.

He almost laughed at how quickly the atmosphere changed once players reached these levels. In youth leagues, you could shine by being strong and agile, by hustling for pucks. Here, that was baseline—everyone hustled, everyone was skilled. The difference came down to how quickly you processed the game, how well you adapted to pressure, and how relentlessly you outworked the competition.

Doug thought of his father's parting words that morning: *We're behind you no matter what happens, son.* That gave him some comfort. *At least I'm not alone in this.*

When the time came for his second session, Doug stepped back onto the ice with renewed determination. His group formed lines again, working through advanced forechecking drills, then a structured scrimmage with referees calling penalties. Doug found himself matched against some real monsters—stocky defensemen who sealed off the boards with ease. More than once, he got dumped onto his backside. But he refused to be intimidated. He bounced back up, chasing the puck, intercepting passes when possible.

Near the end of that second session, Doug picked off a lazy cross-ice pass in neutral ice, blitzed forward on a partial break, and snapped a low wrist shot past the goalie's blocker. The sound of the puck hitting the mesh was like music to his ears, and a surge of validation tingled through his body. *Yes—that's what I can do.*

The whistle blew, signifying a line change. Doug made his way to the bench, inhaling victory for a moment. He swore he saw a coach scribble something on a notepad just after that goal.

But the euphoria was short-lived. As the tryouts stretched into subsequent days, the intensity only ramped up. The coaches and evaluators became more critical, dissecting every weakness. Media members openly speculated on which players had the best shot to crack the rosters. Doug discovered how brutal the rumor mill could be, overhearing talk about who'd get cut or who "didn't belong."

One afternoon, while heading to the rink cafeteria for a quick bite, Doug overheard two older players discussing him by name. "Mansfield—he's got quick hands, but he's undersized," one said. "Don't know if he'll keep up with older juniors."

Doug halted, pressing his back against a vending machine, breath catching in his throat.

"Well, Coach might see him as a project," replied the second voice, "but there are guys here more developed. I don't see him lasting unless he really stands out."

Doug winced. Hearing it so bluntly stung, even though he knew he faced that uphill battle. But he forced himself to continue walking, head held high. *Don't let that negativity sink in. Prove them wrong.*

That same day, Doug encountered the physical aspect of older competition yet again—he took a bad hit from behind during a scrimmage, crashing hard into the boards. The jolt reverberated through his shoulder, pain flaring. He popped up slowly, testing his arm. It felt bruised but not broken. Refusing to show weakness, he finished the drill, even though a dull ache persisted. He realized how little mercy existed in these tryouts. This was a funnel for players to feed into major leagues, and a single injury could derail everything.

Driven by the recognition that he lacked size and experience compared to many of these players, Doug redoubled his training. Each evening, after on-ice sessions, he'd head to the makeshift gym area where a few free weights and exercise bands were set up. He mimicked workouts he'd learned from his youth team trainer: explosive movements, core-strength exercises, plyometrics to sharpen his first-step quickness. Some older players, done for the night, would pass by with raised eyebrows, but Doug paid them no mind.

The hours took a toll. By the end of each day, his legs felt like lead. His bruised shoulder nagged at him, and he iced it religiously. Sleep was restless; he'd dream of missing passes, or of being overshadowed by bigger, faster guys. And always in the background, there was the looming pressure that if he didn't make one of these teams, he might be stuck in limbo, uncertain of his next step.

And yet, ironically, Doug also felt more alive than ever. Every puck battle, every test of endurance, every chance to prove himself kept his adrenaline pumping. *This is what I wanted,* he reminded himself in moments of doubt. *I wanted to see if I can cut it at the higher level.*

In phone calls to his parents, he tried to sound upbeat, glossing over the bruises and the exhaustion. His mother's voice inevitably quivered with concern—she wanted to make sure he was safe and mentally okay. His father offered practical tips: *Ice that shoulder, do some light band work, don't forget to rest.*

Mike, his older brother, shot him encouraging texts: *No regrets, Dougie. Keep your head up—hit the corners like you own them.*

Those reminders kept Doug grounded, reminding him that success in these tryouts wasn't the only marker of his worth. *But oh, how I want it,* he thought. *I want to show I belong here.*

On the final day of tryouts, the coaches organized a series of full-length scrimmage games, splitting the prospects into teams. These scrimmages would be the ultimate test—a chance for players to exhibit not just skill but also game sense and chemistry with prospective teammates. Scouts, local media, and even some fans crowded the bleachers, anticipating a show.

Doug found himself placed on a line with two older forwards, both of whom had partial seasons of Junior 'A' under their belts. They eyed Doug with an air of cautious acceptance, as if to say, *Show us you can keep up.*

The first period was intense. The pace matched any real junior game—fast, physical, relentless. Doug had to dig deep each shift, pressuring defensemen on the forecheck and backchecking hard when possession flipped. He took a couple of hits that rattled his bruised shoulder, but he pushed through, using his quickness to slip away from the worst collisions.

Midway through the second period, an opponent's turnover in neutral ice gave Doug's line a prime chance. One of his linemates corralled the puck and dished it to Doug sprinting across the blue line. Doug noticed the opposing defenseman shifting too far inside, leaving a sliver of space near the boards. He accelerated, leaning his body to slip around the outside. The moment he broke free, he fired a wrist shot toward the far post.

Time seemed to slow. The goalie lunged with his glove— but the puck kissed the inside of the post and ricocheted into the net. Goal. Doug's heart soared. His linemates shouted in triumph, hugging him. He managed a grin, glancing around at the stands, half-expecting to see his parents' proud faces. But they weren't here this time, just cameras and scouts. *This one's for you, Mom and Dad,* he thought.

The final period saw more back-and-forth play. Doug nearly set up another goal with a cross-ice pass, but the defenseman got a stick on it at the last second. Despite that, Doug's line controlled the puck well, and he felt a growing chemistry. By the final buzzer, his team edged out a 3–2 victory. Doug skated to the bench, panting and sweat-drenched, but proud.

As the players filed off, the head coach for the Major Junior 'A' team stood at center ice with a megaphone, thanking everyone for their effort. "We'll be making final decisions in the coming days," he said. "Some of you will receive invites back. Others might need another year of development. But good work across the board."

Doug locked eyes with the coach for a split second. The coach nodded, a subtle acknowledgment. Doug's pulse quickened, hoping that gesture was a positive omen. *Have I done enough to earn a roster spot—or even a development camp invite?*

After that last scrimmage, Doug changed out of his gear, exhaustion mingling with anticipation. He chatted quietly with Luke, the kid who'd shared that initial anxious introduction in the locker room. Luke admitted he might have a shot at a Junior 'A' team but was worried about his size. Doug commiserated, recognizing the same anxiety in his new friend.

Leaving the arena, Doug stepped into a sunny afternoon. It was oddly incongruous—outside, people strolled around, clueless about the high-stakes drama unfolding in the rink. Doug's father waited by the car, arms crossed, scanning for Doug. The moment their eyes met, Doug managed a weary smile and gave a thumbs-up, though not entirely sure it was warranted.

"How'd it go?" his father asked, popping the trunk for Doug's bag.

"Tough," Doug admitted, rubbing his sore shoulder reflexively. "But I had some good shifts, scored once in the scrimmage. So maybe..." He trailed off, not wanting to sound too hopeful.

His father patted Doug's back. "That's all you can do. Let's grab some dinner and head home. You'll hear something soon, right?"

Doug nodded, swallowing. "Yeah, a few days, maybe." It was a short time, but it already felt interminable.

That evening, in the hotel room they'd rented near the tryout facility, Doug lay on the bed, icing his shoulder. A thousand thoughts pinballed around his mind: every turnover, every half-step too slow, every moment he caught a coach's eye. He thought about the monstrous hits, the advanced systems, the game speed. But he also remembered that goal, that crisp pass, the times he'd outskated a bigger defenseman. *Maybe that's enough to open a door.*

The phone buzzed—a message from one of his youth league teammates, Trevor: *How'd it go, buddy?* Doug typed a quick reply: *Survived. Brutal. Learned a lot. Might have impressed some coaches. Fingers crossed.*

A second buzz: *No matter what happens, proud of you.*

Doug felt a swell of gratitude. He also thought of his mother at home, likely pacing the kitchen, awaiting news. By the time Doug sank into restless sleep, he was both overwhelmed and oddly at peace. He'd given his all in those tryouts, facing older, more refined players in an environment that tested every shred of skill and determination he had. If that wasn't enough, at least he knew he left nothing on the table.

The next morning, Doug and his father checked out of the hotel, loaded the car, and began the drive back to their hometown. Doug stared out the window, replaying the highlight reel of his performance. The farmland and small towns blurred past. "Thanks for bringing me," he said quietly. "I know it wasn't cheap—hotel, gas, my new gear..."

His father glanced over, lips curving in a gentle smile. "You deserve the shot, Doug. We'll figure out the costs. The important thing is that you did it—you showed up. Whatever happens next, you've proven you belong in these conversations."

Doug nodded, a lump in his throat. *I hope I can repay that faith.*

They reached home, unloading gear into the garage. Doug's mother rushed out, hugging him carefully around the uninjured side. "You're bruised!" she exclaimed, fussing. "Oh, Doug, let me see that shoulder."

"It's fine, Mom," he said, half-laughing, half-flustered by her concern. "Just a bump."

Over a late lunch, he recounted the intensity of the tryout, the bigger players, the scoring chance he buried, the mistakes he made. His mother listened intently, her face flickering between worry and pride. Mike, who'd hurried over from a friend's house, peppered him with questions. Doug answered as honestly as he could, trying to remain modest about the goal and the positive signs he'd seen.

In the days that followed, a strange hush settled over Doug's life. He did normal things—went for a jog, hung out with friends, helped out around the house—but every time his phone buzzed, his heart lurched. Every time the landline rang, or an email notification chimed, he braced for news from the coaches. *One call could change everything.*

Meanwhile, local media outlets posted tryout recaps, listing "standout prospects." Doug saw some mention of that returning Junior 'A' star, the monstrous defenseman, and a few new names he recognized from the scrimmages. He scrolled anxiously, searching for mention of "Doug Mansfield." Some blogs praised a "small but crafty winger" wearing #81. Doug's stomach flipped—*that's me!*—but they didn't name him explicitly. It was maddeningly vague.

On a Wednesday evening, Doug stood in the kitchen with his parents, clearing dishes after dinner. The sun had set, leaving a quiet hush over the neighborhood. Doug's father placed a hand on Doug's shoulder. "You okay?"

Doug sighed. "Just anxious. Feels like forever."

"You've done all you can," his mother said. "Try to relax."

Doug nodded, though relaxing was easier said than done. He retreated to his room, lay on his bed, and stared at the hockey posters on the walls—Maple Leafs, Canadians from the OHL, minor-league teams. He imagined himself in one of those jerseys, stepping into a bigger rink, under brighter lights, with the crowd roaring.

His phone buzzed. Doug jolted upright.

IncomingCall:UnknownNumberIncoming Call: Unknown NumberIncomingCall:UnknownNumber

He scrambled to answer, heart hammering in his chest. "Hello?"

"Hi, is this Doug Mansfield?" asked a firm, clear voice.

"Yes, speaking," Doug croaked.

"This is Coach Nadeau, from the Junior 'A' program. I wanted to personally thank you for coming out. We were impressed with your skill set. We'd like to invite you to our main training camp this summer as a next step."

Doug's mind reeled. "Really?" he said, fighting to keep his composure. "I—thank you, Coach. That's... that's amazing."

The coach chuckled. "We see potential in you. You'll need to keep working—lots of off-ice strength training, refine your shot. But we think you have what it takes to compete at the Junior 'A' level, at least as a developing forward."

Doug stammered out a few more words of gratitude and asked a couple logistical questions. The coach gave details about camp dates and a contact person for final paperwork.

Finally, they said goodbye. Doug hung up, phone slipping from his sweaty palm.

For a moment, he just sat there, stunned. Then he let out a whoop loud enough that his father came running, worry etched on his face—until Doug's grin told him everything.

"I got an invite!" Doug shouted, voice trembling. "Junior 'A' main camp this summer!"

His mother, having followed behind Doug's father, gasped in delight. They both rushed to hug Doug. Laughter mixed with tears of joy as Doug tried to convey everything: the coach's words, the caution about hard work ahead, the feeling that he'd broken through an invisible barrier.

"What about the Major Junior 'A' OHL team?" his mother asked cautiously, still holding him by the shoulders.

Doug's phone buzzed in his hand again—*another unknown number.* He stared, wide-eyed. "Guess we'll find out," he said, pressing *Answer.*

In a dizzying few minutes, Doug learned that while the Major Junior 'A' OHL team had taken interest in him, they felt he might benefit from a season or two at the Junior 'A' level first. That came as both a disappointment and a relief—he wasn't quite ready for the top rung of junior hockey yet, but at least they recognized his potential. They invited him for an exhibition skate in the fall, a chance to keep him on their radar.

After the calls ended, Doug slumped into the living room couch, emotionally drained. Mike, who had arrived mid-celebration, smacked him playfully on the shoulder, then remembered Doug's bruise and apologized. "Dude, you did it," Mike said. "Junior 'A' is huge. You're climbing the ladder!"

Doug grinned, eyes brimming with tears. "It's... it's what I've dreamed of. But it's also big changes—moving maybe, balancing school, everything."

His father cleared his throat. "We'll figure it out. This is your shot. We'll do what we can to support you."

His mother, tears shining in her eyes, nodded. "We'll talk details soon, but for now, just be proud. You've earned this."

Doug closed his eyes briefly, letting the relief and excitement wash over him. He pictured the next steps—off-season training, the main camp, adjusting to a new environment. He imagined stepping into a Junior 'A' rink with thousands of fans, older teammates, bus rides across provinces, the intensity of a higher-level schedule. It frightened him, but it also ignited a spark of hungry ambition in his gut. *I can't wait.*

As the family shared the moment, Doug felt the echoes of every bruise, every early morning, every doubt-laden night. All of it had led to this threshold. The reality of elite-level hockey was harsh—bigger bodies, sharper skills, ruthless competition—but he'd faced it, fought through the nerves, and proved he could hang.

He rose from the couch, heart pounding with fresh determination. There was so much to do—conditioning plans, paperwork, maybe even a part-time job to help with costs. But for the first time, he sensed the path forward clearly. Junior hockey might not be the final destination, but it was a monumental gateway.

Doug exchanged a look with his parents, seeing the pride in their faces, and felt his own confidence rise. Tomorrow, he'd hit the weights, hit the ice, keep forging ahead. Because if there was one thing he'd learned in these tryouts, it was that standing on the cusp of your dream was both exhilarating and terrifying—but absolutely worth every bruise, every mile, every drop of sweat.

In that quiet living room, with dusk settling outside, Doug made a silent promise: *I'll give this everything I have.*

11

THE FIRST HAT TRICK

Doug held his breath as he stepped off the bus and into the crisp autumn air of northern Ontario. The tall pines surrounding the parking lot swayed gently in the breeze, and in the distance, beyond the modest arena, he could see the pale shimmer of a lake reflecting the early morning sun. This wasn't the bustling city environment he'd grown used to seeing in OHL highlights on TV. It was smaller, quieter—but it was also his new home.

The bus ride from the team's practice facility to their home arena had been short and unremarkable, except for Doug's pounding heart. Ever since he earned a spot on the **North Shore Wolves**—a small-market OHL team located in the heart of northern Ontario—he'd felt both exhilarated and anxious. He'd made it into one of the most respected junior leagues in the world, a stepping stone for many NHL talents. But now that he was here, the pressure to perform weighed heavily on his shoulders.

He shouldered his gear bag and made his way inside the arena. A few fans lingered in the hallway, decked out in the Wolves' navy-and-forest-green colors. They greeted the players politely, offering good-luck wishes. Doug returned polite smiles, but his stomach somersaulted each time he thought about suiting up at this level. Being part of a small-market team meant the local fans were fiercely loyal, and they adored new faces—especially those rumored to bring fresh energy and skill to a roster that had struggled in recent seasons.

Just past the main entrance, an oversized team logo was inlaid in the floor. Doug paused briefly, remembering an old superstition: never step on the logo. He carefully walked around it, not wanting to jinx anything. His new head coach, **Dave Melrose**, was a serious traditionalist, the kind who believed in respecting the game's unwritten rules. Doug wanted to make the best impression possible.

He found the locker room and pushed open the door. Inside, stalls with nameplates lined both walls. Some players were already there, lacing up or chatting quietly. A wave of unfamiliar faces greeted Doug—he'd only arrived a few days prior, so he knew them mostly by name or number. The veterans gave him reserved nods. The younger players—some just a year older than Doug—offered half-grins, recognizing a fellow newcomer. The room hummed with a subdued tension; their first game of the season was only hours away, and every player felt that blend of excitement and nerves.

Doug made his way to his stall, finding a green jersey with gold trim draped over the bench, the number **29** sewn onto the sleeves and back. A small plastic nameplate—"MANSFIELD"— adorned the top. He carefully ran his fingertips over the stitched letters, feeling an odd surge of pride. This was real, no longer a dream.

North Shore, population just over twenty thousand, lived and breathed hockey. The Wolves, though not a perennial powerhouse, embodied the town's spirit of resilience. Decades ago, they'd made a deep playoff run that people still talked about. In the years since, the team's fortunes had dipped, overshadowed by bigger-market rivals. Every autumn, fans clung to hope that *this* might be the year their beloved Wolves roared back to life.

Local media outlets showered attention on the roster. They ran daily articles speculating on line combinations, praising the few returning veterans, and analyzing the new prospects, including Doug. He'd seen his name in a local paper: "Mansfield: A Spark Plug for the Wolves?" accompanied by a grainy photo from a preseason scrimmage. That alone had made his cheeks burn with a mix of pride and trepidation. He wasn't used to being singled out.

Adding to the intrigue, rumors swirled that Doug had been scouted by other OHL clubs before choosing North Shore for more guaranteed ice time. Some fans saw him as the potential face of a rebuilding squad. Others merely shrugged, having learned not to pin too many hopes on unproven rookies. Regardless, Doug sensed that once he stepped onto the ice, every shift would be judged by hungry onlookers.

The season's opening weeks tested Doug's mettle. Adjusting to the OHL was as difficult as everyone said it would be. The pace was blistering, the players older and physically stronger, the systems more advanced. He found himself matched against top-tier talents—some of whom were already drafted by NHL teams. The Wolves struggled in their first few games, dropping a couple of tight contests and one embarrassing rout at the hands of a league powerhouse.

Doug, slotted on the team's third line, managed flashes of skill—winning board battles, feeding crisp passes through traffic—but often got neutralized by bigger defensemen. By game five, he'd notched only one assist. The local commentary began questioning if Doug was truly the dynamic forward rumored in preseason chatter.

He felt the silent judgment from teammates, too. The older veterans, like **Kyle Sutton**—a rugged forward who'd been with the Wolves for three seasons— eyed Doug with skepticism. Sutton had endured losing seasons, endless bus rides, and the disappointment of not being drafted. He seemed wary of any newcomer who might overshadow him or shift the hierarchy in the locker room. "Rookie," Sutton would call Doug, rarely using his name.

Coach Melrose, to Doug's relief, remained patient. "Keep playing your game, Mansfield," the coach said after a frustrating loss, patting Doug's shoulder pads. "This league is a marathon, not a sprint. Find your stride." Doug nodded, grateful for the reassurance.

Things began to shift about a month into the season. The Wolves returned from a grueling road trip with a 2–5 record, battered but determined to redeem themselves at home. Doug felt a burning desire to prove he belonged in the OHL. His parents had managed to drive up for the next homestand, eager to see him in action. Their presence comforted him, a reminder of how far he'd come since those backyard rinks and youth league scraps.

On the morning of a crucial home game against the **Lakefield Eagles**, Doug woke with an inexplicable sense of calm. The Eagles were a formidable team, boasting some top-ranked prospects. Most analysts predicted a comfortable Eagles win. The local paper even ran a piece titled: "Can the Wolves Avoid Another Blowout?"

Doug read the headline over breakfast in the small house he shared with his billet family. The words sparked something inside him—a blend of anger and motivation. He told himself, *We're better than they think.*

At the arena that afternoon, the atmosphere was tense. Teammates spoke in clipped tones, gearing up for what felt like a must-win scenario. If the Wolves lost again, they'd slide further into the league's basement, risking a morale spiral. Doug dressed quietly, steeling himself. **Kyle Sutton** sat on the opposite bench, glaring at the floor with earphones blasting music. Other veterans fidgeted with tape, some joking half-heartedly, trying to cut the tension.

Warm-ups buzzed with anticipation. The stands began filling, the hometown faithful sporting green jerseys and waving flags. Doug took his customary laps, testing edges and flicking pucks at the net. He tried to shut out the swirl of spectators, focusing solely on the ice beneath his skates and the stick in his hands.

By puck drop, the building was electric. The Wolves stormed out with high energy, but the Eagles answered swiftly. Despite a few strong shifts from Doug's line, the scoreboard read 2–0 in favor of Lakefield by the first intermission. One goal came off a wicked slapshot that beat the Wolves' goalie top shelf; the other a defensive breakdown that left an Eagles forward alone in front.

In the locker room, the mood was grim. Coach Melrose tried to rally them, reminding them to stick to the fundamentals and not chase the game. Doug sat in silence, dreading another blowout. He'd only managed a single shot on net so far, easily gloved by the Eagles' netminder. Was tonight just going to be another disappointment?

Early in the second period, fate intervened. The Eagles, pressing for a third goal, turned the puck over at the Wolves' blue line. Doug, covering defensively, swooped in, knocking the puck loose. He looked up to see open ice in front of him.

Seizing the chance, he burst forward, legs churning. A lone defenseman gave chase, but Doug shielded the puck, cutting to the net with a burst of speed.

The Eagles' goalie sprawled to challenge him, but Doug had just enough composure left to tuck a backhand shot low to the far post. It slipped under the goalie's pad and in. 2–1. A roar erupted in the stands.

Doug pumped his fist, adrenaline surging. The bench leaped up, pounding the boards. For a few seconds, the arena rocked with cheers. "Atta boy, Mansfield!" someone yelled. Doug could scarcely breathe as he skated by the bench for fist bumps. Even Sutton reached out for a glove tap, though his expression remained stoic. But that small gesture meant the world—maybe Doug was earning respect.

That goal seemed to flip a switch in the Wolves. They started winning races to loose pucks, finishing checks, forcing Lakefield onto their heels. Late in the period, the Wolves' second line tied the game on a scramble in front of the net. 2–2 heading into the final intermission. The building vibrated with renewed hope.

Between periods, Coach Melrose hammered home the message: *keep pushing.* "They're rattled," he insisted. "They thought they'd roll over us. Show them we won't back down."

Doug listened intently, heart thumping. He could practically taste the adrenaline in the air. This was the OHL moment he'd craved—a chance to rally a struggling team, to seize a statement win on home ice.

When the third period began, the Wolves maintained their momentum. The top line pressured Lakefield's defense, generating near-misses. Doug's line took the ice five minutes in, determined to keep the energy high. A scramble in the corner led to a turnover; Doug snagged the puck near the half-boards, swiftly dished a pass to the high slot. A defenseman fired a wrist shot that deflected wide—but the bounce caromed perfectly to Doug behind the net.

Everything moved in slow motion. Doug flicked a wraparound attempt, jamming the puck on the near post. The goalie lunged, but the puck trickled behind him. Instinctively, Doug smacked it again just before the goalie could cover. The red light flashed. **Goal.** 3–2 Wolves.

The crowd lost its mind. A wave of hats soared onto the ice—an early, mistaken attempt at a hat trick tradition, or maybe just sheer euphoria. Doug felt dizzy with excitement, sandwiched by celebrating teammates. Two goals for him, and the Wolves led. On the bench, he could hear fans chanting his name: "Mans-field! Mans-field!" He'd never heard that before, not in any league, not with such volume.

But Lakefield wasn't done. They answered with a power-play goal minutes later, capitalizing on a hooking penalty. 3–3. Anxiety permeated the stands. The final minutes ticked away in a tense deadlock. Both teams traded rushes. Doug's line hopped over the boards with ninety seconds left, each shift feeling more desperate.

The Eagles' top center circled behind the Wolves' net, looking for an option. Doug shadowed him, mindful not to lose coverage. A poke-check by the Wolves' defense forced a sloppy pass up the boards. Doug pounced, knocking the puck toward neutral ice. He sped out of the zone, feeling the burn in his thighs but refusing to slow.

Sutton, for once, read Doug's momentum and threaded a perfect pass up the middle. Doug caught it in stride, crossing the Eagles' blue line. A defenseman tried to angle him off, but

Doug cut inside. The goalie squared up, and the stadium noise crescendoed, as if all eyes locked on #29. Doug faked a forehand shot, then shifted to his backhand, hoping to freeze the goalie.

Time seemed to dilate. He saw the goalie bite on the fake, dropping slightly, glove hand twitching upward. Doug yanked the puck back to his forehand, releasing a quick snap shot that soared high near the corner. The goalie's glove soared up, but too late. Doug's shot rippled the netting.

For a heartbeat, the arena hushed, as if disbelieving. Then came the roar—the loudest Doug had ever heard in his life. He raised both arms, a flush of pure elation storming through his body. 4–3 Wolves, with under a minute left. His third goal of the night—his first career hat trick in the OHL.

All around, hats rained down onto the ice in earnest. Fans, delirious with excitement, flung caps in arcs across the boards. "Mansfield! Mansfield!" they chanted again, more emphatic this time. Doug's teammates mobbed him against the glass. Even Sutton's face cracked into a grin, forcibly patting Doug's helmet as if to say, *Alright, rookie, you've earned it tonight.*

The Wolves held on, with a frantic final shift, to clinch the 4–3 comeback victory. When the buzzer sounded, fans leaped from their seats, still cheering for Doug's heroics. As a tradition in many rinks, the hat-trick hero often collected the hats that littered the ice. Doug, however, was ushered into the handshake line first. He could feel his cheeks burning, half in disbelief that this was happening.

During the post-game celebration, the public-address announcer led the crowd in honoring Doug as the game's first star. The fans roared anew when Doug skated out, uncertain how to handle such attention. He'd watched OHL games on TV where big-name prospects netted hat tricks, but never imagined he'd be the subject of that applause.

In the locker room, a frenzy of excitement greeted him: stick taps, laughter, and back slaps. The coach shook his hand firmly. "Outstanding performance, Mansfield. You sparked this team. I hope you see what you're capable of."

Doug could barely articulate a response, just a breathless "Thank you, Coach," as adrenaline still coursed through him. More than one teammate slapped him on the shoulder pads, though some, like Sutton, held a more guarded attitude. Doug saw something flicker across Sutton's face—relief at the win, maybe, but also a hint of envy at the spotlight Doug was suddenly hogging.

Still wearing half his equipment, Doug sank onto the bench and exhaled. He could almost float with happiness. *A hat trick in the OHL? Already?* The moment felt surreal. He remembered all those nights on the backyard rink, daydreaming about big crowds, big goals, and the roar of appreciation. Now it was real.

As Doug soon discovered, the local media wasted no time feeding the hype. By the next morning, his phone overflowed with congratulatory messages—some from old hockey friends, some from people he barely knew. The local sports channel replayed each of his goals on a loop, dubbing him the "Overnight Hero."

Social media lit up, praising the Wolves' "rookie sensation." Some longtime fans suggested that Doug's hat trick was a sign of the franchise's return to respectability. Others noted the intangible "spark" he brought, his hustle reminiscent of local legends. Even the bigger OHL news outlets took notice, running short segments on the "small-market newcomer who scored a hat trick in a come-from-behind victory."

Suddenly, Doug found himself recognized around town. When he grabbed coffee at a local café, the barista gave him a free pastry, gushing about the game. Strangers patted him on the back on the street, exclaiming how they'd never seen the Wolves arena so loud in years. Doug's billet family teased him about needing bodyguards soon. He laughed it off, but deep down, he felt both astonished and overwhelmed by the adoration.

The team staff organized a small press conference at the arena. Doug fielded questions from local reporters about how it felt to get a hat trick so early in his junior career. He tried to stay humble: "It was a team effort; my linemates set me up; the fans were amazing." But each softball question reminded him that the spotlight was glaring now. *One game, three goals, and they think I'm unstoppable.*

In the days that followed, Doug sensed a shift within the locker room. While many teammates congratulated him, giving him well-deserved props, a subtle friction brewed. The older guys, some of whom had paid their dues over multiple losing seasons, now saw the media gravitating toward Doug. Local headlines featured *his* photo front and center; fans chanted *his* name.

Kyle Sutton, in particular, wore a slight scowl during practices. He snapped at Doug once for misreading a breakout pattern, barking, "Wake up, rookie! Being the hero in one game doesn't make you perfect." Doug, startled, could only mumble an apology.

Another incident occurred when a local radio show interviewed the team captain, praising Doug's hat trick. The captain tried to give credit to the entire roster, but the hosts kept steering the conversation back to Doug's performance. That evening, Doug overheard a couple of the veterans complaining about how the rookie was overshadowing the entire squad. "One trick, and they act like he's Gretzky reincarnated," someone murmured.

It stung Doug deeply. He had always cherished the idea of being part of a team, not a spotlight hog. Now, despite his attempts to deflect praise, the media—and the fans—just wouldn't let it go. *I never asked for this hype,* he thought, feeling a pang of guilt. *I just want us to win.*

The pressure weighed on him during the next game. He skated tentatively, worried that any mistake would label him a fluke. He attempted fewer risky plays, passing off the puck quickly to avoid hogging the limelight. The Wolves lost 2–0 in a flat performance. Afterward, a local paper criticized Doug for seeming "invisible." The same fans who adored him a week ago took to social media, questioning if the hat trick was a one-off.

Doug found himself reeling—one day a hero, the next day a target. He confided in his parents over a video call, voice trembling as he admitted how lonely it felt. "I'm stuck between making the guys think I'm not stepping on their toes and trying to prove to the fans I can deliver again."

His father's calm voice offered perspective: "That's the nature of sports, son. Highs and lows. Stay steady. Focus on your team, not the outside noise." His mother added gentle encouragement, reminding him that real success would come from consistent effort, not one single sensational night.

Sensing Doug's turmoil, Coach Melrose called him into the office after a practice. A large window overlooked the quiet ice, where a Zamboni circled. Doug shifted nervously as he sat across from the desk, noticing the coach's furrowed brow.

"I've seen your confidence waver," Melrose said, leaning forward. "You're overthinking. You had a big night, then got spooked by the attention. Now you're playing tight."

Doug swallowed. "I just... the older guys... the media... It's too much."

Coach Melrose nodded, tapping a pen on his desk. "This league's intense. Some players thrive on the spotlight, others crumble. But the real test is how you respond after a big night or a rough patch." He paused, letting the words sink in. "You're not responsible for pleasing the media or overshadowing your teammates. Your job is to play *your* game—hustle, skill, work ethic. Remember that kid who scored three goals because he never quit on a play? That's who we need."

Doug inhaled, a wave of relief washing over him. "Thanks, Coach. I'll try to block out the noise."

Melrose patted the desk. "Good. And don't be afraid to talk to Sutton or the others if you sense tension. They respect hard work, even if they're not the most vocal about it. Bring them into your success, share it. That's what teammates do."

Leaving the office, Doug felt lighter. The weight of expectations had nearly crushed him, but the coach's words offered clarity: focus on the team, not the external chatter.

Determined to address the simmering resentment, Doug sought out Kyle Sutton in the locker room after the next practice. Sutton, half-armored in gear, looked up warily. Doug cleared his throat.

"Hey, Kyle. Can we talk?"

Sutton shrugged. "Sure. What's up?"

Doug rubbed the back of his neck. "I just wanted to say—I know the media's been going crazy about my hat trick. I never asked for all that attention. I'm here to help us win, not to steal the spotlight from guys like you who've been grinding for years."

Sutton's gaze flickered, and for a moment, Doug thought he'd brush him off. But then the veteran exhaled, resting his forearms on his knees. "Look, I've been around this team a while. We haven't had much success, and when some new kid gets hailed as the savior, it's easy to feel overlooked." He shrugged. "But that's not your fault. It's just how fans and media are."

Doug nodded earnestly. "I get it. I promise, I'm not looking for personal glory. I want us to be a team. If you ever have advice, I'm all ears."

A hesitant smile tugged at Sutton's lips. "Appreciate that. You're a good kid. Let's bury the hatchet, yeah?"

They shook hands. It wasn't a grand cinematic moment, but it felt like an important step in forging genuine respect. Doug realized that no matter how many goals he scored, he needed the veterans' support to truly fit in.

Over the next few games, Doug strived to strike a balance. He refused to shrink from opportunities to score or create plays, yet he worked to involve everyone. He studied older teammates' tendencies, fed them passes, celebrated their goals as enthusiastically as he would his own. Gradually, a sense of camaraderie blossomed.

He also learned to cope with external pressures: if the media lauded him after a multi-point night, he reminded them it was "a team win." If he had a quiet game, he avoided beating himself up, focusing instead on small positives. Fans still chanted his name, but now they also recognized the efforts of other Wolves stepping up.

One crisp Saturday evening, the Wolves faced another challenging opponent. Doug scored a single goal, helping secure a 3–2 victory. No hat trick, no front-page headlines—but a solid, consistent performance. In the locker room, the atmosphere was joyous yet balanced. Afterward, a local reporter tried to corner Doug for an interview, but he deftly redirected the conversation to highlight a key shot-block from Sutton that preserved the lead. The tension in the locker room further eased.

A couple of weeks after his hat trick, Doug found a quiet moment in the empty stands post-practice. The arena lights cast long shadows across the ice. He looked out at center ice, recalling that magical night. Three goals, a sea of hats, fans chanting his name. He also remembered the whiplash of spotlight, the team's initial resentment, and how easy it was to lose oneself in the swirl of hype.

He exhaled, realizing that scoring a hat trick was both a highlight and a lesson. With success came heavier expectations, not just from fans but from teammates who needed to trust that your intentions were pure, that you weren't just chasing personal stats. The OHL demanded thick skin, resilience, and a team-first mindset if you wanted to last.

That revelation gave him peace. He would relish big moments but wouldn't chase them at the cost of unity. And if the fans or media crowned him a hero again, he'd share the credit, keep the bigger picture in focus.

Doug stood, slinging his stick over his shoulder, and made his way to the locker room's back corridor. The future still held many unknowns: further highs and lows, possibly bigger opportunities in the league or even glimpses from pro scouts. But for tonight, he felt content. He was exactly where he needed to be, learning exactly the lessons he needed.

Outside, the northern Ontario sky stretched wide and deep, stars glinting. The walk to his billet family's car felt refreshing in the cool night air. In that moment, Doug allowed himself a small smile, remembering the roar of the crowd and the weight of hats on the ice. One day, he'd have an entire highlight reel of accomplishments, but for now, a single hat trick had taught him more about perseverance, humility, and teamwork than any success before.

Somewhere in the darkness, a train whistle echoed across the lake. Doug inhaled the pine-scented wind, grateful for the chance to keep proving himself in a league he'd once dreamed about. Tomorrow, practice awaited—more drills, more bruises, more camaraderie, more growth. And that was enough.

12

BUS TRIP

Doug shivered, hunching lower into his seat on the drafty bus as it rumbled along a lonely highway in northern Ontario. It was the dead of winter, and the Wolves—his small-market OHL team—were en route to an away game in a remote town perched on the edge of a frozen lake. Outside, fat flakes of snow whipped past the windows, forming ghostly streaks in the darkness. Every so often, the headlights caught a swirl of white that seemed to swallow the narrow road. Doug glanced back at his teammates, their faces lit by the bus's faint overhead lights. They looked as weary as he felt.

"We should've taken the train," one of the veterans, Kyle Sutton, grumbled from across the aisle. He was bundled in a thick hoodie, arms folded protectively over his chest, looking half asleep. "I swear, we're gonna get lost out here."

"Shut up, Sutton," teased Jeremy, the usually chirpy defenseman, who was wearing a playful grin. "You're just mad you're not up front with the coaches."

The rest of the team chuckled quietly, though the amusement lacked any real enthusiasm. Everyone's nerves were on edge. They'd played a grueling schedule of late, and this was supposed to be a quick overnight trip—drive a few hours, settle into a motel, then face a mid-tier rival the next evening. But the weather had taken an abrupt turn, and their "quick" trip was now a white-knuckled crawl through a raging blizzard.

Doug tried to stretch his legs, but the cramped seats made it almost impossible. His knees bumped the back of the seat in front of him. Beside him, one of the rookies, Drake, was softly snoring, head lolling against the frosted window. Doug envied the kid's ability to sleep in any condition. Meanwhile, Doug's mind raced with anxious thoughts about the game, about the dangerous road conditions, and about how, if something went wrong, they were basically in the middle of nowhere.

A swirl of white suddenly engulfed the windshield. The bus driver slowed further, muttering curses that were drowned out by the howling wind. Doug clutched the seat in front of him. *Don't panic,* he told himself. *We're hockey players, used to tough conditions. Right?*

Coach Melrose stood near the front, leaning on a seat to brace himself. Even from where Doug sat, he could see the tight lines of concern etched on the coach's face. As the bus labored up a gradual slope, the engine groaned, tires spinning on the snow-packed asphalt. For a second, the bus lurched to one side, eliciting gasps and curses from the players. The driver wrestled the wheel, regaining some traction.

"Easy," Coach Melrose called, voice taut. "Everyone hold on."

The bus slid a final few feet, then abruptly came to a halt. Doug's stomach lurched. Around him, the players looked at one another, confused. The driver tried the accelerator again, but the tires only spun uselessly.

"We're stuck," the driver announced grimly, flicking on the hazard lights.

A hush fell over the team. Doug craned his neck, peering out the window at the swirling white void. The only illumination came from the bus's lights, which barely pierced the blizzard. *Great,* he thought. *Stranded in the middle of nowhere, in a storm.*

The driver cut the engine but left the interior lights on, plunging them into a faintly lit stillness broken only by the howl of wind outside. The bus's heater, already feeble, struggled to compensate. A new wave of cold seeped in through the floor and windows. Doug zipped up his jacket, bracing for the chill.

Coach Melrose marched down the aisle, stopping near the middle. "All right, everyone," he said in a calm but firm tone, "we're stuck. Let's not panic. We'll radio for assistance, see if we can get a plow or tow out here. In the meantime, I need you all to stay put and keep calm." He eyed a few particularly restless players. "We're a team. Let's act like it."

The driver had stepped outside to examine the situation. A blast of frigid air swept into the bus, making Doug's teeth chatter, before the door groaned shut again. Around Doug, the Wolves erupted in worried chatter. *How long are we going to be stuck here? Will we even make tomorrow's game? What if the engine dies and we freeze?*

"Settle down," came a voice from the front. It was the bus driver, returning, teeth chattering. "Road's impassable. Snowdrifts. We're going nowhere unless a plow finds us first."

A collective groan ensued. The driver shrugged apologetically. "I've put in a call, but we're pretty far out. It might be a few hours."

A few hours. Possibly more. Doug swallowed hard. *So we're literally in the middle of nowhere, in a storm. Fantastic.*

Time crawled. Ten minutes, then twenty, then an hour. The bus's heat wavered, and the interior began to cool significantly. Several players dug into their bags for extra layers—sweatshirts, toques, anything to stave off the creeping cold. Doug wrapped a scarf around his neck, grateful his mother had insisted he pack it. Across the aisle, Sutton rummaged for gloves, cursing under his breath at the predicament.

"We can't just sit here and freeze," one of the rookies complained. "Isn't there a motel or something?"

Coach Melrose shook his head. "Next town is another hour away, assuming no snow. If we tried to walk, we'd freeze." He gestured at the windows, now coated in a layer of icy crystals. "We're safer staying put until help arrives."

Jeremy, the defenseman known for his humor, tried to inject some levity. "Could be worse," he said. "At least we're not facing our rivals right now with no goalie."

No one laughed. The tension was too thick. A couple of veterans muttered that they'd rather be anywhere else. The bus driver reported that the radio was giving sporadic updates, but no guaranteed rescue time. The road had reportedly become nearly impassable, with multiple vehicles stuck along the same stretch.

Slowly, a restlessness took hold. The cramped conditions, the looming worry about missing the next game, and the biting cold created an edgy atmosphere. Doug noticed small arguments flaring up—someone complaining about no space to recline, another snapping about trivial matters, like who got the last bag of chips from the overhead bin.

At one point, Sutton nearly lost his temper when a rookie accidentally knocked into him while rummaging for snacks.

"Watch it, idiot!" Sutton snapped. The rookie bristled, and for a moment, Doug worried a fight might break out in the bus aisle.

I have to do something, Doug thought, feeling the tension like a live wire.

Trying to channel his role as a supportive teammate—ever since that hat trick moment, he'd felt more confident stepping up socially—Doug got up from his seat, stepping into the narrow aisle. "Hey, guys," he called, voice raised to cut through the grumbling. "We're stuck, yeah, but we can either brood about it or make the best of it. Anyone up for some cards?"

A few heads turned. Card games had been a staple on smaller trips, but no one had suggested them yet on this miserable night. Doug brandished a deck he found in his duffel. "I've got a decent deck here. Let's gather around an empty row and pass the time."

Someone let out a derisive snort, but a few players' expressions perked up. Jeremy, grateful for any distraction, hopped on board immediately. "Yeah, I'm in. Let's do it. We can play a few hands, maybe keep warm by the sheer rage of losing to me," he joked, winking at Doug.

The corner of Sutton's mouth quirked up despite himself. "Count me in," he muttered, albeit grudgingly.

Within minutes, a small group formed around a pair of seats near the back, where they could rest the deck on a flipped-down tray. Doug dealt out a game of Poker. The presence of a clear activity seemed to diffuse some of the anxious energy. Even those not playing watched, occasionally cracking jokes or calling out suggestions. The air felt less stifling, as if a communal exhale had occurred.

From his vantage, Doug noticed a shift. Guys who'd been quietly stewing now chimed in with commentary. A rookie who'd been sulking over missed rest perked up, laughing when Jeremy lost a big hand to Sutton's surprise flush. The harsh climate outside remained dreadful, but inside, the team was finding a small pocket of warmth—literal and figurative.

After the first few rounds of Poker, Doug switched it up with another card game—President—inviting more players to join. Laughter bubbled through the bus when Jeremy declared himself "Permanent President for Life," only to be dethroned spectacularly by Drake, the once-sleeping rookie. The riotous banter that followed peeled away the gloom. Guys began cracking inside jokes, referencing old practices, embarrassing slip-ups, or comedic moments from previous road trips.

Coach Melrose observed from his seat near the front. Though he maintained a stoic front, Doug could see a trace of relief in the coach's features—maybe he was glad the team was bonding rather than tearing each other apart.

Amid the card games, other forms of entertainment emerged. Some players rummaged for leftover snacks, turning them into an impromptu pot for the winning hand. A couple of the younger guys started trading war stories about the hardest hits they'd ever taken. Laughter rolled through the bus as they reenacted these moments in dramatic fashion. Doug pitched in his own recollection of being absolutely flattened by a monstrous defenseman in a previous game, garnering empathetic groans and ribbing from the veterans.

Every once in a while, tension flickered. Space was limited, everyone felt the cold, and the knowledge that they might be stuck for hours weighed on them. But each time a spark of frustration appeared—like a bump in the aisle or a complaint about the temperature—someone managed to channel it into a joke or a friendly challenge. Doug tried to keep a calm, upbeat presence, remembering how important it was for the team to stay united. If the Wolves hoped for a deep playoff run, forging bonds in adversity was as crucial as any on-ice practice.

Time wore on. The bus driver reported that a snowplow was clearing the road from the opposite direction, but it might be a while before they reached the Wolves. The temperature continued to drop, though the bus driver ran the engine in short intervals to provide bursts of heat. Everyone wore multiple layers, and some huddled under blankets. Doug's breath fogged in the dim interior each time he exhaled. His toes began to go numb despite thick socks.

Still, the card games and banter persevered. Doug noticed that the usual cliques—rookies with rookies, veterans with veterans—had dissolved in the face of shared discomfort. Everyone was in it together, dealing with the biting cold and the cramped seats. Even Sutton, who typically avoided fraternizing with younger players, shared a few stories about his earliest days in the league, lightening the mood with self-deprecating humor about rookie hazing.

A roar of laughter erupted at one point when Jeremy tried to mime how their star goalie, Cameron, often snored on bus rides—complete with comedic impressions. Cameron, in defense, snatched a half-eaten candy bar from Jeremy's seat as retribution, sparking a friendly wrestling match in the aisle. Coach Melrose intervened with a grin, telling them to keep it civil. The bus echoed with real joy, a testament to how adversity can sometimes bring out the best in a team's camaraderie.

Inevitably, fatigue and cold took their toll on a few players, fraying tempers again. Late into the night, as the bus lights dimmed further to conserve battery, a spat broke out between two players over seat space. Words escalated to shoves. The team collectively braced for a blow-up. But Doug, having been watchful all night, inserted himself in the middle. He reminded them softly that they were all freezing, all exhausted, and that fighting each other wouldn't magically clear the road.

His calm intervention worked. The two players huffed, apologized, then retreated to their corners. As the tension subsided, Jeremy offered them the last of his warm cocoa from a Thermos, bridging the rift. Coach Melrose gave Doug a nod of approval from across the aisle, recognizing how pivotal that moment was. If they'd started truly fighting, morale could've plummeted.

Sometime around three in the morning, the bus driver got word that the plow was only a few miles away. The news lifted spirits, though some players had already dozed off in awkward positions, lulled by the exhaustion of the day. Doug fought sleep himself, partly because the cold made it hard to relax, but also because he wanted to stay alert if anything changed.

He gazed out the window. The storm raged on, though perhaps less ferociously than before. The swirling snow had lost some intensity, and every now and then, Doug thought he saw a glimmer of moonlight between the clouds. Another hour crawled by, and at last, bright lights appeared in the distance. A loud engine rumble followed. The cavalry—an enormous snowplow—had arrived.

The bus driver hopped out to coordinate with the plow operator, while the team pressed against the windows, peering at the rescue like it was a mythical beast. The plow cleared a wide path around the bus, pushing aside the massive drifts. Then, with chains on the bus's tires for added traction, the driver carefully revved the engine. The bus jerked, wheels spinning on the icy road, but finally lurched forward onto the newly cleared lane. A collective cheer erupted inside the bus, echoing through the frosty interior.

Once freed, the bus followed the plow at a slow, cautious pace. It felt like they were traveling through a tunnel of snow walls. The radio updates indicated that the next town was about an hour away. By then, the team had been on the bus for nearly seven hours—most of it spent stranded. They had no illusions of arriving at a motel for much rest, but at least they were moving.

Doug, now physically and mentally drained, dozed off for short stretches, head bobbing. Around him, other players either slept or stared blankly at their phones (those who had signals, anyway). The tension had eased significantly; a near-crisis had been averted, and they'd come out the other side more bonded than before.

When they finally reached the small town with a motel, the sky was beginning to lighten with a hazy dawn. An exhausted hush settled as they shuffled off the bus, retrieving only essentials for the few hours they could rest before heading to the rink. The motel staff, having heard their plight, offered a dining area for a quick breakfast. Bleary-eyed players grabbed whatever sustenance they could find—bagels, cereal, coffee—mumbling thanks. Doug nearly fell asleep in his plate of scrambled eggs.

Coach Melrose corralled them into rooms. "We'll regroup in a few hours," he said, sounding just as exhausted. "Game's in the evening, so rest up. And let's not forget the adversity we overcame tonight—use that same resilience on the ice."

Doug nodded, stumbling to the small double room he was sharing with Jeremy. The bed looked like heaven. Jeremy cracked a final joke about "nightmarish bus conditions" before flopping onto the mattress, fully clothed. Doug managed to toe off his shoes and set an alarm on his phone. Then he collapsed, sleep claiming him instantly.

That evening, unbelievably, the Wolves still had a game to play. The late arrival meant only a short pre-game skate and minimal warm-up time. Yet, for all the exhaustion, the team seemed infused with a peculiar energy. They'd survived a harrowing experience together. They'd laughed, argued, froze, and supported each other in that bus. In a strange way, that bond coursed through their veins now.

During the pre-game talk, Coach Melrose tapped into that unity. "Boys," he said, eyes scanning the room, "you overcame real adversity last night—stuff bigger than just a hockey game. You took care of each other. That's the spirit we need on the ice tonight. Stick together, push each other, and let's show them what the Wolves can do."

The synergy was palpable from puck drop. Despite the adversity (little rest, minimal preparation), the Wolves played with an edge, forechecking relentlessly, blocking shots with abandon. Doug, who'd perhaps napped only a couple of hours, found a second wind as soon as his skates touched the ice. He recalled the moment on the bus when everyone was so close to snapping, yet they found unity. That memory fueled him with determination.

It was a back-and-forth battle—both teams traded goals, the lead swinging like a pendulum. Late in the third period, the Wolves clung to a 3–2 advantage. Doug's line took the ice, hustling to keep the puck deep in the opponent's zone. Another shot rang off the post, and the other team quickly counterattacked. Tension spiked in the arena, fans roaring for the home side to tie it up.

Doug dug in, intercepting a pass intended for their top scorer. Heart pounding, he skated it back into neutral ice, just to relieve pressure and keep the clock ticking. The final horn sounded with the puck pinned along the boards—Wolves win, 3–2. Their bench flooded the ice, celebrating with surprising fervor for a mid-season victory. They couldn't help it—this felt like a triumph over more than just an opponent.

In the handshake line, Doug exchanged nods with the other team's players, who likely had no idea how insane the Wolves' previous night had been. As Doug reached the locker room, sweaty and triumphant, he made eye contact with Sutton, who gave him a slight grin. No words were necessary. They'd come a long way since nearly throwing fists over seat space. This bus trip from hell had made them better—tougher, closer, more prepared for whatever the season might throw at them next.

When the team finally boarded the bus again—this time under calmer skies—they were exhausted yet elated. The road had been partially cleared, making the journey home more straightforward. Doug found a seat and exhaled. He thought about how that blizzard-enforced detour had tested them not just physically, but emotionally. They'd confronted the worst of cabin fever, the threat of freezing, and the frustration of possibly missing a crucial game. Yet here they were, victorious and forging a deeper sense of brotherhood.

Players settled in, some listening to music, others chatting in hushed tones about the game. The bus rumbled onward, and Doug leaned his head against the window, eyes heavy. The reflection that stared back at him was tired but content. *We overcame so much in just twenty-four hours,* he marveled. *If we can handle that, we can handle a deep playoff push.*

He closed his eyes, letting the bus's gentle rocking lull him toward sleep. The cold journey, the improvised card games, the heated arguments turned laughter... everything blended into a montage of what it meant to be part of this junior hockey life. While some players on high-profile teams traveled in relative comfort or short distances, the Wolves faced endless miles through harsh Canadian winters, forging resilience in every mile.

In that hazy half-dream state, Doug replayed the key moments: distributing cards in the aisle, joking around, stepping in to break up a fight, and ultimately scoring a victory on the ice. He felt proud of how he'd contributed, not just as a forward who could bury pucks in the net, but as a team guy who could keep spirits afloat. The Wolves' bond had been hammered into shape by the storm's adversity—like tempered steel.

And as Doug drifted off, the bus forging ahead through the freshly plowed road, he felt certain that this camaraderie, tested in the crucible of a winter blizzard, would be the bedrock on which they'd stand when the playoffs arrived. *We might still be underdogs,* he mused, *but we're a real team now.*

The overhead lights dimmed, the hum of the engine blending with the soft snores and whispers. One by one, the Wolves settled into an uneasy but hopeful rest, carrying back the memory of a night that had threatened to break them but instead bound them together tighter than ever before.

13

BENCH CLEARING BRAWL

Doug nearly vibrated with anticipation as he slid into the locker room stall, rummaging in his bag for fresh tape. Tonight's game was big—no, bigger than big. It was *personal*. The Wolves were set to face their fiercest rivals, the **Lake City Sentinels**, in what fans called the "Battle of the North." Tensions had simmered between the two clubs for years, fueled by close playoff encounters, contentious trades, and a few borderline hits that had never been forgotten. Now, the teams would meet again, both clawing to climb the OHL standings.

All week, the local papers had hyped the game as a must-win. Wolves fans recalled last season's heartbreak, when Lake City eliminated them in the first playoff round with a rough, physical brand of hockey. Since then, a single mention of "Sentinels" was enough to stir up heated debates in coffee shops around town. The same energy filled the players. Even in that small locker room, Doug felt the buzz—an undercurrent of adrenaline that pushed each of them to sharpen skates and tape sticks with extra focus.

He could sense it on his teammates' faces, too: jaws set, eyes narrowed, the near-silent vow to leave everything on the ice. It was as if one collective heartbeat united them: *We will not lose tonight.*

As Doug taped his stick, **Kyle Sutton** took a seat nearby, adjusting the chinstrap on his helmet. "You ready for this, Mansfield?" he asked in a low voice. Despite some earlier frictions, the two had grown closer over the season. Their bond was forged by nights on drafty buses, big wins, bitter losses, and the blossoming sense that the Wolves were turning into a real contender.

Doug gave a curt nod. "Yeah. Been waiting for this one."

Sutton smirked. "Good. 'Cause they'll come out swinging. We have to match that intensity—no, *exceed* it. Show 'em we're done taking their crap."

Doug's stomach fluttered with a mix of excitement and something else—maybe a hint of dread. He'd seen Lake City's physical style. He knew the brand of intimidation they brought, and how easy it was for big hits to escalate. But he also remembered his own lines in the sand: how far he was willing to go, and how important it was not to cross that threshold recklessly.

Coach Melrose stepped into the locker room, quieting the scattered conversation. His gaze swept across the team. "We know what this game means," he said, voice low but carrying authority. "Yes, it's about points in the standings. But it's also about pride—about showing Lake City that we're not their whipping boys. We push back if they try their nonsense. We play our game. We fight for every inch." He paused, letting tension build. "But remember: keep your heads. Don't get sucked into cheap shots. We want to beat them on the scoreboard, not in the penalty box."

Doug nodded, heart pounding. He appreciated that last point. He'd learned how easily aggression could tip into mayhem if cooler heads didn't prevail. *We can't let it get ugly,* he told himself. *But we also can't back down.*

Stepping onto home ice for warm-ups, Doug felt the electricity in the arena. Wolves fans turned out in droves, some sporting face paint or brandishing homemade signs. Across the rink, a cluster of Lake City supporters bellowed chants. Even warm-up drills carried an undercurrent of tension: players on both sides shot each other pointed looks, as if to say, *We remember last time.*

The opening puck drop arrived amid a thunderous roar. Doug lined up at center ice, adrenaline thrumming in his veins. Lake City iced their top line, including their captain, **Nolan Radke**, a veteran forward known for delivering punishing hits and stirring up trouble. When the linesman dropped the puck, Radke swiped it back to his defense. Immediately, the Sentinels pressed forward with a surge of physicality.

Within the first few shifts, bodies collided along the boards. The referees whistled a couple of minor penalties early—slashing, roughing—trying to set a tone. But the sheer volume of chirping, cross-checks, and borderline hits suggested that discipline might soon unravel. Doug, on his second shift, found himself shoved hard into the corner after chipping the puck deep. He shook it off, skating back into the play, eyes scanning for an equal opportunity to push back.

Midway through the first period, Lake City struck first on the scoreboard. An odd-man rush concluded with a slick tic-tac-toe passing sequence, leaving the Wolves' goalie helpless. The Sentinels bench erupted, hollering taunts. Doug grit his teeth, bracing for an even more physical response from his team. The crowd booed, chanting for the Wolves to answer back.

They did, a few minutes later, with a power-play goal. Doug had a hand in it, retrieving a puck along the half-boards and feeding it to Sutton for a one-timer that whizzed past the goalie's glove. The home crowd roared, and Doug pumped his fist. Tied 1–1.

Yet, the tension thickened. Even from the bench, Doug could see guys on both sides finishing checks with extra venom. The referees doled out more minor penalties, but it seemed inevitable that tempers would boil over if a single match got lit.

That match was struck late in the second period. The Wolves had just killed a Lake City power play, and the puck was cleared up ice. One of the Wolves' top-scoring forwards, **Matty Roy**, chased it down near the neutral zone. A Lake City defenseman closed in—**Grayson Cook**, infamous for borderline hits. Doug saw Cook line up Roy from behind, crossing the blue line dangerously. Roy had no idea Cook was coming at that angle.

Then it happened: Cook launched himself into Roy's back, smashing him face-first into the boards. The impact reverberated around the arena. Roy crumpled onto the ice, unmoving at first. Doug and the rest of the Wolves on the ice froze in horror. The whistle blew frantically.

A collective gasp rippled through the crowd, which then exploded into boos. Wolves players on the bench leaped to their feet, shouting at the officials. Doug's heart leaped into his throat. Roy lay on the ice, eventually rolling over but clearly dazed. The trainer and paramedics rushed onto the rink.

It was a dirty hit—no question.

Doug's blood boiled. He felt his vision narrow, a wave of rage pounding in his skull. Roy was a teammate and friend, someone the Wolves relied on for leadership and offense. To see him taken down by a reckless cheap shot stoked an immediate hunger for retribution.

By the time paramedics helped Roy off, Cook was already jawing with other Wolves, claiming it was an accident. The referees conferred, eventually calling a major penalty. But many Wolves players believed Cook deserved an ejection. The Sentinels bench erupted in protest, their coach demanding leniency. The tension soared.

As soon as the referees attempted to escort Cook to the penalty box, a knot of Wolves confronted him, led by Sutton, pushing and shoving. Lake City players jumped in to defend Cook. The linesmen tried to separate them. Shouts escalated. Bodies collided.

From the bench, Doug saw the melee forming. Players from both teams left their seats, converging on the scrum. It took only a flash for the situation to become a full-scale brawl— fists flying, skates scrabbling on the ice, curses echoing in the rafters. The fans, stunned for a moment, began either cheering or jeering, depending on their loyalties. In a swirl of chaos, the benches emptied.

Doug found himself in the thick of it, swept along by the wave of fury. He tried to restrain a Lake City forward who was swinging wildly at one of the Wolves' rookies. Another Sentinel grabbed Doug's jersey from behind, wrenching him off-balance. Doug spun, adrenaline roaring in his ears, delivering a reflexive shove. In the corner of his vision, he saw a linesman wrestling a pair of brawling players to the ice. Helmets littered the rink, officials frantically blowing whistles to no avail.

Sutton, fists clenched, was going toe-to-toe with Cook. The memory of Roy's lifeless form hitting the boards spurred many Wolves to join in. Even normally reserved players lost themselves in the storm. Doug caught fleeting glimpses of panicked referees waving for more security.

In that chaos, Doug felt a rush of anger overshadow his usual restraint. He saw a Lake City player land a cheap shot on a Wolves teammate. Doug lunged, tackling the aggressor, fists connecting with shoulder pads. The acrid smell of sweat and ice filled his nostrils. He heard shouting from all sides, but his pulse hammered so loud he couldn't parse the words.

Eventually, security and the officials managed to break up the brawl. It took minutes that felt like hours. Bloodied lips, bruises, and battered egos remained. The referees ejected a slew of players, including Cook, Sutton, and several others from both teams. Doug, dazed and breathing heavily, realized he'd also been told to leave. One of the linesmen pointed him off the ice, citing him for "third-man-in," or for instigating additional fights in the melee.

As Doug trudged down the tunnel, adrenaline crashed into shame. He glanced at the scoreboard, which read 2–2. The game was paused, uncertain if it would continue. The crowd's roar echoed behind him like a tidal wave, half excited, half outraged. *What have we done?*

In the locker room, medical staff tended to cuts and bruises. Doug noticed a small gash on his knuckles—he must have hit someone's visor. His breath still came in shallow gasps. The reality of what just happened settled in: they'd caused a bench-clearing brawl, a spectacle that would overshadow any positive about the rivalry. *This is going to have repercussions.*

He was right. Once the dust settled, the referees declared a premature end to the second period, forcibly sending both teams to their respective locker rooms. The league officials would decide how to proceed. The game eventually resumed after a lengthy delay, but Doug and many of the participants were done for the night.

Later, a formal statement from the OHL arrived: video reviews, a disciplinary committee hearing, possible suspensions. Doug's stomach twisted. He'd never been in trouble with the league before, not to this extent. Now he found himself in the crosshairs. *All because of one savage hit, and the unstoppable rage that followed.*

The next few days were a blur of phone calls, league interviews, and swirling media coverage. Sports talk shows replayed the brawl footage ad nauseam, freeze-framing every punch, analyzing who started what. Fans online debated: some praised the Wolves for defending Roy and punishing the dirty hit, others condemned them for letting the game devolve into chaos. Lake City claimed innocence, painting the Wolves as aggressors.

Doug, singled out in multiple replays, faced significant backlash. Clips showed him diving into the fray, taking swings, tackling a Lake City forward to the ice. Another angle caught him grappling with a second opponent, fists raised. Journalists lambasted the "lack of discipline" from both teams. But Doug, as a younger player with a newly minted reputation for skill, was under an especially harsh spotlight: *"Mansfield Crosses the Line in Ugly Brawl"* read one headline.

The Wolves' general manager and Coach Melrose helped Doug prepare a statement, urging him to be contrite, not defensive. The league's disciplinary board scheduled a hearing via conference call. Doug attended it with sweaty palms, the gravity of the situation weighing on him.

Senior league officials grilled him: "Did you intentionally leave the bench to escalate the fight?" "Were you aware of the referees' orders to disengage?" Doug answered honestly, explaining how adrenaline and the heat of the moment got the better of him. He expressed regret, especially for overshadowing the game and fueling a bench-clearing fiasco that risked player safety.

He admitted that he'd stepped over the line: "I wanted to protect my teammate, but I recognize now that I let my emotions spiral. It won't happen again."

Ultimately, the board issued their verdict: a **two-game suspension** for Doug, with a formal warning about future conduct. A handful of others, including Sutton, received similar or harsher penalties, while Cook was slapped with a five-game suspension for the dirty hit and subsequent fight. Lake City also saw multiple suspensions.

Doug left the hearing physically unharmed but weighed down by guilt. He'd never pictured himself as a "dirty" player or someone who'd get suspended for fighting. Yet, here he was. He dreaded telling his parents, worried how they'd react. The Wolves' front office tried to reassure him, though they also stressed the seriousness of the situation.

Public reaction was mixed. Some Wolves fans rallied behind Doug, praising him for "standing up to Lake City's goon tactics." Others scolded him for "throwing away talent for cheap violence." Social media bristled with opinions, and Doug saw his name trending in local circles, not for a highlight-reel goal but for a bench-clearing brawl. The attention felt suffocating, especially when he recognized the negativity overshadowing the rest of his season's hard work.

His teammates offered quiet solidarity. "We all lost our cool," Sutton said, arms folded, sporting a black eye from the fight. "You're not alone, Mansfield. We *all* contributed."

Still, Doug wrestled with personal shame. He recalled how, earlier in his career, a less serious fight in youth hockey had rattled him. He'd vowed then to handle aggression responsibly, to avoid letting anger consume him. But the stark memory of Roy being cheap-shotted and left prone on the ice had obliterated reason. *I lost control again.*

Meanwhile, Roy recovered from the concussion-like symptoms. He assured Doug he wasn't upset with him, that he appreciated the support, but also encouraged Doug to learn from this. "Look, man," Roy said gently, "there's a line between defending your teammate and risking everything with a brawl. We're pros. We gotta do better."

Being suspended meant Doug couldn't play or even suit up for two games. He had to watch from the stands as the Wolves took the ice without him. Each shift pained him—he saw opportunities where he might've contributed, moments he felt he could have helped. The team won one game but lost another, sputtering at times without key players lost to suspension.

Sitting in the bleachers forced Doug to reflect. He realized how easily passion for the game, righteous anger, and the desire to protect a teammate could escalate into chaos. *Was the brawl worth it? Roy's still injured, I'm suspended, and the team chemistry took a hit.*

In a private conversation, Coach Melrose sat beside Doug in an empty row of seats during practice. "I'm not here to scold you further," the coach said, eyes fixed on the players skating below. "But I want you to understand that real toughness is controlling your emotions, not unleashing them."

Doug nodded, absorbing the words. "I know. I just—when Roy went down, I saw red."

"Of course you did. And in this league, you'll see worse stuff. If you can't channel that anger productively, you hurt the team." Melrose paused, glancing at Doug. "I believe you're a big part of our future. Don't let one incident define you."

Doug exhaled, shoulders sagging. "I won't, Coach. I'll be better."

In that moment, Doug felt a shift within himself—a renewed dedication to the concept of disciplined aggression. He wouldn't lose his edge, but he'd strive to harness it, mindful of the consequences that reckless anger wrought.

After missing two contests, Doug was allowed back. On the day of his return, he skated onto the ice for morning practice with a swirl of nervous energy. Would the fans still boo him? Or cheer him? How about his teammates—did they truly forgive him, or did they see him as a liability?

He needn't have worried too much. When he entered the locker room, the Wolves greeted him with a few good-natured jabs—Jeremy teased, "Try not to beat up the boards today, Doug!"—but otherwise seemed genuinely relieved to have him back. Even Sutton clapped him on the shoulder, muttering, "Glad you're outta time-out, rookie."

Doug laced up with renewed focus. This was his shot at redemption, to prove the suspension and brawl wouldn't derail his season or overshadow his potential. In the ensuing game— a home match against a different rival—Doug showcased precisely the kind of controlled intensity Coach Melrose advocated. He finished checks cleanly, backchecked hard, racked up a couple of assists, but refrained from retaliating when an opposing forward tested him physically.

The Wolves won in overtime, a thrilling 4–3 result. While the crowd cheered the entire squad, Doug earned applause for an especially pivotal shift in the third period, where he stayed disciplined despite a high cross-check from an opponent. He'd drawn a penalty instead of engaging in a brawl. The fans recognized the shift—he was still physical, still protective, but didn't cross the line.

Later that night, Doug found himself in his dimly lit billet room, lying on the bed, phone in hand. He scrolled through social media comments. Some fans praised his new composure: *"Mansfield playing tough but clean—love to see it."* Others still dredged up the brawl: *"One fight away from another meltdown, watch out."*

He closed the app, letting the phone rest on his chest. He couldn't please everyone. But he could stay true to himself, keep growing from the fiasco. The bench-clearing brawl had been an ugly chapter, yet it hammered home a lesson: in hockey, aggression is part of the sport, but it must be harnessed. Unchecked anger leads to chaos and consequences.

He recalled that initial phone call with the league's disciplinary committee—his voice shaking, eyes downcast, admitting fault. He never wanted to feel that shame again. He was determined to protect his teammates without losing himself in blind rage.

Outside, the northern Ontario wind howled. Doug took a breath, imagining future games—rivalries that might provoke him again. He pictured Cook's vicious hit on Roy, the sense of betrayal that had fueled the fight. He also pictured a more measured response, one where the Wolves hammered Lake City on the scoreboard rather than trading blows. That path, he realized, was how teams truly triumphed: by channeling fury into unstoppable performance, not unbridled violence.

He flicked off the bedside lamp, closing his eyes. The bruises from the brawl were healing, but the memory remained vivid. Next time, he'd remember the fine line between standing up for what's right and stepping over the edge. That knowledge, however painful to gain, would shape him into a more complete player—and, hopefully, a better teammate.

Days turned into weeks, and the Wolves pressed deeper into the season. Fans and media eventually moved on from the brawl, focusing on the playoff race. Cook served his suspension, Lake City and the Wolves met again with heightened security but fewer antics, and the OHL hammered home stricter guidelines for bench behavior.

Doug continued playing with a sense of purpose. Each time a scuffle threatened to escalate, he'd take a deep breath, scanning for the bigger picture. If an opponent tried to bait him, he thought of that bench-clearing fiasco—of Roy carried off the ice, of the heartbreak of suspension—and weighed his actions accordingly. He wasn't afraid to drop gloves if absolutely necessary to defend a teammate from real harm, but he'd no longer let rage lead him into a blind brawl.

With each passing game, the Wolves found a new level of chemistry, forging a more composed identity even in the face of tough hits. Doug's personal stats improved—his disciplined aggression translated to better puck battles, more scoring chances, fewer penalty minutes. Fans applauded his growth, some even pointing to him as an example of how a player can evolve after crossing the line.

During a post-game interview, a reporter asked Doug about that infamous Lake City brawl, whether it haunted him. Doug offered a measured reply: "It taught me a lot about controlling my emotions. I stand by defending my teammate, but I've learned you can defend a teammate *and* stay within the game's limits. I'm more focused on helping the Wolves win cleanly now."

The article that followed was titled: **"Mansfield's Redemption: From Bench Brawler to Responsible Enforcer."**

As the regular season rolled toward its conclusion, the Wolves were in playoff contention, boosted by renewed unity. The bench-clearing brawl, while embarrassing, had served as a galvanizing event that forced the team to re-evaluate their discipline. Coach Melrose noted that if they harnessed their passion correctly, they could be a genuine threat.

Roy eventually returned from injury, grateful for the unwavering support from teammates during his recovery. The first time he and Doug lined up together again, the fans roared, remembering how that dirty hit had sparked an all-out war. But Roy's presence, combined with Doug's matured outlook, signaled a fresh chapter.

In one of the final home games before playoffs, Lake City visited again. The tension was high, the scoreboard tight. A nasty collision in the second period threatened to flare up. A few players on both sides skated over, fists raised, triggers poised. But Doug, along with Roy and Sutton, intervened just enough to calm it. No full-blown fight ensued—just some harsh words and minor penalties. The Wolves eventually won 3–2, courtesy of a late goal from Doug, who celebrated by hugging every teammate in sight.

Walking off the ice, he caught Coach Melrose's approving nod. The transformation from the brawl to this moment felt profound. They'd proven that they could meet Lake City's physicality without losing control. The fans recognized that growth, chanting, "Wolves! Wolves!" with renewed fervor.

Later that night, Doug lay in bed, physically tired but mentally at ease. He recalled the chaotic bench-clearing scene—the bright lights, the flailing fists, the swirling rage. He contrasted it with tonight's composure—a near-incident defused by level heads. That difference encapsulated his personal journey: aggression tempered by wisdom, heart fused with discipline.

He closed his eyes, letting the hum of the night lull him. In a few days, the playoffs would begin. The road ahead promised challenges and no shortage of emotions. But Doug felt better equipped than ever. The bench-clearing brawl, though a stain on the record, had taught him a lesson he'd carry for the rest of his career.

And if another storm brewed, he'd meet it with skill, resolve, and the knowledge that true strength lay not in raw violence, but in controlling the fire within.

14

MAKING THE PLAYOFFS

Doug exhaled sharply as he peered through the thick plexiglass of the home arena, scanning the ice during a final team practice of the regular season. The metal bleachers were empty now, but by tomorrow night, they'd be filled with roaring fans. Excitement thrummed in the air as the North Shore Wolves prepared for a do-or-die matchup that could seal their spot in the playoffs. It was early spring in northern Ontario, and while patches of snow still lingered along the arena's outer edges, inside, the temperature felt downright feverish with anticipation.

Despite all the twists and turns of the season—a fight-laden rivalry match, stressful bus trips through blizzards, and personal highs and lows—the Wolves now stood on the cusp of qualifying for the OHL postseason. For many on the team, this was not the first time in the playoffs, but for Doug, it was new territory. He'd grown up watching televised OHL playoff battles, marveling at the intensity. And now, he was on the brink of living it firsthand.

He forced himself to refocus. *One game at a time,* he reminded himself. *Don't get ahead of yourself.* But that was easier said than done. The weight of the Wolves' entire season now balanced precariously on the final stretch, and Doug felt the suffocating pressure like never before.

The Wolves had weathered a roller coaster of a regular season. They'd started uncertainly, forging a chemistry that sometimes felt tenuous. Key injuries and suspensions—including Doug's own bench-clearing brawl fiasco—threatened to derail them. Slumps came and went, with criticism piling on from local media and fans. But in between the lows were flashes of brilliance: come-from-behind wins, inspiring performances from their star goalie, thrilling individual efforts (Doug's hat trick among them), and the unstoppable synergy that formed whenever the entire roster clicked.

Coach Melrose had hammered on the importance of consistency, but it was only in the final month that the Wolves found a more stable stride. A modest winning streak lifted them off the bottom rung, and they hovered near the cutoff for a playoff berth. Then, in a nerve-wracking flurry of games, they managed crucial victories against mid-tier rivals. Other teams stumbled, and the door opened just wide enough for the Wolves to slide through—if they could capitalize.

Now they clung to the last playoff spot, just a single point ahead of two other teams. If the Wolves secured a win in their final game—or at least forced overtime, depending on other results—they'd finally punch their ticket to the postseason for the first time in years. The entire town buzzed with cautious optimism. *We just need one more push,* everyone repeated.

For Doug, the prospect of high-stakes hockey felt thrilling and daunting. Unlike many veterans on the roster, he'd never tasted the playoff atmosphere at this level. He remembered the intensity of his youth league playoffs, but this was the OHL. The stakes were higher, the crowds bigger, the media scrutiny sharper. Every shift would matter, every mistake magnified. His steady performance throughout the season made him a key part of the Wolves' offense, but now he questioned if he could handle the extra weight of these do-or-die games.

In the days leading up to the final regular-season contest, the tension was palpable throughout the entire organization. The front office subtly reminded the coaching staff that a playoff berth would boost ticket sales and local pride. Wolves fans filled social media with hopeful messages, many calling Doug by name: *"Keep that hustle, Mansfield!"* or *"We're counting on #29!"* Doug tried to ignore the swirl, but it found him even when he scrolled mindlessly through his phone.

He buried himself in preparation, studying game tapes of their upcoming opponent—a gritty team from a neighboring conference known for tight checking and opportunistic scoring. During film sessions, Doug took extra notes, analyzing the opposing defensemen's tendencies. Which ones pinched aggressively? Who struggled with lateral movement? Where could he exploit gaps?

Off the ice, Doug amped up his workouts, hitting the team gym for short but intense sessions focusing on explosive power and agility. He borrowed older players' practice routines— shooting hundreds of extra pucks after formal practice ended, working on quick-release shots from sharp angles. He practiced off-balance shots, imagining playoff scenarios where defenders would hound him relentlessly.

And yet, no matter how he tried to keep his mind on the process, the outcome loomed: *Win, and we're in. Lose, and everything might be for nothing.* That harrowing thought lurked in his subconscious, fueling dreams at night where he missed an open net or made a costly turnover in the final minute. He'd wake up in a sweat, heart pounding with a fear of letting everyone down—his teammates, the fans, himself.

On the morning of the big game, the locker room crackled with quiet urgency. Normally, jokes or casual trash talk flitted around, but today, conversation was spare. **Kyle Sutton** worked silently on his gear, eyes distant. **Jeremy**, usually quick with banter, kept his headphones on, face stoic as he tapped his foot. **Roy**, recovered from his earlier injury, meticulously sharpened his skates, ignoring attempts at small talk. Even **Coach Melrose** looked more serious, delivering a concise pep talk about details: clearing the puck smartly, winning faceoffs, not taking lazy penalties.

Doug went through his own ritual—taping each knob on his stick carefully, double-knotting his laces, and visualizing a strong first shift. He could feel his pulse beating in his temples. He was ready, or so he hoped. Outside, a lively crowd had already started gathering, the hum of excitement echoing through the arena's corridors. This final match felt like a playoff game in itself.

During warm-ups, Doug skated crisp laps, looking around the stands brimming with fans sporting navy-and-forest green. Handmade signs read, *"Clawing Our Way to the Playoffs!"* or *"We Believe!"* He glimpsed one that said, *"Mansfield Magic,"* with a drawing of a top hat and a hockey stick. That brought a fleeting smile. The crowd's energy buoyed him, but also pricked his nerves further. *So many eyes counting on us,* he thought.

From the opening puck drop, the tension was suffocating. The Wolves' opponents played hard, determined to spoil the night. Every pass felt contested, every rush ended in bone-rattling hits. The scoreboard stayed locked at 0–0 for the entire first period, with both goalies turning aside point-blank chances. Doug's line managed a few zone entries, but the defense collapsed fast, stifling them. The crowd groaned in frustration when a shot from Roy rang off the post.

Between periods, the locker room was a mix of heavy breathing and clenched jaws. Coach Melrose reminded them of the game plan: keep driving the net, stay disciplined, trust the system. No one spoke much, but the intensity in their eyes spoke volumes. Doug wiped sweat from his forehead, trying to calm his racing heart. *Forty minutes left. We just need one goal. Let's do this.*

The second period began with more physical battles. Doug found himself pinned along the boards by a hulking defenseman, fighting for every inch of space. He escaped with the puck, but the shot attempt was blocked. The Wolves' bench erupted whenever they gained momentum, but the opposing goalie seemed invincible. Midway through the period, the opponents capitalized on a defensive miscue, sneaking a rebound goal past the Wolves' netminder. 1–0 against the Wolves.

A groan swept through the arena. Doug's chest tightened. *We can't lose now,* he thought, panic simmering. The Wolves pressed harder, but ended the second period still down 1–0. Heading to the locker room, the mood was grim, though no one dared speak the worst fear: that they might fumble away their playoff spot at the last hurdle.

In the intermission, Coach Melrose delivered a pointed speech: "This is your season on the line. We're a goal down, but that's nothing. Keep your composure. Force mistakes. Believe in yourselves." His gaze lingered on Doug for a moment, as if silently reminding him that the team needed his spark. Doug nodded, exhaling shakily, letting the pressure roll through him. *Don't freeze up now. Just play.*

The third period opened with the Wolves in desperation mode—yet they remained disciplined, no reckless penalties. Doug's line orchestrated repeated forays into the offensive zone. Finally, six minutes in, Doug corralled a loose puck near the slot. He spun away from a defender, found a small window, and fired a wrist shot high to the blocker side. The goalie managed to get a piece of it, but the puck dropped behind him over the goal line. **Goal.** 1–1.

The arena exploded in cheers, relief washing over the stands. Doug's teammates mobbed him as the scoreboard glowed with new life. He skated by the bench, pumping his fist, heart soaring. *We're back in it.* The game resumed with an electric pace, both teams realizing what was at stake. Time bled away, the scoreboard locked at 1–1. A single goal could make or break the Wolves' season.

With under two minutes left, the tension reached a fever pitch. The crowd remained on its feet, chanting the Wolves' name. Doug felt every muscle humming as he hopped over the boards for what might be his final shift. The puck cycled behind the opponents' net, and Doug fought for position in the slot. A pass from Roy squeaked through traffic, but Doug's backhand attempt missed wide. His frustration flared, but he forced himself to keep moving.

The final horn blared, sending the game to overtime. The stands shook with thunderous applause, and the Wolves retreated to the bench. Overtime meant guaranteed at least a point—maybe enough to squeak into the playoffs, depending on other teams' results. But for Doug, the focus remained on finishing strong. *Win in OT, and no one can question we belong here.*

In the OHL, overtime was a high-wire act—three-on-three, wide-open ice, space to maneuver. A single mistake could end the game instantly. As Doug watched from the bench, hearts hammered across the rink. Sutton, Roy, and Jeremy started on the ice for the Wolves, facing a trio of swift, skilled opponents. The first minute was frantic. The puck zipped from end to end, with odd-man rushes forming every few seconds. Doug perched on the bench's edge, adrenaline surging.

When Doug finally jumped over the boards, he joined Roy and a defenseman named Kesh. They pressed into the offensive zone. Roy circled wide, feeding Doug at the left circle. Doug faked a shot, drawing a defender, then slid the puck to Kesh pinching in. But Kesh's shot soared high, glass rattling behind the net. The puck caromed dangerously, leading to a quick transition for the other side.

Doug scrambled back, legs burning, just in time to disrupt a breakaway pass. The near-turnover set pulses racing across the stands. He exhaled relief, resetting. Another shift ticked by, neither side scoring. Less than two minutes remained in the overtime. A shootout loomed—a scenario that further inflamed tensions.

The Wolves regained possession. Roy led a rush, dropping the puck to Doug near the blue line. Doug took a quick look: Roy was heading to the net, Kesh hanging back, an opposing forward lunging for a poke-check. Doug sidestepped the forward, maintaining puck control, then zipped it back to Roy. Roy pivoted, drawing the goalie out. Doug cut to the near post, and Roy feathered a perfect pass across the slot. Doug's stick connected, deflecting the puck past the sprawling goalie. **Goal.**

For a split second, silence gripped the arena, as if no one believed it. Then, an explosion of euphoria. Doug found himself tackled by Roy, both grinning ear to ear as the lamp lit bright red. The scoreboard read 2–1 in OT. They'd done it—clutched up in the final moments.

The bench cleared onto the ice—not with fists raised, as in that brawl, but with unbridled joy. Fans roared, hugging each other in the stands. Up above, the scoreboard flashed a final score: *Wolves 2, Visitors 1 (OT)*. The official conclusion of the regular season: the Wolves squeaked in. They were going to the playoffs.

On-ice, players doused each other in water bottles, releasing months of pent-up tension. Doug sank to his knees at center ice, breathless, letting the crowd's cheers wash over him. In that moment, he tasted the pure relief of fulfilling a collective dream. They might not have soared in the standings all year, but they'd fought tooth and nail to claim a playoff berth.

Fans lingered long after the final horn, chanting the team's name. Local reporters hovered, eager to capture raw reactions. Doug, drained and ecstatic, gave a brief interview, crediting his teammates for setting him up in OT. *"We believed in each other,"* he told the camera, voice quivering. *"We knew we could do it."*

In the locker room, euphoria reigned. Players laughed, hammered the backs of seats, threw tape around in celebrations. Coach Melrose wore a wide grin, though he reminded them: "We're not done. This is just a ticket to the dance. We have to be even better from here on out." The guys nodded, but in the heat of the moment, they just wanted to soak in the accomplishment.

Doug texted his parents, who'd driven up for the game: *"WE'RE IN! We did it!"* They replied with an avalanche of proud messages. Mike, his older brother, sent an all-caps note of congrats. It felt surreal. *I was a rookie not long ago, unsure if I'd even make the lineup, and now I'm scoring the OT goal that sends us to playoffs.* The magnitude of that sank in as he peeled off his gear. His heartbeat finally began to slow.

In the days that followed, the Wolves discovered their first-round playoff opponent—an established team with a deeper roster and home-ice advantage. Analysts pegged the Wolves as underdogs, citing their inconsistent regular season and squeaker of a playoff qualification. But Doug felt a renewed sense of possibility. *Once you're in, anything can happen,* he told himself, echoing a well-worn hockey mantra.

Despite the swirl of external opinions, the team doubled down on preparation. Practices intensified, focusing on specialized systems for the playoffs. Doug pored over video of their upcoming opponent, dissecting forechecks and power-play formations. In the weight room, he did extra sets, determined to be physically ready for the playoff grind—a known war of attrition. The anxiety he'd felt before was still present—this was new, high-stakes territory—but it morphed into a purposeful energy.

He also realized that the margin for error in the playoffs was razor-thin. *A single miscue can cost us a game, maybe the series.* That knowledge fueled his attention to detail, whether it was defensive zone coverage or making a safer pass on a breakout. He could feel his teammates exhibiting a similar focus, each player grappling with the weight of a city's hopes.

As the first playoff game approached, Doug wrestled with moments of self-doubt. Lying in bed at the billet family's house, he'd stare at the ceiling, recalling every brutal highlight reel of playoff heartbreak he'd ever seen: last-minute collapses, goaltenders letting in soft goals, top players choking under pressure. He shuddered at the thought of being the goat in a big moment, letting the team down when it mattered most.

Yet he also remembered his journey—how he overcame early stumbles, the intense fights, the bus fiasco, the pressures of mid-season. He'd grown from each challenge, forging resilience. That gave him confidence that he could handle whatever the playoffs threw at him. If adversity came, he'd face it head-on, just like he'd done all year.

Coach Melrose and the staff tried to keep the mood balanced: acknowledging the playoffs' significance without letting the pressure paralyze them. The morning of Game 1, the Wolves had a light skate, focusing on breakouts and special teams. Doug took extra reps, perfecting quick one-timers from the high slot. Afterward, the players retreated to a short team meeting, where the coach laid out the series strategy. Then they had the afternoon to rest, eat, and mentally prepare for the biggest stage yet.

On the eve of the playoffs, local media swarmed for interviews. Doug faced a small group of reporters in the rink hallway. One asked how it felt heading into his first OHL postseason. Doug admitted his nerves but stressed that he was eager to embrace the challenge. "This is what we play for," he said. "All season long, we've wanted this shot. I'm gonna give it everything I have."

Afterwards, while walking back to the locker room, Doug noticed new banners hung around the arena that read: *"Playoff Bound—Believe in the Wolves!"* The same fans who once doubted them now bristled with excitement at the possibility of a Cinderella run. Doug recognized the precariousness of that label—*Cinderella stories* often ended in heartbreak. But he appreciated the faith behind those banners. For a small-town market that had endured many losing seasons, just making the playoffs felt like a triumph.

Yet for Doug, it wasn't enough to merely show up. He wanted to help the Wolves push beyond the first round, to keep playing until the final buzzer of the final game. Even if external analysts dismissed them as a stepping stone for the top seeds, Doug believed in the power of a united locker room. *We've seen glimpses of what we can do. If we stay disciplined, who says we can't surprise the league?*

That night, Doug found a rare pocket of solitude in the dimly lit corridor outside the locker room. Practice was done. The arena was mostly empty. He paced slowly along the boards, letting the echoes of his footsteps mix with faint mechanical hums from the ice resurface system. In less than 24 hours, the Wolves would face their toughest challenge yet, carrying the hopes of a city on their shoulders.

He paused at the center line, imagining the stands packed, the playoff logos on the ice, the tension so thick it could be sliced with a skate blade. He pictured himself stepping onto that stage—heart pounding, adrenaline surging, every shift a test of will. He felt a flicker of anxiety, but also a calming thrill. *I'm ready,* he told himself quietly, words dissipating in the hush. *I'm exactly where I want to be.*

Glancing down at the ice, he saw the reflection of fluorescent lights shimmering in the freshly resurfaced surface. He recalled how far he'd come since his first days in the league, shaky and uncertain, just hoping to earn a roster spot. Now, he was a key contributor, a forward capable of changing the momentum of a game. The playoffs would be a new mountain to climb, but the lessons from the season—about camaraderie, discipline, controlled aggression, and resilience—flickered in his mind like guiding beacons.

He inhaled, stepping toward the exit. As he did, he noticed Coach Melrose watching from the corridor. Their eyes met, and the coach gave a small nod. No words were exchanged, but a mutual understanding passed between them: *We're going into battle. Let's give it everything.*

The next day's game would officially launch the Wolves into the playoff realm, but for Doug, the shift in mindset had already begun. Anxiety and expectation coexisted in his heart, fueling a heightened focus on every drill, every shift. He recognized this feeling—a blend of excitement and fear, pushing him to be his best.

Before heading home to rest, Doug spent a few more moments in the empty arena, closing his eyes, soaking in the silent promise of possibility. He pictured the opening faceoff, the roar of fans, the sharp scrape of skates on ice. In his mind's eye, he visualized the final buzzer sounding in the Wolves' favor. He let that vision settle into his bones, giving him a sense of calm.

No matter what the final scoreboard showed in the upcoming series, Doug knew one thing: they belonged here. The Wolves had earned their spot through grit and determination, squeaking into the postseason but forging a team identity that could stand up to any challenge. Now it was time to seize the moment.

And so, as Doug left the rink and stepped into the cool northern Ontario evening, a soft wind rustling the fading patches of snow, he carried that sense of purpose within him.

Tomorrow, we start a new chapter. I'll embrace the intensity, push through the nerves, and give everything I have for this team.

This was his first taste of high-stakes playoff hockey—where legends are born, heartbreak is real, and every shift could define a legacy. His shoulders felt the weight of a city's hopes, but also the strong arms of teammates, staff, and fans ready to lift him up. With a determined set of his jaw, he headed off into the night, heart pulsing with the electric possibility that the playoffs promised.

15

FIRST ROUND OF PLAYOFFS

Doug stood in the narrow hallway that led to the visiting locker room, glancing up at the battered steel door. On the other side, the roar of the crowd reverberated in the concrete corridor, signaling the raucous anticipation of playoff hockey. His stomach fluttered. This was it—his first postseason series in the Ontario Hockey League. The North Shore Wolves had squeaked into the playoffs, and now they found themselves facing a physical, battle-tested team in a best-of-seven opening round.

"You good?" asked **Kyle Sutton**, sidling up to Doug with a stick slung across his shoulders. Sutton's normally brash attitude took on a more serious note in the playoffs, but he still attempted a faint grin.

Doug forced a smile back. "Yeah," he managed, voice tense. "A little nervous, but ready."

Sutton clapped Doug on the shoulder pads. "Better to be nervous than complacent. This is a different beast, Mansfield. Be prepared for war."

The door swung open, and a wave of arena noise crashed into them. Doug steeled himself, stepping into the bright lights of the rink. Their opponents, the Kingston Titans—a heavy-hitting squad known for wearing down rivals—were already on the ice, warming up in their dark red jerseys. Fans clamored on both sides of the boards, caught up in the energy of a new playoff season. It felt like the entire building was vibrating.

Doug inhaled the cold, sharp air, letting it jolt him awake. *Stay focused,* he told himself. The previous week had been an anxious lull of waiting and preparing. Now the Wolves would attempt to prove they belonged in the playoffs. This opening series would test them in ways the regular season never had.

From the opening puck drop of Game 1, Doug realized that playoff hockey demanded a new level of grit and intensity. Every shift was contested with punishing checks. The Titans' defensemen, each built like a freight train, closed gaps quickly and finished hits with authority. Within Doug's first two shifts, he got crushed along the boards, rattling his teeth and sending a dull ache through his shoulder. It was a brutal wake-up call. *They're stronger, faster, and they're not giving an inch.*

The scoreboard remained locked in a tight contest, with both teams trading punishing forechecks. Although the Wolves had found synergy late in the regular season, they struggled to find open lanes against Kingston's defensive shell. Doug's line, featuring Sutton and **Matty Roy**, managed a few shots on net but lacked the time and space they'd grown used to. In the stands, fans from both teams roared at every collision, fueling the heat on the ice.

Late in the second period, Kingston capitalized on a defensive turnover, scoring a scrappy goal off a rebound. 1–0. Despite furious attempts in the third, the Wolves couldn't solve the Titans' goalie, who seemed locked in. The final buzzer spelled a hard-fought 1–0 loss for North Shore.

In the locker room afterward, no one was panicking, but Doug could see the tightness in everyone's expressions. They'd discovered just how grueling playoff hockey could be. "We gotta keep pushing," muttered Jeremy, the chirpy defenseman, wincing as he gingerly removed a shoulder pad. "We can't let them bully us around."

Coach Melrose addressed them calmly. "This was a one-goal game. Stay composed. Find ways to crack their defense. We'll adjust."

Doug sank onto the bench, rubbing the soreness in his elbow. He felt the sting of the loss but also a spark of determination. This wasn't going to be an easy series. *Time to dig deeper.*

The Wolves indeed dug deeper in Game 2, determined to avoid going home down two games. They matched Kingston's physicality from the start, finishing checks along the boards. Doug took a cue from the veterans, planting his body hard on opposing players whenever possible. Though he lacked their sheer size, his relentless effort wore on defenders, forcing quick mistakes.

Midway through the second period, with the game again scoreless, Doug capitalized on a neutral zone turnover. He dashed into the offensive zone, used a quick curl-and-drag move to dodge a sprawling defenseman, and snapped a wrist shot high to the goalie's glove side. The puck zipped into the net, electrifying the Wolves' bench. *One-nothing, we're leading.*

A swell of pride surged in Doug's chest. In the final stretch of the regular season, he'd worked extensively on that curling wrist shot, figuring it might come in handy in tight situations. Here it was, paying dividends at the perfect time. The rest of the team fed off his goal, potting an insurance marker minutes later. Though Kingston fought back, the Wolves' netminder held strong, sealing a 2–1 victory.

Exhausted but elated, Doug and his teammates headed back home with the series tied 1–1. The tension in the locker room felt slightly lighter, but no one underestimated the challenges ahead. If Games 1 and 2 were any indication, this series would be a grind.

For Games 3 and 4, the series shifted to North Shore's home ice. The small-town fans, starved for playoff excitement, packed the arena to capacity. Homemade signs and thunderous applause rattled the glass. Local kids wore Wolves jerseys with Doug's number, emulating their new heroes. The players soaked in the energy—this was precisely why they fought so hard to make the postseason.

Game 3 began with a flourish. The Wolves, feeding off the crowd, struck early. Doug contributed an assist, threading a perfect cross-ice pass to Roy for a backdoor tap-in. The building erupted, chanting "Wolves! Wolves!" at a deafening pitch. Kingston, however, responded with aggression, ramping up the physical play. Big hits and face-washes after whistles became common. Referees struggled to keep a lid on the simmering animosity.

In a hectic third period, the Wolves coughed up a lead, allowing Kingston to force overtime. Tensions spiked. One slip would cost them the game. In OT, a scrappy goal-mouth scramble ended with Sutton poking the puck past the Titans' goalie. The place went berserk—3–2 OT win for North Shore. Doug, drenched in sweat, hugged his teammates, ears ringing from the roar. They led the series 2–1.

However, Game 4 saw the Titans bounce back. Their punishing forecheck pinned the Wolves in their zone for extended stretches. Doug felt like he was battling waves of relentless attacks. The scoreboard eventually read 4–2 in

Kingston's favor. The series was knotted again at 2–2. The drawn-out collisions, bruises, and close scores underscored that neither side would surrender easily.

By Game 5, the physical toll on both rosters was apparent. Players sported ice packs on bruised limbs between games, and the mood grew more short-tempered each passing day. For Doug, every muscle ached. He recalled rumors that playoff hockey was "a different level of war." Now he understood. *This is about who endures, not just who's more skilled.*

On the ice, even routine faceoffs turned into mini-battles. Doug noticed how quickly tempers flared with each questionable hit or jab. The referees tried to maintain order, but scuffles broke out regularly. Game 5, played in Kingston's barn, turned into a defensive slugfest with few clean rushes. Doug's line was effectively neutralized by the Titans' top defense pair, and the Wolves struggled to find scoring opportunities. The Titans squeaked out a 2–1 victory, grabbing a 3–2 series lead.

In the post-game locker room, a somber hush fell over the Wolves. They were one loss from elimination. Coach Melrose addressed them in a low, urgent voice: "We've come too far to fold now. We need more grit, more trust in our game. Believe in each other, or we're done."

Doug sat in silence, eyes downcast, feeling the magnitude of the next game. Returning home for Game 6, they'd have to stave off elimination. The pressure was suffocating, but beneath the anxiety was a flicker of determination: *We're not going out like this.*

The atmosphere for Game 6 in North Shore was electric. No seat was left unsold, and hundreds more fans crowded outside to watch on outdoor screens. The local media ramped up coverage, proclaiming a do-or-die scenario. Doug could hardly breathe during warm-ups, his heart pounding with the knowledge that if they lost, the season was over.

But the Wolves refused to let the story end there. They jumped out with ferocious energy, hammering Kingston at every turn. Doug and Roy combined on a brilliant passing sequence early, resulting in a 1–0 lead. The crowd roared in euphoric relief. Later, Sutton decked one of Kingston's star forwards with a clean but devastating check, setting the tone that the Wolves wouldn't be bullied on home ice.

The third period opened with a tense 2–2 tie. Doug, battered and sore, tapped reserves of willpower he didn't know he had. Midway through the period, on a rare 2-on-1 break, Doug faked a pass, snapped a wrist shot short side, and watched it rocket past the goalie's glove. 3–2. He felt the weight of the world lift momentarily, arms raised in triumph.

Kingston launched a desperate assault in the final minutes, pulling their goalie for an extra attacker. The Wolves bent but didn't break, blocking shots with reckless abandon. When the final horn sounded, Doug collapsed to his knees, relief flooding him as the scoreboard read 3–2 Wolves. The series was tied 3–3, forcing a decisive Game 7. The fans rejoiced, chanting Doug's name, exalting him for that crucial go-ahead goal. Despite the euphoria, Doug knew the hardest challenge lay ahead.

Game 7. The two most harrowing words in playoff hockey. Tied 3–3, the series would come down to a single night—winner advances, loser goes home. The Wolves would have to travel back to Kingston's barn, an arena where the hostility was sure to be palpable. The day before the game felt like suspended time. Doug tried to rest, but his body and mind whirled with anticipation.

He studied game tape like never before, zeroing in on how Kingston might adjust. He gleaned clues: a slower defenseman on their second pair, a forward prone to risky turnovers. Meanwhile, the team medical staff patched up bruises and scrapes. Coach Melrose gave short, pointed instructions, not wanting to overload players with new tactics. "We know them, they know us. It's about execution and heart," he said simply.

In quiet moments, Doug wrestled with nerves. *What if I cost the team with a mistake?* But he reminded himself of the journey so far—he'd grown stronger through every challenge, from rookie uncertainties to suspension controversies to last-minute playoff qualification. *I can do this.* He found solace in thoughts of family, friends, and fans who believed in him.

From the moment they stepped onto the ice for Game 7, the tension in Kingston's arena felt suffocating. Over ten thousand fans jammed the stands, many wearing the Titans' colors, jeering the Wolves at every turn. But a contingent of North Shore supporters—traveling on buses and braving rowdy hostility—stood behind the Wolves bench, hoisting signs and chanting. Doug took heart in their presence, telling himself: *We're not alone.*

The first period was a frenzied mix of physical collisions and defensive posturing. No one wanted to be the first to err. Doug's line established a decent cycle in the offensive zone, generating a few dangerous chances. Yet, the Titans' goalie stood tall. At the other end, the Wolves' netminder made heroic stops, including a sprawling pad save that kept the game scoreless.

Midway through the second, Kingston broke through. A defensive lapse freed their sniper, who blasted a one-timer from the slot. 1–0 for the home side. The crowd erupted, shaking the rafters. Doug skated back to the bench, feeling a clutch of anxiety. *We can't let them run away with this.*

The Wolves answered late in the second, courtesy of a deflection by Roy. The scoreboard read 1–1 heading into the final period. Skating off for the intermission, Doug felt like his legs were weighted with concrete. The cumulative exhaustion of the series pressed on his muscles, but he forced himself forward. *Twenty minutes, maybe more,* he thought. *We can survive this.*

The third period featured heart-stopping rushes both ways, each team laying everything on the ice. A Wolves penalty put them on their heels, but they killed it off with desperate shot blocks. Doug flinched as a slapshot ricocheted off his shin, sending pain shooting up his leg. He kept skating. The scoreboard stuck at 1–1, an agonizing standoff.

Regulation ended in a tie—a microcosm of the entire series. Tension soared as both teams prepped for sudden-death overtime. One goal would decide who advanced and who faced a summer of regrets.

Overtime in Game 7 was hockey at its most brutal and beautiful. The Wolves and Titans exchanged furious chances, each shift a life-or-death scenario. Doug's breath grew ragged, adrenaline the only thing keeping him upright. He refused to let exhaustion crush him, though it nipped at every muscle fiber.

Ten minutes into overtime, the Titans nearly ended it on a breakaway. Their forward streaked in alone, but the Wolves' goalie stoned him with a brilliant glove save. Doug exhaled a shaky breath, relief flooding him. The entire bench hammered their sticks on the boards, gratitude palpable.

Moments later, the Wolves struck back. Roy chipped the puck out to center ice, and Doug scooped it up, noticing a glimmer of open ice. He stormed across the blue line, a Titan defenseman looming. Doug faked wide, cut inside, and unleashed a blistering wrist shot aimed high to the far corner. The goalie lunged, catching a piece of it, but the puck fluttered behind him. Time seemed to slow as it trickled over the goal line. **Goal.**

The red light flashed, and Doug watched the net ripple. A half-second of stunned silence gripped the arena. Then the Wolves bench erupted. Doug let out a roar, raising his arms to the rafters. That was it—the game, the series, decided by a single shot in overtime of Game 7.

Wolves players streamed off the bench, piling onto Doug in a frenzied celebration. Their cheers mixed with boos and shock from the Kingston crowd, who realized their team's season was over. Doug, pinned beneath a mass of hugging teammates, felt tears prick at the corners of his eyes. This series had demanded every ounce of willpower, and the Wolves had triumphed.

The post-game handshake line was emotional. The Titans, stunned by the heartbreak, offered terse "good series" handshakes. Doug could see the devastation in their eyes; it reminded him how razor-thin the margin had been. A bounce here, a bounce there, and it might've been the Wolves sulking.

After that, the Wolves lingered on the ice, saluting their traveling fans, who hollered themselves hoarse. Doug, still riding an adrenaline rush, accepted pats on the back and praise for his lethal wrist shot. His entire body throbbed in protest— he had bruises up and down his arms, hips, and legs. But none of that mattered now. He'd scored the biggest goal of his career to date.

Reporters swarmed, hungry for quotes. Doug, breathless, tried to articulate how it felt to earn his first playoff series win. "This is insane," he said, sweat dripping down his face. "I'm proud of our whole team. We battled so hard all series, and it came down to one shot in OT. I'm just... speechless."

In the locker room, the atmosphere was pandemonium: players shouting, hugging, laughing, some even crying. The staff popped a few bottles of soda in lieu of champagne, given the junior rules. Coach Melrose made a short speech, praising their resilience. "This is what playoff hockey is about," he said, voice thick with emotion. "You went to hell and back, and you came out on top. Now, let's keep it going."

The bus ride back to North Shore was a blur of exhaustion and giddy celebration. Some players dozed off immediately, while others rehashed every key play of the series. Doug found a seat near the window, gazing at the dark highway. His shoulder throbbed, and his shins felt bruised from countless blocked shots. But a deep satisfaction coursed through him.

He replayed the overtime winner in his head: the subtle drag of his stick, the release of that practiced wrist shot, the puck trickling in. Months of extra reps, mental fortitude, and team support had converged in that defining moment. Despite the physical toll—he'd probably need ice packs for days—Doug felt unstoppable in that moment.

A few seats away, Sutton offered a tired grin, raising a plastic water bottle in an impromptu toast. Doug returned the gesture, each acknowledging how far they'd come from the season's uncertain beginning. They'd earned the chance to keep chasing a championship, no matter how daunting the next round might be.

Doug arrived home in the early morning hours, body aching but heart still buzzing. After a quick shower, he sank into bed. Despite the exhaustion, his mind wouldn't rest. Images of the series flashed by—big hits, blocked shots, heartbreak and euphoria. He'd discovered a new threshold for pain, willpower, and emotional intensity. Playoff hockey demanded you give everything, and then some.

He also recognized how reliant he was on his teammates. Each night, someone new stepped up—Roy burying key goals, Sutton delivering momentum-shifting checks, Jeremy flustering opponents with chirps and cunning plays. The Wolves were more than a collection of skilled individuals; they'd become a battle-hardened unit, forging a bond under relentless pressure.

Closing his eyes, Doug reflected on the final horn, the swirl of black jerseys mobbing him, the improbable victory in enemy territory. A grin tugged at his lips. This was only his first series, but it already felt monumental. He'd glimpsed how quickly momentum could shift, how close the line between victory and defeat really was. That fine margin, that desperation, made the payoff immeasurably sweeter.

And as Doug drifted toward sleep, he allowed himself a fleeting moment to savor the milestone. He'd won his first playoff series in dramatic style, proving himself in the crucible of seven grueling games. Tomorrow, he would worry about ice baths, looming opponents, and the next round's challenges. Tonight, he was a victor, exhausted yet exhilarated by the war he'd survived on the ice.

16

SECOND ROUND OF PLAYOFFS

Doug's lungs still burned from the final shift of the previous series when he stepped off the bus in the next rival city. Exhaustion clung to him like a second skin—even the short ride from North Shore to this big-market town felt draining. But the playoff schedule allowed little time for recovery. Fresh off their harrowing seven-game victory in the first round, the Wolves were thrust immediately into the second round against a powerhouse team that carried swagger and resources the small-market club could only dream of.

As Doug rolled his duffel bag off the bus, he stole a quick glance at the imposing arena looming ahead: sleek glass panels, corporate sponsorships emblazoned on every surface, banners of past league champions hanging inside. *This place screams money,* Doug thought wryly. The local press had already pegged the Wolves as heavy underdogs—typical of a small-market squad fighting a glitzy franchise known for deeper rosters, bigger budgets, and well-known prospects.

Doug shrugged off the outside chatter. He was here to compete, to push the Wolves as far as they could go. If last series had taught him anything, it was that grit and teamwork could topple even the most fearsome opponents. *They may be favorites on paper, but we'll see what happens on the ice.*

From the first puck drop, Doug sensed the elevated skill level. This big-market rival—let's call them the **Bayfield**

Falcons—carried lines stacked with top draft picks and veterans who'd logged multiple OHL playoff runs. Their forecheck was punishing, but more impressively, their puck movement was crisp and efficient. Doug and his linemates found themselves chasing the play more than controlling it, forced to rely on disciplined defensive coverage to keep the score tight.

Game 1 unfolded at breakneck pace. Doug's legs still felt heavy from the grueling seven-game slugfest against Kingston, but adrenaline spurred him to keep up. Midway through the first period, he intercepted a pass at the Falcons' blue line, surging in for a partial breakaway. The roar of the crowd echoed in his ears—*a different crowd now,* mostly Falcons fans wearing their stylish team jerseys. Doug fired a quick low wrister, trying to tuck it through the goalie's five-hole. The netminder clamped his pads shut in time, swallowing Doug's scoring attempt. A chorus of cheers (for the save) and groans (from the traveling Wolves fans) filled the arena.

By the third period, the Wolves trailed 3–2, valiantly hanging on. Doug nearly tied it with a late one-timer from the slot, but the goalie slid post-to-post with a remarkable pad stop. The final horn sealed a 3–2 Falcons victory, though the Wolves had shown flashes of competitiveness. In the locker room afterward, Doug tried to focus on positives, but the frustrations leaked out in the form of terse swearing and exhausted sighs. They'd expended so much energy just to keep up.

Coach Melrose delivered a measured post-game talk: "They're deep, yes, but we stayed within one shot. We can push them harder. Recuperate, study tape, and we'll come out stronger next time." Doug nodded, though inside he felt worry gnaw at him. *This second round is going to be even harder than the first,* he realized.

Game 2 arrived after a short turnaround, leaving little time for the Wolves to heal their bruises. Doug's hips still ached from board battles. His left shoulder, jarred in the previous series, flared with each explosive stride. Yet he laced up with grim resolve. It wasn't just him—some players wore protective braces, others taped ankles, wrists, or ribs. The playoffs, he realized, were as much a war of attrition as a showcase of skill.

In that second game, the Falcons flexed their depth. Their top line jumped out to a quick 2–0 lead with dazzling passing that left the Wolves chasing shadows. Mid-game, the Falcons' second line delivered punishing checks below the goal line, cycling the puck relentlessly. The Wolves struggled to maintain possession. Doug fought for every inch, but the scoreboard read 4–2 by the final buzzer, a second straight loss.

Exhausted, he slumped in the locker room, sweat pouring off him. The realization that they were down 2–0 in the series stung. He recalled how in the first round, they'd come back from adversity, but this opponent felt more formidable— faster, deeper, more lethal. A swirl of anxiety twisted in Doug's stomach. *We can't lose confidence now,* he told himself, silently mustering the will to keep believing.

Traveling back to North Shore, the bus ride was subdued. Doug tried to catch some shut-eye, but his mind replayed each shift, searching for missed opportunities. He jotted notes in a small notepad about the Falcons' defense pairs—who pinched aggressively, who left gaps. It gave him a semblance of control over the chaos swirling around him.

Heading into Game 3 on home ice, the Wolves refocused. The local fans packed the small arena, chanting from warm-ups onward. Doug felt that surge of energy whenever the hometown faithful roared, recalling how it helped them in the first round.

This time, the Wolves started strong. Doug's line connected for a quick strike less than five minutes in, a tight pass from **Matty Roy** to Doug in the slot, netting a wrister that finally beat the Falcons' goalie high glove side. The crowd exploded. 1–0. Doug's relief was palpable— *We can do this.*

But mid-second period, tragedy struck. Roy chased a loose puck in the corner, tangling with a Falcons defenseman who delivered a questionable high hit. Roy slammed hard into the boards, and didn't get up. Doug, on the ice at the time, watched in horror as Roy lay motionless. Wolves players converged, tension escalated, but the referees hurriedly intervened. A hush fell over the arena, the worst kind of hush, as medical staff rushed in. Eventually, Roy was helped off on a stretcher, still dazed, blood trickling from a gash above his temple.

Doug's heart hammered. Roy had been a vital presence on that line, not to mention a friend. The bench's mood plummeted. After a brief stoppage, the game resumed, but the Wolves were shaken. The Falcons took advantage, scoring twice to flip the scoreboard 2–1. Doug, reeling, tried to rally his teammates, but they looked shell-shocked. Another late goal sealed a 3–1 Falcons win, handing North Shore a 3–0 deficit in the series.

In the locker room, despair hung thick. Roy's status overshadowed all else. Word soon came that he'd suffered a severe concussion, possibly out for the playoffs. Doug felt anger bubble at the Falcons' physical approach, but also a pang of guilt that he couldn't do more to protect Roy. The battered forward had been a crucial spark, and now he was gone.

Facing a 3–0 hole, the Wolves' situation looked dire. Big-market media outlets dismissed them, proclaiming the Falcons a near-certain sweep. But the Wolves refused to go quietly. Roy's injury became a rallying cry—*win for him,* or at least make the Falcons earn every inch. Coach Melrose shuffled lines, placing Doug alongside new linemates in a bid to spark offense.

Game 4, still at home, felt like a last stand. The crowd roared with urgent intensity, signs reading, *"Do It for Roy!"* Doug took the ice with a heavy heart but a fierce determination. Early in the first period, he assisted on a power-play goal, sliding a cross-ice feed to **Kyle Sutton** for a one-timer that ignited the building. Up 1–0, the Wolves played desperate hockey, finishing checks, blocking shots, diving for loose pucks. By the final horn, they'd eked out a 2–1 victory, staving off elimination. Doug contributed a key insurance goal off his patented wrist shot from the top of the circle. The small arena erupted in cathartic celebration.

In the post-game interviews, Doug dedicated the victory to Roy, expressing hope he'd recover soon. The reporters latched onto the emotional angle. Meanwhile, the Falcons seemed frustrated that the Wolves wouldn't simply roll over.

Returning to the Falcons' arena for Game 5, the tension soared. The city's bright lights and polished rink served as a reminder of the disparity between these franchises. But the Wolves carried newfound momentum. Doug, battered and limping from repeated collisions, refused to let up. He netted two crucial goals, one of them a brilliant solo rush weaving through two defenders—still another demonstration of his blossoming skill under playoff pressure.

That night, the scoreboard favored the Wolves 4–3 in a dramatic finish, pulling the series to 3–2. A hush of disbelief fell over the home crowd, who expected an easy finish. Doug embraced teammates, adrenaline coursing. *We're not done yet,* he thought, breathless, as they hurried off the ice. *We're fighting back.*

By the time Game 6 arrived, the series had morphed into a punishing grind for everyone, especially Doug, whose point production soared but whose body felt like it was being held together by willpower alone. He had bruises on top of bruises, and the constant throbbing in his left shoulder worsened each game. Nights of poor sleep, endless ice packs, and the mental weight of each shift made the exhaustion almost overwhelming.

His billet family noticed how subdued he was off the ice, dragging himself through daily routines. He spoke to his parents in short phone calls, not wanting to alarm them but unable to disguise the fatigue in his voice. They expressed pride and urged him to "listen to your body," but in playoff hockey, resting just wasn't an option.

Game 6, back in North Shore, attracted more media than usual—everyone smelled an improbable comeback. Could the small-market underdogs force Game 7, or would the Falcons reassert dominance? Tensions escalated further when the Falcons started dishing out punishing hits in the first period, determined to quell any upset. A mid-ice collision left one of the Wolves' defensemen hobbling, compounding the mounting injuries.

But Doug kept pushing. He notched the opening goal with a laser wrist shot from the slot, his third tally in as many games. The crowd's euphoria washed over him in waves. He celebrated with Sutton, absorbing the momentary respite from pain. The Falcons clawed back, tying the game. The scoreboard read 2–2 late in the third. Every shift had the crowd on its feet.

In the dying minutes, with the stadium at fever pitch, Doug broke a tie with a quick rebound jam in the crease—3–2 Wolves. The final buzzer unleashed pandemonium: the series was now tied 3–3. Doug leaned against the boards, chest heaving. Exhaustion threatened to drop him on the spot. But triumph reigned. They'd forced Game 7, defying every prediction.

For the second consecutive series, the Wolves faced a deciding Game 7. This time, though, it was in enemy territory, and the Falcons—who had let a 3–0 series lead slip to 3–3— were furious. The local press hammered the team for losing focus. The Falcons coach promised a "no-nonsense performance." Meanwhile, North Shore media praised the Wolves' resilience, with headlines praising Doug as a "clutch performer," highlighting his streak of game-changing goals.

Yet, the cost weighed on everyone. Another do-or-die game, more battered bodies. Doug felt especially drained, physically and mentally. He recalled how draining the first round's seven-game war had been, and now they faced a second such marathon. Could they muster one more upset?

On the eve of Game 7, Coach Melrose kept the message simple: "Play your hearts out. If we lose, let it be with no regrets. If we win, it'll be because we gave everything."

Doug tried to rest. Sleep came fitfully. He dreamt of Roy, still recovering from concussion symptoms. He dreamt of missed shots, of pucks rattling off posts. Waking in a cold sweat, he shook off the nightmares. *Focus on the moment,* he reminded himself.

The Game 7 atmosphere at the Falcons' arena was deafening. Their fans, stung by the near-collapse, were desperate to see their team avoid humiliation. Wolves supporters also showed up in droves, brandishing signs of faith. Doug's stomach churned with adrenaline as he took the warm-up skate, noticing the Falcons circling like predators. *They're going to come at us hard from the drop,* he thought.

He was correct. The Falcons unleashed a furious first period. Their top line pinned the Wolves in the defensive zone for lengthy stretches. The scoreboard soon read 1–0 Falcons off a deflection. But the Wolves refused to break. Their goalie stood on his head, making highlight-reel saves to keep the margin close. Late in the period, Doug's line found a seam on a counterattack. A fast pass from Sutton to Doug in the high slot, and Doug ripped a one-timer that whistled by the goalie's ear. 1–1. The hush that swept the arena was telling—they feared Doug's lethal shot now.

The second period saw a parade of punishing hits. The Wolves lost another player to a leg injury, while the Falcons' star forward took a nasty slash, leaving him hobbled. It was a true war of attrition, each side straining to hold on. By period's end, the scoreboard remained 1–1. The tension around the rink felt like a coiled spring.

In the intermission, Doug could barely stand upright without feeling dizzy. His shoulder burned each time he lifted his stick. But he forced himself to suck down water and protein. *One more period,* he told himself. *Leave nothing behind.*

The third period was a blur of furious back-and-forth action. The Falcons scored early, pouncing on a defensive miscue—2–1. Time ticked ominously. But the Wolves scratched and clawed, eventually equalizing when Sutton banged in a rebound. The scoreboard blinked 2–2 with six minutes left. The crowd volume soared, half roaring with support for the Falcons, half cheering in exasperation, wanting the drama to end.

With under two minutes remaining, the Falcons poured on one last flurry. Doug found himself pinned in the defensive zone, a coil of tension in his chest. Each pass from the Falcons threatened to open a lane. The Wolves blocked shots, scrambled for loose pucks, desperate to cling on. Finally, with under a minute left, a clearing attempt found Doug near the boards. He chipped it out, spun around a hitting attempt, and sprinted up ice.

Suddenly, he realized it was a 2-on-1 break with a younger forward, Drake. The crowd noise crashed in his ears. The defenseman slid across to block a pass, so Doug faked the dish, then snapped a quick shot from the top of the circle. The goalie kicked it aside, but Drake swooped in for the rebound. Another save. The puck popped free behind the net. Doug circled, snagging it, glancing at the clock—thirty seconds. Adrenaline fueling him, he pivoted, fired a tight-angle shot that squeaked through the netminder's pads. The red light ignited. **Goal.** 3–2 Wolves.

Disbelief rippled around the rink, followed by a collective roar from the Wolves' fans and bench. Doug, in shock, skated to the corner, arms raised as teammates mobbed him. Twenty-eight seconds remained on the clock. *Hold the line,* he pleaded silently.

In a final, desperate push, the Falcons hammered the Wolves' zone, but the goalie and defenders blocked every attempt. The final horn blared. 3–2. The Wolves had pulled off an upset, rebounding from a 3–0 series deficit to shock the big-market team in seven games.

The aftermath on the ice was an emotional frenzy. Some Falcons players stood frozen, heads bowed, unable to process how they'd lost. The Wolves, equally stunned, embraced each other in exhausted jubilation. Doug slumped to his knees, tears of relief threatening to spill. His teammates surrounded him, laughing, pounding him on the helmet. He could barely lift his arms but managed a triumphant fist pump for the traveling Wolves supporters.

In the handshake line, a subdued respect passed between teams. The Falcons captain gripped Doug's hand firmly. "Hell of a series," he muttered. Doug nodded, gratitude welling up, thankful for the sportsmanship despite the bruises.

By the time Doug reached the locker room, his body felt like a single, throbbing bruise. Yet, joy and pride warred with the pain. The Wolves had done the unthinkable, surging back from 0–3 to clinch the second-round series, marching onward. The entire squad, battered and worn, erupted in cheers as they recounted key goals, brilliant saves, pivotal moments. Coach Melrose kept it brief, praising their "unbreakable will" and reminding them they had more rounds ahead—though everyone agreed to savor this improbable triumph for the night.

As reporters crowded the hallway, searching for quotes, Doug realized how deeply drained he was—both physically and mentally. The adrenaline that had powered him through the last minutes now vanished, leaving him light-headed and trembling. Still, he forced a smile for the cameras, praising the team's character and giving credit to the injured Roy, who'd texted them supportive messages from home.

In the quiet that followed, Doug collapsed onto a bench, pressing an ice pack to his throbbing shoulder. *Another series awaits,* he told himself with a mix of dread and excitement. The bracket grew narrower, the competition more merciless. *Can I hold up?* Doubt poked at him, but the memory of that final goal glowed inside, reminding him that he could still find magic under extreme pressure.

He joined the rest of the players as they headed to the bus, drifting into the city's neon-lit streets. Fans in Wolves jerseys waved them off, chanting Doug's name. It felt surreal, like a vivid dream. A big-market team had fallen to the scrappy underdog. The Wolves' improbable run continued, and Doug's lethal wrist shot had become a symbol of hope for the entire small-town fanbase.

En route to the next challenge, Doug stared out the window at passing headlights. His body screamed for rest, but his mind refused to settle. *We overcame the second round,* he reminded himself, still in awe of it. Two seven-game wars in a row. The emotional roller coaster had hit new peaks and valleys. Injuries piled up, star players sidelined, new heroes emerging each game. Doug realized how few teams survive such gauntlets unscathed—and how each victory carved a bond in the Wolves' locker room that no adversity could shatter.

He recalled Roy's absence, how painfully they'd missed him, how they'd rallied in his name. In a perfect world, Roy might return, though a concussion was no minor injury. The playoffs demanded sacrifices. Doug vowed to keep carrying Roy's spirit onto the ice, channeling that gritty determination. *We'll do this for ourselves, for Roy, for the town that adores us.*

Coach Melrose dozed in a nearby seat, lines of fatigue etched on his face. Jeremy half-sat, half-lay across two seats, eyes closed. Sutton scrolled through his phone, possibly reading congratulatory messages from family or checking social media for news of the next round. The bus hummed, a lullaby that made Doug's eyelids grow heavy. But even as he drifted, the throbbing pain in his body reminded him of the price that each playoff victory exacted.

And yet, despite everything—fatigue, injury, pressure—he felt strangely alive. This was playoff hockey at its core: triumph over adversity, forging an unbreakable will, stepping up when the odds seemed impossible. He'd discovered reserves of mental and physical toughness he hadn't known existed.

The Wolves now advanced to the Conference Finals, an achievement few had predicted at the start of the season. The bracket awaited, another formidable opponent eager to crush them. Doug smiled faintly in the darkness of the bus, letting the seat cradle his exhausted form. He wasn't naive—more punishing hits, more stressful overtime periods, more heartbreak or glory awaited them. But after surviving two epic rounds, Doug and the Wolves felt unstoppable in their unity.

He closed his eyes, recalling the final vision of that game-winning goal floating past the Falcons' goalie. The pure joy that exploded within him. He clung to that memory like a talisman, letting it guide him forward. Tomorrow, the spotlight and hype would intensify, but tonight, he let relief and satisfaction wash over him. The second round had tested his resilience, demanded he step up after losing a key linemate. He answered with clutch performances and unwavering heart.

In the hush of the bus's dim interior, Doug drifted toward restless sleep, content that, for now, the Wolves had conquered another giant. The roar of the crowd, the bitter taste of blood on his lip, the frigid shock of ice packs on battered limbs—

these were the raw materials of a playoff journey that shaped him at every step. He embraced it all, prepared to stand tall against whatever lay beyond this night.

17

THIRD ROUND OF PLAYOFFS

Doug paced the locker room floor, helmet cradled under his arm, trying to quell the surge of jitters coursing through his veins. He had been here before—twice, in fact, in these playoffs alone. Seven-game wars, do-or-die nights, triumphant upsets. But now, stepping into the conference finals, the stakes soared higher than ever. If the last two series tested the Wolves' resolve, this next one threatened to shred it to ribbons.

They were up against the **Midland Monarchs**, a stacked powerhouse boasting multiple future first-round NHL picks and a star forward who led the league in points during the regular season. Media pundits across the OHL predicted a short series, convinced the small-market Wolves would finally meet their match. But Doug and his teammates refused to listen. After toppling two formidable opponents already, they believed they had the heart to go all the way.

Yet, conviction didn't dissolve the anxiety swirling in Doug's stomach. His body still ached—his left shoulder perpetually tender, shin bruises from blocked shots, countless sore spots from relentless hits. The same was true for every Wolves player: everyone's body was battered, each fresh collision layering new pain on top of old. And they hadn't even dropped the puck yet in Game 1 of the conference finals.

Coach Melrose eventually strode in, commanding the group's attention with a subtle wave. Around the tight ring of players, the hush was absolute. Doug felt eyes flick toward him; after a grueling second-round comeback, he'd emerged as more than just a young forward with a lethal wrist shot—he'd become one of the locker room's emotional sparks. Tonight, he sensed the team needed more than just his goals. They needed his voice.

The Midland Monarchs were everything the Wolves were not: a big-market team loaded with top prospects, wealthy owners, state-of-the-art facilities, and a rabid fanbase accustomed to deep playoff runs. Their top line featured a star forward, **Ethan Blackwood**, whose blistering speed and highlight-reel goals dominated OHL coverage. Meanwhile, the Monarchs' second and third lines were hardly any weaker, each humming with skillful, physically imposing players.

When Doug had studied game footage in the days leading up to the series, he marveled at how effortlessly the Monarchs transitioned from defense to offense. Their special teams units were lethal—power-play cycles that often looked unstoppable, penalty kills that turned into breakaway threats. On paper, it seemed the Monarchs had no weaknesses.

Still, the Wolves refused to adopt a defeatist mentality. They'd forged an identity through adversity: small-market underdogs fueled by camaraderie, grit, and a refusal to quit. They'd rallied behind injured players like **Matty Roy**, who still lingered on the sidelines after a brutal concussion. They'd survived multiple overtimes, a 3–0 series hole, and the wear-and-tear of two best-of-seven wars. Now, in the conference finals, they stared down another mountain. If they were to climb it, they'd need every ounce of perseverance left in their battered bodies.

The first game arrived on Midland's home ice, an arena that dwarfed North Shore's by a wide margin. Spotlights danced across the rafters, and thousands of fans in the Monarchs' regal purple jerseys roared as their team hit the ice. Doug stepped out to a cacophony of boos that barely registered as personal—this was playoff animosity incarnate. He scanned the stands, noting the small pocket of Wolves supporters valiantly waving banners. That small cheering section would have to be enough moral support in hostile territory.

From the initial puck drop, the Monarchs showcased why they led the league. Their crisp passing left the Wolves chasing the play. Blackwood, the star forward, orchestrated attacks with uncanny vision. Within ten minutes, Midland struck twice—one goal on a perfectly executed odd-man rush, another on a lethal power-play one-timer. The scoreboard flashed 2–0 before the Wolves had even found their legs.

Doug tried to calm the bench, reminding his teammates to stick to Coach Melrose's game plan: tight defense, disciplined positioning, quick counterattacks. Late in the first period, the Wolves mustered a response. Doug fed a puck to **Kyle Sutton** streaking down the right wing, and Sutton's snipe made it 2–1. But the Monarchs fired back in the second period with two more goals, turning the game into a lopsided affair.

Desperation seeped into the Wolves' play. Bodies collided more fiercely, but the Monarchs seemed unphased, matching every hit and then using their superior depth to wear down North Shore's lines. By night's end, the final buzzer sealed a 5–2 victory for the Monarchs. Doug felt frustration gnaw at him. They'd been outclassed, outskated, outshot. The scoreboard told the story, but the bruises forming on Doug's shins and shoulders underlined it even more harshly: this series would be a war of attrition on a new level.

In the locker room, Coach Melrose reminded them not to overreact to a single game. "We've seen adversity before," he said firmly. "They're strong, yes, but we can push them off their game. Adjust, focus, and come back harder." Doug soaked in the words, though the 0–1 hole weighed heavily.

Before Game 2, Doug sensed the mood in the Wolves' locker room dip precariously. Some guys had glazed looks, likely replaying the previous defeat. Others were taping sticks in grim silence, bracing for another potential thrashing. Realizing the risk of mental collapse, Doug decided to speak up. He rose from his stall, addressing the group.

"Look," he began, swallowing the lump in his throat. He wasn't used to giving speeches, but the quiet tension demanded it. "We knew they were good. No surprises there. But if we play scared or intimidated, we're done. We've shown we can handle big-market teams, we can handle star forwards, we can handle it all. We just need to believe, to stick to our identity." He glanced at battered teammates. "We didn't fight through two insane rounds just to fold now. Let's dig deeper."

He saw nods from a few veterans, a flicker of determination lighting their eyes. Coach Melrose watched from across the room, a faint smile acknowledging that Doug had become more than a quiet contributor—he was stepping into a leadership void left by Roy's absence. The speech wasn't fancy or polished, but it carried sincerity, and the locker room rallied behind it.

When the puck dropped for Game 2, the Wolves burst out with renewed fire. They finished every check, clogged shooting lanes, forced the Monarchs to fight for each zone entry. Doug noticed frustration creeping into the faces of Midland's top line as the Wolves stifled their usual fluid passing. Scoreless well into the second period, tension in the stands built. The Wolves thrived in these grinding, low-scoring affairs.

Late in the second, a scuffle behind the net left the Monarchs penalty-killing. Doug's power-play unit took the ice. Showing remarkable patience, they cycled the puck around the perimeter, searching for a seam. Finally, Doug faked a slapshot, dishing a perfect cross-ice pass to a wide-open defenseman, who rifled it top shelf. 1–0 Wolves. The bench erupted, and Doug felt a surge of relief—he might be overshadowed by the Monarchs' star, but his steady playmaking was making a difference.

The third period devolved into a defensive slog as the Monarchs threw everything at the Wolves' net. With under a minute left, the Monarchs netminder left for an extra attacker. Doug blocked a shot at the blue line, chipped the puck forward, and watched it skip into the empty net. 2–0. Triumph soared through the Wolves. They'd stolen Game 2, tying the series at 1–1. Doug's two-point night reaffirmed how crucial his leadership could be—on the scoreboard as well as off.

Bringing the series home, the Wolves faced a frenzy of local fans eager to see if their team could truly knock off the heavily favored Monarchs. Doug stepped into the small-town arena, the noise hitting him like a gale. Signs praising "Doug's Dishes" and "#29 for the Win" dotted the stands, while others simply roared the team's name. The swirling excitement pressed on Doug's battered body, fueling him with adrenaline.

Game 3 proved another tight contest, though the Monarchs struck first on a slick breakaway from none other than **Ethan Blackwood**. The Wolves battled back, with Doug assisting on a key second-period goal that knotted the game 2–2. In the third period, the Monarchs showcased their depth once more, scoring twice in the span of three minutes. Despite a late flurry from Doug's line, the Wolves fell 4–3, giving the Monarchs a 2–1 series lead.

Game 4 was a classic playoff epic: intense, physical, and overshadowed by Blackwood's star power. He potted two highlight-reel goals, overshadowing Doug's steady play. Still, the Wolves refused to cave. Late in the third, tied 3–3, Doug orchestrated a beautiful passing sequence that ended in a Wolves forward tapping the puck into a gaping net. 4–3, final. The series tied again at 2–2. The crowd's roar left ears ringing, and Doug's heart hammered as he left the ice. Another war, another tie series. The mental and physical toll crept higher by the day.

At 2–2, the conference finals had become an all-out war of attrition. The Wolves and Monarchs ventured back to Midland for a pivotal Game 5. This time, the game spilled into multiple overtimes, a marathon of pure endurance. Doug skated shift after shift, lungs searing, legs trembling from exhaustion. Each line change felt like an unsteady cliff edge, with every pass or shot carrying the power to end the night.

In the second overtime, the Monarchs capitalized on a chaotic scramble in front of the Wolves' net. A rebound slipped through the goalie's pads, crowning the Monarchs 3–2 double-OT winners. Doug hunched over his stick, gasping for air. The scoreboard glowed ominously: series 3–2 Monarchs. If the Wolves wanted a shot at the finals, they'd have to stave off elimination—again.

As the Wolves trudged to the locker room, the atmosphere weighed heavy, hearts pounding with an uncomfortable sense of déjà vu. They'd been here in the first round, they'd been here in the second. Could they keep summoning the will to push beyond another 3–2 deficit?

Before Game 6, back in North Shore, Doug sensed morale wavering. The younger guys looked utterly spent. Some veterans nursed undisclosed injuries that limited their shifts. Even the coaches wore the strain of a playoff run extended by multiple OT games. The Monarchs, with their deeper lines and star power, seemed unstoppable if they pressed the advantage.

But Doug refused to let despair sink in. He gathered the team in a small circle near the whiteboard after Coach Melrose concluded his customary talk. Clearing his throat, he spoke:

"I know we're hurting. Hell, I'm hurting everywhere. But no one gave us a chance to get this far. And each time we've been cornered, we've found a way. We're more than just a Cinderella team. We've proven we can win these battles. If we let our hearts lead us, we'll force Game 7. We'll push them to the edge, just like we did in every round."

He saw nods around the circle, a flicker of determination kindling in tired eyes.

Doug drew a breath. "This is our building. Our fans. Let's feed off that. They think their star forward can overshadow us? Fine—let him have his highlight reels. We'll beat them as a team. Now, let's go out there and fight like we have nothing left to lose."

In that moment, Doug fully realized he'd become a leader, not just in goals or assists, but in spirit. The group scattered to finalize gear, each player carrying renewed grit. Coach Melrose shot Doug a small nod of respect. The mantle of leadership weighed heavily on Doug's shoulders, but he wore it with pride.

In the swirling cacophony of fans chanting "Wolves! Wolves!", Doug took the opening faceoff with a grim set to his jaw. The first period was a bruising stalemate, each side delivering thunderous hits. Doug's body screamed with every shift, but the scoreboard remained 0–0 heading into the second.

Early in the middle frame, Midland drew first blood— Blackwood slipped behind the defense, burying a sharp-angle shot. The hush fell over the Wolves crowd. Doug clenched his teeth. *We're not done.* Moments later, on a power play, he threaded a pass from the half-boards to a cutting defenseman, who blasted it in. 1–1. The arena erupted. Midway through the third, Doug assisted again, this time flipping a backhand dish to **Kyle Sutton** at the edge of the crease, making it 2–1 Wolves.

The Monarchs cranked up the pressure, bombarding the Wolves net. Doug found his legs turning to lead, each stride a monumental effort. With under a minute left, Midland pulled their goalie, nearly scoring on a frantic scramble. Doug lunged to swat a loose puck out of the crease, absorbing a slash to the forearm that made him yelp. But the puck cleared the zone, time bled away, and the horn sealed a 2–1 win. The building erupted in a cacophony of triumph.

Series tied 3–3. Once more, a Game 7 stared them down like a final boss. Doug, battered and gasping, couldn't help but laugh at the improbability. Another do-or-die match, another night of fighting through fatigue. The entire team shuffled off to the locker room, half jubilant, half petrified. They'd come this far, but what else did they have left to give?

A swirl of media hype preceded Game 7. This was the third consecutive seven-game series for the Wolves, an OHL record in recent memory. The narrative hinged on two players: Ethan Blackwood, the Monarchs' unstoppable star leading all postseason scorers, and Doug Mansfield, the "quiet hero" whose timely assists and leadership had kept the Wolves afloat. The press framed it as a showdown—flashy prodigy vs. understated workhorse.

Doug felt uncomfortable with the spotlight. He knew Blackwood was generating triple the headlines. The kid was projected to go top five in the upcoming NHL Draft. Doug, overshadowed, quietly accepted that role. He didn't mind—*all I care about is the win,* he told himself. If overshadowed or not, he'd focus on the game.

When the Wolves bus arrived at the Monarchs' gleaming arena for Game 7, Doug felt the weight of the moment press down like a lead blanket. The final in this best-of-seven, a chance to punch a ticket to the league finals, the biggest stage of junior hockey short of the Memorial Cup. The local fans thronged in purple merchandise, booing the Wolves as they emerged. The tension crackled.

Doug's limbs felt heavy in warm-ups, each stride reminding him of bruises, each shot making his wrists ache. But he forced a routine calm, focusing on technique. As the national anthem finished, both teams lined up at center ice, eyes locked in mutual respect and rivalry. The puck dropped, and the frenzy began.

Blackwood took the puck on his first shift, weaving through defenders. The Monarchs established an early lead— 2–0 by the first intermission. The Wolves struggled with energy, pinned in their zone by the Monarchs' relentless cycle. Desperation flickered in their eyes. Doug could feel moral sag.

Between periods, Doug and Coach Melrose did their best to rally the squad. "We've come back from worse," Doug reminded them, voice quavering from sheer exhaustion. "Two goals is nothing if we believe." He slapped sticks with Sutton and a few others, summoning the last vestiges of hope.

The second period saw a furious push. The Wolves hammered the Monarchs' net, outshooting them 14–6. Doug assisted on a deflected shot that found twine. 2–1. The scoreboard gave them a lifeline. Then, with under a minute left in the second, the Monarchs' star forward again worked magic, scorching a top-corner shot past the Wolves' goalie. 3–1. Doug clenched his fists. The crowd roared, sensing the kill.

Backs against the wall, the Wolves threw everything into the third period. They dominated puck possession, hammered the Monarchs physically, and chipped away at the lead with a greasy goal in front—3–2. Doug's line generated rush after rush, but the Monarchs' defense held firm. With two minutes left, the Wolves pulled their goalie. A frantic scramble ensued in the Monarchs' zone, bodies colliding, sticks tangling.

With 34 seconds to go, a glimmer: the puck squirted to Doug at the side of the net. He fired instantly, but the Monarchs goalie lunged, deflecting it wide. Doug hammered his stick in frustration, but the rebound popped out. Sutton flung a backhand through the crease, and it rattled off a defenseman's skate into the net. 3–3 with 28 seconds left. The building erupted in chaotic fury—Wolves fans celebrating, Monarchs fans howling in shock.

Regulation ended in a stalemate. Another Game 7 overtime. Doug stared at the scoreboard, half in disbelief.

We're truly living a script of madness, he thought. The bench was silent except for heavy breathing, half the team bent over in exhaustion. The Monarchs looked equally spent. Blackwood, their star, rested with trainers massaging his cramped legs. Doug's body felt like it was held together by tape and adrenaline.

Stepping onto the ice for overtime, Doug forced clarity into his mind. *We can do this. Stay composed.* The first few minutes saw the Monarchs dominate possession, peppering the Wolves' net with shots. Doug joined a defensive scramble, blocking two attempts in quick succession, wincing at the pain that shot up his ankle.

An accidental high stick drew a Wolves penalty at the seven-minute mark. Doug's heart plummeted. The Monarchs lethal power play, with Blackwood at the helm. The penalty killers (not including Doug, who needed a breather) heroically collapsed in front of the crease, blocking shot after shot. The Wolves goalie made a sprawling glove save on Blackwood's bomb, preserving the tie. The building rattled with tension.

Seconds after the penalty expired, Doug hopped over the boards, feeling a burst of adrenaline. The puck squirted loose in the neutral zone. A perfect pass from Jeremy on defense found Doug breaking wide. He caught glimpses of a Monarch defenseman closing the gap, so he pivoted, waiting for support. Sutton arrived, receiving the handoff. Then, a quick pass returned to Doug in the slot. He fired—clink, off the crossbar. The crowd collectively gasped. So close.

Minutes turned to tense, sweaty hours. The scoreboard read 3–3, the shots piling up. Another intermission loomed if no one scored soon. Doug's legs throbbed with each stride. The Monarchs scrounged a breakaway attempt, but the Wolves netminder stoned them again, disbelief rippling through the stands.

Finally, as the clock neared the fifteen-minute mark of OT, a fluke bounce behind the Monarchs net gave Doug a puck in stride. He curled around the boards, flicked it to a cutting teammate in the slot. The teammate let fly a quick one-timer. The Monarchs goalie slid across but missed it by an inch. The net bulged.

Goal. 4–3 Wolves.

For a split second, hush. Then bedlam. Doug's teammate raised arms in disbelief, the bench spilled onto the ice, and Doug nearly collapsed in joy and sheer exhaustion. They'd done it—**again.** Another seven-game thriller, another OT stunner. The Wolves, battered beyond belief, had upset the star-studded Midland Monarchs to punch their ticket to the OHL Finals.

The handshake line was a blur. Doug found himself face-to-face with Blackwood, the overshadowing superstar. Blackwood removed his helmet, extended a handshake. "Hell of a series, man," he said, voice low. "You guys have serious heart." Doug nodded, speechless with respect and exhaustion. The rest of the Monarchs wore similar shell-shocked expressions; big-market budgets and star players couldn't guarantee a playoff series win against raw determination.

In the locker room, the Wolves celebrated with a mixture of euphoria and tears. Coach Melrose's voice cracked as he congratulated them, reminding them they'd just made franchise history with three consecutive seven-game victories. Some players slumped on benches, too physically spent to cheer. Others cheered for them, pouring water over their heads in spontaneous celebrations. Doug accepted quiet hugs and backslaps, grateful but nearly numb with fatigue.

When local reporters cornered him, praising his steady performances and key assists, he gave half-coherent answers, lauding the entire team's resilience. He deflected comparisons to Blackwood, insisting the Wolves won as a group—unflashy, bruised, but unwavering. One reporter, pressing, asked how it felt to be overshadowed by a star yet still emerging as a crucial piece. Doug shrugged, mustering a smile. "He's an amazing player, no doubt. But we all have roles to play. I'm just proud to do mine."

Only after the adrenaline subsided did Doug realize how deeply he'd grown into a leadership role. He'd delivered speeches to lift morale, offered calm on the bench during frantic sequences, and provided consistent on-ice production that balanced the star power across the ice. Though overshadowed by bigger names, he'd become an anchor— someone the Wolves looked to for reliability. The locker room demanded his voice as much as his wrist shot.

Now, advancing to the OHL Finals, the pinnacle loomed. They'd face another top-tier team, presumably just as formidable, if not more so. The exhaustion from three consecutive Game 7s weighed heavily. The injury list was extensive, with players fighting through fractures, concussions, and battered joints. Doug's own shoulder likely needed thorough rehab come offseason. But for now, there was no turning back. One last series to determine if the small-market Wolves could claim ultimate glory.

At a quiet moment amid the celebration, Doug slipped away to check his phone. Dozens of congratulatory messages poured in—family, old coaches, fans he'd never met. He spotted a text from Roy, who wrote: *"You're unstoppable, man. Finish the job—win it for all of us."* Doug's chest tightened with emotion. They missed Roy's presence, but he'd been with them in spirit. They'd do everything possible to keep pushing.

Eventually, the team boarded the bus back to North Shore, a long, overnight journey with battered bodies dozing in awkward positions. The hush that fell over them wasn't sadness but utter exhaustion. Doug found a seat near the front, letting the hum of the engine and the knowledge of another victory lull him toward rest. The last thing he saw as he closed his eyes was the faint reflection of bruises along his arms—battle scars of a playoff run that refused to end.

He drifted in and out of dreams: Game 7 heroics, Blackwood's speed, the roar of fans, the weight of the upcoming final. Come morning, they'd have a brief window to regroup—ice baths, medical check-ups, strategy sessions. The war of attrition would only grow more brutal. But if the Wolves had proven anything, it was that no adversity could break them.

In the dim quiet, Doug allowed himself a flicker of excitement. They were going to the Finals. Another best-of-seven series, another shot at rewriting small-market history. A swirl of nervous anticipation filled him. Could they conquer a fourth adversary in a row? No one dared to dream of it two months ago, yet here they were.

As the bus's gentle sway cradled him, Doug breathed a silent vow: *We'll fight again, no matter how battered we are. We'll show the league that heart can surpass any star power.* Then, letting his mind drift, he pictured lacing up for the next round, hearing the final buzzer of the final game. He had no illusions—this final step would be the toughest. But that, he realized with a small grin in the darkness, was the nature of playoff hockey. He and the Wolves wouldn't want it any other way.

18

CHAMPIONSHIPS

Doug's breath plumed in the crisp morning air as he stepped off the bus at a small roadside pit stop. Despite the euphoria of winning the conference finals, exhaustion clung to him and his teammates like a second skin. Three seven-game series in a row had left the entire roster battered—he carried bruises on his arms, a tender shoulder that screamed with each shot, and a mental fatigue that no amount of coffee could fully erase. Yet there was no time to rest. The Wolves had done the improbable, earning their place in the OHL championship series. Another best-of-seven battle loomed just days away.

As the team stretched their legs, a dull ache radiated through Doug's thighs. He tried to roll out the stiffness, reminding himself that *this* was why they played junior hockey—to chase a championship. Despite being the underdogs from a small northern town, they'd outlasted teams with bigger budgets and star-studded lineups. Now, only one more mountain remained.

Coach Melrose caught Doug's eye, offering a weary but proud nod. Doug smiled faintly, heart thrumming with anticipation. For all the pain and fatigue, something else simmered inside him: hope. With each improbable comeback, the Wolves had shown a resilience that defied logic. Maybe they had one last magic trick in them for the final series.

Back in North Shore, the local media frothed with excitement at the Wolves' championship berth. No one had expected them to get this far—neither the pundits nor the fans. But the entire town was electrified, storefronts draped in Wolves colors, homemade signs congratulating the team on making the finals. Doug walked through the streets to the arena for practice, greeted by strangers with shouts of "Go Wolves!" or "Bring it home!"

In the locker room, an odd mixture of pride and trepidation hung in the air. The players exchanged banter, but it felt more subdued than usual—everyone recognized the significance of what lay ahead. Doug, who had grown into a de facto leader, tried to lighten the mood. Jokingly, he asked if they should all take "after-midnight runs" like Rocky Balboa. A few chuckles emerged, gratitude for some comedic relief. Yet the undercurrent remained: one final best-of-seven could define their entire season, possibly their junior careers.

The upcoming opponents, the **Eastbrook Blades**, boasted a formidable lineup. They'd dominated their conference, dispatching teams in fewer games, leaving them relatively fresher than the Wolves. They had speed, size, and a goaltender rumored to be the next big NHL prospect. The Blades didn't rely on miracle comebacks—they simply steamrolled opponents.

But the Wolves had defied conventional wisdom throughout these playoffs. Each series demanded heart and endurance at levels Doug never imagined. Why stop believing now?

When Game 1 of the championship opened on Eastbrook's home ice, the spectacle dazzled Doug. Packed stands, swirling spotlights, a roar that shook the rafters. The Blades wore crisp black jerseys with silver trim, their logo emblazoned in gold. The Wolves, meanwhile, donned their scuffed navy-and-forest-green sweaters—battle-tested gear that had seen countless overtimes.

The puck dropped, and the Blades unleashed a furious pace. Within minutes, Doug felt his legs burning, forced to chase the puck as Eastbrook's forwards flicked perfect passes tape-to-tape. The scoreboard read 2–0 Blades by the end of the first period. Doug, panting on the bench, exchanged worried glances with **Kyle Sutton** and the others—had their run finally met an immovable force?

But the Wolves refused to crumble. In the second period, a sudden counterattack sprang Doug on a partial breakaway. His left shoulder stabbed with pain, but he pushed through, unleashing a wrist shot that deflected in off the goalie's pads. 2–1. The flicker of hope ignited. The Wolves hammered away, eventually tying the score in the third. Though the Blades responded with another marker, Doug's line set up a power-play goal late, forcing overtime at 3–3.

In that extra frame, Eastbrook's big line took control, peppering the Wolves' net. But the Wolves goalie stood on his head. At the fifteen-minute mark of OT, a turnover along the boards gave Doug a chance. He retrieved the puck and fed a cross-ice pass to a cutting defenseman, who buried it top shelf. 4–3 Wolves, final. They'd stolen Game 1 in improbable style, stunning the Blades faithful.

Exhausted and jubilant, Doug skated off, fist-bumping teammates. *One down, three to go.* But beneath the celebration, he felt that twinge of apprehension. If the Wolves had spent all their energy eking out this opener, how much did they have left?

Game 2 showcased the Blades' furious response. They pinned the Wolves in the defensive zone for much of the night, relentless in their forecheck. Doug and Sutton combined for a late goal that cut the lead to 3–2, but Eastbrook sealed it with an empty-netter, winning 4–2. The series knotted at 1–1, heading back to North Shore for Games 3 and 4.

By now, the toll on bodies was staggering. Doug iced his shoulder after every practice, wincing each time trainers applied pressure. Several teammates nursed undisclosed injuries, each shift a test of will. Meanwhile, the Blades seemed fresher, rotating four lines seamlessly. Still, the Wolves harnessed their underdog spirit, determined not to be overwhelmed.

Game 3 in North Shore devolved into a low-scoring defensive struggle. The Wolves scratched out a 2–1 victory in regulation, courtesy of Doug's crucial third-period assist—he threaded a pass from the corner to a waiting forward in the slot. The home crowd roared, chanting Doug's name as he left the ice. They now led the series 2–1, prompting talk of another improbable upset.

But Game 4 saw the Blades reassert dominance, punishing the Wolves with a 4–1 result. Their top line clicked, culminating in a highlight-reel goal that left Doug shaking his head in awe. The scoreboard read 2–2 in the series, with no illusions that the final path would be easy.

Time blurred as the series progressed, each game separated by minimal rest. Doug's role as a leader intensified— he frequently found himself giving pre-game speeches, rallying the bench when heads began to droop, and consoling younger players who worried about glaring mistakes. *This is bigger than me,* he told himself, sensing how the Wolves needed an emotional anchor. With **Matty Roy** still out from a concussion, Doug filled the void, ensuring morale stayed afloat.

"Keep believing," he reminded them before Game 5, pointing around the locker room. "We've come back in every series. These guys might be strong, but we have heart. One more push." He recalled the exhausted nods of approval, the faint smiles through bruised lips. Each man in the locker room shared the same battered determination.

Game 5, back in Eastbrook, delivered a microcosm of the entire series. Brutal hits, precise scoring chances, back-and-forth leads. Doug contributed a power-play goal—his wrist shot screaming over the goalie's shoulder. The Blades answered repeatedly, their top line carrying them to a 3–2 lead late. Yet the Wolves forced overtime with a fluke bounce off a defenseman's skate. Doug hobbled back to the bench, heart pounding. Another OT?

Yes, another OT. In the extra frame, Eastbrook's depth shone. Their second line pressured the Wolves for a solid minute, culminating in a wraparound that ended behind the Wolves netminder. 4–3 final. The Blades claimed a 3–2 series advantage. Doug bent over, hands on knees, panting, wondering how they could muster yet another comeback.

Returning home for Game 6, a hush of nervous anticipation settled over North Shore. The local newspaper ran headlines like: *"Can Wolves Beat the Odds Once More?"* The entire town yearned for a Game 7, though everyone recognized that Eastbrook was the toughest challenge yet. If the Wolves fell short, no one could fault them for running out of steam.

Doug, however, refused to let that logic seep in. He convened a players-only meeting the morning of Game 6, letting everyone speak. Veterans reminded the group how far they'd come; younger players expressed fear of messing up. Doug stood at the end, voice quiet but firm: "If we lose, let's lose going all-out, no regrets. I believe we can force a seventh game. Let's empty the tank."

That night, the arena overflowed with fans, many wearing homemade "BELIEVE!" shirts. Doug took the ice, every muscle protesting, but his spirit fired up by the roaring crowd. The Wolves exploded with a first-period flurry—two quick goals that sent the building into euphoria. Eastbrook clawed back, tying it 2–2 by the third. The tension soared.

In the final minutes, Doug's line pinned the Blades in their zone. A crucial faceoff saw Doug dig deep to win the draw, sliding it back to a defenseman who hammered a point shot through traffic. The puck found the net. 3–2 with under 90 seconds left. The Wolves held on, fueling an ecstatic wave of celebration. Once again, they forced a Game 7, the fourth time in these playoffs. The improbable journey continued.

Game 7. The phrase alone rattled the entire OHL community. Doug had heard the chatter—never before had a team played four consecutive seven-game series en route to a championship. This final showdown in Eastbrook would be Doug's last stand in junior hockey, regardless of outcome. The Wolves had run their bodies ragged; the Blades, though tested, retained some advantage in depth and freshness. But the Wolves possessed momentum, the intangible belief that had carried them so far.

Doug's parents made the trip, braving the sold-out Eastbrook arena. He glimpsed them in a corner section, wearing Wolves scarves, faces alive with pride and worry. It reminded him how far he'd come—once a shy rookie, uncertain he'd even crack the lineup; now a seasoned playoff warrior, recognized league-wide for tenacity and leadership.

The final game dawned with an unspoken weight. In the locker room, a hush persisted as players dressed, each lost in the enormity of the moment. Coach Melrose kept his speech brief: "You've proven you belong. Now, go claim what you've fought for." He glanced at Doug, who acknowledged with a nod, stepping forward to add, "We all have injuries, we're exhausted, but for sixty minutes—maybe more—let's give it everything. Whatever happens, we leave here as brothers."

From the opening faceoff, Game 7 felt like a microcosm of the Wolves' entire playoff run—tense, physical, unpredictable. The Blades scored first, a rocket from their top line. The Wolves tied it 1–1 on a messy goal in front. By the third period, the scoreboard read 2–2. Doug was sure his heart would pound out of his chest. The crowd noise drowned out even his thoughts.

With under a minute left, Eastbrook struck, taking a 3–2 lead seemingly sealing the Wolves' fate. Doug's stomach twisted in heartbreak. But in a script all too familiar, the Wolves pulled the goalie and launched a final assault. A last-second scramble in front saw Doug fling a puck on net, and it bounced off a defender's skate across the line as the horn sounded. Pandemonium—*Goal or no goal?* The referees consulted replay. After an agonizing wait, they signaled good goal. 3–3. Overtime yet again.

The entire building buzzed, fans on both sides half in disbelief. Doug's limbs screamed in protest as he lined up for overtime, but adrenaline fueled him onward. This was it—the final, final push.

Less than five minutes into OT, Doug's line found a cycling opportunity deep in the Blades' zone. Sutton kicked the puck loose behind the net. Doug circled from the corner, eyes scanning. He spotted a defenseman pinching in at the far point. For a split second, the lane was open. Doug dished a perfect pass.

Crack. The puck whizzed toward the net, soared past the goalie's glove, bulging the twine. *Goal.* The red light burst alive. Wolves spilled off the bench, Doug nearly collapsing in elation. They'd won, 4–3 in overtime, capturing the OHL championship. The ultimate exclamation point on a fairytale run.

In that swirling chaos, Doug found himself pinned under a sea of hugging teammates, tears of joy stinging his eyes. He'd scored big goals, delivered timely assists all playoffs—but this assist, setting up the championship-winner, felt beyond dreams. The underdog Wolves, exhausted and battered, stood atop the league.

Except, in the delirium, a linesman skated over. Confusion flickered around the net. Eastbrook's players argued. The referees converged at the penalty box, apparently reviewing the play. The overhead scoreboard's replays suggested something: a high stick deflection? Or goalie interference? The tension soared again. Doug's heart clenched.

After a tense few minutes, the head referee raised his arm. "No goal," the public-address announcer declared. The puck had been deflected off a high stick en route to the net, negating the goal. The crowd erupted in a cacophony of relief (for Blades fans) and despair (for Wolves fans). The scoreboard reset to 3–3. The game resumed. Doug felt a dizzy wave of heartbreak, forced to gather himself for more battling.

The additional minutes drained the last reserves of energy. Then, in an abrupt break, Eastbrook's top forward corralled a rebound in the slot and slipped it behind the Wolves netminder. 4–3. This time, the light stood, no controversial review, no miracle comeback. The final horn blew. Eastbrook's bench flooded the ice in celebration—**they** were champions, not North Shore.

Doug dropped to one knee, burying his face in his gloves. The heartbreak was acute, a dream snatched away in double-overtime heartbreak. Around him, Wolves players slumped, tears in some eyes. Fans in the stands clapped sympathetically. Eastbrook fans rejoiced. Doug forced himself up for the handshake line, congratulating the Blades with as much grace as he could muster.

Inside, his chest felt hollow. So close—one deflected call away from a potential championship. But that was playoff hockey, merciless in its finality. A swirl of bittersweet exhaustion enveloped the Wolves as they retreated to their locker room, heads low. Yet amidst the sorrow, a quiet pride loomed. They'd given everything. They'd proven doubters wrong. They'd soared further than anyone expected.

In the days that followed, the hockey world buzzed about North Shore's improbable run. Scouts and agents hammered Doug's phone, praising his calm leadership, his timely goals, his ability to raise his game in clutch moments. NHL teams took notice. **He** was no longer overshadowed—**Doug Mansfield** had become a name on everyone's lips.

Some referred to him as the "blue-collar hero" of the playoffs, a player who might not have had the flash of certain top draft picks, but who showcased unshakable passion and resilience. The devastating Game 7 defeat didn't erase his accomplishments. If anything, it underscored his character in adversity.

The Wolves' season officially ended. Doug spent a few days reeling from heartbreak. The small-town celebrations for the team still unfolded—parades for the "runner-up heroes," a wave of appreciation for a season that reignited local pride. Doug tried to join in, though a part of him couldn't shake the what-ifs about that disallowed goal. Over time, however, he found acceptance. They had done everything possible, forging a legendary playoff run that overshadowed the final scoreboard.

And there was a new horizon. Word trickled down that multiple NHL and AHL scouts had inquired about Doug's availability. Agents, too, reached out, extolling the possibility of a pro contract. Doug swallowed that reality with awe. *I started this year hoping just to keep my spot in the lineup,* he marveled. Now, he was a coveted prospect, all because of how he'd thrived under the playoff crucible.

In a final, emotional team gathering at the Wolves' rink, the players hugged and parted ways—some aging out of junior, some returning next season, others headed to pro camps. Doug, standing with a gear bag on his sore shoulder, shared a lingering handshake with Coach Melrose. The coach's eyes glistened. "You've been the heart of this team, Mansfield. Don't ever lose that fire."

Doug felt a lump in his throat. "Thank you, Coach. For everything."

He said goodbyes to Sutton, Jeremy, and the rest, each harboring their own future paths. Roy, still in concussion recovery, vowed to come back stronger. "If you go pro," Roy teased, "I'll brag that I taught you everything." Doug grinned, hugging him carefully.

That evening, as Doug loaded his equipment into his father's car, he glanced one last time at the small-town arena's entrance. Painted banners read *"Thank You, Wolves—The Best Run Yet!"* Doug's mother approached, pressing a gentle hand to his back. "We're proud of you," she said softly. "All of this is just the start."

Doug exhaled, letting a sense of closure wash over him. The OHL championship was out of reach, but in its wake, he discovered who he truly was—a player capable of leading, of elevating his team under brutal conditions. NHL or minor-pro leagues beckoned, and he felt ready to chase the dream.

He turned, nodding at his parents, then climbed into the passenger seat. As they pulled away, the reflection of the fading arena lights mirrored in the car window, and with it, the memories of overtime glories, heartbreaks, and a season that had tested every fiber of his being. He'd ended his junior career on a high note, recognized for skill and passion even in defeat.

Doug's heart thumped with quiet excitement. The road ahead was uncertain, but he'd proven he could thrive in adversity. For now, he'd rest—ice up, recover, let the bruises fade. Then, when the call came from scouts and agents, he'd be ready to lace up once more. That final step from junior to pro lay just over the horizon, shimmering with possibility. And Doug Mansfield intended to seize it with the same fearless spirit that had become his hallmark.

19

THE DRAFT

Doug shifted nervously in his seat, gaze flitting across the sea of suits and dresses, bright lights and camera flashes. The smell of polished wood, expensive cologne, and barely contained excitement permeated the massive stadium in Montreal where the NHL Draft was being held. It felt surreal—less than a year ago, he was just another junior player fighting to keep his spot on the roster. Now, after an improbable playoff run that cast him into the spotlight, he was seated among the league's brightest young hopefuls, waiting for his name to be called.

His father sat on his right, posture stiff with pride and tension, while his mother, on his left, squeezed Doug's hand every so often. Mike, Doug's older brother, stood behind them, scanning the bustling crowd. Agents, scouts, media personnel, and thousands of fans packed the floor and seats, the air alive with chatter and anticipation. Giant screens loomed over the stage, each displaying a rolling list of prospects and team logos.

Doug exhaled, trying to steady his heart rate. *This is it,* he thought. *The chance to fulfill a lifelong dream.* As a boy, he'd taped pictures of Maple Leafs legends to his bedroom walls, imagining the day he might don an NHL sweater. Now, reality pressed in all around—frenetic energy, serious men in suits taking calls, GMs huddled in groups, owners scanning their lists. The PA system boomed every few minutes, announcing picks that changed young men's lives in an instant.

Yet, Doug's stomach twisted in nervous knots. The earlier rounds were ticking by, each selection stoking pangs of anxiety. The big names went quickly—household-later talents with unstoppable highlight reels. Doug sat through the first few picks, then ten, then fifteen, pressing his lips together each time another name echoed through the stadium that wasn't his. He'd known he wasn't a consensus top pick. But the memory of his heroic junior playoffs, the invites from scouts and agents, the positive talk from insiders—he'd dared to hope he'd go earlier than the predictions.

As the draft approached the late first round, uncertainty dogged him. *Am I slipping?* he wondered, face warming with anxious embarrassment. He tried to recall every meeting he'd had with teams—some GMs seemed intrigued, others politely disinterested. The swirl of data analytics, skill breakdowns, intangible "character" assessments—nobody knew for sure how teams weighed them. Doug's father gave him a reassuring pat on the shoulder. Mike leaned over, whispering, "Hang tight, Dougie. They'd be crazy not to pick you."

Doug nodded, forcing a small smile. *Easy for them to say, but this wait is brutal.*

Doug had pictured the draft so many times in daydreams—an immediate call-up to the podium, slipping on a Maple Leafs or Canadiens or Red Wings sweater, bounding onto the stage with a grin. Reality was a slow burn. Each time the league commissioner strode to the microphone, hush fell across the floor, replaced by thunderous applause when the pick was announced. Name by name, potential landing spots evaporated. Doug's mind rattled with each selection:

- **Pick #1:** A generational center, widely expected. Cheers erupted.
- **Pick #2:** A star defenseman from the WHL. More applause.
- **Pick #3:** An American forward with gaudy scoring stats.
- ...
- **Pick #10:** Another widely scouted talent.
- **Pick #15:** A speedy winger from the QMJHL.
- **Pick #20:** A big defenseman from Sweden.

All the while, Doug's chest tightened. *Will I even go first round?* He felt beads of sweat forming at his temples. Agents had murmured he was a bubble first-rounder, maybe early second. Yet he was *here*, invited to the draft floor, proof that at least some teams saw him as a potential first-round gem.

When the draft clock ticked near pick #25, Doug's heart hammered so loudly he feared others might hear it. He checked his phone for the hundredth time—no messages. The teams he'd had the best meetings with had already selected or traded picks. Another wave of despair flickered. *Maybe I'll slip into the second round.* He swallowed, mustering acceptance. If that was his fate, so be it. Still, disappointment cut deep. He'd pictured that stage moment, the commissioner calling his name in the first round, the sweater presentation, the handshake. *Maybe that's not my story.*

His father cleared his throat, offering a tight smile. "We're proud of you no matter what happens," he said quietly. Doug's mother squeezed his hand again. "Everything you've done... it's already incredible, Doug," she whispered. That helped quell the swirling self-doubt, but only a little.

Suddenly, the hush of the crowd signaled another pick, #26 overall. The league commissioner stepped to the podium.

"With the twenty-sixth selection in the 20XX NHL Draft," he began, his measured voice reverberating, "the **Toronto Maple Leafs** are proud to select... from the North Shore Wolves of the OHL... **Doug Mansfield**."

A jolt of electricity shot through Doug's spine. He stared at the stage, adrenaline crashing in a dizzy wave. *Did he just say my name? The Maple Leafs?* Realization hit. That was his lifelong dream—his hometown team, the franchise he'd idolized since childhood. He felt his mother's grip tighten, her gasp blending with father's exclamation of joy. Applause broke out around them, cameras swiveling to capture his stunned expression.

In that instant, the decades of Maple Leafs fandom he'd cultivated, the battered backyard rinks, the improbable playoff runs, the heartbreak and triumph—they all coalesced into a single surreal moment. Rising on unsteady legs, Doug blinked away tears, hugging his parents. Mike enveloped him in a back-thumping embrace. He felt cameras flashing in every direction, capturing the biggest moment of his young hockey career. *The Toronto Maple Leafs. I'm going to the team I've dreamt about forever.*

Shaking with excitement, Doug stepped into the aisle, heading toward the stage. Each step felt weightless, like floating in a dream. Agents and other staff parted to let him pass, offering nods of congratulations. The Maple Leafs' front office contingent, wearing suits and the iconic leaf lapels, stood on stage, clapping. Doug's heart pounded, pulses of disbelief swirling. He was about to don the jersey he'd worshipped as a kid.

Once on stage, Doug received handshakes from Maple Leafs executives, a small flurry of "Welcome to the organization!" comments. They handed him a blue-and-white Leafs sweater with "MANSFIELD" stitched on the back, #XX as a placeholder. Doug pulled it over his shoulders, still trying to process the surreality. The logo's iconic leaf over his chest felt like destiny. Flashbulbs erupted from the press row; the audience cheered. The commissioner offered a warm handshake and a friendly pat on the back. Doug managed a shy grin, mind spinning with possibility. *I'm actually a Leaf. For real.*

In that moment, he recalled the nights spent playing pond hockey with his brother, the battered Maple Leafs posters on his childhood walls, the swirl of heartbreak when the team fell short in playoffs. And now... he was part of that storied legacy, a piece of the future. For an instant, joy overshadowed everything else—pain, exhaustion, doubts, heartbreak. The selection had arrived like a thunderbolt.

While the rest of the ceremony continued, Doug was guided backstage for interviews, official photos, handshake sessions with the Leafs' GM and player development staff. His phone buzzed incessantly with messages from friends, teammates, coaches. He felt dazed, heat flooding his cheeks as reporters thrust microphones in his face:

- "Doug, how does it feel to be drafted by the Maple Leafs, your childhood favorite?"

- "You had that remarkable junior playoff run—did you expect to go in the first round?"

- "What do you hope to bring to Toronto's future?"

Doug tried to keep answers humble yet confident. "It's surreal," he admitted. "I grew up idolizing the Leafs. I just want to bring my work ethic, do whatever the team needs. This is a dream, but it's only the start." He repeated variations of that, blinking under bright camera lights, the jersey feeling simultaneously thrilling and heavy on his shoulders.

Eventually, they let him return to his seat. He reconnected with his family, enveloped in congratulatory hugs. Mike teased him, "So you're basically living every Leafs kid's fantasy, huh?" Doug laughed, tears in his eyes, nodding. His father's expression glowed with unwavering pride, and his mother's cheeks shone from emotional tears. *We did it,* Doug thought. *We actually did it.*

As the draft rolled on into subsequent picks, Doug's initial high ebbed, replaced by a quiet sense of wonder and the faintest tremor of apprehension. The Maple Leafs had called his name—fantastic. But he realized, with a stirring of nerves, that the real work began now. Being a first-round draft pick came with weighty expectations in a city like Toronto, desperate for a championship. Media scrutiny soared, fans demanded success, management pinned hopes on each top prospect. Doug's chest tightened at the thought of living up to that.

"We'll celebrate tonight," his father said, noticing Doug's pensive look. "But you know, from tomorrow on, you've got a whole new journey, right?"

Doug forced a half-smile. "I know, Dad. One step at a time, I guess."

The rest of the draft day blurred into a swirl of photos, meet-and-greet with Leafs staff, phone calls from extended family, and well-wishes from fellow draftees. Late that evening, he retreated to the hotel with his family, drained yet electrified. In the quiet of the suite, Doug stared at the Leafs jersey lying folded on the bed. *This is real. I'm a Maple Leaf.*

It felt incredible, but also a tad terrifying. The last few months had been a whirlwind—exhausting playoffs, heartbreak in the final, now immediate stardom and pressure. Could he handle it? Would the fans devour him if he stumbled? The legacy of Toronto hockey weighed heavily on him even now.

His mother, reading the concern etched across his features, laid a gentle hand on his arm. "We're here for you, honey," she said softly. "No matter what." His father nodded, and Mike, flopping on the couch, added, "Dude, you just got drafted by the Leafs. Relax. You'll smash it."

Doug gave a shaky laugh. "Yeah. I just need to breathe."

The next morning, Doug woke early. He'd hardly slept—his phone lighting up every few minutes with congratulatory texts, social media notifications, calls from agents wanting to discuss representation. The Maple Leafs media team had scheduled an orientation day. Doug felt a swirl of excitement and dread. He was about to step deeper into the pro hockey machine.

At a designated location near the draft venue, he joined other newly drafted prospects for a Maple Leafs welcome session. They snapped official photos: him holding up the #XX jersey, beaming in front of the iconic Leaf crest. The staff gave them a rundown of upcoming development camps, training schedules, potential rookie tournaments. Doug's head spun with details, but he forced himself to note everything carefully.

A brief meeting with the Leafs' GM and scouting department hammered home the message: "We liked your playoff performance, your leadership, your two-way skill. We see a bright future, but this is only the beginning. Make no mistake, the NHL is an unforgiving place. You'll need to earn every shift." The GM offered a handshake. Doug's heart pounded at the seriousness behind those words. *I can't just coast on a first-round label. I'll have to prove myself in camp, day after day.*

The team's PR staff whisked Doug into more interviews. Toronto-based media asked about his junior experiences, the big goals, how it felt to represent the Leafs. One reporter pressed him on the overshadowing star forward he'd faced in junior, pointing out how he might face even bigger names in the NHL. Doug answered politely: "I've learned that success comes from consistent effort, not just flash. I plan to keep that approach."

That evening, Doug's family arranged a small dinner in Montreal to celebrate. It was a modest affair, just immediate relatives, a few close friends who'd traveled for the draft, and no elaborate pomp. They toasted Doug's accomplishment with sparkling juice—he wasn't old enough for a real celebratory drink in some provinces. Laughter and relief bubbled around the table. For a moment, the swirl of professional obligations and high-stakes future receded, replaced by gratitude.

When the meal ended, Doug excused himself to the sidewalk for fresh air. He gazed at Montreal's vibrant nightlife—the city always alive, always humming with hockey passion. Reflecting on his childhood dream, he felt tears prick the corners of his eyes. The day had brought him from anxious waiting to triumphant euphoria. He was a Maple Leaf, officially. The gravity of it nearly knocked him off his feet.

Mike joined him, leaning on a lamppost. "So," Mike teased lightly, "are you going to buy me Leafs tickets when you become a millionaire?"

Doug laughed, wiping his eyes. "Sure, if I actually make the big club. I still have to sign a contract, go to training camp..."

Mike sobered. "We know you, Dougie. You'll smash camp the way you smashed those OT goals. Don't let the city's pressure freak you out. Just do your job like always."

Doug nodded, drawing confidence from his brother's unwavering faith. *One step at a time,* he repeated silently.

After the short stay in Montreal, Doug and his family traveled back home briefly. The local media swarmed them upon arrival, capturing the heartwarming scene of a small-town hero returning as a first-round draft pick. The mayor invited Doug to a town ceremony, but he graciously declined, citing a jam-packed schedule. He needed to rest and then begin preparing for Toronto's development camp.

A swirl of new responsibilities consumed Doug: finalizing an agent contract, scheduling medical check-ups, reviewing the Leafs' rookie orientation documents. He fielded calls from potential sponsors and equipment reps. The attention felt surreal, but also draining. Each conversation hammered home that being drafted was a door opening, not a guaranteed NHL roster spot.

His father, noticing the fatigue creeping into Doug's voice, reminded him, "Focus on hockey, son. The rest is just noise. The Leafs picked you because of your game. Don't let the circus pull you away from that."

Doug took that advice to heart, carving out time each day for on-ice drills, cardio, and stretching. Despite the physical toll of a long junior season and playoffs, he strove to maintain sharpness. He realized how quickly the Maple Leafs' development camp would arrive—he had to show up in shape, ready to impress.

A few weeks after the draft, Doug found himself at the Leafs' training facility, walking hallways adorned with photos of legendary players. The weight of the franchise's history pressed in. He spotted other new draftees, second- and third-round picks, free agent invites—each carrying the same mix of nerves and ambition.

In day one's team meeting, the Leafs' development staff laid out their philosophy: "We draft players who embody skill, hockey IQ, and strong character. Being selected in the first round is an honor, but you must still earn your path to the NHL. Some of you will go back to junior. Others might see time in the minors. It's up to you to prove you can handle the pro level."

Doug listened intently. He recognized the truth in those words. No matter his first-round status, he was starting at the bottom rung of the pro ladder, needing to stand out among a wave of prospects all vying for limited spots. The staff singled out certain players for customized plans, including Doug— he'd soon discover intense scrutiny from coaches checking if his playoff heroics translated to consistent performance.

On the ice, he felt the difference in pace. Prospects from major junior powerhouses, NCAA standouts, European imports—everyone flew around the rink. Doug's battered shoulder twinged, but he gritted through, showcasing his quick release and passing game. He noticed coaches nodding whenever he dished crisp tape-to-tape passes. Yet, the star power around him was undeniable—some prospects boasted flash and speed that outstripped his.

During a post-practice chat, a Leafs development coach gave Doug blunt feedback: "We love your grit and hockey sense, but you'll need to keep improving physically—more strength in your frame, faster edgework. We see you as a potential top-six forward eventually, but it's a process. Stay patient, keep working."

That night, Doug collapsed into bed in his small dorm-like room near the practice facility, mind swirling with questions. *Am I truly good enough for the NHL? How long until I might crack a roster?* He missed the camaraderie of the Wolves, but this was a new environment with cutthroat competition. Yet, a flicker of excitement burned. *I'm here, wearing Leafs colors, training at their facility. This is the next step on my dream path.*

He texted a quick update to his parents: *Camp's intense, but I'm learning a ton. Miss you guys.* Then he scrolled social media, glimpsing fresh coverage about how "Mansfield, the Leafs' 26th overall pick, displayed promising two-way skill in scrimmages." Some fans debated his potential—*Is he just hype from the playoffs?* others asked. Doug shut his phone, heart pounding. He couldn't control opinions. He could only keep working.

In the following days, he tackled every drill with unwavering focus, ignoring the persistent aches in his body. He attended film sessions, took notes, and approached coaches after practice for extra pointers. Bits of confidence trickled in: an assistant coach praising his improvement on zone entries, a teammate complimenting his passing vision.

An unexpected highlight arrived on the final day of development camp—a scrimmage open to media and some fans. Doug notched a goal and an assist, including a sweet feed through a defenseman's legs. The Leafs' GM, watching from above, later offered him a handshake, praising his performance. Doug felt a surge of validation. *I can hang with these prospects, even if overshadowed by bigger names.*

When camp wrapped, the Leafs' staff met individually with prospects to discuss the next phase. Doug's meeting offered clarity: he'd likely return to junior for another season to refine his game, gain more muscle, and lead a young Wolves roster if eligible. Or, if the Wolves staff and Leafs staff believed he was ready, maybe a stint in the AHL. Doug braced himself for the recommendation.

Ultimately, the Leafs proposed returning him to the OHL for further top-line minutes, plus an invite to the main NHL training camp as a taste of pro pace. "We see you as a future piece," the GM reiterated, "but we want you to keep developing without sitting in the press box. Trust the process."

Doug nodded, understanding. A swirl of emotions—relief that they had a plan, disappointment that he wouldn't jump straight to the NHL, acceptance that few players soared directly from the draft to stardom. This was all normal. He felt grateful to have a path forward.

Leaving Toronto's facility, Doug realized how profoundly life had changed in just a few months. From a battered junior player overshadowed by star forwards, to a first-round pick for the Maple Leafs, recognized as a major piece of their future. It was both exhilarating and daunting. He recalled the heartbreak of losing the championship in double OT, but also the unstoppable drive that propelled him to that stage.

He stepped outside, breathing in warm summer air, a fresh sense of purpose filling his chest. The draft was over, the jersey donned, interviews done. But the real journey was just beginning: camps, training, another junior campaign, all stepping stones to the dream of someday patrolling the Scotiabank Arena ice in Leafs blue and white.

As Doug's father pulled the car around, Doug hopped in, resting the Leafs jersey folded neatly in his lap. His mother turned in the passenger seat, smiling softly. "Still feel like you're dreaming, dear?"

Doug chuckled. "Yeah, a bit. It's crazy. But I'm excited."

Mike, from the backseat, teased, "Just wait until preseason, Dougie. Then you can show all those fancy prospects who's boss."

Doug nodded, heart fluttering at the idea of wearing the Leafs crest in an NHL preseason match, even if just for a chance to prove himself. "One step at a time," he repeated. "It's only the beginning."

The car pulled away, merging into city traffic. Doug gazed out the window at the bright cityscape, mind drifting to childhood memories of cheering the Leafs on TV. He felt a surge of gratitude—for his family's support, for the Wolves' unwavering bond, for the coaches who believed in him. He'd represent them all in this next chapter.

And so, as the roads led away from the draft's hustle, Doug let a grin tug at his lips. The tension from waiting multiple picks, the swirl of cameras, the triumphant moment of hearing "Doug Mansfield" called by the Maple Leafs—it was all behind him now. The dream had cracked open. He wasn't naive—**getting drafted is only the beginning of the battle**. He'd fight every day to justify the Leafs' faith, to earn a real NHL spot, to stand among the league's best.

But for this moment, in the hush of the ride home, Doug allowed himself to bask in the afterglow of a childhood dream realized. He was a first-round draft pick for his beloved Maple Leafs. The next steps would be demanding, but the future glimmered with possibility. **He was ready to embrace it all.**

20

ROOKIE SEASON

Doug stood in front of his locker stall, heart pounding with an excitement that verged on disbelief. The iconic blue-and-white Maple Leafs jersey hung freshly laundered just inches away, and the smell of brand-new gear filled his nostrils. All around him, established NHL veterans moved with a confident ease, chatting and joking in that casual, comfortable way of players who'd been here for years. Doug felt a tremor of nerves. *I'm really here,* he reminded himself. *An actual rookie in the Toronto Maple Leafs locker room.*

He wiped his damp palms on the towel slung over his shoulder and drew a breath. So much had happened since the night of the draft—summer workouts, the Leafs' rookie camp, a few preseason games, and now the final roster announcement that he'd be starting the season in the NHL. *At least for now,* he thought, always aware that roster spots in pro hockey could be fleeting. Still, that first official day of the regular season—stepping into the locker room as a Maple Leaf—sparked a rush of adrenaline that nearly took his breath away.

Kyle Sutton had messaged him a simple "Congrats, rookie" earlier that morning. Doug smiled at the memory, missing the camaraderie of the old junior squad but equally eager to immerse himself in this new environment. Here, in the heart of Toronto hockey, the stakes were higher than ever, the spotlight more intense, and the city's longing for a Stanley Cup had grown to an almost feverish level.

The veterans carried themselves with an easy confidence. Some joked about dinner plans, others taped their sticks in a habitual, practiced manner. Doug felt both awe and intimidation; these were players he'd watched on TV not long ago—stars and well-known personalities. Now they were his teammates, expecting him to deliver on the potential that had made him a first-round pick. He swallowed, reaching for the Leafs sweater, determined to show he belonged.

The first preseason games had offered Doug a hint of the NHL's breakneck pace: faster decision-making, bigger hits, tighter defensive coverage, and no mercy for hesitant rookies. Once the real season started, it only intensified. On the ice, Doug struggled initially to find time and space. Every pass required pinpoint precision; every shift demanded swift adaptation.

During his debut game at Scotiabank Arena, the stands roared in a sea of blue and white. Doug's pulse hammered as he skated out for warm-ups, scanning row after row of die-hard Leafs fans. The city craved a championship, and the media coverage leading up to the season opener had been relentless. Each new arrival, including Doug, faced intense scrutiny. *Will this rookie help end the drought?* headlines asked. Doug tried not to read them, but they found him anyway.

In that opening match, the physicality and skill difference blindsided him. The opposing defenders read plays instantly, sealing off his angles. Doug took a few checks that rattled his teeth, once coughing up the puck in the neutral zone leading to a dangerous counter. He returned to the bench, heart pounding, chastising himself for the blunder. Veteran teammates patted his shoulder, telling him to shake it off, but the presence of tens of thousands of Leafs fans—and countless viewers on Hockey Night in Canada—magnified every mistake.

Eventually, in the third period, Doug made a sharp breakout pass that led to a secondary assist on a tying goal. The crowd erupted. Doug felt a wave of relief. *At least I contributed something.* The Leafs lost 3–2 in overtime, but Doug's quiet assist offered him a silver lining. *I can play here,* he thought, though part of him still reeled from the speed and skill he'd witnessed.

The morning after that debut, the media throng greeted Doug and the rest of the team at practice. Cameras and microphones hovered. Even though Doug was just a rookie, journalists asked about his impressions of the NHL pace, how he felt about the Leafs' storied history. He did his best to give measured answers, but he could see how easily an offhand comment might spiral into a headline in this hockey-crazed market.

Coach Reynolds, a seasoned NHL bench boss known for his even-keeled demeanor, called Doug aside post-practice. "We drafted you for your hockey IQ, your work ethic. Don't let the city's expectations crush you. Keep your head down, keep improving, one shift at a time." Doug appreciated the reassurance, nodding. He recognized that public glare could be overwhelming, but the staff was there to guide him.

Off the ice, he began forming new friendships with some younger players who'd also navigated the intimidating jump from junior or college to the NHL. They'd compare notes over coffee, lamenting the endless media requests, laughing at mishaps like accidentally taking a veteran's seat on the plane (a rookie no-no). These small bonds anchored Doug in the chaotic environment, giving him a sense of belonging.

Nonetheless, adjusting to pro life was intense. Doug learned quickly that a single day off in the NHL was rare and that the schedule was punishing—back-to-back games, extensive travel, minimal rest. He texted old teammates from the Wolves, recalling those tough junior bus rides. *The planes here might be nicer, but the grind is the same—just cranked to a new level,* he told them.

Toronto's hunger for a Stanley Cup shaped the media narrative daily. After each game, the press dissected line combinations, criticized power-play setups, and zeroed in on every detail. Doug discovered that he couldn't take a single shift for granted. If he missed a coverage assignment or failed to clear the puck, local sports radio hosts would question the rookie's readiness. Conversely, if he scored or assisted, the hype flared—*Is Mansfield the next star forward?*

Early in the season, Doug experienced both extremes. He endured a mini-slump, going several games without a point, prompting some commentary about whether he should be sent down to the minors for more seasoning. A week later, he broke out in a game with a goal and two assists, becoming the story of the night. Doug tried to balance the highs and lows— *Don't get carried away by the praise, and don't get crushed by the criticism.* That was easier said than done.

One morning, he stepped into a coffee shop only to see his name splashed on the front page of a tabloid: *"Mansfield Magic? Leafs Rookie Shows Glimpses of Brilliance."* The article praised his last performance, but hinted that fans expected more consistency. Doug tossed the paper aside, wishing he could ignore it altogether. He reminded himself that ignoring the noise was crucial—he had teammates, coaches, and a daily routine to follow. *Focus on the game, not the headlines,* he kept repeating.

The locker room's established veterans included a few players who'd spent years under the Toronto microscope. They noticed Doug's wide-eyed wonder and occasional nerves, offering quiet mentorship. One such mentor was **Jonas Leroux**, an alternate captain with a decade of NHL experience. He invited Doug to dinner after a tough loss, offering perspective: "The key in this town is consistency. Don't let them crown you after a good game or bury you after a bad one. Stay steady."

Doug soaked up the advice, grateful for the guidance. Another older defenseman, known for stoic leadership, gave him tips on building mental resilience—meditation exercises, journaling about daily progress. At first, Doug felt odd journaling, but found it helped him process the day's experiences, good or bad.

Meanwhile, camaraderie with younger players blossomed. They teased each other about rookie duties—carrying extra gear, picking up pucks after practice. Doug didn't mind the harmless ribbing; it mirrored the respectful hazing from his junior days, forging team bonds. The banter after wins felt infectious, but after losses, the mood was subdued, the city's disappointment an ever-present weight on their shoulders.

As weeks turned to months, Doug tasted the physical grind of the 82-game NHL schedule. Long road trips took him across the continent, from the raucous arenas of the western conference to the historic buildings on the east coast. Jet lag, hotel living, and minimal downtime replaced the simpler routines of junior. He missed the tight-knit Wolves environment at times, but marveled at the grandeur of the NHL stage.

His performance stabilized. He wasn't lighting up the scoresheet nightly, but he contributed timely assists, chipped in a few clutch goals, and gradually earned more trust from Coach Reynolds. Doug's line assignment evolved from bottom-six cameo to a middle-six role, especially after a strong stretch of playmaking. The highlight came in a mid-season home game against a division rival, where Doug notched a game-winning goal in overtime. The crowd's thunderous celebration echoed the euphoria he'd felt back in junior's biggest moments, but on a grander scale.

Off the ice, Doug faced new challenges. Endorsement opportunities popped up, local companies wanting to align with the Leafs' promising rookie. He relied on his agent and family to filter the offers, choosing to keep life uncluttered. The last thing he needed was more stress from marketing obligations.

The real stress came from the city's Cup drought talk. TV analysts hammered the point nightly: the Maple Leafs had gone decades without a championship. Each new season began with hope and ended in heartbreak. Doug felt that burden as fans pinned new hopes on fresh faces like him. He learned to answer politely, "We're working hard every day," whenever asked about ending the curse. Inside, he hoped he'd be part of the group that finally delivered.

In this environment, Doug found solace in forging genuine friendships. One of the Leafs' other rookies, a Swedish winger named **Anton Bergstrom**, clicked with Doug instantly. They discovered shared tastes in music and bonded over the challenges of navigating an intense hockey market. They'd watch film together, highlight each other's mistakes and victories, and try local Toronto restaurants on off-nights.

"Feels like we live under a microscope," Anton once remarked after a tough loss, scanning the headlines labeling them as underperforming. Doug nodded, empathizing. "But at least we're not alone, right?" The shared experience of rookie pressure made them close allies.

Another younger defenseman, **Callum Price**, brought comedic relief to the group with irreverent locker-room jokes. He teased Doug about his "baby face" or about the social media buzz whenever Doug scored. That comedic spirit helped defuse tension in the midst of the unrelenting grind. Step by step, Doug's new teammates became a second family, echoing the camaraderie he'd cherished in the Wolves.

Halfway through the season, the Leafs hit a rocky patch—several key injuries decimated the lineup, and the team stumbled through a losing streak. The media storm escalated. Doug, as a rookie, faced tough post-game questions about how the locker room was handling adversity. Even though veterans led the official responses, the press singled out Doug, pointing to him as a "spark plug" who needed to step up. The pressure felt stifling at times, but he reminded himself of his junior playoff battles, forging mental strength from those experiences.

He found small milestones to celebrate: scoring his 10th career NHL goal, cracking 20 assists in mid-February, earning a mention in the team's highlight reel. Each personal achievement was overshadowed by the Leafs' urgent quest to secure a playoff spot. Doug felt satisfaction in contributing, but also recognized that in Toronto, team success dwarfed individual feats. *If we don't make the playoffs, none of these personal stats will matter to the city,* he mused.

By March, the team rallied behind returning injured veterans, stringing together crucial wins. Doug's line found chemistry, with him racking up consistent points and re-establishing his crisp passing from the half-boards. Coach Reynolds praised Doug's maturity in media scrums: "He's a rookie, but plays with composure. He's learning quickly."

As the calendar shifted into April, Doug encountered what veterans referred to as "the rookie wall." His energy dipped alarmingly. The novelty of travel, the mounting physical fatigue, the barrage of media attention—it all bore down. In one four-game stretch, he looked slow and indecisive, racking up a minus rating and minimal offensive impact. Critics pounced: *"Is Mansfield hitting a wall?"*

Anton Bergstrom, facing similar doldrums, commiserated. "I've never played so many games in such intensity. I'm gassed." Doug found solace in that shared exhaustion. Still, they had to push onward. The Leafs were locked in a tight playoff race, each game a final. Doug leaned on the older leaders like Jonas Leroux, gleaning tips on recovery—ice baths, better sleep habits, nutrition beyond the typical rookie approach. Gradually, Doug began to rebound, his youth and resilience shining through.

A pivotal late-season match saw Doug net a clutch third-period goal, sealing a 3–2 win that nudged Toronto closer to a playoff berth. The post-game media hailed his "rookie bounce-back." Doug just breathed relief, tasting the adrenaline that a sold-out Scotiabank Arena can deliver. He recognized the city's mania for meaningful hockey in spring. The building roared as if reminding him: *This is the place you dreamed about.*

When the final game of the regular season concluded, Doug and the Leafs had secured a wild-card playoff spot, injecting the city with fresh hope. Doug's rookie stats weren't Calder Trophy levels, but they were solid—an impressive total of goals and assists, plus intangible evidence of his grit and leadership glimpses. The media consensus: Mansfield exceeded modest expectations, cementing himself as part of the Leafs' future core.

In the locker room after that last regular-season contest, Doug sank into his stall, reflecting on how far he'd come in a single year. From the heartbreak of losing the OHL final, to hearing his name called at the draft, to navigating the rookie season's punishing schedule and microscope. Yes, he was tired—exhausted, actually—but also brimming with pride. Surviving a full NHL season, earning respect from teammates and coaches, forging new bonds. *I did it,* he thought, though he recognized the next challenge lay just ahead: the playoffs.

Coach Reynolds gave him a congratulatory nod as he walked by. "Good first season, Mansfield. Ready for playoff hockey at this level?" The question sparked a swirl of excitement and nerves. Doug replied with a grin, "That's what we play for, right?" The coach chuckled, clapping him on the shoulder. Indeed, Toronto's mania would only ramp up now that the postseason arrived.

The city's fervor for a Stanley Cup soared. Fans jammed Maple Leaf Square with watch parties, local radio dissected every detail, and the Leafs' star players faced intense interviews. Doug, as a rookie, fielded queries about his readiness for the playoff stage. He recalled the wars he fought in junior: multiple game sevens, heartbreak in the final. *I know a thing or two about big games,* he told a reporter softly, though he realized the NHL playoffs were another beast entirely.

Still, Doug approached the coming days with quiet confidence. The rookie jitters had matured into a calm acceptance of the spotlight. If the Maple Leafs were to end decades of frustration, each player needed to contribute—veteran or rookie alike. Doug set personal goals: keep creating offense, remain defensively responsible, handle the swirling media with humility. *Stay even-keeled—just like the vets taught me.*

In a final press conference before the postseason began, a reporter asked Doug to summarize his rookie year. He paused, searching for the right words. "It's been... everything," he said earnestly. "Harder, faster, and more intense than I ever imagined. But the Leafs organization and the city welcomed me, pushed me. I learned every day. And now, heading into the playoffs, I just want to help us go as far as we can." The cameras flashed. Doug felt the city's gaze intensify, but in that moment, he felt grateful—he was a Maple Leaf, living his childhood dream.

As the Leafs prepared for their playoff opener, Doug revisited the memories that led him here: the magical OHL playoff runs, the heartbreak in the final, the NHL Draft night, the rookie season's highs and lows. Each step shaped him, forging resilience and a willingness to learn. He recognized that forging an NHL career demanded constant adaptation—being drafted or playing one strong year didn't guarantee anything. He'd continue to face adversity and competition for roster spots.

Yet, Doug approached this new challenge with an unwavering sense of purpose. Even if overshadowed by the

Leafs' established stars, he understood his role in galvanizing the locker room, providing secondary scoring, and wearing his heart on his sleeve each shift. The Maple Leafs faithful wanted a Cup, yes—but they also rallied around players who left everything on the ice, a quality Doug had carried from his junior days.

Stepping onto the practice rink for the final prep session, Doug caught a reflection of himself in the glass boards—donned in that navy-blue Leafs sweater, the iconic crest over his chest. He no longer felt like an imposter or a starry-eyed kid; he felt like a legitimate piece of Toronto's hockey fabric. The next stage—NHL playoff hockey—would test him again. But he was ready, forging ahead with the same unstoppable determination he'd always relied on.

In the hush of that moment, as coaches barked drills and teammates skated by, Doug closed his eyes briefly. He pictured the future: deeper playoff battles, the quest for the Stanley Cup, a city waiting. A small grin quirked his lips. *This is just the beginning,* he thought. With a final breath, he pushed off the boards, rejoining drills, heart thrumming with anticipation of what the next chapter might bring.

21

THE OFF SEASON

Doug exhaled deeply as the plane finally touched down in Toronto's Pearson Airport. It was late spring—the Maple Leafs' season had ended a few weeks prior, cutting their playoff run shorter than Doug and the city had hoped. Despite the disappointment of not going deeper, Doug walked off the plane feeling an immense sense of relief. His body and mind craved a break from the relentless grind of the NHL rookie campaign. Now, for a few precious months, he could shift gears. Home beckoned with its comforting familiarity—a chance to reset, see his family, and gather himself for whatever came next.

He navigated the terminal with a minimal carry-on bag, wearing a simple hoodie and jeans rather than the Maple Leafs jacket or anything that would draw attention. Even so, a few hockey fans recognized him, offering subdued nods or quiet "Hey, Doug, good season!" greetings. Doug managed polite smiles and thanks, but he wasn't in the mood for lengthy conversation. He yearned for his own space, to decompress, to let the city's hockey mania fade into background noise—even just for a little while.

Outside arrivals, Doug spotted his father leaning against the car, wearing a grin that radiated pride. The same father who'd driven him to peewee games and supported him through junior's heartbreaks. Doug hoisted his small duffel and trudged over, the tension in his shoulders loosening the moment his dad pulled him into a quick embrace. "Welcome back, son," his dad said. "Let's get you home."

The ride to their suburban Ontario home took about an hour, weaving through highways and then quieter backroads that Doug knew by heart. Nostalgia washed over him, noticing the familiar convenience store, the old community rink he'd once visited as a starry-eyed kid. His father drove with a contented silence for the first few minutes, letting Doug simply stare out the window, reacquainting himself with the landscape that shaped him.

Eventually, Doug's father spoke softly, "I know the season ended sooner than you hoped. But you did great, Dougie. The whole family followed every game." Doug exhaled, nodding. "Thanks, Dad. I learned so much. Just... the pace, the city's expectations. It was all bigger than I imagined."

His father glanced over with compassion. "Now you're home. You can rest, see your mother, your brother, friends. And we'll help you get ready for next year. No rush."

The sun dipped lower, casting long shadows across the farmland. By the time they pulled into the driveway, Doug felt both exhausted and weirdly invigorated. His mother waited on the porch, waving with delight. Doug hopped out and she met him halfway, arms wide, tears glinting in her eyes. "My NHLer is back!" she teased, voice thick with emotion. He hugged her tight, cherishing the warmth of her welcome.

Inside, the house smelled of a home-cooked meal. On the kitchen table sat some old hockey magazines, nostalgic reminders of how Doug used to obsess over Maple Leafs stories as a kid. He sank into a familiar chair, letting the scent of roasting vegetables fill his lungs. This was the off-season he'd craved: a haven from the media swirl, a chance to be plain Doug Mansfield, not just a rookie draftee under Toronto's bright lights.

Over the next few days, Doug slipped easily into a restful routine. Mornings began with a late wake-up—something he rarely afforded himself during the season—and a leisurely breakfast with his parents. His mother fussed over him, ensuring he ate hearty meals and got the vitamins she insisted he'd neglected. Doug teased her in return, but privately, he was grateful for the pampering. Life in the NHL had been a relentless cycle of training, travel, and scrutiny. Home offered safety and calm.

In the afternoons, he strolled the neighborhood, sometimes venturing to the old pond where, as a boy, he'd discovered his passion for hockey. It was no longer frozen at this time of year, of course, but even seeing the placid water stirred memories. He'd recall crisp winter days, the blade of his skates cutting fresh ice, the echoes of laughter from his brother Mike and neighborhood friends. That pond had awakened his hockey dream. Now that he'd lived that dream in a Maple Leafs sweater, returning to the pond felt like closing a circle.

Evenings were quiet, often spent in the living room with his parents, chatting about everything from the Leafs' playoff exit to random family gossip. Sometimes Mike would drop by, joking around as they revisited their sibling banter. The family dynamic remained comforting, a reminder that behind all the big-city hype, he was still just Doug, a kid from Ontario who loved the game.

One of Doug's priorities was reuniting with his old junior teammates from the North Shore Wolves. Though scattered across different pro or college paths, many returned to the area in the off-season, giving them a chance to meet at the local diner or a small bar. There, they swapped war stories: who endured the toughest injuries, which had the craziest fans, how junior hockey's bus rides compared to pro travel.

Sutton, the older forward who'd practically mentored Doug in his last junior year, had caught on with an AHL team out west. He recounted the grind of minor-league life, marveling at how Doug jumped straight to the NHL. "Man, you hopped over me," Sutton teased. "But I'm proud of you, Mansfield. I always knew you'd tear it up." Doug grinned, a flush of gratitude warming him. The bonding felt like old times, though each had grown in different ways.

They also reminisced about their improbable playoff run in junior, the heartbreak of that final series. Doug realized how far those experiences had carried him—fueled his mental toughness in the NHL. "It's weird," he admitted, "some nights I'd think back to those game sevens, telling myself if we survived that, I can handle Toronto." The table chuckled, though some also admitted envy at Doug's Maple Leafs gig. He reassured them he wasn't living in a perfect dream—there were trade rumors, intense media, and the staggering pressure of playing for a Cup-starved franchise.

Nonetheless, that sense of brotherhood lingered. They parted with a group handshake, promising to skate together soon. That impetus reaffirmed Doug's plan: blend rest with targeted training, maybe on the same ice with these old friends.

A week into his break, Doug contacted some of his old minor-hockey coaches to set up personalized off-season training. He recognized that the NHL off-season was about skill refinement and adding muscle, but also addressing weak spots. During the year, opposing defenders had sometimes outmuscled him along the boards. He wanted to get stronger, more balanced on his skates.

Coach Farley, who'd coached Doug in bantam, invited him to a private rink where a handful of local prospects trained in summer. Doug arrived in sweats, greeting the familiar lines of the place with nostalgia. Coach Farley welcomed him with an easy smile. "Let's see how that shot's evolved, Dougie," he teased. "We'll fine-tune a few things." Over the next few sessions, they drilled footwork, puck protection, and small-area battles. With fewer bodies on the ice, Doug could focus on technique, analyzing how to absorb hits and maintain puck control.

It felt oddly comforting to take orders from an old coach, far from the harsh spotlight. They talked candidly about the rookie year—how the NHL's endless pace tested him physically. Coach Farley commended Doug for leaning into the intangible skills that took him beyond raw talent: "Your smarts, your hustle, that's what stands out. Keep that identity." Doug nodded, glad to ground himself in those fundamentals.

He found similar synergy working out in the old high school weight room with an ex-trainer who'd once guided him through adolescent growth spurts. The trainer marveled at the muscle Doug had added but saw room for more. "To survive a full 82 and playoffs," he said, "you need core strength. We'll push your limit." Doug welcomed the challenge, mindful to avoid overtraining after a grueling season. Balance was key— he needed to heal as much as he needed to push forward.

Despite the structured training, Doug carved out time to skate just for fun at the backyard pond of a neighbor who maintained a small, informal rink even in warm weather with a makeshift artificial chilling system. The ice wasn't perfect, but it was enough for Doug to recapture the pure joy of the game without official scrutiny. He'd lace up old skates, slip onto the bumpy surface, and lose himself in casual puck handling. Sometimes, neighborhood kids would gather to watch, wide-eyed at seeing an NHLer in their midst. He'd invite them for a short shinny match, remembering how, not too many years ago, *he* had been that awestruck child gazing at older players.

One evening, the soft glow of setting sun lit the pond, and Doug skated lazy circles, passing the puck to a friend or two. No coaches, no cameras, no pressure. The delight of slicing the blade across real ice, the subtle crackling sound echoing in the still air, reminded him why he fell in love with hockey in the first place. He soared around makeshift cones, attempting goofy trick shots, letting laughter bubble up. The season's intensity melted away, replaced by that warm sense of wonder he felt as a child.

He left the pond that night with a revived spark—his mind free from media demands, trade rumors, and the looming drumbeat of next season. This was the essence of the off-season: rediscover the game's pure love, absent the burdens of a business.

Of course, the off-season wasn't all tranquility. Doug's agent forwarded a handful of endorsement opportunities that emerged after his rookie success. Local car dealerships wanted him as a spokesperson, a sports drink company offered a marketing campaign. Doug was cautious, remembering wise words from older teammates who cautioned against brand alignments that might overshadow actual performance.

He combed through each proposal with his father and agent, seeking deals that felt authentic. The hockey-sense and humility that shaped Doug on the ice also guided his approach to business. He didn't want to plaster his face on every billboard. Moderation felt key. He eventually signed a moderate endorsement with a sports equipment brand that had supported him in junior, ensuring synergy with his playing style. That alone triggered a small press release, generating local headlines. "Mansfield Partners with SwiftGear," they wrote, rehashing how SwiftGear sticks apparently complemented his lethal wrist shot. Doug cringed slightly at the hype, but recognized the necessity of building an off-ice profile.

Such commitments chipped into his rest time, forcing him to schedule photo shoots or sign promotional items. After one long day posing for marketing materials, Doug collapsed on the couch, longing for the simpler days of just practicing and playing. *This is part of the pro life*, he reminded himself. *I need to adapt.* The off-season, ironically, carried its own brand of busyness.

Midway through the summer, a new source of stress surfaced: trade rumors. Doug scrolled social media, seeing fan speculation about the Leafs' need for immediate Cup contention. Some articles suggested the organization might offload younger players or picks to acquire a big-name veteran. While nothing official surfaced, Doug found himself a subject of rumor: *Could the Leafs trade Mansfield for an established star center?*

At first, he shrugged it off—he was a first-round pick, a bright spot in the rookie class. Why would they move him? But as talk radio and online forums kept fanning the gossip, Doug's chest tightened. He recalled older players warning him that pro hockey was a business, loyalty ephemeral. He forced himself not to spiral, reassuring himself that management had told him they viewed him as part of the future. However, the possibility stung. *I just got here. Could they really trade me?*

He confided in his father about the rumors, and his father shrugged calmly. "It's out of your control, Doug. You can't let speculation hamper your focus. If a trade happens, you adapt. But I doubt they'd let you go so soon after drafting you."

Still, the rumor overshadowed his mind at times, occasionally creeping into his off-season training. On the pond or in the weight room, he'd push a little harder, picturing that he needed to prove he was indispensable to Toronto. Maybe a part of him worried he'd lose the chance to realize the childhood dream of wearing the Leafs crest for years to come.

As August neared its end, Doug assessed his summer's work. His shoulder had improved significantly, helped by targeted physio. He'd gained a few pounds of muscle, hopefully helping him handle the NHL's rigors. Mentally, he felt more balanced. The pond sessions and laid-back gatherings with old friends had rekindled that pure passion. He found a measure of calm regarding the media swirl, trade rumors, and endorsement fuss. If a trade came, he'd tackle it then; for now, he was a Maple Leaf, excited to build on his rookie foundation.

One breezy afternoon, he sat outside on the deck, the distant hum of cicadas in the warm air. The off-season was waning, training camp looming just a couple of weeks away. He stared at the old photographs pinned on his phone's screen—him as a junior star, the improbable Wolves' playoff run, wearing the Maple Leafs sweater in that first official rookie game. *So much had changed in a year,* he mused.

His mother joined him, offering a glass of lemonade. They chatted quietly about everyday life, how proud she was, and how she still worried about him being alone in a huge city. Doug reassured her he was making new friends, adjusting to adult responsibilities. "Just don't forget to call home once the season starts," she teased. He grinned, promising he would.

Before departing for preseason activities in Toronto, Doug spent one final evening at the neighbor's pond rink. Although it was late summer, the neighbor's unique cooling system allowed the small patch of ice to hold out. Some kids from the block gathered, plus a few of Doug's old youth teammates. They laced up in the mild twilight, a warm breeze drifting across the yard, an odd contrast to the crisp ice beneath their blades.

They played a casual pickup game—no positions, no set teams, just free-flowing shinny. Doug skated with easy grace, turning tight corners, delivering deft passes, occasionally letting a shot rip. The kids laughed whenever he flicked a behind-the-back pass or tried a playful deke. He found himself beaming, caught between memories of simpler times and the knowledge he was now an NHL player returning to his roots.

At sunset, the final goal brought the game to a close. Doug leaned on his stick, breathing in the orchard-scented air. The small audience clapped politely, but for Doug, the applause wasn't the point. He recalled the phrase that had guided him in junior: *Never lose the love.* The love of the game, unencumbered by contracts, endorsements, or trade speculation. Under the soft glow of a yard lamp, he realized that no matter what city he ended up in, no matter how big the crowd or bright the spotlight, that love was his anchor.

The last day at home arrived in a blink. Doug packed up his gear, hugging his parents goodbye, once again exchanging his father's proud smile and mother's tearful well-wishing. Mike slapped him on the back, telling him to "stay humble and crush it." They teased him about setting aside tickets for them in the season opener. Doug rolled his eyes good-naturedly, promising to do his best.

As he drove toward the city, alone this time, Doug realized how different this departure felt from the rushed scramble of his rookie year. Then, he'd been bright-eyed and naive. Now, he was tempered by the reality of an NHL season—knowing the insane pace, the city's intense gaze, the daily demands. Yet he also carried confidence, forged by a strong rookie showing, plus the knowledge that he'd reconnected with his roots this summer.

He arrived at his modest Toronto apartment in the early evening, hauling in suitcases and hockey bags. The city lights shimmered in the distance. He stood on his small balcony, letting traffic noise and the swirl of urban life remind him of the environment he now called home. The off-season had given him rest, both physically and mentally, but also hammered home that the next step was crucial. No one soared in the NHL by coasting on a decent rookie year. He'd need to prove he could avoid the so-called "sophomore slump," remain healthy, and keep delivering in a league hungry for fresh stars.

That night, Doug tidied up, glancing at the Leafs gear neatly stacked in the corner. Nostalgic pangs for the pond and his family's house threatened to tug him backward, but he also felt anticipation for the upcoming training camp. He recalled the swirl of trade rumors, deciding once more to set them aside. The only path forward was to excel, to make himself indispensable.

He texted some teammates, confirming optional workouts at the Leafs' practice facility the next morning. Then, he sat down on the couch, flipping through a small notebook he'd used all summer—notes on training improvements, personal goals, and mental reminders gleaned from mentors and old coaches. A final page read:

- **Stay disciplined**: diet, workouts, mental fortitude.
- **Focus on the controllable**: your attitude, your effort.
- **Keep the joy**: never lose sight of the reason you started playing.

Doug read the words carefully, letting them sink in. They felt like a personal mission statement. The off-season had reaffirmed each point. Now, he'd carry them into Year Two, an even more challenging NHL season. He closed the notebook, exhaling a slow breath. Outside, city lights glowed. In the hush of that moment, he felt ready—balanced between the comfort of home and the ambition that fueled his pro career.

Rising from the couch, Doug walked to the window, gazing at the city skyline. The next day's training, the looming storyline of a new Leafs campaign, the fanbase's unstoppable Cup dreams—it all lay ahead. But for tonight, at least, he was content with the knowledge that he'd made the most of his off-season. He'd reconnected with the people he loved, rediscovered the pure essence of hockey on a small pond, and prepared mentally and physically for the battles to come.

A small smile ghosted his lips. The journey continued, one step at a time, just as it always had. Tomorrow, the rink awaited, and with it, the renewed demands of a proud, storied franchise wanting to hoist the Cup after decades of longing. Doug

Mansfield, no longer just a starry-eyed rookie, felt more grounded than ever. Bring on the new season—he was ready for whatever came next.

22

TRADE RUMOURS

Doug glanced at the phone on his bedside table for the hundredth time that morning, mentally willing it *not* to buzz. In the past week, every ping of a new message, every call, every social media tag seemed to carry a new swirl of speculation. The Maple Leafs had stumbled in the early part of Doug's second NHL season, going on a brutal losing streak that turned the entire city into a cauldron of frustration. Media outlets hammered management for not constructing a Cup-caliber roster; fans demanded immediate changes. And amidst it all, Doug's name had unexpectedly found its way into trade rumours.

He sat up in bed, running a hand through tousled hair. His second season with the Maple Leafs was supposed to be an opportunity to build on a promising rookie year—improve his offensive production, solidify his role in the top-six, maybe even help push the team deeper into the playoffs. Instead, the Leafs' slow start triggered talk about potential blockbusters: shipping out younger players (including Doug) in exchange for a star forward or top defenseman.

It felt surreal, and more than a little unnerving. Doug's rookie year had ended on an optimistic note; coaches and management had praised his steady improvement and intangible leadership. But as he'd learned repeatedly, professional hockey was a business—loyalty lasted only as long as the results on the ice. And the Leafs, desperate for a Cup and battered by fan discontent, were now rumored to be exploring every option. Including, apparently, trading Doug Mansfield.

His phone lay quiet for now. Doug exhaled, forcing himself out of bed to dress for morning skate. If he fixated on rumors, he'd unravel. Best to block the noise, focus on his day-to-day performance. Still, the dread refused to vanish entirely, a nagging reminder that no one in the NHL was untouchable. *All I can do is play my best,* he reminded himself, heading out the door, bag slung over his shoulder.

At the Leafs' practice facility, an uneasy hush pervaded the locker room. The losing streak weighed on everyone—veterans snapped at each other over minor mistakes, younger guys walked on eggshells, glancing nervously at the coaching staff. The local press had reported that Maple Leafs' management was under pressure from ownership to either rebuild around a new core or land a superstar via a high-stakes trade. No one knew what that meant for the current roster.

Doug navigated to his stall, bracing for the usual morning banter, but found only tense greetings. **Jonas Leroux**, a veteran forward who'd mentored Doug during his rookie year, offered a curt nod. The typically jovial younger players were subdued, eyes glued to their phones or the floor. Rumors circulated that two or three big names were on the block. Doug's ears burned whenever the topic arose, certain that his name might be bandied about.

He suited up quietly, trying to stay calm. He half-listened as a couple of teammates whispered about the GM's rumored desire to package "promising youth" for an immediate impact star. The harsh reality struck him: *I am that promising youth.* Another swirling rumor: a star center from out west might be available, and the Leafs wanted to outbid other teams with a package of picks and prospects. Doug forced the thoughts aside, lacing his skates with uncharacteristic fervor. *Focus on the ice,* he told himself. *Let your game speak.*

Coach Reynolds eventually strolled in, briskly announcing lines for the upcoming practice. Doug's line assignment remained unchanged—for now. But the sense of collective uncertainty made every drill feel like a spotlight test, as if each shift in practice would determine if you'd still be a Maple Leaf tomorrow.

On the ice, Doug skated with as much intensity as he could muster, pushing through breakout drills, refining his net-front presence. He found fleeting comfort in the mechanics of the game, momentarily forgetting the swirling rumor mill. Then, mid-practice, a team staffer abruptly pulled Jonas Leroux aside. The rest of the players exchanged worried glances, wondering if a trade had just dropped. Turned out it was just an equipment matter, but the anxiety in the air was palpable. Everyone jumped at the slightest abnormality.

After practice, reporters swarmed the corridor, hoping for any tidbit on the potential moves. Doug did his best to duck out quickly, but one persistent beat writer cornered him near the exit, recorder in hand. "Doug, any comment on rumors that the Leafs might be packaging you in a trade to acquire a marquee forward? Have you spoken with management about your future here?"

Doug forced a measured response: "I'm just focused on playing hockey, helping the team win," he said, trying to keep his voice steady. "Everything else is out of my control." The reporter pressed for more, but Doug politely excused himself. *So this is how it's going to be,* he thought, frustration simmering. *They'll chase me for a quote every day until the situation resolves.*

He slung his bag over his shoulder, heading toward the players' lounge, where a few teammates sat around a table, picking at post-practice snacks. The tension was thick. Another reporter hovered outside the lounge windows, snapping photos. Doug sank into a chair, shaking his head. Anton Bergstrom, his Swedish friend from the previous year, gave him a wry smile. "Trade rumors. If it's not you, it's me," Anton muttered. "This city's insane."

Doug nodded in resigned agreement, nibbling on a protein bar. The pressure in the city for a Cup run twisted normalcy into a swirl of speculation, especially when the team struggled. "We can't control management decisions," Doug sighed. "All we can do is show up tomorrow, keep working." Anton patted his shoulder sympathetically. Yet, both knew that advice felt flimsy amidst the daily swirl of potential trades.

The losing skid continued that week, culminating in a dispiriting 5–1 home defeat. As the final buzzer sounded, fans booed, fueling the rumor mill further: *Surely major moves are imminent.* Doug skated off, gut churning, wishing they could silence the critics with a big win. But wins seemed hard to come by these days.

Back in the locker room, frustrations boiled over. Some veterans tossed gear with curses, a few players snapped at each other for missed assignments. The tension escalated when a longtime Maple Leafs player—**Devon Wallace**, an alternate captain and Toronto staple for nearly a decade—began ranting about "lack of effort." He singled out younger guys for not stepping up. Doug, removing his helmet, felt Wallace's glare in his direction.

"Rookies, second-year guys... you all gotta realize what's at stake," Wallace spat, voice trembling with anger. "We've tried to build a Cup team around here for years, and if you can't handle the pressure, maybe you should be gone." The emphasis on "gone" felt like a dagger.

Doug bristled. He respected Wallace's seniority, but the blame felt unfairly broad. He mustered a calm tone. "We're all trying. No one wants to lose. I'm giving everything I have."

Wallace slammed his stick into the floor. "Trying isn't enough. You see these trade rumors? Management's gonna blow it up if we don't start winning. Better shape up or ship out." The raw bitterness in his voice stung.

Doug's frustration flared, fed by the swirling uncertainty. "Look, I can't control trade rumors. We do our best every shift. Don't pin this all on younger players."

"That's easy for you to say," Wallace fired back. "You're not the one who's stuck here a decade with no Cup. You're just a piece that might get moved for a star. Maybe you'd prefer a smaller market with less pressure."

The entire room fell silent. Jonas Leroux tried to intervene, placing a hand on Wallace's shoulder, urging him to cool down. But the damage was done. Doug's cheeks burned with a mix of indignation and hurt. Wallace's outburst hammered home the possibility: *Maybe Toronto will trade me. Maybe they see me as expendable.*

Doug bit back a sharper retort, recalling how escalations in a locker room rarely ended well. He just shook his head and turned away, grabbing his gear. The tension lingered like a storm cloud overhead.

That confrontation rattled Doug more than he wanted to admit. He left the arena that night with a pit in his stomach, the city's lights blurred by mounting frustration. *Is he right? Am I just a piece to be moved?* he wondered. The idea that management might trade him to acquire a bigger name or more immediate help stung. He'd dreamed of playing for the Leafs since childhood, picturing himself raising the Cup in that iconic jersey. Now, it felt precarious.

He phoned his father on the drive home, needing a stabilizing voice. "Dad," he began, "I've never felt so uncertain here. The rumors, the losing streak, and even teammates turning on each other." His father offered calm reassurance: "Son, you know how pro sports can be. If a trade happens, it happens. Focus on what you can do—play your game, keep professional. If you end up somewhere else, you'll adapt."

The logic was sound, but heartbreak flickered at the idea of leaving the Leafs. That night, Doug scrolled social media in bed, seeing fans split: some demanded the Leafs package him for a marquee star, others insisted he was part of the future. The noise made his head spin. He closed his phone in frustration, trying to block it all out.

The next morning's practice began with a players-only meeting. Coach Reynolds, aware of tension, let the leadership group speak first. Wallace apologized somewhat reluctantly for the outburst, explaining how the years of heartbreak weighed heavily on him. Doug nodded quietly, still smarting, but accepted the olive branch. They needed unity if they hoped to climb out of this slump.

On the ice, Doug tried to recapture a sense of normalcy— battling in corner drills, firing crisp passes, and focusing on the coaching staff's instructions. The swirl of trade talk remained in the background, but at least the confrontation with Wallace had eased somewhat. Jonas Leroux gave Doug a supportive pat after a particularly strong shift, whispering, "Keep your head up, kid. We need you here." Doug nodded, grateful for the vote of confidence.

After practice, management made a statement to the press, refusing to comment on "baseless speculation." The GM insisted the Leafs believed in their young core, hoping to quell rumors. But privately, everyone knew that if the losing streak continued, changes could come swiftly. Doug still felt that heaviness—like a storm cloud that might break at any moment.

That week, a scheduled match against Doug's hometown rival presented a chance at redemption. The arena buzzed with anxious energy, Leafs fans craving a spark to quell the negativity. Doug was determined to use the game to reaffirm his value to the organization.

In the first period, he notched a slick primary assist—threading a backhand feed through traffic for a teammate's tap-in. The crowd roared with relief. Then, in the second, Doug snagged a rebound and snapped it top shelf, doubling the lead. He pounded the glass in celebration, heart pounding with the feeling that maybe, just maybe, they could turn this around.

The final horn sounded with a 4–1 victory, the Leafs' best showing in weeks. The building erupted in cheers, fans chanting, "Let's go Leafs!" Doug exhaled, a rare moment of joy overshadowing the rumor gloom. After the game, reporters clamored for quotes—some praising Doug's two-point night as a sign he was too integral to trade. Doug offered polite answers, crediting the team effort. Still, beneath the satisfaction lay a lingering question: *Would one good game stop management from exploring deals?*

A day later, Doug found himself summoned to the GM's office, a dreaded scenario for any player living under swirling speculation. Heart hammering, he entered the glass-walled room overlooking practice ice. The GM greeted him with a professional smile, inviting him to sit.

"Doug, I know the rumor mill's been insane," the GM said, voice level. "I wanted to speak to you directly. We value you. You're a first-round pick, and we see a bright future. That said, we're exploring all avenues to improve the team. I can't guarantee zero trade discussions, but I want you to know you're not being shopped actively."

Relief battled with anxiety in Doug's chest. "I appreciate the honesty," he managed. "I want to stay in Toronto, to help this team succeed. I know we've hit bumps, but I'm committed."

The GM nodded. "That's good to hear. We're under pressure—this city demands results. But we drafted you for the long haul. Keep doing your job on the ice, and let us handle the rest."

Doug left the meeting slightly reassured, though the GM's cautious language left the door open. *No active shopping, but maybe if the right offer comes along...* Regardless, at least he had some direct communication rather than swirling gossip.

For the next few weeks, Doug juggled attempts to stay locked in on his performance with the ever-present rumor chatter. The Leafs hovered around the playoff bubble, not entirely out of contention but far from secure. Each victory felt like a band-aid on management's inclination to make a move; each defeat reignited trade talk among fans and analysts.

Doug poured himself into every practice, trying to model the leadership traits he'd cultivated back in junior. Jonas Leroux, sensing Doug's turmoil, occasionally dragged him out for coffee, telling old stories about how he'd faced trade rumors earlier in his career. "It's all part of the big show, kid," Jonas would say. "One minute they love you, next minute you're rumored to be on the block. Just survive the roller coaster."

The confrontation with Wallace eventually faded, replaced by a quiet acceptance that the whole locker room had to unify or risk being dismantled. Wallace even approached Doug after a morning skate, patting him on the shoulder. "Sorry for unloading on you," he said gruffly. "We're all frustrated. I do appreciate what you bring to the team. Let's bury these trade rumors ourselves—by winning."

Doug nodded, grateful. Indeed, if the Leafs played better, management might see no need for a massive shake-up.

By the season's mid-point, the Leafs had stabilized somewhat, going on a modest winning streak that re-energized fans. Doug posted a respectable point pace, cementing his role on a line that provided secondary scoring. The rumor mill calmed, though occasional headlines still mentioned Doug's name as a potential piece if the Leafs suddenly pivoted toward a rebuild or parted with key veterans.

Doug's resolve hardened. He realized how little control he had over the business side of the league, but the one thing in his power was how he played. He refused to let the noise undermine his confidence. If management saw his steady improvement and heart, maybe that alone would shield him from trade blocks.

One afternoon, local TV caught him leaving practice, asking if he worried about being dealt. Doug answered with a small smile: "I love being a Maple Leaf. I want to help this team win. That's my focus." It was a succinct response, but it made headlines anyway, fans debating whether his words indicated unwavering loyalty or naive positivity. Doug shrugged it off—beyond his pay grade.

The Leafs' front office eventually publicly denied rumors of a major teardown, calling them "overblown speculation." The panic subsided. Doug exhaled, feeling a measure of relief. But the entire saga had been a wake-up call: in pro hockey, your place is never guaranteed.

By late in his second season, Doug felt a changed perspective on the NHL. He'd experienced the euphoria of being a hometown draftee, the exhaustion of a rookie year, the heartbreak of a losing streak, and the nerve-wracking swirl of trade chatter. The result was a deeper mental toughness. He discovered he could handle adversity better, forging an edge that veterans recognized. Even in practice battles, Doug approached drills with extra tenacity, driven to prove he was essential to the Leafs' future.

Media members picked up on his evolving game. His name appeared less in trade rumor columns and more in stories praising his consistent development. Meanwhile, Doug quietly recognized that if the Leafs were truly to break their Cup drought, stability might be key—rather than swapping out young talent for a quick fix. At least that's what he hoped management believed.

He also found new motivation in that near-confrontation with Wallace. The longtime Leaf had apologized, but it served as a reminder: guys who'd been chasing the elusive championship for years had their own frustrations. Doug wanted to be part of a solution, bridging the generational gap, bringing fresh energy without ignoring the veterans' urgency. He harnessed every rumor as fuel, determined to make management see he was untouchable in their quest for a Cup.

As the final months of the season approached, the Leafs clung to a wild-card playoff spot. The rumor mill still flickered, but less ferociously. Doug stepped into each game with renewed calm, focusing on details—board battles, quick zone exits, timely passes. The city's mania might not vanish, but Doug had learned to compartmentalize the noise.

One evening, after a satisfying win that boosted Toronto's playoff hopes, Doug found himself lingering on the ice, scanning the stands. He recalled the day he'd first arrived as a rookie, wide-eyed and naive, never expecting trade chatter to swirl so soon. Now, he felt older in hockey years, more attuned to the NHL's unpredictable nature. He'd discovered a resilience he didn't know he possessed.

As the crowd filtered out, a few kids waved from the glass, sporting Doug's #29 jersey. He skated over, tapping his stick against the glass in thanks. In their eyes, he saw the reflection of that same dream he once carried—playing for the Leafs, being a hero in a hockey mecca. If a trade ever happened, it wouldn't be by his choice. But for now, he was still a Maple Leaf, fighting for this city's elusive Cup dream, fueled by the unwavering love he'd had for the franchise since boyhood.

Doug skated away with a small smile. Tomorrow would bring another practice, another wave of speculation, another push in the standings. But he felt ready. Because no matter the rumors or the pressure, he'd keep giving everything. And maybe, just maybe, in this city so hungry for a Stanley Cup, his unwavering dedication would finally help break the cycle of heartbreak—if management let him stay long enough to see it through.

23

A NEW CONTRACT

Doug sat at the kitchen table in his modest Toronto apartment, laptop open to a spreadsheet of player salaries and cap breakdowns. He wasn't used to sifting through so many numbers—a far cry from the usual focus on game tape and practice drills—but such was the reality of the contract negotiations swirling around him. The Maple Leafs had, in a surprising move, tabled an offer for a multi-year extension. After the tumult of trade rumors, Doug had half-expected the door to remain open for a potential move. Instead, management had pivoted: they wanted Doug in Toronto for the long haul.

He exhaled, a mix of relief and cautious optimism fluttering in his chest. The negotiations were tense, no question. Doug's agent believed Doug deserved a bump in pay commensurate with his steady production and intangible leadership qualities, while the Leafs' front office aimed to keep their payroll flexible for other pieces. Both sides recognized the significance of forging a new contract that wouldn't hamper the team's Cup ambitions or undervalue Doug's contributions.

His phone buzzed. An incoming call from his agent. Doug braced himself, hitting the accept button. "Hey, Mark," he greeted, voice steady.

"Doug, just got off the phone with the Leafs' cap guy," Mark said. "We're close. They're inching up on the annual average value, but they want an extra year tacked on. It's actually a decent figure, but we can push a bit more on term."

Doug stared at his scattered notes—comparables to other second-year players signing their first big extension, each with differing stats. "You think it's enough to reflect my potential? I don't want to come off as greedy, but..."

Mark's tone softened. "I get it. That's why we're fighting to ensure your next few years—and your role—are locked in. The Leafs see you as a core piece; you've proven your worth. Let me handle the final wrinkles. I'll circle back soon."

With that, the call ended. Doug sat back, heart thudding with excitement and nerves. The dream from childhood—playing for the Maple Leafs—might not just continue but become a long-term reality. He tried not to think about the weight of the city's expectations, or the next day's headlines. Instead, he let himself briefly relish the fact that he'd come this far— from a first-round pick overshadowed by bigger names, to a rumored trade piece, to now a potential cornerstone of Toronto's future.

Days bled into a tense week of negotiations. Doug juggled daily practices, film sessions, and occasional media scrums with the background hum of contract talk. The Leafs were in the thick of a playoff chase—a narrative overshadowed by the key question of whether Doug Mansfield would be locked up.

Reporters peppered him with questions: "Any progress on the contract?" "Do you want to stay in Toronto?" Each time, Doug offered a measured answer—"I love the team. My agent's handling negotiations. I'm focusing on hockey." Meanwhile, social media speculated on contract figures, fueling debate about whether Doug was demanding too much for a second-year forward, or if the Leafs were lowballing a crucial piece.

His agent Mark remained confident they'd strike a deal. "Both sides want to get this done," he assured Doug. "Management sees you as vital, you're happy in Toronto. The only friction is the exact dollars and the term. But that's how these things go."

During a routine morning skate at Scotiabank Arena, the Leafs' GM quietly pulled Doug aside, wearing a small smile. "We're close," the GM said, voice low. "You've earned this, Mansfield. We want you here. I expect we'll finalize in the next 48 hours."

Doug nodded, a surge of relief flooding him. After months of uncertainty—trade chatter, doubts—this direct assurance felt like a breath of fresh air. He left the rink that day with a renewed spark, even potting two goals in a tight 3–2 win that night, fueling the Leafs' playoff aspirations.

Yet the final step was never seamless. Another day passed without a formal announcement. Doug's agent reported a minor snag: the Leafs wanted a no-trade clause to kick in only after a certain year, while Mark argued for earlier security. Doug tried not to let the details rattle him, trusting Mark's expertise. But as hours dragged, he couldn't help refreshing sports news sites, half-expecting an article about negotiations collapsing.

That evening, he sat in his apartment's small living room, scrolling social media. Leafs fans posted anxious messages: *"Sign Mansfield already!"* Some shared mock-up cap breakdowns, dissecting each line on a hypothetical contract. The city was invested. Doug realized this was another hallmark of playing in Toronto—fans lived every transaction as though it determined the Cup's fate.

Finally, near midnight, Mark texted: *We got it. Meet me at the Leafs facility tomorrow for the signing.* Doug's pulse quickened. *This is real.* He typed back an enthusiastic response before sinking into the couch, relief and excitement tangling in his chest. By tomorrow, he'd be a Maple Leaf for years to come—officially.

The next morning, Doug arrived at the Leafs' practice facility, heart pounding with a mix of pride and disbelief. A small group of staff and PR people awaited him in a conference room. The GM greeted him warmly, motioning him toward a seat. On the table lay a neatly printed contract, multi-year terms spelled out in black and white, numbers that made Doug's eyes widen slightly. He'd never dreamed of earning this kind of money—especially playing for the team he'd adored since he was a kid.

Mark guided Doug through each line, ensuring he double-checked the term length, average annual salary, performance bonuses, and the partial no-trade clause. The final figure was a fair compromise: a decent paycheck that recognized his potential, while allowing the Leafs to maintain cap flexibility. Doug swallowed, pen poised, as everyone watched quietly.

After a deep breath, he signed his name. The GM shook his hand, and the staff applauded politely. A wave of relief crashed over Doug—the moment that solidified his place in Toronto. No more swirling rumors about being a trade chip for a superstar. He was, for better or worse, locked into the Maple Leafs' future.

Flash photography erupted as the PR staff took pictures of Doug with a Leafs jersey. Then came official statements: press releases, website announcements. Doug answered a few quick questions, confirming he was "ecstatic" to remain in Toronto, praising the management's trust, and reaffirming his commitment to bring a championship to the city. The PR staff teased that a more formal press conference might happen soon, but for now, they'd keep it low-key.

Word traveled fast. Within hours, local sports channels broadcast the news: *Doug Mansfield Signs Multi-Year Extension With Maple Leafs.* Pundits debated if it was a "steal" for the team or an overpay for a still-developing forward. Doug found it dizzying—but overshadowed by sheer gratitude. He stepped into the locker room post-signing, greeted by teammates' cheers and playful ribbing. Jonas Leroux teased, "Hey, big-money man, lunch's on you, right?"

Doug laughed, shrugging. "I guess I owe you guys a meal." The overall mood was celebratory. Veteran **Devon Wallace**, who'd once confronted Doug during the losing streak, shook his hand firmly. "Congrats, kid," he murmured, sincerity in his eyes. "Now you're a core piece. Let's chase that Cup."

A private press scrum followed, with city media clamoring for quotes. Doug faced the cameras, attempting to project calm confidence:

Reporter 1: "Doug, how does it feel to sign this extension in a city so hungry for a championship?"

Doug: "It's an honor. I grew up a Leafs fan, so to commit long-term is surreal. I want to be part of the solution—bringing the Cup to Toronto."

Reporter 2: "Were you concerned about trade rumors? Does this contract put those to rest?"

Doug: "I can't control rumors. But yes, I'm relieved. I want to stay, and management believes in me. Now I can focus fully on helping the team."

Reporter 3: "What do you say to fans who hope you become a star that leads the Leafs to glory?"

Doug: "I say I'll do everything I can, every shift, every game. The city deserves success. I'm here to give my all for that goal."

The final question: "Any nerves about living up to the contract?"

Doug offered a small grin. "Every NHL player with a new deal feels that pressure. I'll channel it as motivation. The city's behind me, and I'm behind this team. Let's see what we can achieve."

That night, Doug ventured out briefly with a few teammates to a local restaurant, a quiet celebratory dinner. Fans who recognized him offered handshakes and congratulations, praising the "kid with the heart" for committing to the Leafs. The city seemed to exhale a collective sigh of relief that their promising forward would remain. Leafs jerseys with his name popped up in shop windows, some fans even scrawling "Mansfield 4-Ever" on homemade signs. Doug found it both touching and slightly overwhelming.

His phone overflowed with texts: old junior teammates, family friends, even some Maple Leafs alumni he'd encountered wishing him luck. He read each with a grateful smile. The overshadowing fear of being traded was gone, replaced by a new weight: fulfilling the high expectations that come with a multi-year contract in the heart of the hockey universe.

In the weeks that followed, Doug discovered a subtle shift in how coaches and media approached him. He was no longer just the plucky second-year player; he was an integral part of the core, expected to produce nightly, to lead on and off the ice. Management peppered him with leadership responsibilities—appearing in community outreach events, speaking up in the locker room, mentoring the younger rookies. He welcomed it, though the sense of responsibility felt heavier than ever.

During games, fans chanted his name more vigorously. Each goal or assist was lauded as evidence that the extension was money well spent; each slump or mistake brought mild grumbling about "return on investment." Doug navigated these ups and downs with a thicker skin, reminding himself that the joy of being a Leaf came with unrelenting scrutiny.

One game at Scotiabank Arena, Doug scored a tying goal in the final minute, then assisted the game-winner in overtime. The crowd roared as if a Cup had been won. Cameras panned to him on the bench, the commentators lauding his extension as already paying dividends. Doug felt a jolt of pride. *This is why I wanted to stay,* he thought, *to create moments like these for these fans.*

Beyond the on-ice results, Doug made a public statement of devotion to the Leafs, echoing what he'd told the press on signing day: "I'm here to bring a Cup to Toronto." Over social media, he repeated that vow in a short, heartfelt post. Leafs Nation ate it up, retweeting it widely, proclaiming him part of the city's future. For Doug, it wasn't just a PR line; he believed it deeply, envisioning that sweet day a championship banner might hang over the city that had waited so long.

Some critics cynically pointed out that players always say they want to bring a Cup, but few deliver. Doug accepted that. Words weren't enough—he had to put them into practice, fueling the team's progress. The pressure weighed on him, but he'd grown adept at harnessing pressure as motivation, forging a mental toughness reminiscent of his junior days.

As the season progressed, Doug's performance solidified. He built chemistry with a couple of star forwards, forging a formidable line that combined skill with Doug's gritty board work. The Leafs, though still flawed, found themselves in a healthier playoff position. And with Doug locked in for multiple years, management had less reason to panic. The rumor mill quieted. Instead, fans pinned new hopes on this stabilized core, including Doug, to evolve into a Cup contender.

In early spring, with the playoff picture looming, the Leafs announced a "Core Four" event—spotlighting four cornerstone players expected to lead the franchise. Doug was among them, along with two established stars and a breakout defenseman. They posed for a promotional shoot, each wearing Leafs gear, eyes locked on the camera. The tagline read: *"Our Future, Our Fight."* Doug felt a surge of emotion. He'd dreamt of being a key Maple Leaf since boyhood; now the organization publicly declared him as such.

That evening, he called his father. "It's official, Dad," Doug said, voice brimming with excitement. "They see me as part of the core. That's more than I ever dared hope for." His father's voice beamed with pride: "Just keep working. We believe in you, and so does the city."

And so, in the midst of a tense playoff chase, Doug found himself stepping into a fresh chapter of his hockey journey. The trade talk had dissolved, replaced by a multi-year contract that entwined him with Toronto's quest for an elusive Stanley Cup. The city roared approval each night he took the ice, his jersey flying off shelves, fans eager to see him mature into a genuine star.

In the locker room, he carried himself with more confidence, leaning on older veterans but also voicing his perspective when needed. The confrontation with certain teammates during the rumors had shifted into mutual respect, each acknowledging that Doug was here to stay. He'd handle the city's mania, the unstoppable media presence, and the Cup hunger. He'd embrace it all.

One night, after a thrilling 5–4 overtime victory, he lingered on the ice, tapping gloves with fans at the boards. He recalled that boyhood moment on the frozen pond, imagining wearing the Maple Leafs crest, vowing to bring success to Toronto. Now he wore that crest for years to come, financially secure and embraced by the fanbase. Yet, deep inside, he knew the real measurement would be in playoff success, in whether they eventually lifted that hallowed trophy. *I'll do everything possible to make that happen,* he thought, a determined smile tugging at his lips.

As he left the rink, the city's lights sparkling in the distance, Doug Mansfield felt more assured than ever that his place was here—fighting, thriving, and growing with the Maple Leafs. The off-ice battles over trade rumors, the negotiations, the whirlwind of endorsements—none of it mattered as much as stepping onto that ice, wearing blue and white, forging a brighter future for a franchise that believed in him. And with the multi-year deal inked, he'd have every chance to keep that promise: bringing a Cup home to Toronto.

24

THE GRIND

Doug flexed his stiff shoulder in the dimly lit corridor behind the locker room, rolling out the tension that had settled in after yet another grueling matchup. His muscles ached in ways he'd never imagined back when he was a wide-eyed rookie—back before he'd learned the true toll of an 82-game NHL season, year after year, each new run blending into the next. The Maple Leafs had just eked out a 3–2 victory, snapping a mini-losing streak. It was only November, but already the demands of Toronto's relentless hockey market pressed down on Doug and his teammates like the onset of a heavy winter storm.

He loosened the tape from his wrist, letting the unraveling sound echo in the quiet corridor. **Jonas Leroux**, the veteran forward who'd once mentored Doug, offered a wry grin as he passed, calling out, "We needed that one." Doug nodded in agreement. Wins in this city were never just two points—they were small reprieves from the torrent of media pressure, fan expectations, and locker-room scrutiny that came with every Leafs campaign.

Doug's second contract was well in the rearview mirror now, with multiple seasons in the bag. He'd outgrown the "promising rookie" label, morphing into a reliable two-way forward the Leafs counted on. The trade rumors of earlier years had faded, replaced by a steady presence on the roster.

Yet, each season's grind took its toll, physically and mentally. Some nights, Doug found himself longing for the simple purity of the small-town pond where it all began—before the big contracts, the bright lights, and the swirling frenzy of Toronto hockey.

But as he made his way into the locker room, the reality of the path he'd chosen settled in. This was his life—**the grind**—one that tested him daily and defined him as a pro athlete in a city starved for a championship.

Time seemed to blur once you found your groove in the NHL. Doug had accumulated enough seasons to look back on a mosaic of ups and downs: shocking winning streaks that lit up the city's hopes, demoralizing slumps that had entire radio stations calling for heads to roll, playoff heartbreaks in epic seven-game sagas, and the quiet heartbreak of injuries that sidelined him for weeks at a time. He'd experienced new coaching staffs, roster overhauls, and leadership changes among the team's core. Through it all, he'd maintained his role as a dependable two-way presence, someone who could be trusted in critical defensive moments yet spark offense with a timely shot or incisive pass.

His jersey, once shiny and new, bore the scuffs and nicks of countless collisions. Over the years, he'd moved up from second-liner to an alternate captain role, a reflection of the respect he'd earned in the dressing room. When asked about it, Doug had simply said, "I just keep my head down and work. This city demands that you never stop pushing."

The city itself could be unforgiving. Losses never felt like just a tally in the wrong column; they became micro-crises, dissected by talk radio, dissected by headlines screaming on the next morning's sports pages. Rumors and speculation about the Leafs' Cup drought—now decades in the making—never truly went away. Doug learned to tune out the static, focusing on daily execution: defense, forecheck, transition, special teams. But ignoring the noise didn't mean it disappeared; it only meant he carried it with a certain practiced resilience, each year thickening his emotional armor.

The 82-game season loomed large every autumn, a marathon that started with high optimism and ended with bodies battered and morale tested. Doug discovered that every off-season he needed to reevaluate his training. Over time, he'd improved his conditioning, adopted specialized recovery protocols, and remained vigilant with nutrition—anything to stave off the injuries that inevitably came with so many collisions in so many games.

In particular, he recalled a harrowing stretch in January of one season, when the Leafs embarked on a ten-day road trip through the Western Conference. Long flights, compressed schedules, a new city each night. Doug had played through a nagging hip flexor strain, re-injuring it mid-journey. Instead of resting, he forced himself through the pain for the sake of the team's precarious standings position. By the time they returned to Toronto, doctors insisted on a short IR stint. Doug hated missing games, but the grind had reached its breaking point. Another lesson learned: you had to manage your body if you wanted longevity in this league.

Yet, even injuries didn't fully shield him from the avalanche of media and fan questions. "How soon will Mansfield return?" "Does his absence reveal the Leafs' lack of depth?" Each day, new speculation. Doug tried to keep perspective. "It's part of the job here," he'd say calmly. "You do your best to recover and help the team however you can."

Quietly, though, he'd reflect on that small-town pond—where the only voices that mattered were friendly shouts of a pick-up game.

Year after year, Doug's Leafs found themselves in bruising battles against division rivals. The matchups against Montreal or Boston carried a different energy—hitting soared, tension crackled, the media hype soared to a feverish pitch. By the time the playoffs arrived, Doug's body and mind teetered on the edge of exhaustion, yet he craved the postseason, the chance to chase the Cup that Toronto yearned for.

Some runs ended early, overshadowed by heartbreak in the first or second round, plagued by an ill-timed defensive lapse or an unbeatable opposing goalie. Other times, the Leafs clawed deeper—Conference Finals appearances that had the city delirious with hope, only to face heartbreak in seven-game heartbreakers. Doug recalled those nights vividly: leaving the ice with a mixture of sweat and tears, apologizing silently to the fans who'd believed, knowing he'd left everything out there.

One year, the Leafs advanced to the Eastern Conference Final, clashing with a big, physical team that turned every shift into a war. Doug's line played valiantly, he scored a few pivotal goals, but the series dragged into triple-overtime games that left entire rosters battered. By the time the Leafs were eliminated in Game 7, Doug could barely stand without wincing. He'd sustained a hairline fracture in his foot that had gone unnoticed for two games. But he kept playing—**that** was the demand of a city starved for a chance at glory.

Despite the heartbreak of elimination, those deep runs forged his sense of belonging. Each time, he returned the following season with a grim determination, forging a stronger leadership presence in the locker room. He carried the scars of prior campaigns as badges of experience—reminders that the Cup demanded everything.

Toronto's management also underwent periodic upheaval—new GMs, coaching changes, reshuffling among the assistant coaches. Doug, as he matured, became a steady figure for younger players to turn to whenever the winds of change blew in. He shared the lessons gleaned from old mentors like Jonas Leroux, now retired. At times, captains shifted, leading to fresh voices in the dressing room. Doug accepted each transition with professional grace, adapting his role as needed.

He recognized that, in a city like Toronto, a coaching staff's lifespan often depended on immediate results. One slump might see a new face behind the bench. Doug's background— having survived trade rumors, signing a multi-year extension—positioned him as a "bridge" between different eras. He sat at the intersection of older veterans hanging on for a Cup run and fresh draftees eager to prove themselves.

That bridging role was invaluable. Doug learned to unify the dressing room, smoothing generational gaps, reminding rookies that mistakes were part of the process, and cautioning older players against frustration that could fracture team chemistry. The media soon labeled him a "quiet leader," a label Doug wore with humble pride. After all, he never aimed for the limelight, only to ensure everyone pulled together through the turbulence that was Leafs hockey.

Doug sometimes chuckled at how quickly time passed. Where once Jonas Leroux or Devon Wallace had guided him, now he was the one noticing wide-eyed rookies fresh from junior or overseas, uncertain how to handle Toronto's mania. He'd see them drifting near the bench after practice, anxious for direction, and he'd step in:

"Hey, man, let's work on those board battles. I noticed you're bracing yourself too early. Keep your center of gravity lower."

Or:

"Don't sweat that turnover. We all make mistakes. Next shift's a clean slate. Trust me, I've been there."

He'd recall his own youth and how a single encouraging word from a veteran had boosted his confidence immeasurably. Now, paying it forward felt right. Some of the rookies would eventually surpass him in raw scoring or star potential, but that didn't faze Doug. The team's success overshadowed any personal pride. He relished seeing younger talent blossom, forging a deeper sense of continuity for the Leafs' future.

One afternoon, a rookie named **Jason Kim**, just 19, approached Doug timidly after practice, confessing he was struggling with media scrutiny following a poor performance. Doug empathized deeply—he'd walked that path. Over a half-hour talk in the lounge, Doug imparted lessons gleaned from his small-town pond days, how playing for pure love of the game could ground you against external noise. "Just remember why you fell in love with hockey," he told Kim. "Hold on to that, and the media stuff shrinks." Kim thanked him quietly, eyes shining with relief.

But even as he embraced his mentorship role, Doug couldn't avoid the harsh physical toll. One season, he suffered a separated shoulder after a bone-jarring hit along the boards. He spent weeks rehabbing, missing a significant chunk of the schedule. The tabloids hollered that the Leafs needed reinforcements, fueling speculation the team might accelerate a trade. Doug's recovery spelled endless days in the training room, where he wrestled with self-doubt: *If I can't stay healthy, am I failing the team?*

He returned just in time for a late playoff push, feeling half a step slower initially. The Leafs scraped into the postseason but fell in six games to a gritty Western Conference opponent. In the off-season, fans lamented the "what ifs" of Doug's injury, a storyline amplified by Toronto's unquenchable hunger for success. Doug accepted it stoically—**the grind** was not just a matter of playing, but of coming back from each setback with resilience.

Year after year, columns debated: *Could Mansfield step into an even bigger leadership role? Was he capable of elevating the Leafs to Cup contention?* The speculation never ended, but Doug learned to manage it with seasoned calm. He recalled how, in that small Ontario backyard, he never needed the press's approval—only the joy of the puck on his stick.

One day, rummaging through his gear, Doug discovered an old photograph tucked into a side pocket—a snapshot of himself in junior, beaming after a big playoff goal. The innocence on his younger face moved him. He realized that kid, once overshadowed by star forward rivals, had become a recognized name in the NHL, the steadiest presence on a Maple Leafs team that had changed coaches, captains, and rosters multiple times. He'd endured heartbreak, soared in triumph, and lived the roller-coaster that was pro hockey in Canada's biggest market.

Now a veteran, he felt the city's Cup drought more keenly than ever, each season that ended without a parade adding to the burden. Still, he channeled that weight into leadership, hoping to mold the next generation of Leafs so that, together, they could break the cycle. If fans pinned their hopes on him as a pillar of stability, he'd do everything possible to justify that faith—even if it meant playing through pain or deflecting media pressure from younger teammates.

Rivalries also took on new shapes with each season. Teams that once overshadowed the Leafs—like Montreal or Boston—remained fierce adversaries, but now younger squads from out west or up-and-coming expansion teams also threatened their standing. Doug relished those intense games, the ones brimming with post-whistle shoves, raucous fan energy, and the chance for highlight-reel heroics. He wore bruises from those battles like badges.

Whenever an overzealous rival delivered a cheap shot on a Leafs rookie, Doug found himself intervening—no longer a scrawny second-year kid, but a hardened two-way forward unafraid to stand up for his teammates. On the bench, the younger guys watched with gratitude. Many told him he felt like a "big brother" figure. That touched Doug's heart. The example he set on the small-town pond—of protecting your teammates, playing with passion—lived on.

Throughout the regular season's routine, from road trips to back-to-back games, from morning skates to late-night flights, Doug kept forging his place in Toronto's tapestry. The city's relentless hockey media never let up, but Doug gave thoughtful quotes, deflected undue criticism from the rookies, and advocated for calm whenever the Leafs slid into losing spells.

A typical day for Doug involved early alarm calls for optional morning workouts, hours of film review with coaches, a full practice with the team, plus endless demands for interviews or charity appearances. He'd grown adept at compartmentalizing. The skill and passion that once purely fueled him now combined with discipline and emotional endurance. When people asked how he handled it, he'd shrug, offering: "It's the job. If I love this city enough to chase a Cup here, I have to embrace the daily grind."

In quieter moments, he stayed in touch with his family, who still lived in Ontario. Sometimes, they'd gather at the old pond or local rinks in the offseason, just for a casual skate. On those days, Doug's spirit rejuvenated—reminded that beyond the big contracts and bigger scrutiny, the essence of hockey remained the same: the crisp slice of skate blades on ice, the simple joy of chasing a puck with friends.

In one especially poignant off-season moment, Doug returned to that small town pond where he first discovered his love for hockey. A group of local kids, in awe of an actual Maple Leaf visiting, asked him to run a mini-skate clinic. Doug obliged. As he guided them through basic drills, memories of his younger self flooded him—uncertain yet hopeful, dreaming big from that same patch of ice.

He used those glimpses of nostalgia to remind the kids that dedication and heart could carry them far. *"Keep loving the game,"* he'd told them with an easy grin. *"That's how you survive the hardest battles."* They listened raptly, some likely daydreaming of following in his footsteps. Doug realized he'd grown from receiving that advice to giving it, and the circle felt complete.

Even after returning to Toronto for the start of another relentless season, the pond's spirit stuck with him. Some mornings, amid the hustle and bustle, he'd find solace recalling that quiet patch of ice, free from media glare. It rejuvenated his determination to keep grinding, keep setting an example, keep believing the Leafs could ultimately hoist the Cup.

Time marched on, and so did Doug's career. The lines on his face sharpened slightly, the once-rookie was now a seasoned presence wearing an "A" on his jersey. He tracked up-and-coming prospects, offering pointers to the new wave of Maple Leafs draftees. They asked him about dealing with Toronto's media circus, about staying consistent through 82 games, about navigating the ups and downs of playoff runs. He offered honest answers:

- "Focus on your craft every day. The noise will always be there—good or bad."
- "Play for your teammates, not the critics. That unity carries you deeper than any hype ever will."
- "Never lose the joy that brought you to hockey in the first place. That joy outlasts pressure."

Each season brought fresh heartbreak or fresh hope. Some years, the Leafs bowed out in early rounds. Other times, they pushed deeper, stirring the city's hunger again. Through it all, Doug served as a steady pillar. Fans came to see him not as a flash superstar, but as a heart-and-soul piece: the guy who took on tough minutes, chipped in vital goals, and never wavered in his devotion to a franchise that had been chasing a Cup for generations.

In a quiet moment, late in the night after a second-round playoff exit—another bruising seven-game heartbreak—Doug sat alone in the trainer's room, icing a battered knee. He felt the familiar ache of disappointment, but also the unwavering vow to return stronger. Jonas Leroux had long since retired, many of Doug's old mentors had moved on, and now he was the oldest forward in the lineup. He marveled at how the roles had reversed.

He contemplated the future. He still had years left on his contract, but he was no longer the bright-eyed kid. Did he still yearn for a Cup here? Absolutely. The city's desire for glory matched his own. If anything, the heartbreak fueled him. He decided that no matter the heartbreak, he'd keep forging ahead. The new generation needed his guidance, just as he'd once needed others' belief.

Sitting there, he closed his eyes, recalling the pond's reflection. The promise he'd made to himself in youth, to bring something special to the Maple Leafs. That vow had carried him through injuries, rumors, heartbreak, and the daily rigors of an NHL career in the big city. *Yes,* he thought, *the grind is real, but so is the dream.*

He rose, discarding the melted ice pack, stepping out into the corridor. The echoes of the empty rink, the city's lights glowing outside, reminded him that another off-season awaited—another chance to regroup, heal, and come back for more. He'd stand by the Maple Leafs crest, representing the team as a loyal soldier of the cause, and passing on the lessons he first discovered on a frozen pond, back when hockey was brand-new and infinitely pure.

And so, with battered knees and unwavering spirit, Doug Mansfield, the once-overshadowed rookie turned indispensable veteran, walked forward into the hallway's darkness, carrying the weight of a city and the unwavering hope that next year, or the year after, they'd all finally taste the triumph that only a Stanley Cup could bring.

25

THE QUEST FOR THE CUP

Doug stood at the threshold of the home locker room in Scotiabank Arena, his breath catching as he surveyed the row of Maple Leafs sweaters. Each one bore a name, a story, and a shared goal: the Stanley Cup. This season, more than any other in his career, felt like it could be *the one.* All around him, the city had erupted with renewed faith—some combination of strategic trades, blossoming young talent, and a maturing veteran core made for the strongest Leafs roster in decades. Even the cynical local media had toned down its usual alarmism, acknowledging that this lineup might truly contend.

He glanced down at his sweater, where the shiny **"A"** was stitched beneath the Maple Leafs crest. Doug had worn an "A" for years now, but tonight, the weight felt both heavier and more invigorating. *We're on the cusp,* he told himself. *We finally have the pieces.* He couldn't deny the surge of adrenaline coursing through him.

From the corridor, he heard the muffled roar of the crowd—fans chanting, stamping their feet in thunderous unison. The Leafs were about to open the first game of the playoffs, hosting a well-respected but lower-seeded opponent. The tension in the city was palpable: they wanted not just a deep run, but the ultimate prize. And so did Doug. That promise he'd made as a child—*to bring a Cup home to*

Toronto—echoed in his mind, fueling his resolve. He took a breath and stepped fully into the room, where teammates laced skates, taped sticks, and exchanged determined nods.

Reflecting on the regular season that had just concluded, Doug marveled at how everything aligned. The Maple Leafs boasted a lethal top line featuring a generational sniper, balanced by a second line with enough grit and scoring touch to handle any matchup. The defense corps had been bolstered by a marquee acquisition, finally providing steady presence at the blue line. And behind them, a veteran goalie, in top form, carried the confidence necessary to backstop a champion.

Doug's line—anchoring the middle-six—had flourished. He set career highs in points, but more importantly, embraced a leadership role both on the bench and off it. Younger wingers thrived under his guidance, and the synergy carried them to near the top of the standings. Night after night, the city roared as the Leafs found ways to win crucial matches. By season's end, they secured a first-round matchup that many pundits predicted they'd advance from with relative ease.

Still, this was Toronto, land of perpetual heartbreak. Fans tempered any cockiness with cautious optimism. Doug sensed it in every interview: "This group looks special," reporters would say. "But do you worry about the baggage of past failures?" Each time, he answered politely, emphasizing the team's new culture, discipline, and unity. Inside, he believed wholeheartedly that this year was different.

Indeed, the first round started with a bang. The Leafs jumped to a 2–0 series lead, dominating with speed and lethal power plays, spurring hopes of a quick series. But the opposing team rallied, as all NHL playoff squads do, clawing back to force a tense Game 6. Doug's line contributed key points, and their goalie stood on his head, earning a 3–2 series-clinching win that had the city breathing sighs of relief. One step down, three to go.

The second round, however, tested their mettle in seven heart-stopping games. Doug found himself in a familiar scenario: each shift a battle of attrition, each scoreboard tie ratcheting up the pressure. He recalled the swirl of heartbreak from past playoffs, refusing to let it cloud his approach. Through double-overtime finishes and narrow victories, the Leafs emerged triumphant, winning Game 7 in a raucous home crowd environment. Doug notched a decisive assist in the final, feeding a cross-ice pass to a wide-open defenseman for the game-winning shot. He could hardly hear himself think over the thunderous crowd eruption.

By the time the third round arrived—a conference final matchup against an old rival—Doug's body showed the usual signs of playoff wear: bruises on his forearms, a nagging twinge in his knee, and the constant dull ache of exhaustion. But the unstoppable momentum of the Leafs' run rallied him anew. Fans draped the city in blue and white, parades of supporters swarming Maple Leaf Square for watch parties. The media labeled this the best Leafs team in decades, perhaps since the franchise's last Cup appearance. Doug felt both proud and anxious, cognizant that nothing short of a championship would satisfy the city's hunger.

That conference final soared in drama. The rival team matched Toronto blow for blow—turnovers, big hits, highlight-reel goals—pushing the series to yet another epic seven-game showdown. Fatigue plagued both rosters, with trainers working overtime to keep players taped and functional. Doug found himself battling a re-aggravated shoulder injury from a mid-season collision. It hurt to raise his arm high for a slapshot, but adrenaline and team doctors' magic carried him through. In a decisive Game 7, the Leafs overcame a third-period deficit, culminating in an empty-netter by Doug to seal a 5–3 victory. He skated to the bench, delirious with relief, as the horn echoed the city's collective joy.

With the conference title in hand, the Maple Leafs advanced to the Stanley Cup Final for the first time in decades. It was a generational moment. The entire city erupted in euphoria. Doug, wearing the "A" on his chest, found himself face-to-face with the dreams he'd harbored since childhood. *We're four wins away from a Cup,* he marveled. *Four wins from making history.*

Their final opponent: a Western Conference powerhouse that had claimed multiple recent Cups. Seasoned, balanced, and physically imposing, they boasted a star-laden top line and a rugged defensive core that battered opponents into submission. The media framed it as an old-school clash of unstoppable force (them) and immovable object (Toronto's newly revitalized roster). Doug's phone lit up with best wishes from old teammates, coaches, even from those junior days. Everyone wanted a piece of the potential glory.

Game 1 in Toronto started with electric energy. The city held its breath as the Leafs jumped to a 3–1 lead, only to see the Western team storm back with skillful counterattacks, tying the game in the final minute. Overtime felt like a heart attack on ice. Doug's line nearly ended it twice—he whistled a shot off the crossbar, then set up a golden chance that the opposing goalie snared with a miraculous glove save. Ultimately, a scramble goal near the net sealed a 4–3 OT win for Toronto. The building shook, fans chanting Doug's name as he saluted the crowd. For a fleeting moment, the dream felt that much closer.

But the Western powerhouse answered back, winning Game 2 convincingly with punishing forechecks. They stifled Toronto's breakouts, laid heavy hits on Doug's line, and left the Maple Leafs reeling in a 4–1 defeat. The series stood at 1–1, heading west for the next pair of games.

The flight out West felt surreal—two games in enemy territory, facing a fanbase equally starved for another Cup. Doug slept fitfully, his battered shoulder demanding round-the-clock ice packs. His daily routine boiled down to practice, therapy, and quiet reflection in his hotel room. The tension soared with each day, each team trading barbs in the media. The final series was more than skill—it was will, survival of whichever team could endure the physical and mental grind.

Game 3 witnessed a brutal, punishing affair that spilled into multiple scuffles. Doug took a high hit in the second period, leaving him momentarily dazed. He returned in the third, determined to push through the pain, managing an assist on a tying goal. In double overtime, the Western team's star forward capitalized on a turnover, scoring the game-winner. 2–1 series for them. Doug slammed his stick in frustration heading down the tunnel, his frustration mirrored by teammates.

In Game 4, the Leafs found a new level, responding with discipline and fiery offense. Doug's line clicked, notching two goals in a 5–2 statement win. The scoreboard read series tied 2–2, guaranteeing the Cup Final would return to Toronto for at least a Game 6. The city exhaled, seeing the tide shift again— **any** small miscue could tilt the entire outcome.

By the time Game 5 concluded—an overtime thriller taken by the Western side 3–2—the Maple Leafs returned home for Game 6 on the brink of elimination, trailing the series 3–2. The city collectively held its breath. Could the Leafs stave off heartbreak again? Doug, fueled by adrenaline and the unshakeable vow he'd carried since childhood, stepped onto the ice for Game 6 with unwavering resolve. He scored the opening goal, assisted on the second, and blocked a crucial shot late, leading the Leafs to a 4–2 victory that forced **Game 7**. Toronto roared in euphoria, a city dancing on the edge of a dream realized.

Game 7. In Toronto. The building was a cauldron of noise, fans chanting anthems hours before puck drop. Doug walked into the dressing room, catching glimpses of his reflection: the "A" on his sweater, the Leaf crest shining under the bright lights. This was the moment he'd yearned for as a boy, the chance to bring a Cup to this city. His bruises and battered shoulder be damned—he'd go through a wall for one more night.

The first period was nerve-wracking, each side landing hits, each goalie standing on his head. The scoreboard read 1–1 after twenty minutes. In the second, the Western team jumped to a 2–1 lead, capitalizing on a defensive lapse. Doug felt the city's tension like a physical force. The third period arrived with everything on the line. With six minutes left, Doug snagged a rebound near the crease, jamming it in to tie 2–2. The building exploded in noise so loud Doug's ears rang.

Regulation ended, deadlocked. Overtime for the Cup. The entire city perched at the edge of seats, hearts pounding in unison. Doug's breath felt ragged as he lined up for the faceoff. A single shot, a single break, could define the rest of his life.

Each shift in overtime was a swirl of desperation. Doug's line nearly ended it with a backdoor chance, the opposing goalie making a desperate pad save. The Western side responded with a 2-on-1, forcing the Leafs netminder to sprawl out, miraculously stopping a sure goal. Doug's chest hammered with fear and exhilaration. This was the pinnacle—a moment suspended between immortality and heartbreak.

Finally, after nearly fifteen minutes of overtime, a turnover near center ice gave the Leafs a rush. Doug took a pass at the blue line, carrying the puck deep, swirling away from a defender. He spied a lane at the circle and unleashed a scorching wrist shot. The goalie blocked it but coughed up a rebound. A scramble ensued, skates and sticks tangling in frantic chaos. The puck squirted free behind the net, another Leafs forward snagged it and sent it back to the slot where Doug, adrenaline surging, hammered it through a narrow gap. The puck soared inside the near post. **Goal**.

Time froze. Then the red light flared. The crowd's roar was cataclysmic, so loud Doug could barely breathe as his teammates mobbed him in the corner. Confetti rained from the rafters. The scoreboard blinked a final: 3–2, Maple Leafs. Overtime. Game 7. Cup clinched.

Doug's mind reeled—**they** had done it. The entire team poured off the bench, piling on him, tears and screams of disbelief. He felt a surge of euphoria so vast it drowned out the physical pain. The city erupted into delirious celebrations. The dream, the vow, that boyhood promise to bring a Cup to Toronto, all culminating in that moment of victory.

In the swirling chaos, Doug skated around, dazed with joy, hugging coaches, teammates, equipment managers. The trophy emerged, shining under spotlights, a symbol of the city's decades-long hunger. Captain and alternates stepped up to hoist it first, passing it around. When Doug's turn came, he cradled the Cup, tears in his eyes. The memory of that small-town pond flashed through his mind, the vow he'd made: *to bring this Cup home.* And here it was, real and triumphant in his hands.

Toronto's faithful roared, chanting his name as he lifted it overhead, arms trembling from both exhaustion and rapture. Cameras flashed, capturing tears on his cheeks. He'd dedicated his entire hockey life to this dream—facing heartbreak, rumors, injuries, relentless expectations. Now, in the throes of this delirious celebration, all of it felt validated. The storybook final: an overtime winner from the boy who loved the Leafs.

In the days that followed, the city exploded into a carnival of parades, fan gatherings, and unending press coverage. Doug's face adorned every newspaper front page, banners across downtown proclaiming the Leafs' conquering hero. Even the cynics who once doubted the team's viability had to concede the mesmerizing truth: the Maple Leafs were Stanley Cup champions at last.

Doug navigated interviews, talk-show invitations, and a raucous championship parade. Millions thronged the streets, a sea of blue-and-white, chanting Doug's name along with the rest of the team's. He didn't sleep much that week, reveling in the wonder of it all. The media pinned him as a defining figure—**the** forward who had blossomed from overshadowed rookie to unstoppable two-way star, culminating in a Cup-winning goal.

At the official Cup parade, an emotional meltdown nearly overcame him when he spotted his parents among the throng, tears streaming down their faces. They'd believed in him from the backyard pond days, guided him through every rung of the hockey ladder. He hopped off the float, hugging them tight, the Cup perched on his shoulder. Cameras captured the moment—a testament to the family's unwavering support.

Late one evening, after the final wave of celebrations died down, Doug found himself alone in the Leafs' locker room, the Cup displayed on a table, awaiting its next day's journey to a different teammate's hometown. Doug approached it quietly, brushing his fingers along its engraved names—legends who once captured the same dream. Now his name and his teammates' names would join them, etched into history.

He recalled, in a rush, the pond where he first put on skates, the friction with old teammates, the impossible heartbreaks in junior, the swirl of trade rumors, the punishing 82-game schedules, the pressure from fans and media. Each puzzle piece formed a tapestry that led to this culminating triumph. Pride and relief mingled, tears gathering in his eyes once more.

Gently, he lifted the Cup in his arms. "I promised this city," he whispered, voice trembling, "and we did it." A small grin tugged at his lips as he set it down. Tomorrow, the trophy would continue its tour, but for this moment, Doug simply savored the quiet intimacy of the greatest prize in hockey, alone in the place he'd fought so hard to win it.

He left the arena, stepping into the Toronto night, the city's lights twinkling in quiet adoration. The vow he made as a kid—to bring the Cup home—was no longer just a dream. It was reality, sealed in silver, etched for eternity, and shared with millions of fans. **The quest for the Cup** had ended in ecstasy, marking the pinnacle of Doug Mansfield's hockey journey. And though the future might hold new challenges, trades, or retirements, nothing could eclipse this season—**the** season, when a dedicated forward and his beloved Maple Leafs conquered the game's ultimate mountain.

26

LEAVING A LEGACY

Doug stepped into the hush of the empty locker room at Scotiabank Arena, the overhead lights dim and subdued. It was early morning, well before any of his teammates would arrive. The corridors outside were silent, a far cry from the usual hustle and noise on game day. In that quiet space, Doug found a sense of calm—a final moment of reflection in a building that had shaped much of his adult life.

He set down his equipment bag, gazing around at the stalls lined neatly along the walls. Each one told a story of a current Maple Leafs player, holding sticks and jerseys still scented with faint traces of sweat and victory, or heartbreak. It was in this very room that Doug had watched his career unfold for nearly two decades. From a nervous young rookie overshadowed by bigger names, to a steadfast leader who'd once helped bring a long-awaited Stanley Cup home, every inch of this place was steeped in memories.

Somewhere in the back of his mind, he still saw the wide-eyed kid he'd once been, stepping into a professional locker room for the first time. Now, that kid was gone, replaced by a veteran in the twilight of his career. The gentle ache in Doug's knees and shoulders reminded him of all the collisions, all the bruising shifts. *You can't play forever,* he told himself, feeling a pang of sadness at the thought.

Just a day earlier, he'd made the decision official—this would be his final season, his last run with the team he had always loved. And as he looked around at the quiet stalls and the half-lit Maple Leafs logo on the floor, an unfamiliar mix of anxiety and peace fluttered in his chest. He was ready to stop, yet scared to leave behind the only life he'd known. And he couldn't help wondering: *What legacy will I leave?*

Doug's story had started on a modest frozen pond in small-town Ontario, where he and his brother Mike learned to skate by pushing an old wooden crate across rough ice. Back then, the only crowd was the swirl of wind and the occasional call of a winter bird overhead. No cameras, no screaming fans, no million-dollar contracts. Just the pure joy of skating, that sweet friction of blade meeting ice, and a sense of infinite possibility in each breath of cold air.

From those earliest days, Doug had nourished a singular dream: *to bring a Stanley Cup to Toronto.* It was a vow he carried in his heart, even through the tumult of junior hockey, overshadowed by more hyped prospects. It propelled him through that tense NHL Draft day when the Maple Leafs surprisingly called his name, granting him a chance to fulfill his childhood promise.

And fulfill it he had—years ago, his crucial goal (or assist, depending on the memory) in the Cup-clinching game had etched him permanently into Leafs lore. The city had erupted in an uproar of jubilation, burying the heartbreak of a generational drought. Doug was hailed as a hometown hero, the embodiment of small-town determination and Maple Leafs devotion. His name joined the pantheon of legends who'd bled blue and white. *I did it,* he would sometimes remind himself, marveling at how life could circle back to a boy's dream of backyard heroics.

Yet, it wasn't the Cup or the contract extension or the highlight-reel plays that resonated most deeply for Doug. What gave him lasting satisfaction was knowing he'd ignited hope in kids who wore battered skates on ponds just like he once had. They saw themselves in his journey: a normal kid with outsized ambitions, playing for the emblem he cherished. That connection to the next generation transcended anything else.

Time, however, remained unyielding. Season after season, Doug had soldiered on: battling injuries, guiding younger players, dealing with the city's perpetual media frenzy. He'd watched some rookies come and go, saw coaches hired and fired, endured trade rumor sagas, and learned how to stay resilient in a market where every misstep was magnified. He had become, almost accidentally, an institution in Toronto hockey—sturdy, reliable, and unwavering in the face of pressure.

But in recent years, age had begun to intrude on his game. He lacked the raw speed he once used to blow by defenders. His wrist shot, once lethal, sometimes faltered in high-pressure moments. The Maple Leafs had welcomed new stars into the roster, each shining with youth and vigor. While Doug took pride in his evolving mentor role, each new season also reminded him of his own physical limits.

Eventually, he recognized the signals. The swirl of regret after every shift, the discomfort in his joints whenever a practice ended, the subdued glances from coaches who, out of respect, kept him in the lineup but balanced his ice time. At last, he acknowledged that the twilight of his playing days had arrived. He'd set a personal deadline: one last push, one final season. Whether they repeated as champions or not, he would retire a Maple Leaf.

This final year had been a tapestry of small heartbreaks and unexpected triumphs. Doug found ways to remain indispensable on the penalty kill, mentoring younger forwards about corner battles and transition play. He still managed to produce in key moments, netting timely goals that drew roars from Scotiabank Arena's loyal fans. Media occasionally speculated if he might keep going another year—*He's still got it!*—but Doug stayed firm in his heart, reminding himself of the quiet vow: this is it, no matter what.

He took extra care to connect with young players—**Zack Townsend**, the wide-eyed winger hungry for direction; **Anton Bergstrom**, the Swedish center who'd once been overshadowed by bigger prospects, much like Doug in his early days. Whenever they struggled under the glare of Toronto's critics, Doug reassured them. "Focus on the love of the game," he'd say, channeling the old lessons from that pond. "If you keep that spark alive, you'll outlast the noise."

That sense of mentorship became the highlight of his final season. He saw younger Maple Leafs stepping confidently into roles once anchored by veterans who'd departed. He recognized the cyclical nature of hockey—a baton constantly passed. If he could help them avoid the mistakes he'd wrestled with, if he could instill hope, then he'd leave the franchise in stronger shape than when he'd arrived.

Yet, as the final weeks approached, Doug confronted a wave of uncertainty about life after hockey. Each day away from the rink—on off-days, for instance—felt oddly empty, like a preview of the vacuum retirement might bring. The routine of morning skates, team meetings, pre-game naps, and post-game pressers had shaped his adult life. When that vanished, what would fill the space?

Some suggested he might move seamlessly into coaching or a front-office position. Others believed he had the poise to excel in broadcasting. He appreciated the suggestions but felt no rush to commit. A break might be necessary first, a period of quiet reflection free from the demands of professional sports. The idea of returning to his hometown pond, maybe building a local hockey academy, lingered as a sweet possibility.

He confided in close friend Jonas Leroux, now retired and forging a modest coaching career. Jonas told Doug how he'd struggled initially—missing the camaraderie and the surge of competition, feeling lost without daily structure. "Give yourself grace," Jonas advised. "You've poured your life into this. You deserve time to rediscover who you are off the ice." Doug nodded thoughtfully, storing the words for later.

As the season wound down, the Leafs found themselves once again on the outskirts of a deep playoff run. By the final home game, it was clear they wouldn't advance far. Age, injuries, and tough opposition spelled an early exit. This time, fans braced for heartbreak. For Doug, the final home match of the regular season loomed as his last time stepping onto Scotiabank Arena's ice in a Maple Leafs uniform—at least as a player.

The organization, with the city's fervent blessing, arranged a subdued but heartfelt acknowledgment of Doug's impending retirement. They didn't plan an over-the-top farewell—Doug had insisted on minimal fuss. But word spread among fans, and the arena sold out swiftly. Banners draped from the upper levels, many scrawled with messages like "Thank You Doug!" and "From the Pond to the Cup."

When Doug emerged for warm-ups, the crowd erupted in prolonged applause, chanting his name with an intensity he hadn't heard since their Cup year. He forced himself to stay in the moment, each lap stirring emotions in his chest. Teammates tapped their sticks on the ice in respect. Opposing players, aware of the significance, offered nods of admiration.

Throughout that final game, Doug played with the unburdened joy of a rookie, determined to leave nothing behind. He hustled on every shift, drove to the net, clashed in corners. Despite the Leafs trailing in the scoreboard, the night felt celebratory, the crowd cheering every subtle contribution Doug made—each blocked shot, every crisp pass. Late in the third period, with the Leafs down by two, he found himself on a half-breakaway and flicked a backhand that soared past the goalie's glove. The building exploded, fans on their feet, a last taste of Doug's scoring magic.

Though the Leafs ultimately lost by one, the final horn signaled more than a defeat. It was the closing chapter of Doug Mansfield's Maple Leafs career on home ice. As he took a slow lap around the rink, removing his helmet to soak in the roaring ovation, tears brimmed in his eyes. He thought of the vow made decades ago—**to bring a Cup to Toronto**. He had done it once, achieved something that many had deemed impossible. *It's enough,* he told himself, pressing a hand to his heart.

After the handshakes, and as the opposing team filed off, Doug lingered on the ice alone. The crowd refused to leave, chanting, "Mans-field! Mans-field!" in a thunderous echo. Smiling through tears, he raised a gloved hand in farewell. A thousand flashbulbs captured his final wave, final tear, final moment in a Leafs sweater under the bright arena lights.

The scoreboard's glow dimmed, but the fans stayed, offering him that final standing ovation. Doug glided slowly to the tunnel, heart pounding with emotion. As he stepped into the corridor, a hush fell behind him—the city acknowledging the close of an era. He paused, turning one last time to glimpse the stands, the rafters where a Cup banner hung, the logo at center ice. "Thank you," he whispered under his breath, voice quavering.

Then he slipped into the hallway, disappearing from the stage that had defined his adult life.

The next morning brought an odd calm. No rush to attend practice, no game to plan for. Local papers ran heartfelt covers praising his legacy: *"Mansfield's Final Bow," "Our Hometown Hero."* Social media overflowed with tributes, highlight reels, anecdotes about his kindness to fans. He recognized many of these stories from personal experiences, but seeing them aggregated struck him anew. *I've touched so many lives,* he realized, a wave of gratitude mingling with nostalgia.

He spent the day quietly, fielding calls from old teammates scattered across the league, from family in his hometown, from young players he'd mentored. Each conversation carried an undercurrent of disbelief that he was done. Some insisted he might come back for one more year. Doug only smiled, repeating, "No, I've given all I can."

Jonas Leroux texted a short message: *Welcome to retirement, brother. Let's grab a coffee soon. You'll be okay.* Doug appreciated the reassurance. The uncertainty about life without hockey lingered, but the supportive voices gave him hope.

In the days that followed, fans petitioned for the Maple Leafs to hold a bigger ceremony, to retire Doug's jersey. The organization responded by scheduling a "Doug Mansfield Night" early in the following season. Doug found the idea humbling—he'd never considered himself on par with the greatest legends. But management and fans insisted his contributions ran deeper than pure stats: he'd bridged eras, anchored a Cup run, and inspired kids from small towns everywhere.

He decided to graciously accept the honor. *If this city wants to celebrate me, I owe them that.* Because truly, he owed Toronto everything: the chance to fulfill a dream, the unwavering support even during the worst slumps, and the euphoria of hearing them roar when he hoisted the Cup. So he stood at center ice on that special night months later, wearing a suit, a glimmering Maple Leaf pinned to his lapel. The rafters glowed with a commemorative banner, not an official jersey retirement but a symbol of the city's gratitude.

Addressing the crowd, he spoke about how a little boy on a pond discovered a love so powerful it lifted him to the NHL. He recounted adversity—rumors, injuries, heartbreak—and how each forged his resilience. Then he spoke about the kids, those who might follow in his footsteps. "You can come from anywhere," he said, voice thick with emotion. "If you have passion and heart, nothing is out of reach. This city taught me that."

And there, in that moment, with tears in his eyes, he felt the intangible truth: his legacy wasn't merely the Cup or the stats, it was the living proof that a small-town kid with big dreams could succeed in the most pressurized hockey market on earth, inspiring others to chase their own improbable goals.

Amid the swirl of tributes and media retrospectives, Doug returned to his hometown one last time, slipping out quietly to avoid a crowd. Early morning frost blanketed the fields as he approached the pond where his love of hockey had bloomed. The caretaker had tended the ice that winter, ensuring it was clean and safe for any local kids wanting a pick-up game.

Doug arrived alone, stepping from his car with an old pair of skates. Though his knees still ached from his final season, a lightness filled his heart. He crossed to the pond, laced up in near silence. The air smelled of pine and frozen water, reminiscent of those early days with his brother. He tested the ice with a gentle glide, feeling the blade's friction, the crisp crackle of the surface. A rush of childhood wonder overcame him. *So many years, so many changes,* he thought. *But the ice... it's the same.*

He spent a while skating lazy circles, lost in memory. Eventually, a couple of local kids arrived, eyes widening in shock at the sight of him. He grinned, waving them over. With minimal fuss, they started an impromptu pick-up game—two kids against the Maple Leafs legend. The kids were wide-eyed, uncertain if they could keep up. But Doug just laughed, encouraging them to try their moves, savoring the unadulterated spirit of the sport.

After a short while, he called for a break, the crisp air making his breath cloud. The kids peppered him with questions—*How'd you do it? Did you ever think you'd get so far?* Doug answered with gentle honesty: "I believed in my love of the game. Everything else—hard work, discipline—came from that love. If you keep that flame alive, you can handle any hurdle."

As he packed his skates, one of the kids tugged his sleeve, whispering, "I want to play in the NHL too. One day, can I wear your Leafs number?" Doug's heart squeezed with emotion. He crouched to the kid's level. "You can wear any number you want," he said, voice warm. "Just chase your dream. That's what matters."

Leaving the pond, Doug felt a gentle finality. His playing days were finished, but a new future stretched out. Perhaps he'd found his calling in guiding youth. Or maybe a role with the Leafs' development staff, bridging the gap between prospects and big-league reality. Whether he resided in the city or retreated to the quiet of small-town Ontario, he carried a wealth of knowledge, a passion that hadn't dimmed even if his body insisted it was time to stop playing.

He recognized that life beyond the boards could be rich in its own way—family, friends, the possibility of shaping the next generation. The Maple Leafs would always remain a part of his soul, no matter where he ended up physically. Toronto's fans had woven him into their hockey lore, just as he'd woven the city's spirit into his identity.

Looking back, Doug saw the narrative arc of his life as a testament: from an 11-year-old on a backyard rink, discovering a surprising knack for skating, to an OHL up-and-comer overshadowed by flashier talents, to a rumored trade piece, to eventually a champion who quieted a city's decades of longing. He'd learned that legends weren't just about scoring titles or highlight reels; they were about perseverance, humility, and the willingness to keep forging ahead when the entire hockey world demanded results.

In the end, his impact ran deeper than goals and assists. Young kids from rural corners of Canada, or any underdog environment, saw in Doug's path a reflection of their own hopes. Rookies in the Leafs locker room, anxious about living up to Toronto's mania, found solace in his mentorship. And loyal fans, once battered by heartbreak, discovered fresh faith when he lifted that Cup overhead—a living, breathing reminder that nothing is impossible.

Now, in retirement, he left behind a legacy: not just a name on the Cup, but an imprint on every kid who believed they too could transcend small-town ponds to the highest stage. His devotion to the Maple Leafs, to the city's dream, wove him into Toronto hockey's tapestry as a figure revered for heart over flash, substance over style.

As he turned the key to his car after leaving the pond for the final time, Doug reflected on that vow he'd made so long ago. *I brought a Cup to Toronto,* he thought, *and hopefully, much more than that.* He smiled, tears of contentment glinting in his eyes. His watch beeped, reminding him of the next step in life—whatever that might be. Hockey had shaped him, given him purpose and heartbreak and triumph, but it was no longer his entire existence.

Thus, with quiet pride and a heart full of gratitude, Doug Mansfield closed the chapter on his playing career. He had proven, once and for all, that a small-town kid from a backyard pond could rise to the pinnacle in the biggest hockey market in the world. And in doing so, he left behind a legacy that would echo in corners of Toronto's rinks and beyond—a living testament that dreams, chased with unwavering love, could come true, carrying others along in the slipstream of hope.

The End

ABOUT THE AUTHOR

Blair Edward Russell (B.E. Russell) was born in 1979 in Etobicoke, Ontario, the second son of Bob and Marie Russell. Growing up in Oakville and Bradford, just outside Toronto, Blair was surrounded by the quintessential Canadian hockey experience. As the son of a former Edmonton Oilers player, hockey wasn't just a sport; it was a way of life. Whether he was playing the game, cheering on the Maple Leafs with his family every Saturday night, or heading out fishing any chance he got, Blair's childhood was filled with adventure, camaraderie, and a deep love for the outdoors.

Summers were a blur of outdoor escapades—roaming forests, wading through creeks in search of fish, skateboarding around the neighborhood, and playing endless games of street hockey. At 15, Blair moved near Shelburne, Ontario, to attend The Hockey Training Institute and play Junior 'A' hockey with the Shelburne Wolves in the Metro Junior 'A' Hockey League.

After hanging up his skates, Blair pursued his education at York University in Toronto, graduating in 2007. Not long after, he embarked on a new adventure, relocating to Miami, Florida, with his wife, Ginna, to build their life together in the Sunshine State.

Blair's creativity doesn't stop at writing. He's also an avid oil painter, a domain name investor, and an accomplished internet entrepreneur. Most of all, he's a passionate angler, especially when it comes to fly fishing. His novels draw heavily on his love of fishing, blending themes of mystery, light horror, and the great outdoors into stories that hook readers and take them on thrilling, unforgettable journeys.

Today, Blair lives in Aventura, Florida, with his wife Ginna and their cherished 17-year-old cat Roco (or Rocky as Blair calls him). Whether he's crafting a new original tale, painting in his studio, or casting a line into tranquil waters, Blair finds inspiration in life's simple yet extraordinary moments.

In 2019, always up for a new adventure, Blair and Ginna spent several days camping and portaging through the stunning wilderness of Algonquin Park. One unforgettable moment came on a portage trail when they came face-to-face with a massive bull moose. Thankfully, the moose was just passing through, leaving Blair and Ginna with a thrilling story—and a memory they'll cherish forever.

ACKNOWLEDGEMENTS

I would like to thank the following people who have helped inspire me and supported me throughout my life in all the various projects and endeavors I have been through.

My wife Ginna, My father and mother Bob and Marie, My brother and sister Bobby and Stacey, all of my friends and extended family as well as you my passionate reader.

You are all the ones who inspire me to share my dreams and ideas with the world.

FURTHER READING

Please be sure to check out the other fine books from **B.E. Russell** including:

- *Stories From the Grave – Book Two*
- *Stories From the Grave – Book One*
- *Life in the Woods*

If you enjoyed reading this novel be sure to join my mailing list at **www.BlairEdwardRussell.com**.